DEATH OF A CHANCELLOR

Other titles in the series

Goodnight Sweet Prince
Death & The Jubilee
Death of an Old Master

DEATH OF A
CHANCELLOR

A Murder Mystery featuring
Lord Francis Powerscourt

DAVID DICKINSON

CARROLL & GRAF PUBLISHERS
New York

Carroll & Graf Publishers
An imprint of Avalon Publishing Group, Inc.
245 W. 17th Street
11th Floor
New York
NY 10011-5300
www.carrollandgraf.com

First Carroll & Graf edition 2005

First published in the UK by Constable,
an imprint of Constable & Robinson Ltd 2005

ISBN 0-7867-1492-1

Printed and bound in the EU

In memory of Mary Muriel,
And of Sue who liked Evensong

Part One

Epiphany

January 1901

1

There was just one figure on the deck of the ship at four o'clock in the morning. Surely only a madman would venture into the open on such a night, the sky above black as pitch, illuminated by neither moon nor stars, the fierce wind cutting across the decks, a relentless rain slanting down from the invisible sky, the spray from the prow of HMS *Fearless*, one of the Royal Navy's newest destroyers, washing and swirling round the madman's feet, sloshing its erratic way towards the gunwales where it returned to the foaming sea. On the bridge the Captain stared at his instruments and wondered whether he should decrease his speed in case his most eccentric passenger turned into a man overboard.

But Captain William Rawnsley did not alter his course or his speed. One part of his mariner's brain was permanently, subconsciously, attuned to the beat of the great engines beneath him, the finest and the most modern that the engineers of the Clyde could produce. As long as that heart beat strong and sure he was confident that his ship would do whatever he asked of her. And Captain Rawnsley had made a promise to the madman on the deck in Cape Town at the very start of their journey back to England. He would deliver his passenger on to dry land at Portsmouth at eight o'clock in the morning of Friday the twenty-fifth of January in the year of Our Lord 1901. No earlier, no later. The Captain knew his passenger the madman was anxious to see his wife and family who had been informed of his time of delivery. The Captain himself, as he told the madman, was equally anxious to return to his home. He had a pair of twins waiting for him. And Captain Rawnsley had never seen them since they were born three long months before.

The madman was clutching the rail of the ship very tightly in his lookout post some twenty yards from the prow where the sea crashed over the Glasgow steel in angry torrents. Sometimes he peered up at the empty sky as if willing some stars or some fragment of moon to come out and cast light on his journey. Sometimes he stared straight ahead, mesmerized by the relentless crashing of the waves or the white line of spray along the side of the vessel. Sometimes he stared out to his left as if he might spy land, a faint outline that would mark the coast of England.

Always he thought of the people waiting for him at the other end. Lady Lucy, wife of his heart and love of his life, Thomas, his son, and little Olivia, his daughter. He had not seen any of them for over a year, four hundred and five days since he had waved goodbye at that melancholy railway station. For the madman was Lord Francis Powerscourt and he was going home. He wrapped his great sou'wester ever more tightly round his body and stared yet again at where he thought England must be. Darkness was upon the face of the deep, he muttered to himself, and the spirit of God moved upon the waters.

Thirteen months before, the Prime Minister himself had despatched Powerscourt and his small private army to South Africa to improve the British Army's intelligence in the war against the Boers. Even now Powerscourt could still remember the exact words of his orders: 'The whole structure of military intelligence in South Africa is wrong. War Office can't sort it out. Useless bloody generals can't sort it out. They think the Boers are here. They're not. They're over there. The generals plod over there. By the time they arrive, Mr bloody Boer has disappeared again. Difficulties in the terrain, they keep telling me. Rubbish. Faulty intelligence, maybe no intelligence at all.' It had taken Powerscourt and his companion in arms Johnny Fitzgerald a year to sort out the problem, but he had left in place a whole new system of intelligence gathering, based on the speed and mobility of the African scouts he recruited, and the information gleaned from hundreds of black spies.

Some thirty miles north-east of HMS *Fearless* another figure was peering out to sea. Lady Lucy Powerscourt was rubbing at the window of her hotel room on the sea front in Portsmouth. Surely, she thought, the hotel people could keep their glass cleaner than this. The visitors wanted a proper view of what was going on down below in the harbour. But all she could see were the lights on the shore and a dark, impenetrable blackness behind.

When she married Lord Francis Powerscourt some eight years before, he had left his career in Army Intelligence and become one of the foremost investigators in Britain, solving mysteries and murders that once went right into the heart of the Royal Household itself. Neither she, nor indeed he, had ever imagined that he would be recalled to the colours and sent to the other side of the world to help in a grubby and difficult war. She had found his absence very hard to bear. Only the children rescued her from depression. Thomas sometimes had a way of flicking his hair off his forehead that replicated to the last detail the behaviour of his father. Then, for what seemed to Thomas to be completely unaccountable reasons, she would sweep him up into her arms and smother him with kisses.

Lady Lucy was fully dressed. She turned from her lookout post and glanced at the sleeping children. She smiled. They had taken their father's absence in totally different ways. Thomas had an enormous map of Southern Africa on the wall in his bedroom, covered with stars and dates for the places his father had been. The map itself was now scarcely visible. What the little boy did not know was that his father never put his real location in his letters in case they were captured by the enemy. When he was in Natal, he told Thomas he was in the Transvaal, and vice versa. So Thomas's map was accurate in the sense that his father had been in all the places ringed with stars, but never at the time marked on his wall.

Olivia had never seen the point of the map and the stars. Instead she had appropriated a photograph of her Papa from the drawing room and she drew dozens and dozens of pictures of him, scarcely recognizable to anybody else, but a constant record of her devotion. She made her Mama keep a list of all the things she had to tell her father about, her new shoes, the pony in her grand-mother's stable in the country, her new friend Isabella on the other side of their house in Markham Square in Chelsea.

Lady Lucy checked the time once more. Half-past four. Not time yet to wake the children. She prayed that the ship would arrive on time. Perhaps they would be able to spot it better from the quayside. At six o'clock, she said to herself, I shall wake Thomas and Olivia and get them dressed. They will be so excited. She smiled again. After four hundred and five days, an hour or two was nothing, nothing at all.

On board HMS *Fearless* the rain seemed to have grown still more powerful. Captain Rawnsley and his officers on the bridge could just see a second madman come to join the asylum on deck. Even through the roar of the elements they could hear him shouting to the first lunatic.

'For Christ's sake, Francis, why do they have to put these bloody guns in the middle of the floor? You'd think they'd put them higher up somewhere.' Johnny Fitzgerald had banged his knee on one of the Navy's latest and most lethal weapons as he crossed the deck to join his friend. 'It's bloody inconsiderate of them, that's what I say.'

'Good morning to you, Johnny. Mind how you go now. You don't want to fall overboard at this stage.'

'One of those bloody officers up there,' Johnny Fitzgerald gestured vaguely towards where he thought the bridge must be, 'has just taken a bet with the Captain person that one of us will fall in.'

The *Fearless* sank at that moment into a particularly deep trough. As she rose out the other side a wall of water flooded over Powerscourt and Fitzgerald.

'That's the other bloody thing,' said Johnny bitterly, never a happy sailor. He was hanging on to the rail with both hands. 'Ever since we left, this bloody boat has been either going up and down like this,' he ducked as another helping of ocean cascaded over them, 'or rocking from side to side. It's drunk all the time this boat, that's what it is. Why can't the damned thing move along on an even keel? They cost a fortune, these bloody boats, Francis. You'd think they could make them go along steadily, like a train. I mentioned the fact to the Captain the other day.'

There was a temporary lull in the weather. Fitzgerald plunged his right hand deep inside his clothes and produced an enormous flask.

'This is what you need on a night like this, Francis. Naval rum. Fellow in the catering department gave it to me. Said it's the stuff they give the sailors before a battle. Makes them fighting drunk, he said. Seems to me you'd need to have the bloody stuff twenty hours a day, battle or no battle, to survive on these wretched vessels.'

Powerscourt smiled. He suddenly remembered Johnny Fitzgerald turning green and being sick over the side on a yachting expedition years before when there was barely enough breeze to fill the sails. 'I'm very curious, Johnny,' he shouted into the wind, 'to know what the Captain said.'

'What the Captain said when?' Fitzgerald yelled back.

'When you complained about the ship not travelling like a train.' Powerscourt had turned very close to his friend's ear. Johnny Fitzgerald laughed.

'He said to me, Francis, "You're a hopeless case. Don't think I could convert you to ships any more than I could convert the Hottentots to Christianity. Here, you'd better have another drink."'

Fifty miles to the west of Lady Lucy's hotel, Andrew Saul McKenna finally decided that he must get up, even though it was five o'clock in the morning. McKenna was butler in the great house of Fairfield Park, situated in the tiny village of Hawke's Broughton in the county of Grafton in the west of England. He knew something was wrong. He had heard strange noises in the night. He thought, or had he imagined it, that he heard a muffled scream. Now there was no noise, just this overpowering sense that something was terribly amiss in his little kingdom. He lit a candle and climbed rapidly into his clothes for the day, left out in neat piles the night before.

McKenna's first thought was for the master he had served for the last fifteen years. Mr Eustace's bedroom was one floor below. McKenna could still remember his master coming round the desk to shake him by the hand when offering him the job.

'I do hope you'll be able to stay with us for a long time,' he had said with a smile. Eustace was Chancellor of the Cathedral of Compton, responsible for the archives and the famous cathedral library.

Now McKenna was tiptoeing down the back stairs in the middle of the night, his stomach churning with worry and fear. A floorboard creaked as he made his way along the corridor. Outside he could see, very faintly, the trees shaking slowly in the wind. He passed an ancient statue of a Roman goddess, lost in thought. For a big man, he moved very quietly.

Andrew McKenna paused before he opened the door to his master's bedroom. There was a loud creak when you opened it, he remembered. He'd meant to have the door oiled for weeks now. He gripped the handle firmly and twisted it open as fast as he could. There was no noise this time.

Nothing, he thought, nothing could have prepared anybody for what he found inside. As he moved slowly across the room towards the great four-poster bed, he found the long discarded habits of childhood had returned to take temporary occupation of his brain. His hands moved automatically into the folded position. He said two Our Fathers. He closed his eyes briefly to avert them from the horror. Hail Mary, full of grace, his lips muttered, his hands moving along the beads of an invisible rosary, blessed art thou among women, blessed is the fruit of thy womb, Jesus. As he took in the full horror lying across the bedclothes, he realized that the words in his brain suited his master much more than they suited him. Pray for us now and in the hour of our death, Amen. Charles John Whitney Eustace, Master of Fairfield Park, Canon and Chancellor of the Cathedral of Compton, had died in the most terrible fashion. There were still two hours left before the dawn. Pray for us now and in the hour of our death, Amen.

The rain on the deck of HMS *Fearless* had stopped. The spray and the waves were as powerful as ever. The night was still an impenetrable black. Powerscourt was wondering if this happy return might become an anticlimax. He had heard stories from men in the Army about upsetting reunions, so passionately desired over such a long time, so eagerly awaited on the long journey home, but where people found they had little to say to each other after the initial euphoria had worn off. Time had ensured that there was too little experience left in common after a long separation. After a fortnight, one man had told him, he realized he was living with a complete stranger he didn't know at all. Powerscourt didn't think that was going to happen to him. He groped about inside the folds of his sou'wester and produced a pair of binoculars. They were of the finest and the latest German make. The Kaiser had sent whatever he could to the Boers to confound perfidious Albion, guns to kill the British, ammunition to keep killing them, binoculars to find them. He peered despondently into the gloom.

'Don't suppose you'll see anything yet, Francis.' Johnny Fitzgerald was peering into the water below. 'How deep would you say this bloody water is?' he went on, as if he saw himself being sucked overboard right down to the bottom of the ocean floor where there were no reviving bottles to console the living or the dead.

'Very deep, I should think,' said Powerscourt.

> 'Half owre half owre to Aberdour
> It's fifty fathoms deep
> And there lies good Sir Patrick Spens
> Wi' the Scots lords at his feet.'

Lady Lucy checked her watch again. Time seemed to be moving very slowly this morning. Twenty to six. Still an hour and a half to go before the dawn as the helpful hotel people had told her the night before. Francis is coming, she said to herself, remembering the mantra she had used like a comfort blanket when she had been kidnapped by a gang of villains and locked up on the top floor of a Brighton hotel. He had found her then. She checked the children once more and returned to her vigil by the window. Francis is coming. She smiled again.

Andrew McKenna was shaking slightly as he stood by his dead master's bed. Part of it was shock. Part of it was anger that anybody human could have done such a brutal thing to his gentle master. Part of it was that he simply didn't know what to do. He felt suddenly that he was the lone representative left on earth of Charles John Whitney Eustace, charged with special duties towards the dead. His master had been quite small in life. Now, lying on this bloody bed, with blood dripping on to the floor, he looked smaller still.

McKenna knew that terrible scandal could follow the discovery of the body. The newspapers would invade this remote corner of rural England and titillate their readers with exaggerated stories of vicious and violent death before dawn. The rest of the staff would want to come to pay their last respects. The women would turn hysterical if they saw this bloodied corpse, the men would turn homicidal towards the unknown perpetrators. The only thing to do for now, he said to himself, is to fetch the doctor who lived but a few hundred yards away. But he couldn't leave the remains of his master where they were. Somebody else might come in and find him. So the only thing to do was to move him. To move him now. McKenna shuddered violently as he thought of carrying this

9

corpse, of all corpses, anywhere at all. And where should he take it? To the doctor's? Some early-rising farmhand might spot him walking along the village's only street with blood and gore running from the package in his arms. Then he remembered the spare bedroom above the stables, recently refurbished and remote from the main part of the house.

McKenna took a deep breath. He found that his hands were making the sign of the cross. He pulled out all the bedclothes and rolled them round his master till he looked like a wrapped-up sausage or an Egyptian mummy en route to the burial chamber deep inside a pyramid. He tried putting the body over his shoulder like a fireman rescuing somebody from a blazing building. That didn't work. The body kept slipping. Between the bed and the door he found that the best way to carry his master was in his arms, like an overgrown baby wrapped – the biblical reference came to him again from Christmases past – in swaddling clothes. Going to a stable, he said, his mind on the edge of hysteria now, like they did all those years ago.

The journey to the kitchen passed off without incident, apart from the fact that Andrew McKenna had started to weep and had no hands to wipe away his tears. Outside the back door they were hit by the force of the wind. McKenna reeled like a drunken man. The real disaster came on the way up the stairs to the bedroom above the stables. McKenna slipped and almost fell over. Desperately he reached out his left hand to steady himself against the wall. The body fell out of his grasp and began rolling down the stairs. It stuck four steps from the bottom. Summoning the last of his strength McKenna picked his master up once more and went up the stairs as fast as he could. He dumped John Eustace on the bed and went down the stairs two at time. Out in the fresh air he stood still for a moment, panting heavily, tears still rolling slowly down his cheeks. He noticed that a spot of blood had escaped from the wrapping and fallen on to his hand. He set out to wake the doctor. His hands were out of his control by now. They were shaking violently from the strain of carrying a corpse a couple of hundred yards in the dark. Pray for us, his lips were moving as he swayed up the village street, pray for us now and in the hour of our death, Amen.

Six o'clock at last. Just two hours to go now. Lady Lucy decided the time had come. The children would never forgive her if they missed the boat's arrival. They could have breakfast downstairs in the great dining room that looked over the harbour. Just over four hundred days have passed, she said to herself happily as she woke Thomas and Olivia on the morning their father came home from the wars.

Powerscourt and Fitzgerald had company in their night watch on deck. A cheerful 'Good morning, gentlemen' announced the presence of Captain Rawnsley himself, fresh from his command post and his instruments on the bridge.

'There's just an hour and a bit to go before the dawn,' he announced as if sunrise and sunset followed the orders of the Royal Navy. 'I hope to take the ship into the harbour at first light. We shall dock at about a quarter to eight. The first passengers should be able to disembark on the stroke of eight. Then,' he smiled broadly at Johnny Fitzgerald, 'you will owe me fifty pounds.'

Johnny had placed the bet one day out of Cape Town, refusing to believe that anybody could calculate their journey time so precisely in such an unreliable and dangerous thing as a boat. He laughed.

'Touché, Captain,' said Johnny. 'I don't have the money on me at this moment, forgive me. Too dangerous carrying money around on the deck of one of these things.' He waved an arm dismissively at the surrounding bulk of HMS *Fearless*.

'But come, gentlemen, we are having a special breakfast at seven o'clock. I hope you will be my guests. A little champagne might ease the memory of the fifty pounds, Lord Fitzgerald?'

Johnny tried to persuade Powerscourt that his only reason for placing the bet had been to make sure that they did actually reach Portsmouth at precisely eight o'clock in the morning. 'Fellow like that Captain, Francis, nothing like a bet of fifty pounds to make sure you got home at the time you'd told Lucy. Stands to reason, if you ask me.'

Powerscourt didn't believe him.

'Dear God, why would anybody want to do that to John Eustace, of all people?' Dr William Blackstaff was fastening his boots on the edge of his bed with Andrew McKenna in dutiful attendance. Blackstaff, like John Eustace, was in his early forties. They had known each other for over ten years. Every Wednesday, without fail, they had lunch together in the upstairs dining room of the White Hart Hotel in Northgate in the little city of Compton . At weekends they walked together over the hills. In spite of his walks Blackstaff was thickening out. The beginnings of a paunch were showing through the tweed suits he always wore, a collection so large and varied that the children in Compton always referred to him as Dr Tweed, amazed in later years to discover that his name was not Tweed at all but Blackstaff.

'We must have a plan,' he said, making the final adjustments to his tie. He had served in the Army for five years and some memory of the need for proper staff work had stayed with him all his life.

'Yes, sir,' said McKenna, looking out into the dark night beyond the doctor's windows. 'It's going to be light in under an hour or so.'

Blackstaff stared vacantly at his friend's butler. 'Let me just try to think this through, McKenna,' he said. 'Please tell me when there is a flaw in the plan.' Dr Blackstaff paused, well aware that his mind was so tinged with grief and shock that he probably wasn't thinking straight.

'We take him out of the stables at once,' he said. 'But where do we take him? We could bring him here, but that's not going to solve the problem, is it?'

'The chief difficulty, it seems to me, sir,' said McKenna, 'is that the family are going to want to look at the body in the coffin. And that's impossible.'

'This is the best I can do for now, McKenna,' said the doctor, moving heavily towards his front door. 'I take my carriage with the covers up along the road towards the house. I stop about a hundred yards away in case anybody hears the noise. You bring the body down from the stables into the carriage. I shall take it into Wallace's the undertakers in Compton. Old man Wallace knows how to keep his mouth shut. He can put the body in the coffin and seal it up so tight that nobody can get at it.' Blackstaff and McKenna were climbing into the carriage by now, groping their way with the reins in the dark.

'The cover story is slightly different. You must make up the bed as if nobody had ever slept in it. And of course you must clear up the blood in the bedroom. I shall say that your master came to see me late last night, feeling very unwell and complaining of chest pains. I kept him here overnight as I judged that the walk back to Fairfield might kill him. I watched over him all night. Later this morning I shall return to Compton and bring Wallace back again, as if to fetch the body. We'll say he died shortly after ten o'clock this morning. I shall send word up to the house once Wallace has gone with the imaginary body.'

Dr Blackstaff paused. 'Are we breaking the law?' he whispered. 'Are we going to end up in jail?'

'Don't see how we are breaking the law, sir. Poor Mr Eustace is already dead.'

'And,' said the doctor, stopping his carriage shortly before the entrance to the stables, 'I shall tell anybody who asks that he most definitely did not want people peering at him when he was dead. Indeed, I shall say that he repeated that wish to me only last night as he sat by my fire, looking very pale and ill. Got that, McKenna?'

'Yes, sir,' said Andrew McKenna, and he loped off along the path to start his late master's journey to the undertakers and to the grave.

Powerscourt was back at his post on deck. He watched as the black turned to dark grey, then to a paler grey as visibility grew from fifty yards to two hundred and then to half a mile. A thin pencil of land was visible ahead of him. When he raised his binoculars he could see a tall spire somewhere near the centre of Portsmouth. He could see the naval buildings lined up along the quayside and the multitude of dockyards, repair workshops and training stations that marked it as the centre of the Royal Navy, the greatest seafaring power on earth. His heart was beating faster. He remembered the words Lady Lucy had said to him in the drawing room of their house in Markham Square on his last evening in London and again on the station platform the following morning as the train took him away. 'Please come back, Francis. Please come back.' Now the moment, of all moments the one he had most longed for, had nearly arrived.

It was Thomas who claimed he saw him first. He had appropriated the binoculars from his mother, in true male fashion, and thought he recogniszed another figure with binoculars on the deck of HMS *Fearless*.

'There he is!' he shouted. 'There's Papa! Up at the front of the ship with the binoculars!' He shouted at the very top of his voice, 'Papa! Papa!' and waved furiously as fast as his hands could move. The other people waiting at the quayside for their loved ones smiled at the little boy and his enthusiasm. Now they were all waving, all three of them, Olivia standing on tiptoe so her father would recognize her across the water.

Then Powerscourt saw them. He put his binoculars down and waved for all he was worth. Johnny Fitzgerald had stolen a naval flag from somewhere and was waving it above their heads like a banner. Powerscourt thought he was going to cry. These three little figures, waving as though their lives depended on it, these three, not the mighty ships with their great guns, not the peaceful English countryside that rolled back behind the city, these three were his homecoming, his landfall.

He came down the gangway as the church bells of Portsmouth rang the hour of eight. He embraced Lady Lucy. She was crying. He picked up Thomas in his arms and kissed him violently. He hid Olivia inside his cloak and squeezed her till she thought she might break.

Lord Francis Powerscourt was home.

2

John Eustace came from a family of four. His elder brother Edward had died serving with his regiment in India. His twin brother James had moved to New York where he dabbled unsuccessfully in share speculation. His elder sister Augusta Frederica Cockburn was the first to hear the news of his death, and the first to set out for Hawke's Broughton.

Life had not been kind to Augusta Cockburn, née Eustace. She had been born with some of the features thought desirable in a young woman. She was rich, very rich. She had a great deal of energy. She was tall, with a face adorned with a long thin nose and large protruding ears. Her fine brown eyes, one of her best features when she was young, had grown suspicious, almost bitter with the passing years. Her marriage at the age of nineteen, an act, she told her friends at the time, largely undertaken to escape from her mother, had seemed glorious at first. George Cockburn was handsome, charming, an adornment to any dinner table, a good fellow at any weekend house party. Everyone thought he had money when he led Augusta up the aisle at St James's Piccadilly all those years ago. He did have money, after a fashion. But he had it, as his brother-in-law once remarked, in negative quantities. He was always in debt. Some scheme, launched by the artful dodgers on the fringes of the City of London, was bound to attract him. The schemes invariably failed. He began to chase after other women. He began losing heavily at cards. After ten years of marriage Augusta had four young children, all of them looking distressingly like their father. After fifteen years of marriage they were all she had left to live for, George Cockburn being seldom seen in the family home and then usually drunk, or come to steal some trinket he could take to the pawnshop or use as a stake at the gambling tables. The very generous settlement bestowed on her by her father at the time of her marriage had almost all gone.

Many families progress upwards as they move through life. They move into larger houses to accommodate their growing numbers. Augusta found herself carrying out the same manoeuvre, only in reverse. The family moved from Mayfair to Chelsea, from Chelsea to Notting Hill, from Notting Hill to an address that Augusta referred to as West Kensington but that everybody else, particularly the postmen, knew as Hammersmith.

Augusta did not take these changes well. She grew sour and embittered. Only the appeal to his nephews and nieces persuaded her brother John to keep her financially afloat. So when she heard of his death she resolved to set out at once, without the children, on a visit of mourning and condolence to Fairfield Park. Her real purpose was to discover what had happened to her brother's money, and, if possible, to appropriate as much of it as possible for herself and her family. Thus could she restore the fortunes her wastrel husband had thrown away.

It also has to be said that Augusta had not been a welcome visitor in her brother's house. John Eustace found her constant complaints, the endless whingeing about poverty and the cost of school fees rather wearing, particularly as it began over the break- fast table when a man wants to read his newspaper. And she was bad with the servants, peremptory, short-tempered, always secretly resentful that there were far more of them than she could afford back in West Kensington or Hammersmith. They, in turn, had devised subtle forms of revenge. Her morning tea was never cold, but never hot either. Tepid perhaps, lukewarm. The junior footman, who was almost a genius at pipes and plumbing, would contrive an ingenious and elaborate system for the course of her stay whereby the water in the bathroom, like the tea, was never hot but never cold. In the autumn and winter her room would be so thoroughly aired that the temperature would sink almost to freezing point. Then the fire would be made so hot it was virtually unbearable. They had, to be fair to them, the servants, decided that in view of the tragic circumstances they would behave properly in the course of her visit to the bereaved household. But only, said the junior footman who doubled as a plumbing expert, only if she behaved herself.

It was now three days since the passing of John Eustace. Andrew McKenna, waiting nervously in the Great Hall to greet Augusta

Cockburn, had found them very difficult. He had never liked lying. He didn't think he was particularly good at it. As he told the servants the sad news of their master's death, he tried to sound as authoritative as he could. Grief overwhelmed them so fast they had no time to notice the anxiety in his voice, the slightly shaky legs. That too, he told himself, could have been put down to shock. But now, he knew with deep foreboding in his heart, he would face a much sterner test, Mrs Augusta Cockburn with the light of battle in her eyes. The trouble was, he said to himself as he waited for the sound of the carriage coming down the hill, that he still wasn't certain he and Dr Blackstaff had done the right thing.

Then the nightmare started. Leaving the servants to carry in her small mountain of luggage, she swept him off to the great drawing room at the back of the house, looking out over the gardens and the ornamental pond.

'McDougal, isn't it?' she said imperiously, settling herself into what had been her brother's favourite chair.

'McKenna, madam, McKenna,' said the unfortunate butler, wondering if he was about to develop a stammer.

'No need to say it twice,' snapped Augusta Cockburn, 'I'm not stupid. I knew it was Scottish anyway.'

She was twisting slightly in her chair to get a better view. McKenna was hovering at what he hoped was a safe distance.

'Come here, McKenna! Come closer where I can see you properly! No need to skulk over there like a criminal.'

Criminal was the very worst word she could have used. For Andrew McKenna had often suspected in the previous seventy-two hours that he was indeed a criminal. Some phrase about obstructing the course of justice kept wandering in and out of his mind. He blushed as he advanced to a new and more dangerous position right in front of Mrs Augusta Cockburn.

'Tell me how my brother died, McKenna. I want all the details. I shall not rest until I am satisfied that I know absolutely everything about it.' She made it sound like an accusation.

'Well, madam,' said McKenna, wondering already if his legs were holding firm, 'he went over to see the doctor three nights ago. That would have been on Monday night. I believe Mr Eustace was feeling unwell, madam. The doctor thought he was not well enough to come home so he kept him at his house overnight. That way he could keep an eye on Mr Eustace, madam, and give him any attention he needed. Unfortunately the doctor could not save him. He died at about ten o'clock the following morning, madam. His heart had given out. Dr Blackstaff came to tell us just after eleven.'

Augusta Cockburn thought there was something wrong about this account. The man spoke as if he had learned it off by heart, or had just translated it from a foreign language. Precisely what was wrong she did not yet know. But she was going to find out.

'Hold on, McKenna or McDougal or whatever your name is – '

'McKenna, madam.'

'Don't interrupt me when I am speaking to you. You have begun at the end. I want you to begin at the beginning. What happened on the Monday? Was my brother feeling unwell? Did he complain about pains in his chest or anything like that? People don't usually drop down dead with no warning at all.'

'Sorry, madam. Your brother went off to the cathedral in the normal way on Monday morning. He came back about five, I believe, madam, and had some tea in his study. James the footman brought it in to him. We served his dinner in the dining room at eight o'clock, madam. He would have been finished about a quarter to nine. Then Mr Eustace went back to his study, madam.'

He paused. Now came the difficult bit. For if everything he had said so far was totally or partially true, the words he was about to utter were complete fabrication. And there was no mercy from his interrogator.

'Get on with it, McKenna. All of this only happened three days ago. It's not as if you're telling me the line of battle at Trafalgar.'

'I went to see Mr Eustace at about nine thirty in his study to ask if there was anything he wanted. He said I was not to wait up as he might be working till quite late. That was the last time I or anybody else in this house saw him, madam.' Until I found him dead in bed in the middle of the night, he thought, blood all over the sheets.

Augusta Cockburn sniffed the air slightly, like a bloodhound. If she had suspected something was amiss before, she was almost certain now. How unfortunate it was that a man so bad at lying should have encountered a bloodhound like Augusta Cockburn at such a time. For if he was bad at lying, she was an expert in its detection. She felt she could hold down a chair, the Regius Professorship in Lie Detection, at one of the ancient universities. After all her long years of marriage she had listened to so many lies from her own husband. Lies innumerable as the grains of sand on the seashore or the stardust on the Milky Way. Kept very late at

18

dinner, couldn't get away. Need some money to buy some railroad shares. Damaged my ankle so badly at the club I couldn't even walk down the stairs. Some damned woman spilt her perfume right down my shirt. Fellow insisted I go home with him for a nightcap. Bloody trains cancelled yet again, couldn't make it home. Those were just the preface. Now she stared at McKenna as though he were a common criminal.

'And where is the body?'

'The body, madam?'

'My brother's body, McDougal. Where is it and when can we pay our last respects and say our goodbyes?'

'I believe the body is at the undertaker's in Compton, madam.'

'And when is it being brought back here for the family's last respects?'

'I'm afraid I could not say, madam. The doctor has been looking after the arrangements.'

'Are you not meant to be the butler here? Are you not meant to be looking after the arrangements, as you put it? Is that not what you are paid to do?'

Andrew McKenna turned bright red at the insult to his professional abilities. 'I have been butler here for the last fifteen years, madam. I have never had any complaints about the performance of my duties.'

Augusta Cockburn snorted. The whole house obviously needed taking in hand from top to bottom.

'I have not found this interview at all satisfactory,' she said, drawing herself erect in the chair, her eyes flashing. 'You may go now. I shall be writing to this doctor, Blacksmith or Blackstaff or whatever he is called. Perhaps you could arrange for its immediate delivery.'

'Dr Blackstaff, madam,' said McKenna, heading as fast as he dared for the escape route. Before Augusta Cockburn had time to speak again, McKenna had reached the safety of the door. He closed it firmly, possibly too firmly, behind him and fled to the sanctuary of the servants' hall below.

'Just look at this, Anne. I'm really pleased with it.' A slim young man with dark brown hair and dancing eyes was sitting at the kitchen table in a little house right on the edge of the Cathedral Close in Compton. The young man was called Patrick Butler and he was talking to Anne Herbert, the twenty-eight-year-old widow of the Reverend Frank Herbert, previously vicar of St Peter under the Arches in the city. When he met a tragic death in a train accident the Dean and Chapter had given the use of this house to his widow.

Butler had an early issue of the county newspaper in his hand. He was the editor of this weekly journal, the *Grafton Mercury*, not one of the mightiest organs of opinion in the land, but a post where a man might make a name for himself and progress to greater things. He had been in Compton for nine months now, promoted from a position on an evening paper in Bristol.

Anne brushed a couple of her children's drawings on to a chair and opened up the newspaper. Patrick was hovering enthusiastically by her shoulder. She read of the tragic death of John Eustace. There were glowing tributes from the Bishop, 'always a humble and devoted servant of the cathedral and the people of this city,' 'beloved by all who knew him, a terrible loss to the community,' from the Dean, 'taken from us in his prime, when he had so much left to give,' from the Archdeacon.

Then came the paragraph of which Patrick Butler was particularly proud. He felt sure it would cause a sensation. He had already been in contact with a couple of the great national dailies in London about its contents. It might make his name.

'The *Grafton Mercury*,' Anne read, aware that Patrick was somewhere very close but not sure exactly where, 'has learned that the former Chancellor of the cathedral, John Eustace, was one of the richest men in England, possibly the richest of all. His father was a very successful engineer in Britain who went on to make a vast fortune in America. His mother was an American heiress. On their death he was left an enormous portfolio of shares whose value has grown ever larger. It is believed that he was also left another fortune by his elder brother Edward. Mr Eustace was single at the time of his death.'

Anne Herbert looked up at her friend. 'This is amazing,' she said. 'How do you know it's true?'

Patrick Butler looked at her with a teasing smile. 'I'm not sure I can reveal my sources,' he said. 'We're not meant to divulge where our information comes from, you know. It might get somebody into trouble.'

'If you think, Mr Patrick Butler,' said Anne firmly, 'that you can come into my house and drink my tea and sometimes eat your supper here and not tell me how you know this, you'd better prepare for some changes about the place.' She tried to look at him severely but knew she was failing.

'I'll give you three guesses where the information came from,' he said.

'All right,' she replied, 'let me think. He told you himself. How about that?'

'No good,' said Butler, 'I only met the man a couple of times. Next?'

Anne was looking down at the newspaper as if Patrick might have put his source right at the bottom of the page. 'Dr Blackstaff told you. He was always very friendly with the Chancellor.'

'Wrong again,' said Butler cheerfully. 'Last go. If you don't get it this time, then you've had all your chances.'

Anne thought carefully this time. It must be somebody at the cathedral, she felt. People in those closed communities usually knew everybody's secrets.

'It's the Dean,' she said authoritatively. 'The Dean told you.'

Patrick Butler looked impressed. 'How on earth did you guess that? It's not actually the Dean in person but you're as close as could be.'

'Don't think it could have been the Archdeacon,' she said thoughtfully, 'you're lucky if you get the time of day out of him. I know, it's the Bishop. It's the Bishop!'

Patrick Butler clapped his hands vigorously and smiled right into her eyes.

'Absolutely right. Gervase Bentley Moreton, the Lord Bishop of Compton Minster, told me himself about five or six months ago.'

'But won't he be cross with you, Patrick? Won't you get into trouble?'

Patrick picked up his newspaper from the kitchen table and waved it about. 'Where in this article is there any mention of the Bishop? Have I written that the Bishop told the *Grafton Mercury* this exciting piece of news? I have not. And he did not tell me at the time that it was confidential or anything like that. And the information would have come out at some point in the future. It's just that we have got it first. It's a world exclusive for the *Grafton Mercury*, Anne! It's tremendous!'

Anne smiled at the enthusiasm of her friend. 'But when did he tell you? He wasn't drunk or anything, was he?'

21

Patrick Butler smoothed out his paper and put it back on the kitchen table. 'It was all rather odd, really. It was at a cricket match at the end of last summer. The Friends of Compton Cathedral Eleven were playing a team from Exeter. The Bishop wasn't enthroned in state in the pavilion or anything like that, he was just sitting on the grass like any ordinary mortal, watching the match. Compton were batting, with Chancellor Eustace well set batting at number four. He was a very tidy batsman, Anne, if you know what I mean. Nothing violent, nothing agricultural about his play. He just stroked the ball about, a flick here, a nudge there, the odd cover drive that looked completely effortless. He had just placed the ball way into the outfield and they were running three. The Bishop tapped me on the shoulder, I remember. "You'd never think now, looking at John Eustace play cricket, that he is one of the richest men in England." Then he told me about his parents and all that stuff. The really odd thing was what happened when he got to the end of his story.'

'What do you mean?' said Anne.

'Well, I wonder now if it mightn't have been an omen. All the time he was batting you would have said Eustace was going to bat for ever, that he'd never get out. But the minute the Bishop finished his story, he was clean bowled next ball.'

Augusta Cockburn stared angrily at her breakfast in the dining room of Fairfield Park. Her fury was as cold as the scrambled eggs in front of her. The toast was limp and soggy. Her tea was almost cold. War had been declared between the servants of the late John Eustace and the living presence of his sister. The vote in the servants' hall the previous evening, Andrew McKenna the Speaker of this tiny democracy, had been unanimous. In less than twenty-four hours Augusta Cockburn had insulted every single member of the household. Now she was paying the price. She looked again at this insult, this degradation of a breakfast. They'll all have to go, she said to herself. Every single last one of them, out the door and with no references to help them in a hostile world.

The footman, at least, was managing to uphold the sullied banners of propriety.

'Dr Blackstaff, madam, is waiting in the drawing room.'

This was going to be another trial. She had met the doctor on previous visits. She had not cared for him, sensing perhaps that he was much closer to her brother than she would ever be. He, in his turn, did not care greatly for Mrs Augusta Cockburn. Dr Blackstaff had developed over the years a particularly annoying habit of asking whereabouts she was currently living. 'Still in Chelsea?' he would inquire with a smile. When, reluctantly, she reported yet another retreat, another withdrawal of her living quarters to a less socially desirable part of the capital, he would repeat the last address as though the area contained, if not the plague, then at least elements that might not be entirely respectable. 'West Kensington?' she remembered him saying at their last encounter, 'West Kensington?' as though he could scarcely believe the place existed at all.

But this morning Dr Blackstaff seemed to be on his best behaviour. He was wearing a dark grey suit of impeccable cut in place of the usual tweed. He began by offering his most sincere condolences for such a tragic bereavement. He went on to explain that the Dean had taken charge of the funeral arrangements. It was only right in the circumstances that the Chapter of Compton Minster should oversee the last rites of one of their own. The Dean, he went on, liked taking charge of arrangements for almost everything. That, probably, was why he was Dean in the first place. The service itself was planned, subject, of course to Mrs Cockburn's approval, for the Wednesday afternoon the following week. The delay was because the Dean had managed to locate John Eustace's twin brother James in New York. He was returning on the fastest transatlantic liner available and would be back in time to attend the funeral service in person. The cathedral authorities, Dr Blackstaff went on, intended to say farewell to her brother with the ecclesiastical equivalent of full military honours. There was talk of a memorial plaque in the north transept under the cathedral's finest stained glass window, hundreds of years old. The burial itself would be in the graveyard of the little church just behind the house where they were sitting. It had been the wish of Eustace himself.

For the first time since she had been in Fairfield Park Augusta Cockburn was impressed. She might have to fire all the servants in the house. But it seemed that the Dean and Chapter could be left in post for a little longer.

'I am very happy with these arrangements,' she said. 'Things seem to have been very competently handled.' She graced the

23

doctor with a thin suspicion of a smile. 'But forgive me, doctor, if I ask about my brother's last hours. It is only natural for his closest relatives to want to know everything possible. And you were the last person to see him alive.'

Dr Blackstaff was well prepared for this, possibly too well prepared. Andrew McKenna had given him a blow-by-blow account of his inquisition by Augusta Cockburn. 'It was as if she didn't believe a single word I said,' he had told the doctor. 'She's got eyes that seem to look right into your head.' Blackstaff had considered blinding Mrs Cockburn with medical science. He had checked out in his medical books a fleet, a veritable armada, of terms relating to heart conditions that only the fully qualified would understand. Then he thought he would probably have to explain every single one of them. He resolved on a different approach. He had practised it over and over again till he felt prepared for anything.

'Let me speak as a friend as much as a doctor,' he began, his eyes fixed on a Dutch painting over the mantelpiece. 'Over the years your brother and I had grown very close. I think I can truly say that he was my closest friend in Compton as I was his. Of course he was close to many of the people in the cathedral but I always felt he found it more relaxing to talk to somebody who came from a different, a less exacting world.'

Why isn't he looking at me? said Augusta Cockburn to herself. She too stole a quick glance at the painting on the opposite wall. It showed a domestic scene in an Amsterdam household, a group of servants cleaning a great hall under the watchful eye of a person Augusta presumed to be their mistress. She noticed that they had missed a very obvious pile of dust on one of the dressers. Really, she thought, even then standards were dropping fast. More staff to be fired.

'I had noticed over a period of a year or so that your brother's heart might be deteriorating,' the doctor went on, shifting his gaze now to the logs burning in the grate. 'He became tired quite easily. He wasn't able to walk as far as he had done in the past. Sometimes when he had to take one of the great services in the cathedral or preach a sermon on some important occasion, it wore him out. This could, of course, be the normal process of people slowing down in middle age. Nothing concrete was ever revealed under examination. And believe me, Mrs Cockburn,' suddenly he did look her straight in the eye, 'I examined him many times.'

'Was he worried about something, Dr Blackstaff? I have been

24

told that anxiety can cause all sorts of problems.'

'No, no, he wasn't worried. I would have been the first to know if he had been. He wasn't worried at all,' said the doctor, who knew better than any man on earth just how worried John Eustace had been in the last months of his life.

A sliver, a scintilla of a suspicion passed through Augusta Cockburn's mind. Did the man protest too much? Was he too telling her a pack of lies?

'To come to his last hours, if I may.' The doctor paused briefly, running through his story in his mind yet again. 'He came to see me about ten o'clock on the evening before he died. He was feeling unwell. On examination he was suffering from a condition known as cardiac disfibrillation, a sort of racing of the heart. It could be that all sorts of things were going wrong, but we do not at present have the means to detect what those might be. I gave him something to ease the condition and a draught to help him sleep. I advised him against returning to his own house at that time. I thought it was merely a precaution. I did not imagine that John would never see his own house again.' The doctor turned from staring into the fire to look at Augusta Cockburn and he shook his head sadly.

'The next morning, there was little change. I examined him again. I gave him some more medicine. But it was no good. Whatever was wrong with his heart, whatever pieces of human equipment were malfunctioning, his God called him home just after ten o'clock.' The doctor paused again. 'I don't believe he was in any great pain. His heart just stopped working and he was gone.'

'And why is nobody allowed to see him before he is buried? Why is he locked up in the undertaker's as if he had the plague?'

Dr Blackstaff had known this was coming. 'He told me several times over the last few years that he didn't want any procession of people peering in at him when he was gone.'

The doctor was not prepared for the next salvo.

'When did he tell you? What were you doing? Were you in this house or in his?'

'I can't remember exactly where it was,' the doctor said, 'not exactly. But he certainly said it.'

'You can't remember where you were when my brother said such a strange thing? You can't remember?' Augusta Cockburn's voice rang with scorn.

'Mrs Cockburn,' the doctor said in his most authoritative tones, 'believe me, in the course of my professional duties, I have a great many confidential conversations with my patients. I carry around in my head all sorts of wishes and requests relating to what people want to happen when they die. I cannot be expected to recall exactly where I was on each and every occasion.'

'But you might have muddled them up, might you not, doctor? Somebody else might have told you they wished to remain locked up in their coffin like a criminal. If you can't remember where you were, how can anybody be sure that you've got the right person? Somebody else might have told you they didn't wish to be seen.'

Dr Blackstaff shook his head. 'I know I am right,' he said.

Nothing, absolutely nothing, could have prepared him for the next blast.

'Are you a beneficiary under my brother's will, Dr Blackstaff? Has he left you a lot of money?'

Blackstaff turned bright red. Augusta Cockburn thought this denoted guilt. In reality it was anger that such a question, such an imputation, be directed at him.

'No, to the best of my knowledge, I am not, madam. And now, if you will excuse me, I have patients to see to. The living have rights as well as the dead. I wish you a very good morning, madam.'

With that the doctor picked up his bag and strode from the room.

Augusta Cockburn stared at the doctor's departing back. She continued to stare at the door long after he had gone. She was not a bad woman, Augusta Cockburn. She had loved her brother. She loved her family, except, of course, for her lying husband. But the circumstances of her life brought out all the worst aspects of her character.

She picked up the latest edition of the *Grafton Mercury*, lying on the table in front of her. She wondered if there was anything about her brother inside. She gave a little cry when she came to Patrick Butler's favourite paragraph. Charles John Whitney Eustace one of the richest men in England. An enormous portfolio of shares. Mother an American heiress. She read it again. She knew her brother was rich but not as rich as this paper said he was. It definitely did say he was one of the richest men in England. How did they know that, the people in this little backwater, miles from civilization? How did this twopenny-halfpenny scandal sheet, the *Grafton Mercury*, filled with information about the price of pigs and meetings of the parish councils, know it? Had all of Compton known it? Did the money, heaven forbid, have anything to do with his death?

Augusta Cockburn stood and stared out of the window at her late brother's garden. A couple of robins were hopping energetically on the lawn. A light rain was falling. She hadn't believed the butler. She hadn't believed the doctor either. Dr Blackstaff might have been a more professional liar than McKenna or McKendrick or whatever the wretched man was called – doctors have to lie every day of their working lives, she thought – but there was something suspicious about his story too.

One phrase kept echoing round her head. One of the richest men in England. Maybe she could move house again, back to a proper address. One of the richest men in England. She could provide properly for her four children. She could pay off all the debts her wretched husband had accumulated. One of the richest men in England. She could pay her husband off with a large sum of money so that she never had to set eyes on him again. They would, for once, have enough money to live on without worrying about how the next bill was going to be paid. One of the richest men in England.

Augusta Cockburn moved to the far side of the room and went into her brother's study. She locked the door, gazing quickly behind her to make sure she was not being watched. She opened the drawers of the great desk where her brother did his work. She checked through all of them. She looked in the little cubby-holes on the top, full of writing paper and envelopes. She checked that there were no secret compartments where important documents might be hidden away. She didn't find what she was looking for. She unlocked the door and rang the bell.

'McKendrick, or whatever your name is,' she said, 'I wish to go to the railway station. I have to go back to London. I shall return in a few days' time. Order the carriage.'

'Certainly, madam.' Andrew McKenna rejoiced as he heard of their tormentor's departure. He and his colleagues had escaped from jail for a few days at least.

Mrs Augusta Cockburn was returning to London to find a private investigator to look into her brother's death. She suspected very strongly that he had been murdered.

3

Anne Herbert was waiting for Patrick Butler in the coffee house on Exchequergate, a couple of hundred yards from the west front of the cathedral. Patrick was late. He was, Anne smiled to herself, usually late. Just had to talk to a couple of fellows, he would say with that great smile of his.

Anne Herbert was tall and slim, with dark hair, a regular nose and very fetching green eyes. It was two years now since she had lost her husband, and been left with the two young children in the little house on the edge of the Cathedral Close. 'She's so pretty, that Anne Herbert,' the Dean had said to John Eustace after arranging her new accommodation, 'I'm sure she'll be married inside a couple of years, if not sooner.' Marriage had seemed a distant, an impossible option to Anne for the first year. She had loved her husband very dearly and found the prospect of a replacement inconceivable. One or two of the younger curates had tried and failed to woo her. Then five months ago, she had met Patrick at one of the Dean's tea parties. He had simply walked up to her, cup of tea in one hand and a large piece of the Deanery's best chocolate cake in the other, and said, 'How do you do. I'm Patrick Butler.' They had been seeing each other with increasing frequency ever since. The Dean had prophesied once more, saying this time to his housekeeper that he expected them to be married within the year. The Dean planned to conduct the service himself. He was searching, he told the Bishop, for a suitable passage of scripture concerning the scribes in the Bible to pay tribute to Patrick's profession.

Then Butler himself walked in and ordered two cups of coffee. 'Sorry I'm late,' he said with a smile. 'Had to talk to a man down at the cathedral. How are the children?'

Anne smiled back at him. 'The children are fine,' she said. 'Have you had any reaction to the article about Mr Eustace? Everybody in Compton is talking about it.'

'Good,' said Patrick. 'I've got some news on that front. But first I need to ask you this.' He leaned forward in his chair in case they could be overheard. 'You've lived here all your life, haven't you? I mean you were born here, weren't you?'

Anne's father was the local stationmaster. 'Yes, I have.'

The young man pulled a small notebook out of his pocket. 'Ten months ago, just before I came to work here, one of the vicars choral simply disappeared. That's right, isn't it?' He looked down at his notes. 'Singing person by the name of William Gordon, my man in the cathedral tells me.'

'Yes, that's right. But what of it? Everybody's forgotten about it by now.'

'But he wasn't the first one to disappear, was he? There was another one, about eighteen months back. I can't find anybody who remembers his name, though. Even the old boy in the cathedral couldn't remember him.'

Anne Herbert looked at Patrick. He was very excited. Then she remembered a young vicar choral called Peter Conway coming to lunch when her husband was still alive. He had great plans for his future, he had told the young couple, hoping to end up as a choir-master in one of the great cathedrals of England. Then he vanished without trace. Nobody paid very much attention to either disappearance. Vicars choral, for some unknown reason, had a reputation for flighty and irresponsible behaviour.

'I think he was called Peter Conway,' she said very quietly. A couple of middle-aged ladies were planning a shopping expedition to Exeter in very loud voices a couple of tables away, their voices bright with expectation and greed. 'But what of it, Patrick?' Something in the nature of the young man's occupation always worried Anne Herbert. It was all too excitable. Patrick and his colleagues were often obsessed with the dark side of human nature. As usual, he had laughed when she told him of her anxieties.

'Heavens above, Anne,' he had said, 'do you want everything to run like your father's trains, punctual down to the last minute, schedules planned months in advance? In the newspaper world, believe me, variety is the spice of life!'

Now he looked over at the middle-aged ladies. 'Think of the

reaction of respectable people like that when they read the article, Anne.'

'Which article, Patrick? The one about how rich Mr Eustace was?'

'Sorry,' said Patrick Butler, turning back to inspect Anne Herbert's eyes. They were still green, still the same colour he often thought about last thing at night before he fell asleep. 'I'm getting ahead of myself. Two vanished vicars choral, missing, possibly deceased. Late vicars choral. Singing for their suppers no more. One dead Chancellor Eustace, called to his maker long before his time was up. Three of them altogether. I think I'm going to call it the Curse of Compton Minster. That should cause quite a stir!'

Anne was appalled. She had spent most of her adult years surrounded by the clergy and the choristers of this cathedral city. Now Patrick was going to blaspheme against her household gods, bringing the sordid techniques of his occupation to bear against the traditions of her upbringing. It was the profane assaulting the sacred.

'You can't possibly write such an article, Patrick. Nobody knows those two men are dead. I don't think anybody even suggested it at the time. And you can't be suggesting that there was anything suspicious about Mr Eustace's death. That's ridiculous.'

Patrick Butler thought it was time to beat a tactical retreat. Maybe certain things had to be sacrificed in the cause of love. But he wasn't going to give up easily.

'I wasn't going to run this article soon, Anne, if it ever runs at all. I shall have to wait until after the funeral. And if it really upsets you, then I may never run it at all.'

Lady Lucy Powerscourt had been planning her campaign for over six months. Like all great generals she had carried out a number of reconnaissance missions. The final details had been fixed for some time. All that mattered, as with most military missions, was the timing. If that misfired, her strategy could collapse in a matter of minutes. She looked over at her husband, peacefully reading the newspapers in his favourite chair by the fire. It was now a fortnight since Powerscourt had stepped ashore in Portsmouth. Life was beginning to return to what she would regard as normal. He had spent a great deal of time with his children, mostly listening as they filled him in on the details of their lives while he was away, details that now seemed as important to Powerscourt as the schemes and stratagems he had hatched against the Boers thousands of miles from Markham Square. The previous evening he had taken Lucy to a concert where a young German pianist had taken their breath away with his interpretation of Beethoven's Emperor Concerto. Afterwards there had been a romantic dinner by candlelight where Powerscourt had repeated his private vow to her. Semper Fidelis. Forever Faithful.

'Francis,' said Lady Lucy to the figure in the armchair. It was a slightly hesitant 'Francis,' as if she was not quite sure about what was to come. Like all famous commanders she was slightly nervous at the start of her operations.

'Lucy,' said Powerscourt, putting down his newspaper and smiling with pleasure at the sight of his wife, 'something tells me you are up to something.'

Lady Lucy was momentarily taken aback. How could he know what she was about after just one word? Then she rallied. 'It's just there's something I wanted to discuss with you.'

Powerscourt rose to his feet and leant on the mantelpiece. 'Can I have a guess as to what this is all about?' he said cheerfully. 'Let me see, perhaps the kitchen is in need of modernization, though I don't think it is going to be that. Change the bedrooms all around? New carpets for the hall? I don't think it's any of those but I could be wrong. Maybe it has something to do with this room we're in now?'

Lady Lucy blushed slightly, embarrassed at the nature of her plans having been so easily rumbled. 'It does have to do with this room, Francis, you're quite right.'

'And what were you proposing to do here, Lucy?'

Before she could reply there came a slight apologetic cough. Rhys, the Powerscourt butler, always coughed apologetically when he entered a room. Powerscourt had often wondered if the man had coughed slightly before proposing to his wife or stating his marriage vows in church.

'Excuse me, my lord, my lady. There is somebody waiting downstairs who wishes to speak with you, my lord.'

Powerscourt looked apprehensive all of sudden. Was his peace, so ardently desired, so long awaited, about to be disturbed? 'Does this person have a name, Rhys?'

'Of course, my lord. Sorry, my lord. She is a Mrs Cockburn, Mrs Augusta Cockburn.'

'Then you'd better show her up.' Lady Lucy looked at her husband carefully as she left the room. He was looking miserable and he hadn't looked miserable once since his homecoming. Just when her plans were coming to fruition too.

Augusta Cockburn had decided to dress in mourning clothes for her visit. She thought it might make a better impression. Perched demurely on the edge of the Powerscourt sofa, she poured out her story. Powerscourt decided not to interrupt. Her suspicions about her brother's death. The butler whose account she did not believe. The doctor whose account she did not believe. The strange, almost inexplicable fact that nobody could pay their last respects to the dead man because he was sealed up for all eternity in his coffin in the Compton undertaker's. Her overpowering sense that something was being concealed and that that something might be very terrible indeed. The fact, if it was relevant, that her brother had been one of the richest men in England.

'I would like you to investigate the matter, Lord Powerscourt,' she concluded. 'They say you are one of the finest investigators in the country.'

Powerscourt wondered precisely what her motives might be. Was she a humble seeker of the truth about her brother's death? He rather doubted it. Where did the money fit in? But most of all he wished she hadn't come. He didn't want to be bothered with another investigation so soon after his return.

'I have to tell you, Mrs Cockburn, that it is most unlikely that I shall be able to take the case on. I have only just returned from a year and more on service in South Africa. I have hardly had time to reacquaint myself with my wife and children.'

'I'm sure it wouldn't take you long, Lord Powerscourt. Not a man of your abilities.'

'Perhaps I could just ask one or two questions, Mrs Cockburn. Do you know the details of your brother's will?'

'I'm afraid I do not,' said Augusta Cockburn vaguely. 'Not exactly. It's just possible that he left it in our house or at our solicitor's, I'm not sure. I believe my husband may have helped him with it, but George, Mr Cockburn, is away at present.'

Augusta Cockburn was a much more accomplished liar than Andrew McKenna or Dr Blackstaff. Maybe the years with her deceitful husband had taught her something after all.

'Did your brother ever give any indication about his intentions in his will?' asked Powerscourt.

'Not specifically, Lord Powerscourt, no. But he always said that my family would be well provided for. Sorry, I should have told you before. My brother was not married. There were no children.'

'And what do you think actually happened to your brother?' asked Powerscourt, the investigator in him always fascinated by puzzles and mysteries.

'That's what I want you to find out, Lord Powerscourt.'

'Do you think he was murdered?'

Silence fell over the Powerscourt drawing room. It lasted quite a long time. Powerscourt waited for her reply.

'He certainly could have been, Lord Powerscourt. I don't think we can rule it out.'

'He didn't by any chance suffer from a debilitating illness? Something that could have disfigured his face?'

'Not as far as I am aware, Lord Powerscourt. And I'm sure the doctor would have mentioned it if he had been.'

'Very good, Mrs Cockburn, you have presented the facts of the affair very clearly.' And not all of them completely truthfully, Powerscourt thought, but which part was fiction and which the truth he did not yet know. He checked the address on her card. 'If you can leave me until this afternoon, I will let you know then whether I can take the case on or not. I must speak with my wife.'

Two minutes after Augusta Cockburn's departure Lady Lucy was back in the drawing room. She found her husband pacing up and down. She thought he was swearing under his breath.

'Johnny and I used to do a lot of this walking up and down on that ship on the way home, Lucy. Helped to pass the time.' Now it was her turn to wait until he was ready to speak. It was a full five minutes before he sat down and told her the details of the death of John Eustace.

'That poor woman, his sister,' said Lady Lucy sadly.

'You wouldn't say poor woman if you spent any time with her. She's bitter and twisted inside as though she had a corkscrew in her heart.'

Lady Lucy winced. 'What are you going to do, Francis? Are you going to take it on?'

Powerscourt started walking up and down again. 'I really don't know. I've only just got home.'

'Well, it's not as if you're going back to South Africa.'

'Do you think I should do it, Lucy?' said Powerscourt, stopping by his wife's chair.

'You know what I think about these things,' said Lady Lucy very quietly, looking at her husband's face. 'Let's suppose this poor clergyman was murdered. Somebody else may get murdered after that. And then there may be more victims. I think you have to remember the number of people who may be left alive after you've finished, the ones who might have been killed if you hadn't come along.'

Powerscourt smiled suddenly. 'Lucy, what were you just about to say earlier this morning when that woman was announced?'

Lady Lucy blushed. Interior decoration didn't seem quite so important now. 'I was just going to suggest, only a suggestion, Francis, that we might . . .' She paused briefly, then her courage returned. 'We might just redecorate this room. New sofas, new wallpaper, that sort of thing.'

Powerscourt took her in his arms. 'You go right ahead, Lucy, my love. Just as long as I can hang on to that chair of mine. After all, I may not be about very much for a while.'

Five days later Lord Francis Powerscourt was sitting in the nave of Compton Cathedral, waiting for the funeral service of John Eustace to begin. He was early. The ancient bells, high up in the great tower, were tolling very slowly for one of their own. Powerscourt had arrived at Fairfield Park as a guest of the family, an old family friend from London come down to help Mrs Cockburn through the ordeal of the funeral and the revelation of the will. So far Powerscourt had asked no questions. He had chatted inconsequentially with the servants. He had spent a lot of time in the dead man's bedroom and in his study. He had walked the short journey between the Park and the doctor's house a number of times. He was waiting until he became a more familiar figure before he talked to anybody, but he was careful to be as charming as he could to every servant he came across. Augusta Cockburn was astonished at the improvements in daily life in Fairfield Park since Powerscourt's arrival. Baths were actually hot. Meals were served at the proper temperature. It's probably because he's a man, she told herself bitterly.

There was still some time before the service was due to start. One row behind him on the other side of the nave Anne Herbert, dressed in sober black, was sitting next to Patrick Butler whose tie was not sitting properly on his collar. Patrick was thinking about the special edition of his paper to commemorate Victoria's death several weeks before. It was going to include tributes from all the major towns in the county. He had prevailed on the cathedral archivist to write an article on the changes to the minster during Victoria's reign. The headmaster of the main secondary school, a noted if slightly erratic local historian, had agreed to contribute a similar piece on the changes in the city. The Lord Lieutenant, who had served briefly at court some thirty years before, was going to write his personal reminiscences of his sovereign. Patrick Butler was pleased that his material had all arrived on time, the headmaster and the archivist both having let him down on previous occasions at the turn of the century. He had launched an appeal to the major advertisers in his journal to take out larger than usual notices in his pages. 'Most newspapers,' he had told the proprietor of the main hotel with disarming honesty only that morning, 'are thrown away after a while. But this special edition of the *Grafton Mercury,* each page specially edged in black, will be a permanent memorial to Victoria's death. People will keep it safe. It will pass down the generations. Surely you would want a proper memorial to your business in such a paper?'

Still the bells rang out on this wet and windy afternoon. High up on the roof the crows, regular attendees, if not actually confirmed members of the Church of England, added their raucous tribute to the dead. Powerscourt was looking at the military colours of the local regiment that hung in the north transept and thinking about the dead Queen, in whose armies he had served, and in whose service he had seen too many lay down their lives. He looked around the congregation, late arrivals filling up the last few pews right at the back of the cathedral. How many, he wondered, in this great throng, come to pay their last respects to a different person, how many could remember a monarch other than Victoria? He certainly couldn't. As he looked across the tightly packed pews on the other side of nave, he thought six or seven persons might remember the reign of William the Fourth. Victoria had seen her island kingdom rise from being an important power to the greatest empire the world had ever seen. Powerscourt had not been the only person in Europe and North America to wonder if the Boer War in South Africa might seem in future years to have marked the slow beginning of that empire's end. And now there was a new King, Edward the Seventh. Powerscourt tried desperately to recall who Edward the Sixth had been. Was he warrior or wastrel, playboy or saint? Dimly he remembered that Edward the Sixth had been an ardent Church reformer, sandwiched between Henry the Eighth and Bloody Mary, eager to force the Protestant religion on a reluctant people. Maybe Compton Minster had its own martyrs to the zealotry of the Reformation. He struggled further back to earlier Edwards, Confessor and Hammer of the Scots.

The bells stopped. The entire congregation turned to look as the body of the former Chancellor, John Eustace, was carried into the cathedral. Six pallbearers, three staff from Fairfield Park led by Andrew McKenna, and three vergers from the cathedral, all clad in black, bore the coffin in a slow procession behind the choir and three members of the Chapter. A junior vicar carried a large silver cross in front of the Dean and the Bishop.

Powerscourt suddenly remembered walking round one of England's finest cathedrals with his father years before on one of their rare trips from Ireland to England, Wells had it been, or Gloucester, and his father explaining to him the different roles of the various dignitaries. The Bishop in spiritual authority over every priest and every parish in his diocese. The Dean responsible for the administration and running of the cathedral. The Chancellor, secretary to the Chapter and responsible for the archives and the famous cathedral library. The Precentor in charge of the music and the organist and the choirmaster, the two posts often held by one man. The Archdeacon the link between the cathedral and the work of the Bishop in the diocese. Powerscourt remembered his father taking particular pleasure as they watched a vicious game of croquet in the gardens of the Bishop's Palace where all the players were in dog collars. 'The Church Militant rather than the Church Spiritual,' his father had said as a red ball disappeared off the lawn into the Bishop's rose-beds.

The little procession was passing Powerscourt now, the pallbearers straining to keep in step, always fearful that one of them might slip and drop the dead man to the ground. The coffin was laid on a table in the centre of the choir. If he strained his neck right out to one side, Powerscourt could just see the side of it through the screen. 'I know that my Redeemer liveth,' the Dean had a strong tenor voice, well able to fill the great spaces around him, 'and that he shall stand at the latter day upon the earth.'

The choir began to sing the 60th Psalm, 'Lord thou hast been our refuge from one generation to another.' Powerscourt looked around again at the mourners. They were not, on the whole, the rich of Grafton though there were many who had turned out in fashionable clothes. These, he thought, must be the respectable middle classes of Compton, shopkeepers, teachers, lawyers with whom John Eustace had come in contact. Patrick Butler was eyeing the congregation too, wondering if there were any more advertisers he could lure into taking space in his memorial issue to Queen Victoria. Anne Herbert was sitting beside him, fretting about his restless staring up and down the nave.

The congregation sang 'Abide with Me' and 'Lead Kindly Light' by John Henry Newman. The Bishop read one lesson, the Archdeacon of Compton the other. Then the acolyte with the silver cross preceded the Dean to the pulpit. The congregation settled themselves noisily in their hard pews to hear him.

Connoisseurs of the sermons of the dignitaries of Compton Minster had long ago noted that the Bishop, although a considerable scholar in the Gospels of the New Testament, always preached from texts in the Old Testament. He would tell the stories of the ordeals of the Children of Israel against Philistines and Gideonites, Danites and Ammonites, Benjamites and Schechemites, and Keilites and Amalekites. There were often some bloodthirsty battles. There was, usually, triumph and victory for the Israelites, after many hardships along the way. Thus, the Bishop would always conclude, does the Lord of Hosts finally triumph over the enemies of his chosen people. The Dean, the connoisseurs noted rather sourly, always tried to bring in some references to the latest theological thinking when he preached. Neither the connoisseurs nor the congregation cared for the latest theological thinking. They preferred the older theological thinking, many feeling that the world would be a better place if everybody still believed every word of the creation story in the Book of Genesis. The Chancellor seldom preached, but his sermons were always mercifully short. He would speak of the transcendent importance and power of God's love, a love handed down to his servants in so many forms, love of parents to children, love of children to parents, love of husband to wife, wife to husband, love of the natural world created for God's glory.

'My text for today,' the Dean began, peering out at his congregation over the tops of his glasses, 'comes from the fifth verse of the fifth chapter of the Gospel According to St Matthew. Blessed are the meek, for they shall inherit the earth.' The connoisseurs had not

37

heard this sermon before. It must be a new one, specially composed for the occasion, rather than an old one revamped. Powerscourt looked closely at the Dean, a tall strong figure of a man, with powerful hands which turned the pages of his sermon.

'It is now twelve years since John Eustace came to this cathedral as Chancellor,' the Dean went on, 'and I can still remember his first meeting with the full Chapter of this cathedral as if it were yesterday. He was slightly shy. He was invariably courteous. He did not push himself forward. That meekness, which shall inherit the earth, was a constant in his behaviour with his colleagues in all the years he graced the minster with his presence.'

Patrick Butler was wondering if he should reprint the Dean's sermon in his next issue. Depends on how long it is, he said to himself. Patrick didn't think the Dean would approve if his words were cut. Powerscourt was remembering the words of the Latin tag. *De mortuis nil nisi bonum.* Speak only good about the dead. And then he remembered the impious adaptation given by his Cambridge tutor after attending the funeral service for a famously unpopular professor, *De mortuis nil nisi bunkum.* People only speak rubbish about the dead.

'One of the definitions of the word meek in the Oxford Dictionary,' the Dean went on, 'is kind. To be meek is to be kind. Meek is merciful. To be meek is to be merciful. John Eustace was famous throughout our little city for his generosity. He was a man blessed with great wealth. Blessed are the meek for they shall inherit the earth. Chancellor Eustace had already inherited a large portion of the wealth of this world. Such people do not always take the time or the trouble to seek out the hungry and the afflicted, the poor and the bereaved. John Eustace did. Our late Chancellor was one of the greatest benefactors the poor of Compton have ever known. The houses he had built for the poor and the destitute of this city will be a permanent memorial to his life and his generosity.'

Some of the congregation's heads were beginning to slip as the sermon went on. Behind the coffin the six pallbearers waited to resume their duties. The acolyte with the cross waited patiently at the bottom of the pulpit steps.

'Today is a time of great sadness,' said the Dean, laying aside his spectacles and looking around at his listeners, 'for one of our number has been taken from us before his time. He would have had many years of service to give to this cathedral and to this city.

But is also a time for rejoicing.' The Dean's delivery lost a fraction of its former conviction at this point. The most acute of the sermon connoisseurs, the second tenor in the body of the vicars choral, who had attended theological college before losing his faith, later attributed the change to the Dean's suspicion that his listeners no longer believed in heaven or hell. Assuming they ever had. The Dean ploughed on.

'For if ever a man was going to take his place in the kingdom of heaven, that man was John Eustace. We rejoice today that he has gone to be with his Father in heaven. Though worms destroy my body, as the prophet Job tells us, yet in my flesh shall I see God whom I shall see for myself, and mine eyes shall behold, and not another. John Eustace, a good man, a meek man. Blessed are the meek for they shall inherit the earth. Blessed are the meek for they shall also inherit the kingdom of heaven.'

The Dean collected his papers. The acolyte escorted him back to his position. As the choir began an anthem by Purcell, the six pallbearers brought the coffin back down the nave of Compton Minster. A fleet of carriages waited to take it and the mourners to the little cemetery behind Fairfield Park. The funeral of John Eustace was over. In forty-eight hours' time, in the offices of Drake and Co., solicitors of Compton, his last will and testament was to be read to his survivors.

4

Lord Francis Powerscourt decided to walk the five miles from Hawke's Broughton into Compton the following morning. He was exceedingly angry. He took no notice of the fine scenery he was passing through, the February sun casting its pale light across the hills and the valleys. The incident that caused his wrath had occurred just after breakfast. Mrs Augusta Cockburn was decidedly tetchy this morning, he had noticed. The nose seemed to have become more pronounced, the cheeks more hollow. She snapped at the servants even more than usual. But nothing could have prepared him for the onslaught.

'And when do you intend to start work, Lord Powerscourt?' had been the opening salvo.

'I beg your pardon?' said Powerscourt, half immersed in the *Grafton Mercury*.

'I said, Lord Powerscourt, when do you propose to start work? You have been accommodated here at my wish and at my expense to investigate the circumstances of my brother's death.' She lowered her voice slightly and peered crossly at the door in case any of the servants were listening. 'So far as I can see you have done absolutely nothing except potter around this house and take advantage of your privileged position to attend various functions like my brother's funeral and the small reception we gave here after the burial ceremony. If I did not know of your reputation, Lord Powerscourt, I should say you were a shirker and a scrounger. We have not discussed money, but I am most reluctant to pay you a penny for anything you have done so far.'

Powerscourt had not been told off like this since he was about twelve years old. Then his reaction had been to hide in the top of the stables for as long as he could. This morning, he felt that charm would be the most potent form of defence.

'My dear Mrs Cockburn,' he began, 'please forgive me if I appear to be moving slowly. As I explained to you the other day I felt it was important to win the trust of the servants here before questioning them closely. If I appear as an unknown person from an unknown world I shall automatically seem hostile to them. Very soon, I know, I shall have to come out in my true colours. But not yet. Not until I judge the time is ripe. On that, I fear, you just have to trust me. In all my previous cases the people who asked me to look into murder or blackmail or whatever it was have always left me to my own devices. I would be more than happy to provide you with some references if you wish. I could start with the Prime Minister.'

Mrs Cockburn snorted slightly. 'I don't think that will be necessary,' she said, 'but I shall be watching, Lord Powerscourt. I shall be waiting for results.' And with that she had marched out of the room.

Bloody woman, Powerscourt said to himself on his walk, bloody woman. He could see the minster spire now, rising out of the valley like a beacon. As he entered the streets of the little city he saw that flags were still flying at half mast from the Bishop's Palace and County Hall in memory of the late Queen and Empress.

He was, he decided, looking forward to this meeting in the solicitor's office. He suspected that there would be trouble with the will. He suspected there might be more than one.

Oliver Drake's offices were right on the edge of the Cathedral Green, in a handsome eighteenth-century building with great windows looking out towards the west front of the minster. Powerscourt was shown into what must have been the drawing room on the first floor. Paintings of the cathedral adorned the walls. There was a long table in the centre, able to seat at least twelve. A fire was burning in the grate.

Oliver Drake himself was very tall, with a slight stoop. He was also painfully thin. His children sometimes said that he looked more like a pencil than a person. But he was the principal lawyer in Compton, with the complex and complicated business of the cathedral and its multiplicity of ancient statutes at the heart of his practice. To his right, appropriately enough, sat the Dean, dressed today in a suit of sober black with a small crucifix round his neck. The Dean already had a notebook and a couple of pens at the ready. Perhaps the man of God is better equipped for the tasks of this world, Powerscourt thought, than the laity he served. On the other side of Oliver Drake sat James Eustace, twin brother of the deceased. Powerscourt hadn't been able to glean very much information about him from Augusta Cockburn. She seemed to think it inappropriate for strangers to know the extent to which some of her family had fallen. Gone to America, lost most of his money, drinking himself to death were the salient facts lodged in Powerscourt's mind. Beside James Eustace sat Mrs Augusta Cockburn herself, looking, Powerscourt felt, like a very hungry hen. He himself was on the far side of Mrs Cockburn, furthest away from the seat of custom.

'Let me say first of all,' Oliver Drake had a surprisingly deep voice for one so skeletally thin, 'how sorry we all at Drake's were to hear of the death of John Eustace. The firm offers our condolences to his family and,' he nodded gravely to the Dean, 'to the cathedral. John Eustace had been a client of mine for a number of years, as are so many of his colleagues.' A thin smile to the Dean this time.

'I regret, however, to inform you this afternoon that there are complications, great complications in the testamentary dispositions of the late Mr Eustace. It is unlikely that there can be any satisfactory resolution to the problems today. I may have to take further advice. I may have to go to London.'

Powerscourt thought he made London sound like Samarkand or Timbuktu. But Augusta Cockburn was out of her stall faster than a Derby winner.

'Complications?' she snapped. 'What complications?'

Oliver Drake did not look like a man who was used to interruptions on such occasions. Powerscourt wondered how he would manage if Augusta Cockburn gave him the full treatment, rudeness, insolence and insults all combined.

'I beg your pardon, Mrs Cockburn,' he said icily, 'if you will permit me to continue my explanation without interruption, the position will become clear.'

Powerscourt felt it would take more than that to silence Mrs Cockburn. He was right.

'Perhaps you will be kind enough to inform us of the nature of these complications.'

Oliver Drake sighed. Outside the morning sun had been replaced by heavy rain, now beating furiously against the Georgian windows.

42

'To put it very simply, ladies and gentlemen, there is more than one will.' There were gasps of astonishment from around the table. The Dean stared open-mouthed at Drake. Augusta Cockburn muttered, 'Impossible!' to herself several times. The twin brother, his face heavily blotched from regular consumption of American whiskey, looked as though he needed a drink. Now. Powerscourt was fascinated.

'I think it may be helpful,' Oliver Drake continued, rummaging in a file of papers in front of him, 'if we take these various wills in time order.' He glared at his little audience as if daring them to speak. Powerscourt was temporarily lost in a very fine watercolour above the fireplace which showed a brilliant sun setting behind the minster, bathing its buildings in a pale orange glow.

'Will Number One dates from September 1898. I remember it because we wrote it together in my office downstairs. Apart from a number of bequests to his servants,' Augusta Cockburn shuddered, 'the main beneficiaries are twenty thousand pounds each to his brother and his sister, fifty thousand pounds to Dr Blackstaff' – Augusta Cockburn glowered significantly at Powerscourt when the doctor's name was mentioned – 'and the remainder to the Cathedral of Compton, for its use and maintenance in perpetuity.'

Powerscourt thought he detected a faint hint of a smile crossing the features of the Dean.

'Forgive me, Mr Drake,' Augusta Cockburn interrupted again. 'Please excuse a simple housewife and mother for asking a simple question. How much money are we talking about? How much was my brother worth?'

Powerscourt thought you could actually hear the greed.

Oliver Drake was ready for this one. 'Mrs Cockburn, that is, of course, a very sensible question. But it is not susceptible to an easy answer. Until the will is proved it will be difficult to establish the entire pecuniary value of your brother's estate.'

'But you could make a guess, could you not, Mr Drake?' She sounded like a small child who had been given a bag of sweets only to have them snatched away.

'It is not the business of country solicitors to make guesses, Mrs Cockburn, but I feel I should give you an approximation.' He paused. The logs were crackling in the grate. A hooded crow had come to perch in the tall tree opposite the window. Perhaps the crow felt it deserved something too. 'I expect the value of the estate, including Fairfield Park, to be well over one million pounds.'

Still Augusta Cockburn would not give up. 'How much more?'

'It could be a million and a quarter, it could be a million and a half. But I feel we should return to the main business in hand.'

'Forgive me, Mr Drake, could you just set my mind at rest?' Augusta Cockburn had been doing some arithmetic on a small pad in front of her. 'In the case of the first will – and I don't believe it to be the real one for a moment – when you take the various other legacies into account, does that mean that my brother and I would receive twenty thousand pounds each and the cathedral,' she paused as if she could scarcely believe her calculations, 'the cathedral,' the scorn and incredulity formed a toxic mixture, 'would have received almost one million pounds?'

Oliver Drake looked at her solemnly. 'That is correct. The second testament dates from March of the year 1900.' Something about his tone made Powerscourt suspect that Drake didn't believe this will was genuine. 'Your brother made this will when staying in your house, Mrs Cockburn. He entrusted it, you say, to your husband for safekeeping. Your husband, in his turn, put it under lock and key at your family solicitors, Matlock Robinson of Chancery Lane. They in their turn forwarded the document to me.'

Oliver Drake held up a typewritten document, less than a page long. The Dean was peering at it with great interest. Now Powerscourt was able to pinpoint one of the areas where Augusta Cockburn hadn't told him the whole truth at their first meeting. Little had been said about this will, drawn up in her house less than a year ago.

'In this document,' Powerscourt wondered why he used the word document rather than will, 'there are no bequests to the servants at all. Fifty thousand pounds for the twin brother, fifty thousand pounds to the Cathedral, the residue, including the house, to his sister, Mrs Winifred Augusta Cockburn, of Hammersmith, London.'

'Nothing for the servants?' asked the Dean. 'Nothing at all? I think that is very uncharacteristic.'

It was the first time Powerscourt had seen Augusta Cockburn smile. For a few moments at least, she was rich.

'The final will, in terms of time, is very recent. It was written in January this year. It too has some unusual features.' Powerscourt wondered what he meant by too. One of the other wills? Both the other wills? 'For a start,' Drake went on, 'it was not supervised by me or by any member of this firm. It was done in Homerton, about fifteen miles from here, at the local solicitor's. The terms are identical to the first one, bequests to the servants, fifty thousand pounds for the doctor, twenty thousand pounds each for the brother and sister. But there is no mention of the cathedral at all. The residue, the sum of almost a million pounds, goes to the Salvation Army.'

'The Salvation Army?' said the Dean and Mrs Cockburn in unison. 'Why should a man,' the Dean simply talked over Augusta Cockburn, 'who has served the cathedral for the best years of life, who has promised on a number of occasions, in my hearing, to leave the cathedral a large bequest, why should he then turn round and leave it to people in pretend military uniforms who try to look after drunks and beggars? I cannot believe he wanted to leave his fortune to a soup kitchen!'

'Please forgive me.' It was the first time James Eustace, twin brother of the deceased, had spoken. The accent was still English, with just a faint transatlantic twang.

'I don't have a will to put before you. But I do have a letter from my brother which I believe has a bearing on things. He wrote it to me after his visit to New York last July. Perhaps you'd like to read it out, Mr Drake?'

Drake's role as a conjuror of wills was over, Powerscourt felt. To produce three in one afternoon was pretty impressive going.

'"Dear James,"' read Oliver Drake. The Dean was leaning across to inspect the handwriting. '"It was very good to see you, even if your circumstances were a little distressing. I hope the money I have left for you will be sufficient for your needs and that you will soon be back on your feet. Please rest assured that if you need any further financial assistance I shall be only too happy to assist. Your loving brother, John."'

The Dean snorted. Oliver Drake coughed. Powerscourt wondered if the twin brothers had had identical handwriting. Outside the window the crow flew off noisily to a better perch.

Oliver Drake took a large white handkerchief from his pocket and mopped his forehead. The fire was warm this afternoon. 'So there we have the current position, ladies and gentlemen. I feel that I myself am somewhat constrained in that I am named as the executor in the two wills drawn up locally. I feel that some of you may also wish to take independent legal advice. I have had my clerks prepare copies of all the wills for you to take away if you wish. I propose that we reconvene here ten days from now. That should allow time for consultations. Are there any final points before I declare this meeting closed? Mrs Cockburn.'

Augusta Cockburn was still in fighting form. 'It seems to me, Mr Drake,' she said with a rare lack of venom, 'that the easiest course would be to declare the Matlock Robinson will the authentic one and proceed accordingly.' Then normal service was resumed. 'I cannot believe that my brother would have wished to leave fifty thousands to a humble country doctor. Nor do I believe he would have wished to leave a million pounds to a heap of ancient stones that are merely a memorial to a long-dead religion. And I think it is quite simply inconceivable that he would wish to leave a million pounds to be wasted on the human scum who infest our great cities.'

'Thank you, Mrs Cockburn,' said Oliver Drake wearily. He wondered if all the women in London behaved like this. If so it must be an even more dreadful place than he thought. 'Dean?' He glanced at the figure in black to his right.

'I have nothing but contempt for the insults we have just heard to our cathedral and, dare I say it, our God. However, I need to take advice. I expect the cathedral will wish to employ legal representation.' Privately the Dean was deeply troubled, but not by all the complications about the will, nor by the insults of Mrs Cockburn. He was going to have to take advice from his Bishop. It was virtually unheard of.

'Mr Eustace?' Oliver Drake turned to the twin brother. 'Do you have anything you wish to say?'

'Nope,' said James Eustace. 'Bloody meeting has gone on far too long. I want to get out of here. I need a drink.' With that he headed for the door and the saloon bar of the White Hart, two doors away.

Five minutes after the last departure Powerscourt knocked on the door of the downstairs office of Oliver Drake.

'Mr Drake? Could you spare me a few minutes of your time? And may I speak in confidence?' Drake pointed to a comfortable armchair beside his desk. Powerscourt couldn't help observing that not a single piece of paper, file or legal reference book was to be seen on the green leather surface. Mr Oliver Drake, he felt, must be an obsessively tidy man.

Powerscourt explained that he was in Compton under false pretences. He was not a family friend of the Eustaces', as represented. He was not a family friend of Mrs Augusta Cockburn's. He was an investigator, hired by Mrs Cockburn to look into the death of her brother. He gave details of some of his previous cases to lend authority to his position. He now found himself, he told the solicitor, in the bizarre situation of harbouring misgivings about his employer.

'Never thought it likely you'd be a family friend of the Cockburns', Powerscourt,' said Drake with a smile, 'don't suppose the bloody woman has any friends at all. Hell's too cold for that woman, if you ask me. I speak in confidence, of course. But tell me, why does she want her brother's death investigated? Do you think there was anything suspicious?'

'I am not in a position to answer that at present. There are three main grounds for her suspicions. She thought the butler was lying. She thought the doctor was lying. She thought it most unusual that the coffin was closed so soon. But consider what we have heard this afternoon. Pretend, for a moment, Mr Drake, that you are also an investigator. Money, like jealousy, is one of the most potent motives for murder. Enormous sums of money, like those possessed by the late John Eustace, are an even more powerful motive. Start counting, Mr Drake. The doctor could have wanted him dead for the fifty thousand pounds. Mrs Cockburn could certainly have wanted him dead to lay her hands on the lot. In her present circumstances even twenty thousand might be worth killing for. The cathedral, taken as a human institution rather than a transmitter of God's truth, could have wanted him dead. You can replace a lot of roof slates with one million pounds. The Salvation Army could have wanted him dead. And the twin brother, almost certainly secreted away in the public house next door as we speak, could certainly have done with the money. That's five, for starters.'

'Good God, man, you're not saying that John Eustace was murdered, are you?' said Oliver Drake, rising to his full height and staring out of his window.

'No, of course not. I think it is extremely unlikely, but not impossible. However, Mr Drake, there are certain aspects I wish to investigate where I need your approval. Talking to the solicitors Matlock Robinson in Chancery Lane, for example. They would wish to know if I had the executor's permission before they said anything. And I should like to bring in some examples of the late Mr Eustace's handwriting, to compare them with those in the various wills in your possession.'

'Lord Powerscourt,' said Drake, 'I feel absolutely certain that you are a man to be trusted. If you wish to say, as part of your inquiries, that you are assisting the firm of Drake and Co. in their handling of these wills, please feel free to do so. There's only one condition.'

'And what is that?' asked Powerscourt.

'That you endeavour to keep that bloody woman out of my office for as long as you possibly can.'

'I take it that you are referring to my current employer?' said Powerscourt with a smile.

'I most certainly am,' said Oliver Drake.

Solicitor and investigator shook hands.

Patrick Butler was sitting once more in the living room of the little house on the edge of the Cathedral Close. It was strange how frequently he found himself in this part of the city between the hours of four and five in the afternoon. Anne Herbert was making tea in the kitchen. The children had gone to their grandparents' house where the two little boys could watch their grandfather's trains come and go to their hearts' content.

'Anne . . .' Patrick came through to the kitchen. He didn't think his news would wait. 'I've made a very exciting discovery.'

Anne Herbert smiled indulgently at her friend. Anybody who came in regular contact with Patrick Butler was the recipient of very exciting discoveries two or three times a day. 'What is it this time?' she said.

'I shan't tell you anything if you're going to be like that, treating me like a child,' said Patrick, lifting the tea tray to carry it into the other room.

'I'm sorry, Patrick. Please tell me about your discovery.'

Patrick looked at her suspiciously. But he couldn't help himself.

'You know that man who's staying at the Eustaces' house at Hawke's Broughton? The one we saw at the funeral service?'

'Was he a tall fellow with dark curly hair and an expensive-looking coat?'

'The same,' said Patrick, helping himself to a home-made biscuit. 'His name is Powerscourt, Lord Francis Powerscourt. I looked him up in Debrett's. They keep a copy over in the cathedral library. He's supposed to be a friend of the Eustace family.'

'How did you discover his name, Patrick?' said Anne Herbert, pouring two cups of tea. She sometimes suspected that Patrick and his staff would stoop to almost anything to find out what they wanted.

'One of the servants at Fairfield Park told me,' Patrick said, managing to spill some of his tea as he spoke. It was a diversionary tactic. He did not care to mention that since the death of John Eustace regular sums of money, moderate but not inconsequential, had been entrusted to the care of the butler in exchange for information. 'But that is not the point, Anne. I was talking to one of those London reporters last week.'

Five of Fleet Street's finest feature writers had been despatched to this obscure part of the country to entertain their readers with tales of the death and funeral of the Chancellor of Compton. His house, in these accounts, had been magnified in size until it was considerably larger than Knole or Chatsworth or Blenheim Palace. The wealth had been increased too, rising to sums of almost unimaginable size as if Eustace had been richer than the Carnegies and the Vanderbilts and the Rockefellers combined. And the grief of the town was portrayed on a truly Homeric scale, frail old men, strange peasant hats on their venerable heads, leaning on their rustic sticks as they lined the coffin's route, clay pipes held in reverential tribute by their sides, weeping mothers holding up their children to watch and mourn as the funeral cortège went past, public houses empty and deserted in tribute to the dead. This last touch appealed particularly to the scribes from the capital. There was no greater testimony to the depth of mourning that they could imagine.

'And what did this London reporter say?' Anne Herbert had read one of these accounts in a great national daily and been appalled. She hoped that her Patrick was not going to be contaminated by these strangers who could arrive in a town and tell packs of lies about the inhabitants, secure in the knowledge that they would shortly be on the next train back to London.

'He said, Anne,' Patrick looked into those green eyes again with great delight, 'that this Lord Powerscourt is an investigator. He is famous for solving murders and mysteries of every description! How about that!?'

'Well, he may well be an investigator, Patrick. He may equally well be a friend of the family as everybody says. You mustn't jump to conclusions.'

'Maybe not,' said the editor of the *Grafton Mercury*. 'But what if he was? What has he come to investigate? Death Comes to the Cathedral? The Curse of Compton Minster?'

Anne Herbert had decided long ago that journalists like her

friend fell in love with their headlines rather more than they did with the truth.

'That's all very interesting, Patrick,' she said, looking at him in rather the same way she looked at her eldest when he came up with some outlandish piece of nonsense. 'I think you'd better have another biscuit.'

The subject of Patrick Butler's speculation let himself quietly out of the side door of Fairfield Park. It was raining heavily again, large puddles threatening to meet and cover the little road with water. In the distance a lone horseman leant forward in his saddle, trotting peacefully towards his destination. Lord Francis Powerscourt was going to pay his respects and ask his questions of Dr William Blackstaff, friend of John Eustace, and the last man to see him alive.

He wondered about the lies and the liars he had known as he splashed his way towards the doctor's house. Some people were just very bad at lying. He suspected that the butler Andrew McKenna was one of those. A furtive air came over him any time his late master's death was mentioned. Others simply convinced themselves that the lie was true, that the falsehoods they were telling had actually happened. And Powerscourt was certain as he entered the drive of Dr Blackstaff's house that it was seldom the words that gave the liars away. Rather it was the gestures, the lack of eye contact, the slight shifting in the chair, the sudden combing of the hair. He remembered one spectacularly successful liar and fraudster in India whose only fault was that the fingers of his left hand would strum very slowly on his knee when he began to dissemble. The greater the lie, the faster the strumming became.

A servant showed him into the doctor's drawing room at the back of the house. Curtained windows led out to where the Blackstaff garden must have been. There were three sofas and a couple of old armchairs on either side of a great fire.

'Lord Powerscourt, good to see you again.' The two men had met briefly at the reception after Eustace's burial. 'How can I help?' The doctor was charm personified, clad for the day in a suit of dark green tweed.

He thinks I've come about my health, Powerscourt suddenly realized, a hacking cough perhaps, influenza brought on by the winter rains of Compton.

'Dr Blackstaff, I owe you an apology. I am afraid I am operating

50

under false pretences.' Powerscourt sank into a chair opposite the doctor by the fire. 'I have been described as a family friend, and it was under those auspices that we met the other day.'

Dr Blackstaff wondered what was coming. Was Powerscourt another long-lost relation come to claim his inheritance? Was he a lawyer come to arbitrate about some problem concerning the will?

'I am a private investigator, Dr Blackstaff. I have been hired by Mrs Augusta Cockburn to investigate the circumstances surrounding her brother's death.'

Dr Blackstaff looked at Powerscourt for about fifteen seconds. Then he burst out laughing. 'That bloody woman,' he said, 'she'll be the death of us all. I shouldn't be at all surprised if she was having us all watched twenty-four hours a day.' He stopped suddenly and looked closely at Powerscourt. 'You're not having me watched twenty-four hours a day, are you, Lord Powerscourt?'

Powerscourt laughed. 'Certainly not,' he said. But he knew, after that meeting in Drake's the solicitors, he knew even better than the doctor that there were no depths to which Augusta Cockburn would not stoop to conquer her adversaries and retire from the field with one million pounds sterling.

'Perhaps the best thing, Dr Blackstaff, if you could bear it, would be if you could tell me the whole story once again. I apologize for asking you. I know how close you were to John Eustace and that further narration of his last hours will not be easy.'

So the doctor told his story once more; the late-night visit of his friend; John Eustace's complaints of feeling unwell; his examination of his patient and his decision to keep him overnight in his own house; his suspicions, already formed, that Eustace was suffering from a heart condition; his death, so sudden and so tragic the following morning. Sometimes Dr Blackstaff looked at Powerscourt. Sometimes he looked into the fire.

Powerscourt found his eyes wandering to the remarkable collection of medical prints and portraits from the past. To the left of the fireplace four men were holding down a fifth. In the centre of the print a man in a long coat was advancing towards the captive with a vicious pair of forceps in his hand. A fifth man was holding the victim's mouth open. Just a routine operation in the life of an eighteenth-century dentist, though Powerscourt suspected the bills must have been very high after all the assistants had been paid off.

'Thank you, doctor,' said Powerscourt when the narrative was complete. 'I'm sure it must be painful, even for a medical man like yourself, to have to recall all the details once more.' Mind you, he said to himself, he's had plenty of practice already. Mrs Cockburn, the coroner – and the Dean, Powerscourt remembered, had told him he'd had a long conversation with Blackstaff about John Eustace's last hours. 'I hope you won't mind,' he said, 'if I ask you a few questions?'

'Not at all,' said Dr Blackstaff.

Powerscourt felt that he needed some unorthodox bowling at this point. Any obvious question about the central points would be easily parried. He needed a googly, the ball that spins in the opposite direction to the one expected. Or an inswinging yorker, the ball of very full length that shoots under the bat and spread-eagles the batsman's wicket.

'Would you say that you were in any financial difficulties at present, Dr Blackstaff?' said Powerscourt, his eyes wandering towards an oil painting above the fireplace.

'Financial difficulties?' said Dr Blackstaff, turning slightly red. 'No. I have no worries about money. Why do you ask?'

'Forgive me, doctor. Let me tell you in confidence that there is a possible bequest to you in John Eustace's will of fifty thousand pounds. In my profession, we are accustomed to looking for the dark side of the moon, as it were. If you were my current employer, you would look for the dark side of Satan himself. Money is often a motive for murder.'

'I had no knowledge of any such bequest, Lord Powerscourt, please believe me. That is the truth.'

In which case, Powerscourt said to himself, what about everything else you have been telling me for the last half an hour? He tried another tack.

'What happened to his clothes?'

'His clothes?' said the doctor, looking slightly lost.

'John Eustace's clothes, Dr Blackstaff. The clothes he came in. The clothes he died in.'

Dr Blackstaff looked uncertain. He paused slightly. 'Sorry,' he said. 'The housekeeper sent them back to Fairfield Park, I'm sure.'

Where they would have been cleaned, if cleaning were necessary, Powerscourt thought. Or thrown away by the butler.

'Can you remember what your friend was wearing when he came to see you that evening?'

Again that slight, barely detectable pause. 'He was wearing a brown suit with a pale blue shirt,' said Dr Blackstaff. John Eustace had at least fifteen brown suits and a dozen pale blue shirts.

'And when he stayed here overnight, I presume you lent him a nightgown or some pyjamas or something similar?' Dr Blackstaff nodded. His interrogator went straight on.

'And in the morning, did he get dressed again, or did he, please forgive me, did he die in his nightgown?'

'He passed away in his nightgown, I'm afraid,' said the doctor. He got up suddenly. 'I'm finding all this rather a trial, Lord Powerscourt. Can I interest you in a whisky? A glass of port?'

'A whisky would be delightful,' said Powerscourt, knowing that time was being bought while glasses were found, bottles opened, drinks poured. He looked at an oil painting on the far side of the fireplace. It showed a naval surgeon at work in the height of battle, probably during the Napoleonic Wars. The centre of the painting showed a line of sailors, covered in blood, with different varieties of arm and leg severed or broken, lying on a long table. At the top of the painting there was a small patch of blue sky. The rest was obscured by the smoke of battle. Mentally, if not physically, you could hear the great guns being run out to pound Britain's enemies into pulp. The surgeon had an enormous knife in his hand. He was covered in blood from the top of his chest. Blood was flowing out of the room as the ship tilted in combat. The surgeon's assistant was trying to pour something, almost certainly rum, Powerscourt thought, down the patient's throat. Another sailor was going to have an arm or a leg amputated.

'Thank you so much,' said Powerscourt, cradling a large glass of whisky as Dr Blackstaff lowered himself into the position opposite. There had been a certain hesitation about the question of clothes. He decided to continue in the same vein.

'Just one last question about Mr Eustace's last hours here, doctor,' he said gravely. 'Was he wearing boots or shoes?'

Again that slight hesitation. For a fraction of a second Dr William Blackstaff wished to confess. He could tell the truth and this interrogation, none the easier to bear for the studied politeness with which it was carried out, could stop. Then he thought of the scandal. Temptation passed.

'Boots, I think. It was rather a wet day, Lord Powerscourt. It usually is round these parts at this time of year.'

He's playing for time again, with these remarks about the weather, Powerscourt felt.

'Black or brown?'

Blackstaff would have said they were purple with yellow stripes if he thought the questioning might stop.

'Black,' he said, almost recklessly.

'One last question, doctor, and then I shall trespass on your time and your hospitality no longer,' said Powerscourt. Dr Blackstaff looked more cheerful. 'John Eustace's request that nobody should look at him in his coffin, was that an unusual one? I mean, have other patients of yours asked for the same thing?'

'Unusual, yes. Uncommon, no. Quite a number of my patients have made similar requests in the past. With some of them, I think it is because they believe more in the old superstitions than in the God of the cathedral. There are a number of ancient pagan sites within twenty miles from here.'

Powerscourt made a mental note to make a pilgrimage to the pagans when time afforded. He looked at his watch. It was five minutes before eight o'clock.

'Thank you so much for your time, doctor,' he said, finishing his glass and rising to his feet. 'Perhaps I could call on you again, and we can discuss more pleasant matters, like your collection of medical prints and paintings. I think they're absolutely fascinating.'

Dr Blackstaff escorted him to the door. 'I used to hang some of the prints in my surgery,' he said, 'but then I had to take them down.'

'What happened?' asked Powerscourt with a smile.

'It was all very regrettable,' Dr Blackstaff replied. 'I used to get lots of small boys with imaginary illnesses who came to enjoy the blood and gore. Then I had a farmer whose arm had been severed in an accident. He took one look at that naval painting and passed out clean, right in the middle of the surgery floor.'

As Powerscourt made his way back to Fairfield Park, he was sure of one thing, that Dr Blackstaff had been lying for some if not all of the time. The uncertainty about the clothes convinced him on that point. And there had been that very strange comment right at the beginning of the interview: 'That bloody woman,' Dr Blackstaff had said, 'she'll be the death of us all. I shouldn't be at all surprised if she was having us all watched twenty-four hours a day.' Us all . . . Powerscourt said it to himself a number of times as he tramped the couple of hundred yards up the rain-drenched road. Who is us? Or rather who are us? More than one person? A single accomplice? A number of accomplices?

In one minute's time, Powerscourt said to himself, I am due to

54

talk to Andrew McKenna, the last man in Fairfield Park to see his master alive. Powerscourt had timed the interview so there could be no opportunity for doctor to confer with butler. He felt an almost overwhelming curiosity coming over him. An over-whelming curiosity about suits and shirts and boots and shoes.

5

Andrew McKenna was waiting for Powerscourt in the drawing room. Outside the wind was rattling the windows and the rain was lying in puddles on the steps of the stone staircase. Powerscourt took a careful look at the Fairfield butler. McKenna was in his forties, clean-shaven, with very dark hair that was beginning to thin on top. His pale brown eyes, Powerscourt thought, were frightened.

'First of all, McKenna, I must make a confession to you and to everybody else in this house. I am not a family friend of the Eustaces' or the Cockburns'. I am a private investigator, employed by Mrs Augusta Cockburn to look into the circumstances surrounding her brother's death.'

'Very good, sir,' said McKenna in a quiet voice. Inwardly he was terrified. This, or something like this, was what he had been dreading ever since the events of that terrible night. At least this Lord Powerscourt wasn't wearing a police uniform.

'I'm sure we can clear things up very quickly, McKenna. There's no cause for any alarm,' said Powerscourt with a smile. He was beginning to feel sorry for Andrew McKenna. 'Can you remember what Mr Eustace was wearing the last time you saw him?'

'Wearing?' said McKenna in a mystified voice. Powerscourt thought that both the butler and the doctor seemed to have trouble with clothes.

'What sort of a suit, if he was wearing a suit that day, what sort of shirt, that sort of thing?'

'Sorry, my lord,' said McKenna, seeming to recover himself. But then a terrible thought struck him. Powerscourt had just come from the doctor's house. He must have asked the doctor the same questions. If his answer wasn't the same, then the police might come and take him away. What would the doctor have said? Why hadn't the doctor worked out that somebody might ask this question?

'He was wearing a brown suit, my lord,' said McKenna, but he didn't sound convinced.

'And the shirt?' asked Powerscourt. Once more there was a pause.

'I think it was a grey shirt, my lord.'

'Grey, you say,' said Powerscourt thoughtfully. Up the road in the doctor's house John Eustace had been wearing pale blue.

'And was he wearing boots or shoes, can you recall?'

Again Andrew McKenna paused. Powerscourt could hear John Eustace's eighteenth-century clock ticking on the mantelpiece. McKenna, he noticed, had turned rather red during the interrogation.

'As far as I remember, it was boots,' he said finally. Powerscourt suddenly remembered the dental print on Dr Blackstaff's wall. McKenna was the victim, held down by four men, a fifth forcing open his jaws, while he, Powerscourt, was advancing towards him, fearful pliers in hand.

'What colour of boots, McKenna?'

'Brown, my lord. Mr Eustace didn't like black boots for some reason. Black shoes were acceptable, but not boots.'

'I see,' said Powerscourt as gently as he could. 'Perhaps you could you just describe the last evening he spent here in this house. Before he went to the doctor's.'

Andrew McKenna began the same narrative he had given to Mrs Cockburn some time before. He was word perfect on this part of the story. He repeated it to himself many times every night in case he had to tell it again. He had even written it all out on three sheets of paper and hidden them under his floorboards.

Powerscourt wasn't really listening. He knew. Well, he didn't actually know in any sense that would stand up in a court of law. It wasn't just the discrepancy between the colour of the boots and the shirts in the two accounts. It was the demeanour of the two men.

'Shortly after he finished his dinner, my lord, Mr Eustace went to his study,' McKenna was still going, telling his story like children at school reciting a poem they had been made to learn for their homework the night before, struggling occasionally to remember the next

57

line. Powerscourt wasn't sure what to do. 'I went to see him some time after that and he told me not to wait up for him . . .'

Just what had happened to John Eustace? Had one of these two men killed him? Killed him for the doctor's cut of the will? Fifty thousand pounds would go a long way, even after you had paid off your accomplice. Andrew McKenna might be a very poor liar but he didn't look like a murderer. But then, as Powerscourt remembered from some of his previous cases, murderers seldom do look like murderers.

'The next time we heard of Mr Eustace, my lord, was when the doctor came round the following morning and told me he was dead.' McKenna's recital was almost over.

Had Eustace killed himself? Powerscourt wondered. Blown the top of his head off with a pistol, rendering himself so disfigured that nobody could have endured the sight of him lying in his coffin, half of his face blown away in the blast? That would explain why the coffin lid was sealed so early. Maybe the shame of a suicide had to be covered up. Powerscourt wondered briefly if he should put this very question right now to Andrew McKenna. 'Did Mr Eustace commit suicide, McKenna? Did you find him with the top of his head blown off and then go to the doctor who concocted this cover story?' He decided against it.

'I got all the servants together – we had to wait a while, my lord, for the gardeners to come in from outside – and I told them the terrible news.'

McKenna stopped. Powerscourt found himself looking closely at McKenna's hands. They were clasped together very tightly, as if to stop them from shaking.

'Very good, McKenna,' said Powerscourt in his most emollient manner. 'Could I just ask you one more thing? Would you have said that Mr Eustace was upset or depressed about anything in the days and weeks before his death?'

McKenna thought for a moment or two. 'I wouldn't have said he was depressed, my lord. He was always a very cheerful gentleman, at least to us servants. Maybe preoccupied would be the word, my lord. But then he was often preoccupied if he had to preach an important sermon or something like that.'

'Thank you so much, McKenna. I am much obliged to you for that account. And now, perhaps, you could be so kind as to bring me a whisky. I shall be in Mr Eustace's study.'

Without realizing at first what he was doing Powerscourt began pacing restlessly up and down the drawing room. Lady Lucy would have smiled had she seen the habits of Markham Square reproduced so perfectly in a country house nearly two hundred miles away, the same abstracted air, the same sense of having completely departed from the immediate surroundings. Suppose it wasn't suicide, he said to himself. Suppose John Eustace was murdered. But by whom? By the butler? By the doctor? By another of the servants with a grudge against his master? By an outside hand, by a person or persons unknown? But how did they get in? How did they get out? McKenna had told him very clearly on his first afternoon in the house that none of the doors or windows had been disturbed during the night of John Eustace's death. The whole household would have had to be involved in such a conspiracy. And what should he tell the ferocious Augusta Cockburn? She was, after all, his employer. Was he bound to pass on his suspicions to her? Powerscourt dreaded to think of the mayhem her tongue and her malevolence could cause if she thought her brother had committed suicide or been murdered.

Andrew McKenna was waiting in the study with the whisky. Powerscourt told the butler he could go, and not to wait for him. He checked his watch. He had just given McKenna the same instructions at virtually the same time as his previous master had done some days before. And in virtually the same place. Maybe, thought Powerscourt fancifully, this is my last evening on earth. Maybe I shall meet a mysterious death in this very house tonight. Maybe my body too will be sealed in its coffin before its time, leaving Johnny Fitzgerald to conduct an investigation into the circumstances of my demise.

'Shut up,' he said quietly to himself and took a drink from his whisky. He sat down at the Eustace desk. Hanging on the wall directly in front of him was a reproduction of a Raphael. Powerscourt remembered reading about this painting. It showed Pope Leo the Tenth flanked by two other cardinals who just happened to be his nephews. The Pope, a powerful figure of a man, is wearing a red cape over an ornate white cassock. The fleshy jowls on his face reveal that whoever may have been his favourite saint it was not one of the ascetic ones like St Francis of Assisi. Leo is seated at a desk, covered with a rich red cloth, examining an illustrated book with a magnifying glass. One of his nephews is to his right-hand side, staring into space, possibly praying. The other, a rather shifty-looking prelate in Powerscourt's view, is looking directly at the painter. Powerscourt shuddered as he remembered that Raphael painted it shortly after a murder plot against Leo had been unearthed in the College of Cardinals. This was Leo's way of telling the world, and the College of Cardinals in particular, that he was still at large. The whole canvas, dominated by reds and scarlets against an almost black background, reeked with pomp and power and privilege.

A sudden thought struck Powerscourt. He got up from the desk and went to the door to look at the painting from a greater distance. His original assumption was that it must be a reproduction. Perhaps it wasn't. Perhaps it was the real thing, an original Raphael hanging here in the quiet hamlet of Hawke's Broughton. He peered at it again. He looked round the other walls to see if Leonardos and Michelangelos might be hanging here as well. He didn't think so. He remembered what he had learnt in a previous investigation involving works of art and forgeries and murdered art critics. Raphaels for some reason fetched incredibly high prices. John Eustace could certainly have afforded a whole gallery of Raphaels. Perhaps the value of his estate would have to be increased by another hundred thousand pounds or so if Pope Leo and his nephews were consigned to the art dealers and the auctioneers of New Bond Street.

Powerscourt sat himself down at the desk once more. He hadn't come here to look at the paintings on the wall. He began a systematic examination of John Eustace's kneehole desk. The drawers to the left-hand side were filled with business correspondence. There were bills from the local shopkeepers, details of repairs to the house, correspondence with his bank. The bottom two drawers were filled with letters from friends and acquaintances. Powerscourt would much rather have seen John Eustace's own letters to his friends. They might have told him something about his state of mind. He took a note of the addresses of his two most frequent correspondents, a country clergyman in Norfolk and an archdeacon in Oxford. Maybe they could tell him something.

If the left-hand side of John Eustace's desk rendered unto Caesar, the right-hand side belonged to God. The first two drawers related to his work in the cathedral. The third contained bundles of sermons. Powerscourt riffled through John Eustace's thoughts about the meaning of Lent, about the Christmas message, about how it was easier for a camel to go through the eye of a needle than for a rich man to enter into the kingdom of God. Powerscourt suspected John Eustace might have had some difficulty with that one. But the bottom drawer was the most interesting of all. It too contained sermons. But whereas all the ones in the drawer above had been stacked in neat piles, in the bottom drawer Powerscourt found that the pages were all confused. Thou shalt love thy neighbour as thyself was jumbled up with the raising of Lazarus, the feeding of the five thousand had alternate pages with the forty days in the wilderness, the parable of the fig tree was mixed up with turning the water into wine. Powerscourt took all the pages out and laid them on the floor. Perhaps I am doing this in tribute to John Eustace's memory, he said to himself. For he felt that whatever desecrations might have happened to the dead man, somehow he would want his sermons left intact. After half an hour they were all reconstituted and replaced in their drawer. All except one. John Eustace's sermon on the first verse of the thirteenth chapter of the First Epistle to the Corinthians, though I speak with the tongues of men and of angels, and have not charity, I am become as a sounding brass or a tinkling cymbal, had two pages missing. Powerscourt realized as he stared at the Roman numerals at the top of the first page that all the sermons had the dates of composition on them. The tongues of men and of angels had been composed fifteen months before. It seemed to have been the last sermon John Eustace ever wrote. Maybe he adapted some of the older ones for other occasions. And two pages of the six had disappeared.

Powerscourt leaned back in his chair and gazed up at the fleshy features of Raphael's Renaissance Pope. Most probably somebody took the missing pages after the death. But why? A dark suspicion crossed Powerscourt's mind. He took two more pages from the sermon. Then he looked back and took a page from Lazarus, preached three years before, and from the parable of the fig tree, written five years earlier in 1896. Handwriting, he knew, changes slightly over time. The next time he went into Compton he would take his pages from the sermons of the late John Eustace into the offices of Drake and Co. and compare them with the scripts of the various wills. He thought he knew what he would find.

'So what are you going to do about that young man?' Hilda Davies, previously Hilda McManus, had been Anne Herbert's best friend at school.

'What do you mean, what am I going to do about that young man?' said Anne defensively. The two were having early morning tea in the little house on the edge of the Cathedral Close. Anne thought she was uncertain about her feelings for Patrick Butler, the editor of the *Grafton Mercury*, so she had invited her best friend around for an exchange of views.

'You know perfectly well what I mean, Anne. Let's not beat about the bush. What are you going to do about Patrick Butler?' Hilda Davies had been described in one of her school reports as a forceful personality in class. The passing years, the acquisition of a rich husband and three children and a large house, had made her almost domineering. Her servants called her a bully behind her back.

Anne felt she was under attack. 'Well,' she said defensively, 'I like him well enough.' A month before, the three of them had attended a concert together and Patrick had taken them out to dinner in the town's finest hotel.

'Such a pity, I always felt, that your first husband died on you, Anne.' Hilda made it sound as though Anne was personally responsible for his passing. 'Such respectable people, clergymen. And such prospects too in a place like this. I'm sure Frank might have become the Dean at least.'

'Are you saying that newspaper editors aren't respectable people?' Anne was beginning to feel cross.

'I grant you he is good-looking, that Patrick,' condescended Hilda, 'but why can't he find a proper job like other people?'

'What's wrong with newspaper editors?'

Hilda Davies felt it was not the time to mince words. 'For a start,' she said, 'I don't think they're quite respectable. Lots of the county people round here'– Hilda obviously thought of herself as being at the very epicentre of county and Compton society – 'wouldn't dream of asking one of them to dinner. You'd have to check the silver after they'd gone.'

'If you're suggesting that Patrick is in the habit of going out to dinner and pinching other people's spoons, then you're sadly mistaken.' Anne, normally so placid, was in danger of losing her temper. She remembered that their schooldays had been punctuated by occasional very vicious rows.

'It all depends on the society one keeps,' said Hilda, casting a superior glance at the fairly humble furniture in Anne Herbert's little drawing room. 'If you want to consort all your life with the minor clergy and the poor vicars of Compton, then I suppose it might be all right.' She paused briefly before firing another salvo. 'It's not just that they're not quite respectable. Journalists are known for having a number of serious deficiencies in their character.'

'And what might those be?' said Anne.

'Horace has had a lot of dealings with them, especially when he goes up to London on business for the firm.' Horace was Hilda's long-suffering husband. He was a partner in a firm of Compton solicitors. Once a year at most, to the best of Anne's knowledge, he ventured forth to the metropolis. She suspected he would have gone more often if he could for a respite from his domestic bliss.

'Drink,' said Hilda firmly, shaking her head at the hazards of a reporter's life. 'They all drink far too much. Maybe not when they start, but it gets most of them in the end. Horace said he knows of a number of them who have ended up destitute, their poor families abandoned for the spirit bottle.'

'Patrick doesn't drink very much,' said Anne defensively.

'He may not now, but he will. They all do in the end. And they're unreliable. Never home at a respectable hour like my Horace. Think what appalling parents they must be.'

'Patrick is very good with the children, he couldn't be kinder.'

'That's only until he gets his hands on you, my dear. Then it will change. You can't possibly contemplate being married to such a creature.'

Anne Herbert wondered suddenly what it would be like if Patrick Butler got his hands on her. She thought it might be rather agreeable.

'And what about his family? Are they proper sort of people?' said Hilda with a sneer on the word proper.

'They're a perfectly respectable family, Patrick's people. His father is a schoolmaster in Bristol.'

'My dear, I think the position is quite clear,' said Hilda Davies, drawing the meeting to a close. 'You should break things off with this young man. He sounds most unsuitable. You must wait for a better offer to come along. I'm sure there must be a regular supply of unmarried clergy passing through the cathedral. One of them will turn up.'

'Wait? Wait?' said Anne Herbert angrily. 'I am now twenty-eight years old. I have two small children. As for waiting, you couldn't wait at all. You threw yourself at the first rich man who came into view. I don't think you're in any position to talk to me about waiting.'

'I certainly am in a position to talk to you about unsuitable young men. And this Patrick or whatever he's called seems to me to be most unsuitable. Now I must go. I have an appointment to keep. When you have had a chance to reflect in peace I am sure you will see that I am right.'

Mrs Hilda Davies departed into the morning air of Compton. Anne closed the door firmly behind her. Well, she said to herself, I may not have been altogether sure of my feelings towards Patrick before this morning but I am much more certain now. She wondered wistfully if he would come round for tea that afternoon.

Lord Francis Powerscourt was smiling to himself as the Fairfield coachman drove him into Compton early in the morning three days after his encounter with the sermons. He had a recent letter from Lady Lucy in his hand. The first page expressed the hope that his mission was going well and that the case wasn't going to prove very difficult. There was news of her vast tribe of relations, two of whom, elderly aunts in their late eighties, Powerscourt learned, had recently passed away. He had once worked out that with the sheer numbers of Lucy's extended family, at least six should perish every year according to the law of averages. Replacements were arriving even faster to fill up the numbers at the other end of the age scale.

But it was the second page that lifted his spirits. 'There has been a most moving meeting in the drawing room this afternoon,' Lucy had written. 'The two children had asked specially to see me. They came in hand in hand, Thomas looking very solemn, Olivia looking as though she had been crying. I asked them what the matter was. "It's Papa, Mama," said Thomas. "Yes, it's Papa," said Olivia in a doleful voice. "What about Papa?" I said. "We don't think he's coming back soon like you said. We think he's gone back to the war." "We think," Olivia went on, sounding as if the two of them were a Cabinet committee just emerged from a special private session, "we think he's gone back to South America. Where he was before." "South Africa, Olivia," Thomas corrected her, "it's South Africa we think he's gone back to. And we think he'll be gone for another year like he was last time." "A year or more," said Olivia who had no idea how long a week is, let alone a year. I showed them your letters, Francis. I promised them you were in England. I got out the map to show them where Compton is and how there was a symbol on there for the cathedral. Part of me wanted to laugh, they were so serious about it all. So you see, when you do come back, and I pray God it is very soon, you'll have to tell them you haven't come back from the wars, only from the west of England.'

Powerscourt had now arrived at the offices of Drake and Co., solicitors, with their fine views over the Cathedral Close.

'Wills?' said Oliver Drake, shaking his visitor warmly by the hand. 'You said you wanted to look at those. Do you mind doing it in my office? With all due respect I don't think I should let you take them away.'

'Of course,' said Powerscourt as he drew out the pages of his three sermons, Lazarus, the tongues of men and of angels, and the parable of the fig tree. Drake took out the three wills and handed them over to Powerscourt. The easiest one to forge, Powerscourt felt sure, would be the one that came from the firm of London solicitors, Matlock Robinson in Chancery Lane. With the text typewritten there were only three signatures to add. He peered closely at John Eustace's signature. The hand looked almost identical to the text of the tongues of men and angels. He could see no difference either in the Eustace signature on the other two wills and the sermons he had brought with him. He knew that there were people, particularly on the Continent, who claimed that they could analyse personality from handwriting and definitively state whether or not a signature was genuine. But he knew too that no English court would accept such evidence. He was not likely, he decided, to make any progress here.

'Mr Drake?' Powerscourt handed back the three wills. 'Thank you so much. I have to confess I am none the wiser after comparing these various bits of handwriting. Now I must make for the station.'

Powerscourt was settling himself into a first class compartment on the London train when a familiar figure, clad in clerical black, swept past. The Dean was carrying a large and impressive-looking briefcase. He looked, as usual, as though he felt the world would not function properly, might indeed fall off its axis, if he was not managing as many of its affairs as possible.

'Powerscourt, good morning to you. Can't stop, I fear. I have a compartment reserved up ahead. There is much to do.'

'Good morning to you, Dean. Are you going to London on the Bishop's business?'

The Dean snorted. 'The words business and our Bishop do not sit together well, Powerscourt. Do you know the story? It is old now, but everybody in Compton knows it.' The Dean paused and looked at his watch. 'I have just time to tell it you. We do not leave for a couple of minutes.'

The Dean abandoned his position by the door of the compartment and sat down opposite Powerscourt.

'Nine or ten years ago it must have been now, the previous Bishop died. Salisbury was Prime Minister, normally very good at ecclesiastical appointments. Not like that old rogue Palmerston who couldn't tell a crucifix from a chasuble. No idea at all. Salisbury takes his time. Eventually he slips the name past the Queen. Moreton's the man for Compton. Moreton. Salisbury tells the happy news to his Private Secretary, leaves him to get on with it. Only one problem, Powerscourt, there are two Moretons at large in the upper reaches of the Church of England. There's Professor Gervase Bentley Moreton of Oriel College Oxford, expert on the textual differences in the early versions of the Four Gospels and precious little else. And there's William Entwistle Moreton, then headmaster of one of our great public schools, Marlborough or Rugby, can't remember which. Private Secretary Schomberg McDonnell looks up Moreton in his church directories. Finds the Oriel Moreton. Writes to him with news of his appointment that very day. Always admirably brisk in the way of executing business, that McDonnell. I sometimes think he'd have made an excellent dean. Oriel Moreton replies by return of post, accepting the position. Tells his college. Tells his friends. Tells *The Times*. Only thing was, McDonnell had got the wrong Moreton. It was Headmaster Moreton who was meant to be Bishop of Compton. But by then it was all too late.'

The Dean, after this splendid example of brotherly love and Christian charity, looked at his watch again. The train was beginning to move.

'Must go now, Powerscourt. I have much business to attend to.' He glanced at his briefcase as if he could see the papers inside through the dark blue cover. 'I should be through with all this by Reading. Probably just on the far side of Reading to be on the safe side. Do come and see me then.'

'And who do you think I am?' Lord Francis Powerscourt was crouching down in his own drawing room in Markham Square later that evening.

'You are Papa, Papa!' said the voices of Thomas and Olivia Powerscourt in unison.

'Do you think I am here in our house?'

'Yes, Papa, yes!' shouted the children.

'Am I in South Africa?' Powerscourt shouted back.

'No, Papa!'

'Are you sure, Thomas? Are you sure, Olivia?' Powerscourt prodded each of them in the chest.

'Yes! Sure!' The noise must have carried as far as Victoria station.

'Am I here in London?' Powerscourt shouted once more.

'Yes, Papa!'

'Not anywhere else?'

'No, Papa! No!'

'Very good then,' said their father, rising to his feet. He thought the children could have carried on shouting all night. 'Off you go now. I'll come and see you later.'

'I hope that may reassure them a bit,' he said, readjusting his waistcoat and smiling at Lady Lucy. Johnny Fitzgerald was looking closely at a wine label on the sofa. Powerscourt had told them both about the strange goings-on in Compton just after he arrived back in London. Now he wanted to take their advice.

'Lucy, Johnny,' he began, 'what do you think I should do about Augusta Cockburn? Should I tell her that I think her suspicions were justified, that there was something strange about her brother's death?'

'It's a contradiction in terms,' said Johnny Fitzgerald, still inspecting the writing on his bottle. 'Couvent des Jacobins, it says here. I know my French isn't world class but *couvent* says convent, nunnery to me, lots of ladies in black habits and wimples praying all day and all night, that sort of thing. Jacobins says French revolutionaries to me, violent and unstable fellows, their brains addled with cheap red wine and garlic, endlessly denouncing their colleagues and sending them off to the bloody guillotine. What are they doing on the same bottle, Francis? If the nuns had their way they wouldn't have let any Jacobins inside the nunnery, if the Jacobins had got in there wouldn't have been any nuns left alive. I don't understand.'

Lady Lucy smiled as she handed him the corkscrew. 'Maybe you can tell from the taste, Johnny. As to Mrs Cockburn, Francis, I think you are morally obliged to pass on your suspicions. I'm not sure but I think that must be the right thing to do.'

'You haven't met the woman, Lucy. Please God you can get through the next few months without that privilege. Augusta Cockburn is a monster.'

Johnny Fitzgerald now had a dreamy look on his face. 'I think the Jacobins must have won out against the nuns,' he said. 'It's sort of spicy, raring to go. Just the thing to sample before you charged a few barricades. I don't think you have to do anything at all about the Cockburn connection, Francis. Let it wait. Any number of things could happen in the next couple of weeks. You haven't been engaged on the case for very long. And,' he went on cheerfully, 'you haven't had me around to help you. Things are about to look up.' And with that he took another large mouthful of his Jacobin Couvent.

'Think of it this way,' said Powerscourt, still wrestling with his conscience. 'What if the brother did commit suicide? I still think that's the most likely explanation. Or, much more unlikely, what if he was murdered, though I can't for the life of me work out how that might have been done. If it was murder, there may be more murders. And if it was suicide and it was your brother wouldn't you want to know?'

'Francis,' said Lucy, trying to ease her husband's way, 'you don't actually know any more than this Mrs Cockburn woman. She had her suspicions. You have yours. But there's nothing more than that, is there? You haven't got any evidence at all. So why not tell her that you are continuing with your investigations and leave it at that?'

Powerscourt didn't look happy with that. Johnny Fitzgerald was looking at the fire through the red in his glass. 'I'm ready for anything, Francis,' he said. 'One or two more glasses of this stuff and I'll be fit to storm the Bastille single-handed. I do wonder, mind you, if it mightn't be necessary to sample another bottle of this revolutionary brew. It mightn't taste quite as uplifting as this one. You do have some more of this stuff, don't you, Francis?'

'Lots more,' said Powerscourt, grinning at his friend. 'But look here, Johnny. There's the business with the wills. Oliver Drake implied quite strongly at the last meeting that there was something fishy about the Cockburn will that left her all the money. It was as if he didn't quite believe in it.'

'When was it dated?' asked Johnny Fitzgerald. 'How long before he died?'

'It must have been about six or seven months before his death, when he was staying with Mrs Cockburn the sister up in London,' said Powerscourt. 'But suppose he wasn't actually staying with Mrs Cockburn at all. Suppose it happened like this. Here's Mrs Cockburn, always hard up, always moving house all the time to cheaper property, as one of the servants in Fairfield Park told me so happily. She decides to forge a will for her brother, which leaves most of the money to herself. Even if there is another will she can still use the fake one to contest it. End of money problems for Mrs Cockburn.'

'You're not suggesting, are you, Francis,' said Lady Lucy, looking slightly shocked, 'that Mrs Cockburn was the murderer, or that she organized some hired killers to murder her brother?'

'I don't think I'd rule it out,' said Powerscourt after a pause for thought.

'But,' Lady Lucy went on, 'there's a flaw in your argument. If she was the murderer, why did she ask you to investigate the business?'

'Cover, Lucy, it could just be cover. What better proof of your innocence could you offer than hiring an investigator to look into a murder you have committed yourself? It's the most disarming thing you could do, virtually guaranteed to make everybody believe automatically in your own innocence.'

'Just because you don't like the woman,' said Johnny Fitzgerald, 'doesn't mean that you have to wish she's going to end up on the gallows.'

'Let me just say one last word on the subject,' said Powerscourt with a smile. 'You two have not actually met this virago in the flesh. You have not faced her insults and her rudeness. If you ask me, hanging is far too good for her.'

6

Blissfully unaware that he had recently been described as a most unsuitable young man, Patrick Butler sat looking at a set of figures in his office in Compton. To call it an office was to pay it a great compliment, for it was really much more like an attic than a place of business. The command post of the *Grafton Mercury* was on the top floor of an old building in a side street some distance from the Cathedral Close. To gain admittance visitors had to climb a rickety set of stairs that creaked out the details of every new arrival. Inside there was just enough room for the three people who worked there, and then only one could stand fully upright. There was a large map of the county on one wall and back copies of the newspaper piled up against the others. A small and rather dirty skylight admitted an inadequate amount of natural light. Patrick felt sure that the newspaper editors in the great cities of Britain must have enormous offices with well-tended fires and handsome paintings lining their walls. But he knew that he would never be as proud of any future office he might inhabit as he was of this tiny garret. This was his first command.

The production of newspapers is a complicated business requiring considerable powers of organization and discipline. Every week Patrick and his colleagues displayed those virtues to the full. In their everyday lives, however, they did not reveal any sign of such powers. Their little office was a shambles. There were scraps of paper, empty bottles, cigarette butts, opened books overdue at the local library, old bills lying all over the floor. The desks, as they referred to the rough trestle tables where they wrote their stories, were virtually invisible. Piles of paper, half-finished articles, draft copies of advertisements, old editions of the national newspapers were scattered about in cheerful abandon. Every now and then Patrick and his colleagues would rouse themselves to action. The floors would be swept, the tables cleared of their accumulated detritus. For days afterwards one or other of them would complain that a piece of paper full of vital information had been lost, or that the full list of all those persons attending the Rotary Club luncheon could not be found. Patrick was a great believer in printing lists of persons attending functions, however humble. He believed that human vanity is always flattered when a person sees his or her name in print. Word of this stupendous fact travels fast round the little community. The person or persons are duty bound to purchase a copy of the *Grafton Mercury* to see their name in print. Maybe even two copies, as this is such an important edition.

The figures he was looking at related to the recent sales of his paper. Since his arrival he reckoned that he had increased the circulation by about twenty per cent. But that was not enough for Patrick Butler. There were thousands and thousands of citizens in the county who were not buying his paper. When he saw the good people of Grafton en masse, on market days or attending a local football match, he wanted to harangue them on the error of their ways. Did they know what they were missing by not buying the *Grafton Mercury*? Did they not realize how their lives would be enriched by reading the pages of his paper? But one recent edition had sold spectacularly well. It was the commemorative special on the death of Queen Victoria which was still on sale all over the county. It was going to make an enormous profit. What else, Patrick wondered, could merit the same treatment and deliver an equivalent volume of sales?

He rose cautiously to his feet and crouched under the grimy skylight. If he craned his neck, he could just see the spire of the minster off to his right. Something was stirring in his restless brain. The cathedral, something to do with the cathedral. Then he had it. The anniversary, the one thousandth anniversary of the cathedral was to come at Easter. There had been announcements in the paper already, details of the plans for the celebrations, of course. But what a perfect opportunity for another anniversary edition. The articles and headlines began to roll through the printing presses in his mind. A Day in the Life of a Medieval Monk. The Role and Responsibilities of an Abbot. Patrick thought the Dean might enjoy writing that one. The Hands of Time, he could find somebody to tell the story of the medieval clock, said to be the oldest in England. The Bells of God, one of the fraternity of bell ringers who still met after practice in the Bell tavern could provide that one. He wondered briefly about the Dissolution of the Monasteries and the Reformation. Had there been any executions at that time? Terror Stalks Compton as Friars Burn, he particularly liked that headline. Then there had been the corrupt and venial Dean early in the last century who had packed the offices of the cathedral with no fewer than fourteen of his own relatives. Corruption in the Chapter. Perhaps that was a bit strong, but the article would please the dissenters and the Nonconformists. Something for everybody in the broad church of the *Grafton Mercury*. As he pulled his head back inside his attic Patrick forgot to duck. He cracked his head loudly and painfully on one of the rafters. 'Damn,' he said very loudly. 'Damn.' He checked his watch. It was nearly half-past four. Maybe he should call on the Dean to ask him to deliver his thoughts on the managerial and administrative role of an abbot in the reign of Edward the Confessor. His route, he realized, would take him right past the front door of Anne Herbert's little house on the edge of the Cathedral Close. And it was tea time.

Mr Archibald Matlock was the proud owner of an office considerably larger and more opulent than that of the Editor of the *Grafton Mercury*. His was on the second floor of a handsome old building on Chancery Lane. Prints of lawyers, old and modern, lined the walls. There were lawyers with enormous pens, lawyers with enormous faces, lawyers with enormous noses, lawyers with enormous bellies. There was even one, Powerscourt noticed, almost hidden on the top rank of this rogues' gallery, hanging from an enormous gibbet for his crimes against humanity. Powerscourt rather liked that one.

'I have come about a will,' said Powerscourt, 'the will of a clergyman called Charles John Whitney Eustace.' Archibald Matlock did not look like a man who might feature in the prints on his walls. He was of regulation height, with a regulation dark grey suit, and a regulation dark blue tie. The most noticeable thing about the man was his hair, or the lack of it. Archibald Matlock was completely bald. Every now and then he would rub the top of his head as if checking to see if his earlier complement of hair had returned.

'Lord Powerscourt, it is not our custom to discuss the wills of our clients with anybody else, however distinguished they may be.' With that he smiled a deprecating smile.

'Forgive me,' said Powerscourt, smiling back, 'I should have said. I have a letter here from Mr Oliver Drake, solicitor of Compton. He is the executor of Mr Eustace's will.'

Matlock took out a small pair of glasses and scanned the document. 'I see. So you are an investigator, Lord Powerscourt. Is there, may I ask, trouble about the will?'

Powerscourt felt sorely tempted to reply that he was not in the habit of discussing his client's affairs with outsiders, however bald they might be, but he refrained.

'There is indeed trouble about the will,' he said. 'The trouble is that there are three of them.'

'Three wills?' said Matlock incredulously. 'I have heard of cases with two wills, but never three. Is it true that the late Mr Eustace was one of the richest men in England? I seem to remember reading about it in the newspapers but you can never really believe what they tell you.'

'I believe it is true,' said Powerscourt, his eye suddenly caught by one of Matlock's lawyers on the wall, who appeared to be reading out to a greedy-looking company from an enormously long piece of paper with the legend Will inscribed at the top.

'It would help me,' he went on, 'if you could tell me everything you can remember about the composition of this will. I believe it was written about six or seven months ago, all of it, except the signatures, typewritten.'

Archibald Matlock paused. He went to a large cupboard at the back of his office. 'We keep copies of all the wills that pass through our hands,' he said. 'These ones here should really be locked up in the basement safe. I shall make a note to have them removed.' Powerscourt noticed that above his head was a splendid print of two eighteenth-century lawyers, wigs slightly adrift, consuming an enormous meal. Discarded bones are lying on the floor. Two empty bottles are lying on the table, a phalanx of further bottles waiting to one side. An elderly, very fat lawyer is just about to carve an enormous side of roast beef.

'I remember this will very clearly,' said Matlock, returning to his desk with a piece of paper. 'The whole process began when Mrs Augusta Cockburn – do you know Mrs Cockburn, Lord Powerscourt?' A faint tremor of distaste, it might even have been fear, passed over the Matlock countenance. Powerscourt nodded. It looked as if the woman was as ferocious in Chancery Lane as she was in Compton. 'Anyway, the whole process began, as I was saying, when Mrs Cockburn turned forty. In my experience, turning forty can be a pretty traumatic event, particularly for women.' Powerscourt wondered briefly how many forty-year-old females Archibald Matlock had helped cross this particular threshold. 'Mrs Cockburn decided it was time to make her will. She grew very excited about the making of wills. She decided it was time for her husband to make his will, though there was nothing there to leave to anybody at all. And she decided that it was time for her brother to make his will. He was staying with her at the time of this particular onslaught.' Powerscourt suspected the moon must have been full at the time, Augusta Cockburn rampant across heaven and earth.

'Both Mr and Mrs Cockburn's wills were made here in this office. They wrote out what they wanted, one of our young women typed it up on the machines downstairs, they were signed here in this office.' Archibald Matlock paused. 'Did you know Mr Eustace, Lord Powerscourt? Did you meet him in the flesh?'

'I have only met his twin brother,' Powerscourt said, 'and he is rather dissolute, to put it mildly. I never met Mr John Eustace in person. But why do you ask, Mr Matlock?'

'Well,' said Archibald Matlock, running the hourly check on his bald patch with his right hand, 'for the Eustace will, there was no signature in this office. Mrs Cockburn brought in her brother's dispositions and we prepared them in the normal way. She asked if I could go to the house to witness the signature and make sure everything was in order. She said her brother was unwell.'

'Why could it not wait until he was better?' said Powerscourt.

'I'm coming to that. Mrs Cockburn explained that he had to return to Compton very soon, but that he was anxious to sign the will before he left London. She said it was preying on his mind, that he would make a better recovery once he had finished the business.'

'Did any of this strike you as odd, Mr Matlock?'

'After twenty-five years in this profession, Lord Powerscourt, nothing strikes me as odd any more. Subsequent events, I have to say, were odder still. May I tell you something in confidence?' Powerscourt nodded. He thought he knew what was coming. 'I have never found Mrs Cockburn to be one of my easier clients. She can be very difficult. At this time, I recall, she was very excited, almost hysterical, particularly about her brother's will. But Matlock Robinson have looked after the family's affairs for as long as I can remember. Obligations have to be respected. It was not the custom to go to the clients' houses for the signing of wills. Much better for them to come here.' And the lawyers can remain in their offices, earning their fees, Powerscourt thought, rather than wasting their time travelling through the crowded streets of the capital.

'At this time,' Matlock went on, 'the Cockburns were living somewhere in West Kensington or Hammersmith, well out in the west. Mrs Cockburn showed me into what might at one time have been her husband's study. Mr Eustace was wearing a large coat with a muffler round his neck. His sister said he was feeling the cold because of his illness. There was very little light in the room as Mrs Cockburn said it was hurting his eyes. She brought in a couple of neighbours as witnesses. Mr Eustace signed it, I signed it and the whole thing was over in less than three minutes. I brought the will back to the office, of course, and despatched it, as requested, to my colleague Mr Drake at the appropriate time.'

'Did John Eustace speak at all?' said Powerscourt.

'He may have muttered good afternoon, I'm not sure. Apart from that, if indeed he did say that, he said nothing at all.'

'Did you see his face?'

'Not properly, no.'

'If he walked into this office now, Mr Matlock, would you recognize him?'

'I very much doubt it. He was so heavily wrapped up.'

Powerscourt wondered if Matlock had reached the same conclusions as himself.

'Did you think at all about what had happened, Mr Matlock?'

'I can't say that I did, Lord Powerscourt. I was in a great hurry that day. It was my wife's birthday and I had sworn to be home early. Then the firm was very busy with a very difficult case. But can I ask you, Lord Powerscourt, what you think was going on?'

Powerscourt looked carefully at Archibald Matlock. He decided to take him into his confidence. 'I think it perfectly possible that the man who signed the will that day was not John Eustace.'

'God bless my soul,' said the solicitor. 'Why do you say that?'

'It's only conjecture, Mr Matlock, not hard facts that lawyers like yourself are so fond of. The key thing, it seems to me, is the signature. I have compared the signature on that will with John

Eustace's hand and I cannot tell the difference. I doubt if anybody could. But suppose you had found a forger. Suppose the forger could reproduce John Eustace's hand, or anybody else's, perfectly. But he could not reproduce his voice. If the man wrapped up against his illness, with the muffler round his neck, had talked to you in a foreign accent, or an East End accent, would you have believed he was John Eustace? You would not. So the lights are low, he is heavily wrapped up, but the signature on the will seems authentic. The will is false. But that is almost impossible to prove.'

'God bless my soul,' said the solicitor. His left hand this time checked in vain for the return of the hairs on his head. 'What are you going to do?'

'I wish I knew, Mr Matlock,' said Powerscourt, beginning to take his leave. 'Thank you so much for your time. I must return to Compton without delay.' He knew perfectly well what he was going to do but he felt he had said enough already. As he walked down the stairs towards Chancery Lane, he saw another of those prints on the wall. It showed three lawyers seated round a table. The surface is invisible for the piles and piles of heavy coins heaped upon it. The lawyers are counting the coins and putting them into little bags. All three are smiling.

Part Two

Candlemas

February 1901

7

The English countryside is turning into fairyland, Powerscourt thought, a white and rather mystical fairyland. Snow was falling fast over the hills and valleys of the county of Grafton, settling on the roads and lanes, smoothing and obliterating everything beneath it. Distant farmhouses looked like the blobs on a child's painting. The horses were treading carefully now as the snow piled up. Soon, reflected Powerscourt, it would be time for the fairies to go home. Perhaps they already had, darting or flying back to their magical castles through this world of enchanted white.

It was shortly after five o'clock in the morning. The Dean's man, a human giant, well over six feet of brawn and muscle, had called for him at Fairfield Park with a cryptic message. 'The Dean says you're to come at once,' was all he would say. Powerscourt's attempts to glean further intelligence on the short journey into Compton had been in vain. The man was a silent giant. In the two days since his return to Compton Powerscourt had not been idle. He had walked yet again the short route between the house and the residence of Dr Blackstaff. He had called on the Chief Constable to announce his presence in the county and to request assistance, should that become necessary. He had walked several times all around Compton itself, spotted on one occasion by Patrick Butler, who had made a mental note that the man who might be an investigator was still in the locality.

Powerscourt didn't think it was the habit in English cathedrals to start the day with a service at five thirty in the morning. Perhaps, centuries before, the Benedictine monks would have been up for hours, with a couple of Masses already under their belts, but not now in this first year of the twentieth century. So what could have happened for him to be summoned at this ungodly hour of day?

Another body? Another corpse? Not far to go now. Powerscourt realized that they were approaching the walls that ran around the Cathedral Close. Then he saw a light burning in the Deanery which lay opposite the minster in a handsome eighteenth-century house.

'Good morning, Powerscourt. So glad you're here. Please come in.' The Dean, Powerscourt noted with interest, was wearing an enormous blue dressing gown. Beneath it, glimpsed occasionally as he walked, were a pair of white flannel pyjamas with dark blue stripes. He had a pair of battered slippers on his feet. He led Powerscourt into a large drawing room. A fire was beginning to splutter in the Dean's grate but it had not yet warmed the room. The Dean's drawing room was bitterly cold.

'The Chief Constable you know, I believe.' Powerscourt bowed slightly to William Benson. Benson, he noticed, had found the time to put on a dark suit, although Powerscourt saw that in his haste and possibly in the dark the Chief Constable had put on an odd pair of socks.

'Chief Constable told me about your occupation, Powerscourt,' said the Dean, trying to warm himself in front of his fire. 'Suggested I should send for you.'

'What has happened?' said Powerscourt, his mind alert from his ride through the snow. 'Has there been a disaster of some kind?'

'Disaster?' snorted the Dean. 'You could call it that. Or maybe worse.' He pulled his dressing gown tighter round his powerful frame. 'Let me give you the facts. On the far side of the cathedral you may have seen a little terrace called Vicars Close. That is where the vicars choral, the people who sing in the choir, live while they are with us. There is a large building at the bottom of the Close, the end nearest the cathedral, called Vicars Hall where they eat their meals. The kitchen there is huge. It has a great spit, large enough to roast an ox. At four thirty-five this morning, the porter found the remains of a man who had been roasted all night on that spit. He was almost unrecognizable, but the porter managed to identify him as Arthur Rudd, a senior member of the community of vicars choral.'

The Dean crossed himself very quickly. The Chief Constable bowed his head. Powerscourt looked at the fire. The flames of hell have come to this tiny city, he thought. For our God, he remembered the lines from the Old Testament, is a consuming fire, a fire that had sucked the last breath from the lungs of the unfortunate Arthur Rudd. Hieronymus Bosch and his apocalyptic vision of the torments of the damned are stalking the inhabitants of Compton Minster. What more tortures did he have in store for his victims?

'This is terrible news,' said Powerscourt. 'Has a doctor been to inspect the body?'

The Dean nodded. In matters of practical efficiency the Dean had no equal in the Cathedral Close. On the higher questions of the nature of good and evil, of sin and redemption, he might not have been so strong.

'Dr Williams is with him now. He is supervising the removal of the body from the Vicars Hall to the undertakers. He is going to conduct a preliminary investigation there. He should be joining us shortly. And,' the Dean went on, with a faint note of distaste in his voice, 'I have asked the Bishop to be here at six o'clock.'

'Could I ask you, Powerscourt,' said the Chief Constable, 'if you have ever come across anything like this before?'

'I have not,' said Powerscourt. 'It is appalling. Could I ask, Dean, if the dead man had a wife and children?'

'He did not,' replied the Dean, 'but I must tell you two gentlemen that I am almost at a loss to know what to do in these circumstances.' Powerscourt rather enjoyed the almost. It implied that the situation might be desperate, the enemy might be at the gates, the vandals might be about to enter Rome, but the Dean would remain master of events.

'I'm not sure I understand you, Dean,' said the Chief Constable. 'The matter must be investigated in the normal way, however distasteful that may prove to the members of the church administration.'

'Think of our situation, Chief Constable, think of it, I pray you,' said the Dean, stretching his hands in front of him as if he was preaching a sermon and imploring the sinners to repentance. 'We have just had various members of the national press on our doorstep after the unfortunate death of Chancellor Eustace. I have to say that in spite of our best efforts that publicity was not altogether favourable. I dread to think what those gentlemen may say if they return to report on a member of the cathedral Chapter roasted to death on a spit in the Vicars Hall. The millennial celebrations for the Abbey and Cathedral of the Most Blessed Virgin Mary are but weeks away. And the last thing the Church of England as a whole can afford is another scandal. Our congregations are not growing any larger, as you know, Chief Constable. One more scandal could see them fall yet further until we minister only to assemblies of devout old women and dying old age pensioners.'

No need to talk to the faithful about imagining the fires of hell any longer, Powerscourt thought flippantly. You had a perfect example of the flames operating here, right inside the Cathedral Close itself. There was a loud knock on the door. Dr Williams, a handsome young man in his early thirties carrying a large medical bag, and the Bishop himself took their seats in the Dean's drawing room. Formal introductions were made. Even in these dreadful circumstances, Powerscourt said to himself, decency and good manners must prevail.

'The doctor has just told me what happened,' said the Bishop, 'we met on our way over here. It's truly terrible.' The Bishop shook his head. Powerscourt remembered what the Dean had told him on the train to London. He doubted if expertise in the textual differences in the early versions of the Four Gospels would be much use to a bishop at a time like this. Maybe that other Moreton, Headmaster Moreton, accustomed to coping with scandals about drinking and debauchery among his pupils, might have been a better man in these circumstances. He looked closely at the Bishop. Episcopus, he remembered it said in Latin on the Bishop's cathedra, or chair, in the ornate and beautiful choir stalls in the heart of the cathedral. Beatus Vir. The Bishop. A holy man. Like the Dean, the Bishop was tall, but not so powerfully built. He had a distinguished shock of grey hair, and eyes that seemed to look elsewhere, at the plains of Galilee perhaps, or the kingdom of God. He kept clasping and unclasping his hands.

'Dr Williams,' said Powerscourt, 'have you had the time to complete a preliminary investigation of the late Arthur Rudd?'

'I have,' said the doctor.

'Could I ask you a question, if I may? Was the man dead before he was put on the spit, or was he killed by the flames?'

The Dean looked shocked that such a question should be asked in his drawing room. The doctor took a quick glance at the Dean as if asking permission to proceed. The Dean, wrapping his dressing gown ever tighter around his body, nodded slightly.

'I cannot be certain yet,' said the doctor. 'I shall have to conduct another examination when, forgive me, the body has cooled down further. But I am fairly sure he was dead before he was placed on the spit.'

'What makes you say that?' asked Powerscourt. He doubted if it would make much difference, but it might cast light on whether they were dealing with a complete madman, or merely a murderer with an advanced taste for the macabre.

'Forgive me, Lord Powerscourt, but if the man had still been alive I am sure he would have screamed out in his agony. Other inhabitants of Vicars Close would have been woken in their beds by the noise. But no screams were heard, so I say I think he was dead.'

'Thank you,' said Powerscourt, 'thank you very much.'

He wondered if the Dean would return to his earlier theme. He did.

'My lord,' he said, gazing down at Bishop Moreton, 'I was raising the question shortly before you arrived of the possible methods of handling these terrible events.'

The Bishop looked up at the Dean as if he didn't quite understand what he was saying.

'I was pointing out,' the Dean carried on, 'that a wave of scandal would erupt over this cathedral and over the Church of England if the full details of what happened in the early hours of this morning were ever to see the light of day. Think of what the newspapers will say, and all this just weeks before the celebrations for the thousand years of the minster.'

He's proposing a cover-up, Powerscourt said to himself. His mind drifted back to an earlier cover-up at Sandringham House years before when the Prince of Wales decided to conceal the murder of his eldest son. That too had been in January. Then too it had been snowing, great drifts piling up on the royal gardens and the royal roof. Then too doctors had been involved, concocting medical bulletins to deceive the newspapers and the public. He wondered about another doctor, Dr Blackstaff, asleep in his bed now, no doubt. Had he too concocted a cover-up story with the butler to conceal the facts about the death of John Eustace?

The Bishop was staring hard at the Dean. One of the pockets on the dressing gown, Powerscourt observed, had simply disappeared. Maybe his housekeeper hadn't noticed.

'I was merely thinking, my lord,' the Dean went on, 'that we could perhaps say that the poor man died in his sleep. Nobody need ever know the terrible circumstances of his passing. You could argue,' Powerscourt sensed that the Dean felt that the Bishop was not in favour of his scheme, 'that such a course would be the least distressing for the dead man's family, least distressing for the wider community of the cathedral, least distressing for the national community of the Church of England.'

The Dean paused. Dr Williams was looking directly at the Bishop, as if measuring him up for any possible illnesses. The Chief Constable was also looking at the Bishop, wondering what he was going to do. The prevailing wisdom in Compton was that the Dean ruled over the Bishop with a rod if not of iron, then certainly of some hard and unbending material. Powerscourt was fascinated by the Dean's expression. He looked, he decided, rather like a gambler who suddenly realizes that he may have overcalled his hand.

'My dear Dean,' said the Bishop quietly, 'I can fully understand why such a course of action might seem superficially attractive. But it is completely unacceptable. The lights of our Church may be burning low at the present time, the candles may even be extinguished, but that does not mean that we should falter in our commitment to the truth. What else, apart from our faith, do we have to cling to? I do not care how wide or how deep the scandal flows round this cathedral and round our city. I do not care how much the newspapers print, or how lurid their stories are. I do not care if the celebrations of one thousand years of religion in this place are dimmed by obloquy and disrepute. The Church must tell the truth. Our own truths, the truths of humility and repentance and the necessity of loving an invisible and often unaccountable God, may be difficult to accept for our own faithful. But what happened to that poor man Rudd is also true. We must recognize and acknowledge that truth. We must also accept that it happened inside a community which is supposed, above all others, to love its neighbour as itself. This terrible death must be as much a part of God's purpose as was that earlier death on the cross. We must tell the truth, Dean. We can do no other.'

The room fell silent. Powerscourt thought that the Bishop might have spent years of his life searching for lost iota subscripts in the early versions of the Gospels, wrestling with the precise meaning of words in a language dead centuries before. But when the time came, even at six o'clock on a cold January morning with the snow falling outside, however unlikely a representative of God's purpose he might have seemed, the Bishop had answered the call. His trumpet had sounded with clarity and conviction against the equivocations of the Dean. And the Dean, Powerscourt recalled, had but a single word above his stall in the cathedral choir, a word with no connotations of civic or ecclesiastical virtue. Deaconus. The Dean. The Bishop, however, had three. Episcopus, Beatus vir, Powerscourt thought to himself, looking at Gervase Bentley Moreton with fresh respect. The Bishop. A holy man.

But the Dean was very quick in his response. Powerscourt thought he was extremely light on his feet for such a burly man.

'My dear Bishop,' the Dean began, echoing his superior's own preamble, 'how very eloquently you put it. How wisely do you recall us all to our Christian duty and our obligations to our fellow men. I could not have put it better myself.'

Powerscourt thought he detected a slight smile crossing the face of the Chief Constable. Perhaps the man was an aficionado, a connoisseur of Bishop–Dean relations.

'So now it is time to make our plans,' the Dean swept on. A total volte-face, a complete reversal of his own position had been carried out in less than thirty seconds. Powerscourt, who was something of a student of successful military retreats, was most impressed.

'Chief Constable,' the Dean began the disposition of his forces, 'could I, as the person responsible for the cathedral, request you, as the representative of the forces of law and order, to commence your investigation into this terrible death? Could I make a humble plea for all possible discretion until we have conducted the funeral?'

The Chief Constable nodded.

'Could I make a suggestion here?' The Bishop unclasped his hands and placed them on his knees as if ready for active service. 'With your agreement, Dean, and yours, Chief Constable, might I propose that we ask Lord Powerscourt to take part in the investigation also, as a representative of the cathedral authorities? I'm sure his experience would be invaluable. If that is agreeable to you, of course, Lord Powerscourt?'

Powerscourt nodded gravely. He had served his sovereign in his time. He had gone on a mission to South Africa for the Prime Minister himself. He had investigated murders and mysteries for the Prince of Wales and for the masters of money in the City of London. Mammon had had its day. Now it was time for the service of God. He felt Lady Lucy would be proud of him.

The Dean embarked on a lengthy discussion with Dr Williams about funeral arrangements. The Chief Constable was staring at the snow still falling outside the window. The Bishop had closed his eyes, perhaps in prayer for the dead vicar choral, perhaps from lack of sleep. Powerscourt was listening abstractedly to the Dean as he reeled off the times when the cathedral would be unable to conduct the funeral because of previous commitments. He seemed to carry in his head the timetables of every service, prayer meeting and school visit over the next ten days.

'My lord Bishop, Dean, Chief Constable.' Powerscourt was beginning his service to his Lord and Master. Later he was to say it was more like the Stations of the Cross than any other event in the Christian calendar. 'I have been thinking about what you two gentlemen have been talking about and your concerns in this terrible affair. I observed that you were both concerned in your different ways about the coverage the death of Arthur Rudd might receive in the newspapers. I would like, if I may, to offer some thoughts on that question.'

'Please do,' said the Dean affably.

'The first point I would wish to make is that the tone of the coverage of the event will almost certainly be set initially by the local newspaper here in Compton. I believe it is called the *Grafton Mercury*. The editor here will have contacts in London. He may earn himself extra income from selling stories to the national newspapers.'

The Bishop looked astonished that such practices might be carried out.

'My second point,' Powerscourt continued, 'is that there are two very different extremes in handling the gentlemen of the press. One is to tell them absolutely nothing. That can, on occasion, be the only available option, but it leaves the journalists suspicious, certain that things are being concealed from them and liable to print whatever comes into their heads. The other extreme is to take them into your confidence, to tell them as much as you possibly can, to try to convey the impression that nothing is being hidden from them. In between, of course, there are any number of gradations. The natural course to pursue in this case would be to say as little as possible. I would recommend the opposite. If this man at the *Grafton Mercury* believes he has been told all there is to know, he will not have his reporters running all over the place inventing stories to fill the empty spaces in his newspaper. I would suggest this man needs to be brought on board, to be made to feel so involved that he feels he is batting for the cathedral eleven, if you see what I mean.'

'He's quite a good cricketer, since you mention it,' said the

Bishop. 'I saw him last summer. He made over fifty in very quick time.'

'Quite so, quite so,' said the Dean, unwilling to be drawn into reminiscences about past performances on the cricket fields of Compton. 'The editor's name, Powerscourt, is Patrick Butler.'

'Old or young?' asked Powerscourt, suspecting that an ageing editor nearing retirement might be more amenable than a young man keen to make his name and fortune.

'He's young,' said the Dean, 'very young. He hasn't been here very long. I should say he was an ambitious young fellow, wouldn't you agree, Chief Constable?'

'I certainly would,' replied the policeman. 'But he's a stickler for accuracy. He and his reporters are always very careful to get their facts right.'

'Well,' said Powerscourt, 'my recommendation would be that you take him into your confidence as soon as possible. And there's one other thing, if I might make another suggestion, gentlemen?'

'Please do,' said the Dean. Powerscourt observed that he had left his position in front of the fire and was now taking notes at a small table by the window.

'This thought comes from my recent experiences on military service in South Africa. I was there, for your information, for slightly over a year. I have only just come back. During my time there I was present at a number of battles. I subsequently read reports of some of these encounters in the newspapers, and I made a strange discovery. When the reporters were not present at the fighting or in the immediate aftermath, their accounts contained the most gory and bloodthirsty descriptions of the action. But when they were there in person, the accounts were very different, much more restrained, much more sober. It was as if the realities of war were almost too much for them, the mutilated bodies, the faces blown off, limbs left hanging from a thread of skin.'

'Quite so,' said the Dean, looking at his watch. 'Perhaps you could enlighten us, Lord Powerscourt, on the relevance of the battlefield conditions of the Boer War in South Africa to a dead man in Compton, found on a spit in the Vicars Hall?'

'Forgive me, Dean. I'm just coming to the point.' Powerscourt smiled diplomatically at the Dean, now turning over to a fresh page in his notebook. 'When you tell the young man about the spit, I suggest that you have the doctor with you. I suggest that the doctor gives the goriest account he can of what had happened to the body. There is no need to go into details now, Dr Williams, but it must have been absolutely frightful. I suggest that you try to make the man literally sick, if you can. That way I think you will find, oddly enough, that the coverage of the last hours of Arthur Rudd is both more limited and more restrained than it might otherwise be. If you let these reporters imagine things, their imaginations run riot. If they have to confront the horrible truth, it sobers them up no end.'

The Dean looked at the clock above his fireplace. 'My lord Bishop, gentlemen, please forgive me. I shall give Lord Powerscourt's recommendations the most serious consideration. But now I am due to conduct the service of Holy Communion in fifteen minutes. Deaths, plague, wars, invasion threats have not succeeded in halting the divine offices of our cathedral in almost a thousand years. One more death shall not succeed either.'

The Dean departed to change into more appropriate clothing. Powerscourt wondered if only suggestions emanating from the Dean in person were capable of instant acceptance. Dr Williams hurried off to his corpse, Powerscourt following behind. The Chief Constable left to brief his officers. Only the Bishop remained in the Dean's drawing room. His eyes were fixed on the fire. His lips moved slowly. He remained there a long time. Outside the snow was still falling.

Later that morning the streets of Compton were all white, the snow turning into slush in places. Anne Herbert was negotiating her way from the butcher's to the grocer's where she needed to purchase some more tea. Patrick particularly liked their new breakfast blend, she remembered. Then she heard a shout from across the street.

'Anne! Anne!' said the voice. She wondered if she shouldn't be addressed in a public place as Mrs Herbert but she doubted if the voice would take any notice.

'Anne,' said the voice again, sliding to a stop beside her. 'Are you managing all right in all this snow? Can I carry anything for you?' The weather, Anne thought, had wrought a sharp improvement in Patrick Butler's manners. She couldn't remember him offering to carry anything for her before.

'I'm fine, thank you, Patrick,' she said, smiling at the young man. His face was slightly red and he looked ever so young as he stood before her in his new suit. Anne had supervised its purchase in

Compton's only decent tailor the week before. Patrick had said he was hopeless about clothes.

'You must come with me at once, Anne. It's very important.' Anne thought these were most unusual circumstances in which to discuss elopement.

'Where are we going, Patrick? I haven't got all morning to gallivant round Compton with you in the snow.'

'You must come to my office. I'd take you for coffee but we might be overheard. I've got something very exciting to tell you.'

Anne Herbert had been once before to the local offices of the *Grafton Mercury*. In spite of all the best efforts of Patrick Butler, the place had looked a most appalling mess to her. She had thought of the extreme tidiness of her father the stationmaster's little office where everything was always in its proper place and dust was banished almost as soon as it appeared. It wasn't that men couldn't keep places tidy, she had decided. Some of them just didn't want to.

'It's not going to take long, is it, Patrick?' said Anne as they set off down Northgate towards the paper's headquarters.

'Not very long,' said Patrick, looking as excited as Anne had ever seen him. 'Do you think you might slip? Would you like to take my arm?'

'I'm fine, thank you.'

One or two of the citizens of Compton smiled knowingly to themselves as the young couple went past, Patrick Butler talking excitedly, Anne Herbert passing the occasional comment. They were well known now as young lovers. The more romantic of those in the know predicted Easter bonnets and an Easter wedding.

'I don't think there's anybody in the office,' said Patrick, as they began the tortuous ascent of the stairs. 'Peter's gone off to look into a flock of sheep said to be stuck in a snowdrift up in the hills and George is in court.'

Anne gazed in despair at the chaos that was Patrick's office. She was just about to ask why they didn't employ somebody to clean up for them when Patrick was off.

'Anne,' he said, closing the door firmly behind them and speaking very quietly, 'something terrible has happened up at the cathedral. Have you heard anything on the Close?'

'How do you know, Patrick? It all looked perfectly fine to me when I left. There were quite a lot of policemen wandering about but that's not unusual.'

'There are policemen all over the place, Anne. You can't get into Vicars Close at all. It's been sealed off. Oh, it's all very quietly done, there aren't lines of men across the street, but if you try to go up there a police officer pops out from somewhere and tells you the road is closed. They won't say why. Orders is all you can get out of them. I've just been there.'

'What do you think has happened, Patrick? Do you think some of the houses are going to fall down?'

'Those little houses, Anne, have been there for hundreds of years. I think I read somewhere that it's the oldest inhabited street in Europe. I think it's something terrible. And there's more. You remember that man Powerscourt, the one who's an investigator? He's wandering round the place, chatting to the odd person, looking as though he's thinking very hard. And there's one other thing. I have received an invitation to call upon the Dean at four o'clock this afternoon. What do you make of that?'

'Didn't you ask the Dean to write an article about the celebrations? Something to do with medieval abbots? Isn't it going to be about that, Patrick?'

'Medieval abbots be damned,' said Patrick Butler, 'this is more than that, I'm sure, much more. Look, I'd better get back and see where else is being closed down. Can I escort you home through the snow?'

Anne Herbert declined. But she did negotiate her way to the grocer's where she bought a pound of Patrick's favourite tea. Something told her she would be making the first cup later on that day.

Lord Francis Powerscourt spent much of the day wandering around the cathedral and its precincts. Normally he would have been fascinated by the building and its long history. But today it was as though he had a film or a glaze over his eyes. The flying buttresses and the chantry chapels, the medieval stained glass and the Angel Choir, the spandrels and the scissor arches, the presbytery and the misericords all left him cold. He wondered all day if there was a link between the death of John Eustace and the murder of Arthur Rudd. He still thought it possible that Eustace had committed suicide with the gun making some terrible marks on his face so he was hurried to his coffin with no relatives allowed to see him. But if he had been murdered, then surely money was

90

the motive. Eustace had so much of it. Powerscourt entertained dark suspicions of Mrs Cockburn. Suppose she had forged that will six or seven months ago when Mr Archibald Matlock had witnessed the signature of a man who did not speak, the entire ceremony over in three minutes. Suppose she waited until the memory of that ceremony would have faded. Then she has her brother killed and claims the money, ignorant of the two other wills in existence. But why, in that case, should she employ Powerscourt at all? Why did she need to establish that her brother was murdered? That could not have any bearing on the wills.

But suppose the two deaths were linked, suppose the cathedral and the Close, so innocent looking as they lay wreathed in the pure embrace of the snow, held the key to the deaths?

He wandered into the ancient chapter house where the abbot and the monks held their business meetings centuries before. Sitting on one of the stone seats he imagined he could hear one of those robed Benedictines start the occasion by reading a chapter from the Bible. It was that custom that gave the chapter house its name. Something obscure from the Old Testament, he felt, some tale from long ago of the sufferings of the Children of Israel out of the Book of Nehemiah or Hosea. Why would anybody want to kill a member of the vicars choral whose only crime was to sing for their supper?

He went to a choir rehearsal where he could observe the late Arthur Rudd's colleagues in action. He learnt something of the strange world they inhabited, how fifteenth-century vicars choral were notorious for drunkenness and womanizing, how in some cathedrals they had formed themselves into guild associations so powerful that they could not be sacked and were entitled to generous pensions. In some places, he was told, reformers had taken up to fifty years to root out the corrupt practices of the past. But of a motive for the death of Arthur Rudd, he learnt nothing. He did learn that there were at least four ways into the kitchen of the Vicars Hall and that none of them were locked at night. Was the burning of the body some obscure biblical reference? Was it some terrible practical joke carried out when the victim was already dead?

He went over and over again to stare at the names on the choir stalls, the names not only of the officials of Compton Minster but of the parishes which had once been part of the diocese and whose income may have helped to build and maintain it. Perhaps they held the answer. He was hypnotized by the names. Grantham Australis, Powerscourt read. Yetminster Prima. Winterbourne Earl. Teynton Regis. Hurstbourne and Burbage. Fordington and Writhlington. If Rudd was already dead, why take the trouble to burn him as well? Was it the same person who strangled him and put his body on the spit, turning round and round in front of the flames? Or two different people? Yetminster Secunda. Minor Pars Altaris. Chardstock. Netherbury in Ecclesia. Weird figures from the Middle Ages were striding out of Powerscourt's imagination now and taking their seats in the choir. Grimston. Grantham Borealis. Coombe and Harnham. Chisenbury and Chute. Was John Eustace a friend of Arthur Rudd? Was there a feud running through the Close? Wilsford and Woodford. Lyme and Halstock. Ruscomb. Bedminster and Redcliffe. There were no answers. Powerscourt suddenly remembered that Mrs Augusta Cockburn was due to return the following day to Fairfield Park. The second meeting about the wills with Oliver Drake the lawyer was only a couple of days away. The names on the choir stalls pursued Powerscourt as he walked down the nave towards the Cathedral Green outside. They were like a code whose meaning he could not decipher. Shipton. Netheravon. Bishopstone. Gillingham Minor. Beminster Secunda.

8

At a quarter to five on the same afternoon Anne Herbert was sitting in the little drawing room of her house on the edge of the Cathedral Close. Her children had gone to make a snowman in their friends' garden four doors away. The snow had stopped but a wind had risen, blowing flakes of snow in random fashion all over Compton. Anne was wondering if she could afford a new sofa. The boys seemed to have worn her present one out completely, bouncing up and down and performing somersaults. Maybe it would be simpler, she thought, just to have this one re-covered. A new sofa would be subject to the same level of assault and battery as the present one.

From time to time she found her eye wandering towards the hall and the front door. And it was not her two boys she was thinking of. Patrick Butler had been due to see the Dean at four o'clock that afternoon. She remembered the time distinctly. The Deanery was two minutes' walk away at most. And the Dean, she knew only too well, prided himself on the rapid despatch of business. The entire transaction of Anne Herbert being transferred from her humble rectory after her husband died into this little house, more like a cottage than a house, had been carried out by the Dean in less than five minutes.

Maybe she should put the kettle on again and make some fresh tea. That would make him come, some of the breakfast blend she had bought in the grocer's that morning. Five to five now, she checked the clock in the kitchen. There was still no sign of Patrick Butler.

Three pots of tea had been made and then thrown out before there was a knock on her door. A pale, distraught-looking editor of the *Grafton Mercury* presented himself and requested refreshment at twenty past five. Anne did not believe he could have been with the Dean all that time.

'Patrick,' she said, 'are you all right? You look very pale. You don't look at all well to me. Hadn't you better go home and lie down?'

Patrick did not like to tell her that the two rooms he rented on the top floor of an old house on the outskirts of the city were usually even more untidy than his office. 'I'll be fine in a moment, Anne,' he said. 'I just need a moment or two in peace to compose myself.'

Anne was certain he must be ill now. Very ill. Possibly in need of urgent medical attention. Maybe she should take him to the hospital. For the one thing Patrick Butler had never done in all the months she had known him was to ask for time to compose himself. The composing and the being Patrick were, in Anne's experience, totally incompatible. He was the most restless, the most energetic, the most mercurial person she had ever known. Composed he was not.

'Tell me what happened, Patrick,' she said, 'only when you're ready.'

By now he was lying back on the sofa. He smiled wanly at her.

'Forgive me, Anne, I'll be back to normal in a moment.'

'Biscuits, Patrick? Even a drop of brandy?' She remembered her friend's warnings about the dangers of drink and journalism and ignored them.

A large gulp of cognac began to restore his powers of speech. 'Let me tell it all to you from the beginning, Anne. It's a terrible story.'

He sat up again on the sofa and polished off a couple of biscuits in quick succession.

'At four o'clock this afternoon, as requested, I checked into the Deanery. The Dean was in a very sombre and serious mood. You know that air he usually has, of wanting to get you out of the door as fast as possible because he has another meeting to go to, well, he wasn't like that at all.'

Anne Herbert wondered if the snow was bringing personality changes all over Compton. First her Patrick, then the Dean. Maybe the Bishop would be singing bawdy songs in the public houses of the city before the day was done.

'This is all very unpleasant, Anne,' Patrick went on, looking very serious, 'and it gets worse as it goes on, much worse. You must stop me if I start to upset you.'

Anne Herbert nodded. Privately she thought women were much less squeamish than men. Just think of childbirth, after all, she said to herself. But this was not the time for such a discussion.

'At a quarter to five this morning,' Patrick checked the time in his notebook, 'one of the porters found a body in the kitchen of the Vicars Hall. The man's name was Rudd. They think he might have been strangled. He was one of the senior vicars choral, with three or four years' experience in Compton. He was in his middle thirties.'

Patrick suddenly realized that he must sound as if he was giving evidence in court or reading one of his own compositions in the *Grafton Mercury*.

'Sorry for sounding so cold, Anne. I've been trying to write the story in my head ever since.'

'The poor man,' said Anne. 'Did he have a wife and children?'

'No, he didn't,' said Patrick, looking once more at his notebook. 'But that's not all. Somebody put him on a spit and roasted the body for most of the night in front of that huge fire they have in the Vicars Hall kitchen.'

'Oh, my God,' said Anne Herbert. She put her face in her hands and said the Lord's Prayer. She couldn't think of anything else.

'That would all be bad enough.' Patrick was leaning forward now. 'The Dean said he was anxious that I and our readers should know as much as possible about what had happened. He said he didn't want to hide anything from me. He had a doctor with him, that chap Williams. I've known him for a while, he's a very sound and reliable fellow. It was he who was responsible for looking after the dead man, the death certificate, all that sort of thing. He took me to the morgue in the hospital where Rudd's body was laid out. They hadn't cleaned him up yet.'

Patrick Butler stopped. He wondered if he should say anything more.

'You see, Anne, it's a strange thing. I've never seen a dead body before. Reporters often have to write about dead bodies killed in fires or train crashes or accidents, but they never actually see them. When you start on a newspaper you have to go to magistrates' courts, you have to go to football matches, you have to write about society weddings. You have to write about all sorts of strange things you have seen. But the one thing you're not used to seeing is a dead body. Nor,' he paused briefly, 'a body that has been roasted all night on a great spit in front of a roaring fire.'

'I don't think I want to hear any more details, Patrick, if you don't mind. I've heard too much already. I'm feeling rather sick.'

Patrick was turning pale again. He was thinking of the terrible scene in the mortuary, what had happened to Arthur Rudd's eyes, what had happened to his skin, what had happened to the hair and the skull, the eruptions that had burst forth from the poor man's intestines. He hoped he would be able to forget it. He took another large gulp of his brandy.

'Sorry, Anne,' he said, 'I'm so sorry. And I don't know what to put in the paper. The *Mercury* goes to press tomorrow. I'm going to have to write this story tonight or first thing tomorrow morning.'

Anne thought that Patrick must be returning to normal. Deadlines were the bread and butter of his business. 'What do you mean, what should you put in the paper, Patrick?'

'It's the details. How much detail should I put in? We're meant to tell the truth the whole truth and nothing but the truth.'

'Nonsense,' said Anne Herbert firmly. 'Nobody wants to read the details in a case like this. Why can't you just say he'd been strangled? That's bad enough, for heaven's sake.'

'But then I wouldn't be telling the truth.'

'The people of this town and this county, Patrick, do not want to read about roasted bodies over their tea and toast first thing in the morning. Nor do they want to read about it over their supper in the evening. They do not want to have to explain to their children who can read what it means to be roasted on a spit all night in the kitchen of Vicars Hall. They may even stop buying your paper if you upset them. And then where would you be?'

Anne suddenly wondered if the snow was having an effect on her too. She could not remember having being so emphatic in her whole life. She did not realize it but she had become, for Patrick Butler, a sort of one woman litmus test of what was and what was not acceptable to his readers. Maybe he should give her an official position, not Censor in Chief, but Taste Arbiter Supreme.

'Are you sure, Anne? Are you sure people might stop buying the paper if there was too much gory detail in it?' The one unassailable deity of the newspaper world, the circulation figures, was uppermost in his mind.

'I'm quite certain of it.'

Patrick Butler munched his way through another couple of biscuits.

'Very well,' he said. 'I shall sleep on it and write the story in the morning.'

'You don't need to sleep on it, Patrick. You know what the right thing to do is. You could write it this evening.'

The young man smiled. 'Very good, Anne,' he said, 'I shall go and write it now. And, don't worry, I'm just going to say the poor man was found strangled in Vicars Hall.'

After he climbed up to his office for the last time that day Patrick Butler found that his informant in the town's most expensive hotel had left him a message. Three visitors from London were expected, the note said. All of them lawyers.

'Have you found him yet?' Augusta Cockburn's knife was poised menacingly over a breakfast kipper in the Fairfield Park dining room.

'Found whom?' asked Powerscourt, taking refuge in a slice of buttered toast.

'The person who killed my brother.' Mrs Cockburn began her demolition of the fish.

'I have to inform you, Mrs Cockburn, that I am still not sure that your brother was murdered. It may all have been perfectly normal. I am not yet in a position to form a judgement.' Powerscourt realized that a rising anger was driving him towards pomposity.

'It's the doctor, it must be the doctor.' Augusta Cockburn began to choke slightly on a bone. 'Look at the amount of money he was left in two of those wills. Have you questioned Dr Blackstaff, Lord Powerscourt?'

'I have, madam, and while there were certain inconsistencies in his version of events, I have at this time no reason to believe that he is a murderer.' Privately Powerscourt wasn't as sure as he sounded about the doctor's innocence. Fifty thousand pounds was a fortune. Even after a donation of five thousand or so to the lying butler you would still be rich for the rest of your life.

'Maybe I should involve the local police, Lord Powerscourt. Perhaps they will be more effective in questioning him than you are.'

Powerscourt didn't reply. The fish bone seemed to have accomplished a task way beyond the powers of most ordinary mortals. It had reduced Augusta Cockburn to silence. But the relief was short-lived. The offending bone, like so many of her enemies, was trampled underfoot.

'Really,' she said, 'I shall have to speak to the cook.' She had turned slightly red. 'Why the servants cannot perform a perfectly simple operation like filleting a fish I do not understand. Any fool could do it.' She paused to take a mouthful of tea, still spluttering slightly. The incident had not improved her temper.

'And how much longer, Lord Powerscourt, do you intend to stay in this house, consuming our victuals, sleeping in one of our beds, using up valuable fuel?' Powerscourt thought she might have been addressing the under butler. But he was prepared for this one.

'Mrs Cockburn,' he said, 'I regret to have to inform you that there has been a murder in Compton. One of the vicars choral was found strangled in the kitchen of the Vicars Hall. The Bishop has asked me to look into it.'

'Another murder?' Mrs Cockburn spat out. 'Another murder? Why are you so quick to take on new cases, Lord Powerscourt, when you have not found the answer to the first one? Is it because you believe it to be beyond your abilities?'

Powerscourt wondered if he should mention the roasting on the fire, a fate he felt sure deserved to happen to Augusta Cockburn after her departure from this life, but he did not. 'If I could just finish,' he went on. 'I am content to continue my investigations into both cases. And I have asked Mr Drake, as the executor of the will, if I could rent this house for the duration of my inquiries. I have offered him a generous sum. I believe he intends to discuss it with you, madam, before the meeting about the wills this afternoon.'

The prospect of money seemed to cheer Augusta Cockburn up. 'I shall certainly discuss it with Drake,' she said. 'But rest assured, Powerscourt, I shall make a full inventory of all the valuables.'

The Dean was reading an early edition of the latest issue of the *Grafton Mercury*. He was so pleased with it he read it three times. It was true that the story was placed in a prominent position in the paper. But the account of the death was short and simple. It merely said that Arthur Rudd, a senior member of the vicars choral, had been found strangled in the kitchen of the Vicars Hall. There were various tributes to the dead man, including one the Dean had given personally to Patrick Butler. There were paragraphs on the antiquity of the foundation of the vicars choral and their role in the services of the cathedral. Chief Inspector Yates, the paper went on, was the officer responsible for the investigation. He was reporting directly to the Chief Constable himself. But of fires and roasted flesh, of the spit that turned all night in the kitchen, there was no mention. The Dean went so far as to congratulate himself on his success. Without his intervention, he told himself, the matter would not have been properly handled at all.

The Bishop was wrestling with a thorny problem about the authenticity and origin of a late Hellenistic text of the Gospel according to St John. Some troublesome German scholars from Tübingen or Heidelberg, he couldn't quite remember which one, had been making the most ridiculous claims about this document. But he too paused from his textual labours and read his copy of the *Grafton Mercury* when it arrived. The Bishop did not congratulate himself. He could see the attractions of concealing the details of the roasted body. But he wondered where it fitted in with his own appeal for the Church to tell the truth. The Bishop was troubled. Maybe the Dean had got the better of him again.

Anne Herbert normally waited until the afternoon for her copy of the paper. Patrick would bring one round with him when he happened to drop in for a cup of tea. But on this occasion she went to the shops and bought her own. Her initial reaction was like the Dean's. She was pleased that she had been able to play her part. But then she too grew troubled, although not for the same reasons as the Bishop. She wondered how much it must have hurt Patrick to leave out the gory details. Here was a man who prided himself on his paper's ability to find things out, to tell the truth to the citizens of Compton and the county. She had even heard Patrick talk once about how important newspapers and the free flow of information were to the proper functioning of democracy. Now he had forced himself to leave something out, not to tell the truth. She wondered if it would prey on his mind.

They were, Powerscourt thought, the three largest briefcases he had ever seen. All three were temporarily parked on the long table in the boardroom on the first floor of Oliver Drake's offices in Compton while their owners rummaged inside for their papers for the meeting. The black one, Powerscourt realized, as Drake made the introductions, belonged to Mr Sebastian Childs of Childs, Goodman and Porter of Lincoln's Inn Fields in London. Mr Childs was representing the interests of Mrs Augusta Cockburn and had the good fortune to be seated beside her. The dark blue one was the property of Mr Benjamin Wall of Wall and Sons of Bedford Square, London, representing the interests of the Salvation Army. Powerscourt had peered briefly into the street as if a marching band in military uniform might have accompanied him on his mission. The dark red briefcase contained the papers of Mr Stamford Joyce of Joyce, Hicks, Joyce and Josephs of Ludgate Hill, also from London, there to guard the interests of the Cathedral of Compton and the Church Commissioners. Stamford Joyce sat at the Dean's right hand.

'Gentlemen,' said Oliver Drake, 'the last time the will or wills were discussed I said that I had to take advice on the question of the various wills left, or purportedly left, by the late Charles John Whitney Eustace of Fairfield Park in the county of Grafton. I have been to London to take advice from Chancery counsel. I propose to inform you of my conclusions at this meeting. You have copies of the three wills in front of you – I'm sure you are all acquainted with these various documents.'

There was a vigorous nod from Childs, a barely perceptible inclination of the head from Joyce and no acknowledgement at all from Wall. Powerscourt thought that was rather ungracious seeing the man was representing the Salvation Army.

'Just to make sure there is no possible confusion,' Drake went on, his thin and bony frame twisting slightly as he spoke, 'I propose to name the three different wills in the order of time of composition. Will A, the oldest, of which I am the executor, left the bulk of the estate to the Cathedral of Compton. Will B, the second most recent, left the estate to Mr Eustace's sister, Mrs Cockburn. Will C, the most recent, left the bulk of the estate to the Salvation Army.'

Three gold pens scribbled very fast across the notepads in front of them. The London lawyers were watching Oliver Drake very carefully. One mistake, Powerscourt thought, and they'll eat him alive.

'The substance of my advice is that the first will, Will A, the one that leaves the bulk of the estate to the cathedral, should be regarded as the most appropriate record of the deceased's intentions. I propose to apply to the Principal Probate Registry in London for it to be proved in common form. If the supporters of Wills B and C wish to contest that, all you have to do is to lodge a caveat at the Registry. Then the case will come before the Probate Divorce and Admiralty Division of the High Court in due course.'

'All perfectly proper,' said Stamford Joyce for Will A and the cathedral. Joyce was a small fat man with a perfectly round face that looked as if it had never had any facial hair at all. He was in his late thirties, wearing a dark suit and a Magdalen College Oxford tie. 'My clients are perfectly willing to argue in court that Wills B and C are invalid.'

'Very well!' said Sebastian Childs for Will B and Mrs Cockburn. Childs was an elderly solicitor with a shock of white hair and at least two chins. 'We shall certainly be advising Mrs Cockburn to lodge a caveat and demonstrate that Wills A and C are not proper.'

'And so shall we,' said Alaric Wall for Will C and the Salvation Army. Wall was the youngest man there, in his late twenties or early thirties, with a physique that said he might have been a rugby player or a rowing blue. 'It is a well-established precedent in English law for the most recent will to take precedence over all earlier testamentary dispositions. I note that this has been ignored in this case. No doubt the court will bear that in mind. I shall be advising my clients that they too should lodge a caveat and contest the validity of Wills A and B. '

Outside the snow was back. It was settling thickly on the roofs of Compton, nestling in the trees, turning everywhere beneath its fall into a carpet of white. Powerscourt could see a couple of snowmen standing like sentries on duty at the edge of the Cathedral Green. On the roof to his left a couple of birds had left symmetrical footprints in the snow. He was trying to remember the legal position from an earlier case years before that had involved the will and the very stupid family of a Master of Foxhounds in Somerset. Once the caveat was lodged, there could be no probate, no release of John Eustace's million and a half pounds. The money would be frozen until the legal proceedings were completed and the court made its judgement.

'My clients believe they can show,' said Stamford Joyce for the cathedral, 'that the two later wills were made under coercion or when the deceased was not in full possession of his faculties. There are many in senior positions in the cathedral and the Close willing to testify that the deceased had frequently informed them how he wished to leave the money. There is indeed, quite extensive correspondence with various members of the Chapter leaving detailed instructions on how he wished his estate to be used.'

A vision of the Dean, Bishop, Precentor and Archdeacon all filing into the witness box in quick succession crossed Powerscourt's mind. He wondered what they would wear. Suit? Cassock? Purple? Would the Staff and Mitre come too?

'I'm sure that's all perfectly possible,' said Alaric Wall for the Salvation Army. 'I'm sure the gentlemen of the cloth would be happy to appear in the witness box in pursuit of a million pounds. But nothing they could say would necessarily mean that the late John Eustace couldn't have changed his mind. Which he obviously did.'

'I beg your pardon,' said Sebastian Childs for Mrs Cockburn, 'my client is able to prove that she, as the sister of the deceased man, was in a much better position to understand his intentions than the people he happened to meet occasionally at his place of work. There is ample precedent for family considerations being given their proper place in the judgements of the Chancery Court. Appledore versus Bailey in 1894, for instance. Or Smith versus Crooks in 1899.'

They're bringing their weapons out now, Powerscourt felt. He wondered if it had been wise of Childs to reveal his precedents so early. Various bright young men in the offices of Wall and Sons and Joyce, Hicks, Joyce and Josephs would be poring through the records of those cases very soon.

'Gentlemen, please.' Oliver Drake was on his feet this time. 'I feel that this argument could go on for most of the day, if not most of the week.' He paused and looked round the combatants very slowly. 'I have a suggestion to make, gentlemen. You are perfectly welcome to throw it out. I do not know,' he smiled benignly at Sebastian Childs, 'if there are any precedents.'

The lawyers were writing in their books no longer. They stared, temporarily transfixed, at Oliver Drake.

'My suggestion is this, gentlemen. It is based on the enormous sums of money available. I propose that we come to an informal agreement among ourselves. Let Will A go forward as I believe it should. But let there be no objections from the other parties. When the business is completed, let the money be divided three ways. One third for the cathedral. One third for the Salvation Army. One third for Mrs Cockburn. If my calculations are correct, each party should receive a sum slightly in excess of four hundred thousand pounds.'

Drake sat down. Neat, thought Powerscourt, very neat, the judgement if not of Solomon, then of Oliver Drake, solicitor of Compton. Everybody wins, nobody wins. Nobody loses, everybody loses.

Then, as he heard the muttered conversations between client and lawyer start up around the table, he saw the flaw. Everybody wins, except the lawyers. No contested will, no expensive visits to the Probate Divorce and Admiralty Division of the High Court, no need for any further representation or indeed any fees at all if the Drake plan went ahead.

There was a slight cough from Alaric Wall for the Salvation Army. 'Ingenious, very ingenious,' he said, 'but I could not in all conscience suggest to my clients that they willingly forgo the sum of eight hundred thousand pounds, a sum which would make such an enormous difference to the poor and needy in our great cities.'

Powerscourt didn't think it likely that Alaric Wall would shortly be joining the ranks of the poor and needy in our great cities in person.

'I fear that my clients,' it was Stamford Joyce's turn now, speaking for the Dean, 'would also find that such a scheme, however superficially attractive, was not in the best interests of the Church or the cathedral or the architectural heritage of Great Britain.'

Powerscourt wondered if Drake had ever thought that his plan might work. Maybe he had a warped sense of humour.

'And for my part,' said Sebastian Childs for Mrs Cockburn, 'I could not recommend to my client that she accepts such an arrangement which could deprive her and her family of their rightful inheritance.'

At least Oliver Drake now had the chance to close the meeting. He told everybody that he was going to seek proof of Will A and the others were free to lodge their caveats if they wished. The three briefcases and their owners and clients shuffled slowly out of the boardroom.

'That business with Fairfield Park, Powerscourt,' said Drake as he collected his papers, 'it's all absolutely fine. Thank you for the very generous down payment of the rent.' He looked out into the street. Two of the lawyers were having a stand-up row on the pavement outside his office. It looked as if they might come to blows.

'What a bad-tempered meeting,' said Drake. 'There was only one redeeming feature, Powerscourt. Did you spot it?'

Powerscourt shook his head.

'That bloody woman,' said Drake. 'That bloody woman Augusta Cockburn. She didn't say a single word. Can you believe it?'

9

The Rule of St Augustine. The Rule of St Benedict. The Imitation of Christ by Thomas à Kempis. Edmund Burke, *Reflections on the French Revolution.* Lord Francis Powerscourt was browsing through the small library in Fairfield Park. Mrs Cockburn and her lawyer had both departed to London to plot further assaults on the will of the late John Eustace. Mrs Cockburn informed Powerscourt that she was going to take her family abroad for a while until the legal business was settled. Her parting shot showed that she had lost little of her venom.

'I shall be most surprised, Powerscourt, if you have solved the mystery of what happened to my brother before I return. But I shall send you an address in case you turn lucky.'

Powerscourt, now temporary master of the house, had invited Lady Lucy and the children to come and stay. He had also asked Johnny Fitzgerald.

Powerscourt was now browsing through a large box with the words 'History of Fairfield' on the cover. He learnt that there had been a house here in Tudor times, that most of the present building had been constructed at the end of the seventeenth century by a man called Crosthwaite, Secretary of State for War and paymaster of the armies of William the Third. There were several references to the French style of architecture fashionable at the time, the enclosed courtyard in the front, the low wings containing nurseries, and the covered passage. Covered passage? What covered passage? Powerscourt said to himself, suddenly wide awake despite the late hour. Where did it go to? Where did it start?

Further researches revealed that the passage was concealed behind a door beside the fireplace in the drawing room. But the drawing room in the sketches of the time did not correspond with where the drawing room was now. Some later Crosthwaite must have moved it. Powerscourt found an earlier map of the house, which contained no reference to this mysterious passage, but did show the previous layout of the ground floor. What had been the drawing room, he decided, must have been turned into the library, where he was now. And, sure enough, there was a door to the left of the fireplace, less than fifteen feet from where he was standing.

Powerscourt pulled hard at the door. It refused to move. He wondered if it was locked. He tried one more time. This time it creaked open very slowly, as if it had not been in use recently. Behind it Powerscourt saw another black metal door with a small knob halfway down. Powerscourt turned it and peered inside. He could see nothing apart from a set of steps leading downwards. The sensible thing to do would be to wait for the morning and descend the steps, lantern in hand. But Powerscourt wasn't feeling particularly sensible. He fetched two enormous volumes, bound in red leather, *The History of Dorset* they claimed to be, and wedged them as firmly as he could in the jamb of the door. He checked carefully to make sure they could not move. Then he set off.

It was easy at the beginning. There was enough light filtering through to make the descent of the first dozen steps fairly straightforward. Then the passageway turned sharply to the left. The steps gave way to a narrow path, leading, Powerscourt thought, away from the house. The walls, he noticed, were a dark and slimy green and rather damp. He could hear water further up, dripping onto the rocky passageway below. He wondered if there were mice or rats or bats down here. Powerscourt didn't mind mice or rats very much but he had an abiding terror of bats from his days in India. The light behind him had almost gone. He was groping his way forward now, his right hand feeling the surface of the wall, one boot brought forward so the heel rested on the toe of the one in front. His earlier calm had been replaced by a growing unease. What if the passage was three or four hundred yards long? What if the gate or the trap door at the far end was locked? If he looked back he could just see a sliver of light falling on the passageway. Soon that too would disappear.

Powerscourt pressed on. He passed the place where the drip came down from the ceiling. It fell on his head instead. It felt very cold. He wondered if he should turn round. He heard a scurrying of very light feet in the distance, rats, he thought, fleeing from the human invader. The wall was growing damper. He realized that

105

his boots were beginning to splash their way along the floor. He heard another drip, more than a drip, a small cascade up ahead. He pressed on, trying to move faster. He forced himself to take a series of deep breaths. Panic, he knew, would be a disaster. He wished Johnny Fitzgerald was with him. Now he could see nothing at all. He thought he heard a different noise, far in the distance, a low moaning sound. Maybe the ghosts of Fairfield spent most of their half lives down here, flitting restlessly up and down this dank corridor, only emerging to haunt the living when one of the doors was opened. Up until this point Powerscourt's right hand had told him that the side of the passage was simply rock. Now it became smoother suddenly. He thought it might be bricks. That gave him hope.

The stairs were almost his undoing. However carefully he was moving his feet, he missed the first step. He fell forward, holding out his hands to break his fall. Something very unfortunate had happened to his ankle. He was now half lying, half sitting on the floor at the bottom of the stairs, in total darkness. Slowly, very slowly, he pulled himself upright. He found it was easier to crawl up the steps than to walk. They were lined with a damp and slippery mould. Twice he nearly slipped backwards. Then he banged his head very loudly on something above. Powerscourt was stunned. He felt as though something was echoing inside his skull. He waited a few minutes to compose himself, his ankle aching, his head throbbing. That must be a trap door, or something similar, above my head, he said to himself. He put both his hands up and pushed as hard as he could. The door fell backwards. Powerscourt crawled slowly out of the terrible tunnel and found himself surrounded by what seemed to be a low wooden wall. Only when he stood up did he realize that he was in the enclosed pew of the inhabitants of Fairfield Park in the little church behind the house. John Eustace, he remembered, was buried in the church-yard outside. There was a faint light coming in through the windows. Various marble tombs were semi-visible on the walls. The pulpit was only fifteen feet away. Powerscourt closed the trap door and made his way out of the church. Thank God the door wasn't locked. He didn't fancy spending the night in there, surrounded by the bats and the dead, even if was preferable to spending it in the passageway he had just left.

He took several deep breaths and hobbled towards the house. His brain was reeling. Maybe Augusta Cockburn had been right all along. For until now the reason he had dismissed her murder theory was that he could not see how the intruders might have got in and out of the house. All the doors and windows, he remembered the butler telling him, had been securely fastened from the inside the morning after John Eustace's death. Now he knew how a murderer could have got in and out without being detected and without leaving any telltale trace behind. Into the church, down the passageway, into the library, up the back stairs, into John Eustace's bedroom. But why, in that case, had the body ended up in Dr Blackstaff's house? Unless the murderer had carried him there? Was the murderer an ally of the doctor's? Was he acting in concert with the butler? But in that case, why did they need the murderer at all? Either or both of them could perfectly easily have walked into the bedroom without anybody else being any the wiser.

It was only just outside the house that Powerscourt noticed something was wrong. The lights in the library had gone out. When he left, not more than twenty minutes before at the most, they had been switched on. It was their light that had shone down the steps and illuminated the first stage of his journey. He checked again. He remembered standing in the garden in the daylight only the day before, making a mental note of where all the ground-floor rooms were. The library was the last room on the left from the garden. There were no lights on. Even if he was wrong, and he didn't think he was, all the lights in this part of the house had been turned off.

Had somebody seen him go? And tried to ensure that he wouldn't have been able to come back? Was somebody in the house trying to send him a message? To frighten him off? But even so they must have known he could just walk out of the church and come down the path towards the back door. Had they thought the church was locked? He wondered, as he limped back into the house, what had happened to the door. Was it still open, waiting for a possible return? Was it closed? He didn't like to think what it might mean if it was closed.

He found McKenna checking the windows at the very front of the house.

'Good evening, McKenna,' said Powerscourt, sidling up behind him.

'My goodness me, my lord, you made me jump there. I thought you had gone to bed. I've just been putting the lights out.'

'You know that passageway in the library, McKenna,'

Powerscourt went on, wondering yet again if he would ever get the truth about anything out of Andrew McKenna, 'do many people know about it? I've just discovered it by accident.'

'I turned the lights off in the library a moment ago, my lord. I didn't see anybody in there. You don't want to be going down there in the dark, my lord. Could be quite dangerous at this time of night. Lots of people know about it round these parts, my lord. If children came to call or to stay Mr Eustace used to take them down there. Scared most of them out of their wits, I shouldn't wonder. But they quite like being frightened, I sometimes think.'

'Very good, McKenna. I've left a book in the library. Goodnight to you.'

'Goodnight to you, my lord.'

Powerscourt was trying to remember how much of the library you could see from the door by the light switches. If you could see the whole room, open door to the passageway included, then Andrew McKenna was in a for a very rough time. He opened the door and turned on the switch. If you didn't actually walk inside the room, he realized, you couldn't see the open door. And was the door open or closed? He took three paces into the room and looked sharply to his right. The door was still as he had left it. The route to the black hole was still open. Lots of people, he remembered, knew about it in these parts.

'Guess who's invited me to lunch on Thursday?' Patrick Butler had just hung his hat and coat in their usual place in Anne Herbert's hall.

'The Dean? The Bishop? I'm not sure bishops ask people like you to lunch, Patrick,' said Anne, smiling as she brought in the tea.

'No,' said Patrick Butler, laughing. 'Much better than that.'

'You can't get much more important than the Dean and the Bishop round here,' said Anne, offering him a piece of cake.

'Powerscourt,' said Patrick Butler proudly. 'Lord Francis Powerscourt has invited me to lunch at the Queen's Head at one o'clock.'

'Why do you think he wants to do that, Patrick? You're not a murder suspect or anything like that, are you?' She looked at him carefully.

'I would think,' said Patrick with his man of the world air, 'that he wants to pick my brain. Local knowledge, that sort of thing.'

'If you were an investigator, Patrick, would you ask yourself to lunch? Yourself, the newspaper editor, I mean.'

'I'm not sure I would,' said Patrick Butler thoughtfully. 'Unless I wanted something, some information maybe. Or unless I wanted to see what would happen if some story was printed in the paper. Maybe that's what he wants.'

'Is there any news about the death of that poor man in the kitchen of the Vicars Hall?' Anne Herbert was wondering, as she looked at Patrick, if she should suggest buying him some new shirts. His present collection were rather frayed. Better wait, she said to herself, he won't want to talk about shirts just now.

'Not as far as I know,' said Patrick Butler, unaware that he had narrowly escaped ordeal by shirt and collar. 'I had a word with that policeman this morning, Chief Inspector Yates. Do you know what he said? I thought it was rather good, but he won't let me use it in the *Mercury*. "Look at these vicars choral when they are singing," said the Chief Inspector. "Look at how wide they open their mouths. The effort seems to exhaust them for the remaining part of every day. The rest of the time their mouths are very firmly, very tightly shut. They don't tell you a bloody thing."'

Lord Francis Powerscourt was walking yet again the short distance between Fairfield Park and Dr Blackstaff's house. Only this time he was going inside, by appointment with the good doctor in his room full of medical prints.

'Dr Blackstaff,' Powerscourt began, 'do you know of that passage between the library and the church up at the Park?' He wanted to test the butler's assertion that everybody in the locality knew about it.

'Oh yes,' said the doctor, 'most people round here know about that passage. How did you find out about it?'

'I discovered it by accident the other night,' Powerscourt said, accepting a small glass of the doctor's whisky. 'I thought it interesting because it showed that some outside body could have gained entry to the house in the middle of the night. All they had to do was to walk into the church, lift up the trapdoor, make their way down the passageway and into the library. Nobody inside the house would have heard a thing. Wouldn't you agree, Dr Blackstaff?'

'It seems perfectly possible, I must admit. But why do you ask, Powerscourt?'

'I am thinking of the suspicions of my employer, Mrs Augusta Cockburn. She suspects that her brother may have been murdered. Until now I have always been sceptical of that theory. I do not believe that any of the servants would have murdered him. I could not work out how any outsider might have gained entrance to the house when all the doors and windows were still bolted the following morning. Now I am not so sure. As you know, it would take less than a minute to walk out of the library, up the back stairs, and into Eustace's bedroom.' Powerscourt paused and looked across at Dr Blackstaff, sitting on the other side of the fire. 'Do you follow me, doctor?'

'I do,' said Dr Blackstaff, 'but I do not see the relevance of all this. John Eustace died here in this house, as you know.'

'But he could have been killed in his own house, could he not, and then brought over here already dead by one of the servants, the butler, for example. Is that not so?'

Dr Blackstaff smiled. 'In your profession, my friend,' he said, 'you are accustomed to looking for the darkest possible interpretation of events. I am sure that you could make a very credible case for saying that our late Queen was murdered in her bed by the agents of some wicked foreign powers. But John Eustace died here in this house, as you well know.'

Powerscourt changed tack. 'Have you heard, doctor, about the death of Arthur Rudd, the vicar choral found strangled in the kitchen of the Vicars Hall?' Dr Blackstaff nodded. 'And have you had a chance to talk to Dr Williams, the medical man from Compton who attended on the dead person?' Powerscourt believed that if the two doctors had met, the true facts surrounding the terrible demise of Arthur Rudd would have been exchanged. The medical profession might pride itself on its tact and discretion when dealing with their patients and people outside their own circle. But doctor will gossip unto doctor just as surely as lawyer will gossip unto lawyer. Blackstaff's reply was a relief.

'I have not spoken to Gregory Williams for some weeks now, not since we met at a party in the Bishop's Palace, to be precise.'

Powerscourt found himself wondering briefly precisely what a party in the Bishop's Palace might be like. Quizzes on the names of the Old Testament prophets? Or which came first in Egypt, the death of the first born or the plague of locusts? He pressed on. 'Let me tell you, in confidence, if I may, the facts that have not been made public about this death.' Powerscourt paused. 'The body was

110

actually found attached to the roasting spit in the kitchen of the Vicars Hall. There was a powerful fire burning. The body had been roasting in the flames for a number of hours, five or six probably, before it was discovered. Somebody killed the poor man and then roasted him as if were an ox or a stag or a deer. I do not need to tell you, doctor, the condition of the body when it was found.'

'How terrible, how absolutely frightful,' said the doctor. Even he, Powerscourt noticed, turned rather pale. 'But why are you telling me all this?'

Powerscourt was looking very sombre. 'Let me be perfectly frank with you, Dr Blackstaff. I have to admit that there were certain inconsistencies, certain discrepancies, between your account of what happened on the night of John Eustace's death and the account of the butler Andrew McKenna.' Powerscourt had no intention of spelling out what the inconsistencies were. If he did, he suspected that the leaky vessel that was their story might be hastily repaired. Dr Blackstaff looked as if was about to speak, but Powerscourt held up his hand to stop him.

'Please hear me out, doctor. And please make your own allowances for the tendency of my profession to be forever looking at the darkest sides of human nature. But suppose for a moment, if you will, that my employer's suspicions are correct, that her brother was murdered. Now we have not one death but two. And in the case of the second one we know that there is a murderer on the loose with a macabre, not to say demented, method of killing his victims. Suppose the two deaths were linked in some way. Suppose that it was the same motive that led to the deaths of John Eustace and Arthur Rudd. And suppose that the murderer has not yet got what he wanted. Suppose there are going to be more victims in the days and weeks ahead, bodies discovered nailed to a cross on the Cathedral Green, maybe, or hanging in chains from the roof of the chapter house. I put it to you, Dr Blackstaff, that anybody in possession of any information that might be relevant to these inquiries should unburden themselves of it immediately. I put it to you that anybody in possession of such information who chooses to remain silent, may be contributing to another terrible death, or even deaths, in Compton and its surroundings. And I would remind you that any such information passed on to me would be treated in the strictest confidence.' Powerscourt stopped for his words to sink in. Then he asked very quietly, 'Is there anything you would like to tell me, Dr Blackstaff?'

The doctor opened his mouth as if to speak. Later Powerscourt wondered if he had come within a second or two of telling him something. Then the doctor thought better of it. He went over to the sideboard and returned with his whisky decanter.

'Let me refresh your glass, Powerscourt,' he said, 'and let me tell you that I have nothing further to add to my earlier account of the last night and day of my friend John Eustace. It may be that there are inconsistencies between my account and that of the butler. I would be surprised if there were not. At times of great strain people often find it difficult to recall things precisely. I have known patients – and this happens more frequently than you might think and not just with the old – who have forgotten most of what I tell them in my surgery before they reach their own front doors. I wish I could be of more assistance, I really do.'

There was an extraordinary variety of equipment on show running down the hill with an equal variety of techniques on display for controlling them. Sleds, sledges, toboggans, some with ropes to steer them, some without, one-seaters, two-seaters, one enormous toboggan that looked as if it could hold four people. More snow had fallen overnight and the great hill at the front of Fairfield Park had become a paradise for the Powerscourt children. James Bell, the coachman, had introduced Thomas and Olivia to the sledges early that morning, making repairs where necessary, checking that the ropes were in good order. He had created one enormous length of rope which stretched from one of the great oak trees at the top all the way down the slope so the children could pull themselves back up to the summit again. He had organized them to build a snow wall round the ancient statue of Neptune, halfway down the run, in case they crashed into the stone plinth and knocked themselves out.

Powerscourt and Lady Lucy were standing at the very top of the hill. From there the house itself was invisible. Only a third of the way down the twisting driveway did the rooftops begin to appear.

'I've always wondered why they didn't build the house up here in the first place, Lucy,' said Powerscourt, rubbing his hands together to keep warm. 'Just look at the view. You can see for miles.' On a sunny day like this the view stretched for about forty miles over the snow-covered hills and the surrounding country-side.

'Maybe it was the wind up here,' said Lady Lucy, taking her husband's arm. 'I think we should go part of the way down so we can see the bottom. The children are more likely to crash further down.' There was a very loud shout of 'Tally-ho!' from halfway down the hill. Johnny Fitzgerald had narrowly missed the statue and was heading at considerable speed towards the giant snowman a hundred yards from the house.

'Are you going to take a ride, Francis?' asked Lucy, squeezing his arm.

'I think I may have to,' said her husband gloomily. 'Thomas asked me if I was too old for it. I haven't been in one of those things for years.'

Powerscourt had been fascinated by the different approaches of his two children. Thomas, the elder, was cautious, proceeding with great care down the white slopes and veering off to the left or right if he thought he was going too fast. Only once, as far as Powerscourt could see, had he reached the bottom of the run. But Olivia was like a thing possessed. She climbed in, pointed her sledge towards the bottom, kicked herself up to a good speed and hurtled down the slope, screaming with delight as she went. Her father was sure he had heard her shouting 'Faster, faster,' at her sledge as she went.

Johnny Fitzgerald was hauling himself back up the slope. 'Francis,' he said, 'this is excellent sport. I thought I was going to crash into that bloody snowman just now.'

'Can I ask you to do something for me, Johnny?' said Powerscourt. 'I want you to go down among the dead.'

'Tombstones, Francis? Opening up the graves in the Compton cemetery, is that what you want me to do?'

Powerscourt smiled at his friend. 'I don't want you to turn into a grave robber, though it might just have its advantages.' Powerscourt suspected that if he could just look inside the coffin of the late John Eustace, some of his problems might be solved. But he also knew that it would be almost impossible to secure an exhumation order. The Compton coroner was Dr Blackstaff's brother and Powerscourt could not see the doctor agreeing to an exhumation. And, as Powerscourt remembered from a previous case, there was a section from the Burial Act of 1857 which stipulated that the Home Secretary had to give his consent to such an exhumation.

'It's the undertakers in Compton, Johnny, that's where I want you to make some new friends. There must be a couple of labourers there who do most of the heavy work, lifting the bodies about, that sort of thing.'

'Why do I always get such exciting jobs, Francis?' said Johnny Fitzgerald, throwing a snowball at the passing figure of Olivia. 'Wasn't there anything more cheerful you could think of, making friends with the people in the morgue, perhaps? Rolling up sleeves with the staff at the local abattoir?'

'I'm sure you'll be able to cope, Johnny,' said Powerscourt. He noticed that Master Thomas had finally plucked up enough courage to get to the bottom of the hill on his sledge. He was waving a small and very dirty fist in the air in triumph. 'They have very recently received the body of Arthur Rudd, the roasted vicar choral. They must have some pretty good stories to tell about him. But what I want to know about is the body of John Eustace, the one transported there at such speed if you recall. Maybe they've got some stories to tell about that one too. That's what we're after, Johnny.'

'Very good, Francis,' said Fitzgerald. 'Maybe I'll just take a turn or two down the hill before I go. I don't suppose you managed to see if there's a decent inn near the undertakers where a thirsty fellow might go after he'd finished packing the dead into their coffins?'

Powerscourt laughed as his friend departed up the hill. 'I think you'll find it's called the Stonemason's Arms, Johnny. Good local beer.' Then he saw that a deputation was coming his way. The two children were pulling their sledges up the hill towards him. Lady Lucy was with them, with a rather larger model. She was smiling at him. She knew what was coming.

'Papa,' said Thomas seriously.

'Yes, Thomas,' replied Powerscourt.

'It's time you took a ride in one of these sledges. You can't just stand around in the snow talking to Johnny all the time. Mama has brought one for you.'

'And it's great fun,' Olivia chimed in, 'you can go really fast.'

'Well, I'm not sure,' said Powerscourt, looking down at the two faces beside him. 'I don't think I've ever done it before. We didn't have much snow in Ireland when I was growing up, you know. It's against the rules.'

Thomas looked at him suspiciously. 'That's not true, Papa. There must be snow in Ireland.'

'Course there's snow in Ireland, Papa,' said Olivia, who had no idea where Ireland actually was.

'Anyway,' said Powerscourt, moving on to a second line of defence, 'I'm far too old for it. Didn't you see the sign in the stables where the sledges are kept? People over thirty are forbidden to use these sledges, it said.'

He looked down at his children with his most serious face.

'That's not true! You're making it up,' said Thomas defiantly.

'You're not too old at all, Papa,' said Olivia. 'You're only sixty-five or whatever it is. That's a lot less than thirty.' Olivia had always been confused by big numbers.

'Very well,' said Powerscourt, 'I give in. Lucy,' he went on as the three of them began their ascent of the hill, 'I hold you personally responsible for this. You will find my will in the bottom left-hand drawer of my desk in Markham Square.'

The workmen found the body in the crypt late that afternoon. Ever since the archivist and the architect decided that the ancient crypt must be slightly larger than it appeared, they had been taking down a low wall at the eastern end of the structure. Once a section of the stones had been removed they could see that there was a space extending away from the main structure for about eight to ten feet. Closer inspection revealed a very ancient wooden coffin. Behind the coffin, as if concealed by it, was a small wooden box, about three feet square. Both were heavily covered with dust and mould.

'Another bloody coffin,' said William Bennett, the foreman in charge of operations. 'That makes six we've found in the last ten years. I'd better tell the archivist and he can decide what to do with this one. I'll bring him the box as well. Maybe it's got buried treasure inside.'

10

'Soup,' said Powerscourt. 'I think I'll have the soup, and then the lamb.' He smiled at the waitress in the dining room of the Queen's Head. 'Will you join me in some wine, Mr Butler?'

The newspaper editor and the investigator were seated at a corner table of the room. Behind them the snow was beginning to melt in the hotel gardens. A flock of sparrows were hopping busily among the bushes.

'That would be very kind,' said Patrick Butler, feeling rather grown up. He felt sure that the great newspaper editors and feature writers must often have lunch with distinguished people. Maybe he'd be entertaining cabinet ministers in ten years' time. Powerscourt had already given the young man the details, in confidence, of some of his previous cases. He had also told him that he had been asked by the Bishop to look into the death of Arthur Rudd. Now he was scanning the wine list. A slight look of pain crossed his features as he surveyed the offerings of the Queen's Head. He didn't think Johnny Fitzgerald would approve of any of it. Then he found salvation hiding at the bottom of the page.

'Nuits St Georges, please,' he said, smiling again at the waitress. 'That should warm us up on a day like this.'

'Mr Butler,' he turned to his companion, 'I need to ask you for some assistance.' Flattery, he felt, would not do any harm at all. 'I am a stranger here in Compton. A man in your position must know everything that goes on here.'

'I have to tell you, Lord Powerscourt,' said Patrick Butler, still slightly overawed, 'that I have not been here very long, only about nine months or so. But I'd be only too pleased to help in any way I can.'

Two enormous plates of the Queen's Head's finest country

vegetable soup were laid before them. The bottle of red wine was placed carefully in the centre of the table so they could help themselves.

'Let me ask you about the cathedral, if I may, Mr Butler. Are there any secrets up there? Any feuds? Any of those long-running disputes about ritual and vestments and so on that have caused such trouble in recent years?'

Patrick Butler was eating his soup very quickly. 'They say, Lord Powerscourt, that there is only one insoluble mystery up at the cathedral.'

'And what might that be?' said Powerscourt, leaning forward to refill the young man's glass.

'Where does the Archdeacon go on Thursdays?' said Patrick with a laugh. 'Sorry to be flippant, Lord Powerscourt, but that is what most people in Compton would tell you. It's become a sort of running joke in the community. Every Thursday Archdeacon Beaumont leaves Compton on an early train. He says he is going to visit the outlying parishes in the diocese. But there are never any reports of him being seen in any of these places. He usually returns in time for Evensong up at the cathedral.'

'And what,' said Powerscourt, tucking into his lamb, munificently adorned with gravy and mint sauce, 'does informed opinion in Compton say is going on?'

'I don't need to tell you, Lord Powerscourt, that gossip can be quite frightful in a little place like this. The least popular theory is that the Archdeacon has another job on Thursdays, teaching Hebrew or Greek in a school or college, maybe, because he needs the money. The second is that he keeps a married woman hidden away somewhere in the country and goes to see her every Thursday. The most salacious rumour – none of these, needless to say, have any foundation in fact – is that the Archdeacon goes to visit the prostitutes of Exeter.'

Patrick Butler took another sip of his Nuits St Georges. Outside one of the waitresses was throwing the rejected bread on to the grass. A battalion of sparrows were circling overhead.

'Forgive me, Lord Powerscourt, for giving you a totally useless piece of information. It's not something I would ever consider publishing in the *Grafton Mercury*.' Butler paused to dissect an enormous roast potato. 'You ask about secrets and feuds and obscure theological disputes. I have no other cathedral to compare it with, so I cannot say how typical our situation here is. There is a certain amount of friction between the Dean and the Bishop. That is well known, but I think it's only the mutual irritation that could arise between one man whose chief bent is efficiency and proper administration and another whose main interest is in scholarship.'

Powerscourt was impressed with the maturity of the judgement. He was beginning to take to Patrick Butler.

'I don't think there are any real feuds or vendettas up there in the Cathedral Close,' he went on, 'not like some of those you hear of elsewhere. Maybe that's the curious thing. You see, Lord Powerscourt, I have quite a lot of dealings with the members of the Chapter in one way and another. They always seem to me to be a bit enclosed, locked up in their own world. Maybe they are all really close to God and that sets them apart.'

'Army regiments can be a bit like that,' said Powerscourt, 'they can seem closed off to outsiders. But then they're more concerned with killing people on this earth than saving their souls for the next one. Tell me,' he went on, 'leaving aside the possible position of the Archdeacon on Thursdays, are there any emotional entanglements in the Close that might lead to murder? I thought when I heard of the death of Arthur Rudd that jealousy might have been the motive.'

'Do you know the full story of his death, Lord Powerscourt? Do you know all the details?' The young man placed a heavy emphasis on the word all. Powerscourt knew full well that Patrick Butler had been taken by the doctor to view the corpse in person. He had, after all, suggested it himself.

'I do, I'm afraid,' Powerscourt said. 'and I'd be curious to know why you didn't print it in your newspaper.'

'I wanted to, I wanted to print it very much,' said Patrick Butler sadly, 'but then I thought it would upset a lot of people, especially the women. I'm sure at least as many women as men read the *Grafton Mercury*. If we really turned their stomachs then they might stop buying the paper. It was pure self-interest in the end, however much I regretted it.'

The main course had been cleared away. An enormous trolley appeared, filled with equally enormous puddings. There were apple pies fit for a giant, monstrous edifices of fruit and custard and cream disguised as strawberry trifles, lemon meringue tarts. Patrick Butler opted for Goliath's apple pie, Powerscourt asked for a small, David-sized helping of the lemon meringue.

'To get back to any emotional entanglements on the Close, Mr

Butler, if I may. Deans and archdeacons, forgive me for saying so, can be as liable to the attractions of other people's wives as everybody else.'

Patrick Butler was looking thoughtful. 'I don't think there are,' he said, 'and I've just realized something I hadn't noticed before. I checked out Arthur Rudd, by the way. None of his colleagues knew of any emotional involvements anywhere at all, or if they did, they weren't telling me. But it's quite odd, Lord Powerscourt. The main reason I don't think affairs of the heart can have anything to do with it is that there are hardly any women up there. The Bishop isn't married. The Dean isn't married. The Precentor isn't married. Chancellor Eustace wasn't married. I don't think any of the vicars choral are married, not that you could afford to have a wife and family on their wages. Oh, there are housekeepers and so on but hardly any wives.'

'I believe that some of the High Anglicans don't think it right to marry,' said Powerscourt.

'High, low, wide, narrow, shallow, deep, I don't think anybody would notice here in Compton,' said Patrick Butler cheerfully. 'If you said High Anglican to any of the citizens here, they'd think you were referring to the elevation of the cathedral spire. Mind you, Lord Powerscourt,' Patrick Butler went on, the wine making him talkative, 'there is a very good story about affairs of the heart in the cathedral but it's about three hundred years old.'

'Are you sure,' said Powerscourt in a mock serious tone, 'that it is a story you would be happy to print in the pages of the *Grafton Mercury*?'

'When I judge the time is right,' replied Patrick Butler, 'it will receive appropriate coverage on the front page of the journal. There was an organist and choirmaster, Lord Powerscourt, in the year 1592 who had fallen in love with the wife of the Dean. One day he appeared in the cathedral at Evensong and began conducting his charges in the usual way. After a few minutes he left the cathedral by the west door and made his way over to the Deanery. There he produced a knife and tried to murder the Dean. But the Dean was an enterprising fellow and managed to escape to a bedroom where he proceeded to lock himself in. Unconcerned by the failure of his murderous mission, the choirmaster returned to the cathedral where he conducted his choir until the close of Evensong. Then he vanished, only to surface at Worcester some weeks later where he applied for the post of choirmaster there.'

'History does not relate, I presume, whether these events took place on a Thursday? The Archdeacon's special day?'

Patrick Butler shook his head. There were only two other clients left now in the dining room of the Queen's Head. Outside the light was beginning to fail.

'Could I ask you one more favour, Mr Butler?' asked Powerscourt.

'Of course,' the young man replied, 'and please call me Patrick. Everybody else does.'

'Thank you,' said Powerscourt. 'I wonder if I could read the back copies of your paper for about the last year or so? It helps me absorb the local colour.'

'Of course,' said Butler. Then a terrible thought struck him. He remembered the chaos, the detritus strewn all over the floor, the cramped conditions, the desks virtually invisible with the material piled all over them.

He looked embarrassed. 'It's just, Lord Powerscourt, it's just . . .'

Powerscourt wondered if some of the back copies were missing. Then he remembered a visit earlier in his career to the offices of one of the London evening papers. The chaos had been indescribable.

'If I am to understand by your hesitation that the offices of the *Grafton Mercury* are not perhaps as tidy as they might be, Patrick, do not worry. I have just spent six months in South Africa with a perfectly charming, extremely intelligent subaltern who had a genius for mess. He could not walk into a room without managing to leaves bits of his uniform or anything else all over the floor. His colleagues referred to his quarters as the Temple of Chaos.'

Patrick Butler smiled. 'As long as you don't mind, Lord Powerscourt. Could I ask you a question?'

'Of course,' said Powerscourt, suddenly on his guard.

'I know you're here to investigate the death of the vicar choral. But didn't I see you here before, at the funeral of Chancellor Eustace?'

Careful, careful, Powerscourt said to himself. Under no circumstances did he wish Patrick Butler to know that there were grave suspicions surrounding the death of John Eustace.

'I was here then,' he said with a smile, 'but that's because Mrs Cockburn, the dead man's sister, had asked me to give her some advice about the will. Very complicated things, wills.'

'So there's nothing suspicious about that death?'

'Good heavens, no,' said Powerscourt with a smile. 'Now then, when can I come and look at your back copies?'

'Tomorrow afternoon would be fine, Lord Powerscourt. And can I mention in the paper that you are here investigating the death of Arthur Rudd?'

'You may indeed,' said Powerscourt as he settled the bill, 'but I don't think I wish at this stage to be connected in any way with the Archdeacon's Thursdays. That's a much more serious matter.'

Patrick Butler was elated as he left the hotel. One of Britain's foremost investigators come to Compton. What a good story! Mayfair Sleuth on Trail of Compton Murderer. He felt it might atone for his earlier withholding of the truth about the end of Arthur Rudd. He checked his watch. It was almost four o'clock. If he walked slowly, almost an impossibility for Patrick Butler, he could be round for tea with Anne Herbert just as the cathedral clock struck the hour.

Lord Francis Powerscourt had enjoyed his lunch. He had only one object in view. He wanted the fact that he was investigating the death of Arthur Rudd splashed across the pages of the *Grafton Mercury*. He hoped the murderer would read it. He was, what did they call them, the toreador or the picador whose job it was to goad the bull into action in the bullfights of Spain. He could see himself now, riding a beautifully turned-out horse, a red cape thrown over his shoulders, not on the edge of the Cathedral Green in Compton, but in some hot and dusty bull ring in Barcelona or Madrid. Beneath his feet lies the finely raked sand that will be stained later in the day by the blood of matador or bull. All around the huge crowds are shouting themselves hoarse. Picador Powerscourt taunts the great bull, its horns raking the sultry air. The bull charges. The matador takes over. Except, as Powerscourt knew, he was not really the picador. He was certainly inviting the bull or the murderer to charge. But he, Powerscourt, was the target. He wanted the Compton murderer to be roused to action. Then, perhaps, he would make a mistake.

Lady Lucy was waiting for her husband underneath the west front of the cathedral. Above her soared the remains of one of the greatest collections of medieval statuary in all of Europe. Once the hundreds and hundreds of niches had each been filled with its own limestone apostle or saint. Now less than half were left as the statues had been torn down at the time of the Reformation with its puritan decrees against graven images or despoiled by the soldiers and supporters of Cromwell's New Model Army during the Civil War. The west front was an enormous dictionary of the Christian faith. All the apostles were up there, with special places for the four evangelists. There were scenes from the Old Testament to the right of the great door, scenes from the New Testament to the left. As the statues rose higher up the façade, bishops and saints took their places in this towering showcase for the Christian religion. At the very top was the Resurrection, so the early pilgrims, gazing in wonder up at the façade, would be transported upwards through time and space, past niche and statue from their earthly place towards eternity. Heaven lay just above the figure of the risen Christ, a paradise beyond the limestone.

Powerscourt stared up at the figures. Suddenly he looked more closely. Could the two missing vicars choral have been encased in plaster of Paris or some similar substance over their cassocks and popped into one of the empty niches? Had the absent angels or saints been replaced by missing members of the Compton choir? Reluctantly he decided it would be too difficult, hard to preserve the corpses without specialist knowledge, virtually impossible to manoeuvre the bodies into position without being seen.

'Lucy,' said Powerscourt, taking her hand, 'I've just been having a most enjoyable lunch. I need a touch of Evensong to wipe out the excesses of Mammon.'

They walked up the right-hand side of the nave. Earlier bishops gazed down at them from the walls. Local magnates were interred in the floor beneath them. Powerscourt paused at the chantry chapel of Robert, Lord Walbeck, with its master lying inside, encased in stone with a great stone sword by his side. This Lord Walbeck, Powerscourt remembered the Dean telling him, had paid for the construction of a special house on the Green to house the priests who would have said the Masses for his soul. Indeed, the house was still there. Powerscourt wondered suddenly what would have happened if the Reformation had never been. Would those chantry priests, even in 1901, be processing every day across the Cathedral Green, up the nave of the cathedral to say Masses for the soul of their dead benefactor, Lord Walbeck? Would the money have run out? And, if not, how much would the man have had to leave in his will to pay for the priests? Did he have a date in his mind for the Second Coming so he knew he had to provide only up till then, and no further?

Lady Lucy was tugging at his arm. They took their seats at the back of choir. There were only two other people in the congregation, bent old ladies who had difficulty with the steps.

'Rend your heart, and not your garments, and turn unto the Lord your God, for he is gracious and merciful.' A terrible vision of the garments of the late Arthur Rudd shot across Powerscourt's brain, literally burnt off his body. The service was being taken by a member of the Chapter he had not seen before, a tall young man with a lilting Welsh accent. The Dean was sitting resolutely in his place. The Bishop's chair was empty. As the choir sang a psalm, Powerscourt noticed that he was sitting in the stall marked with the prosaic name of Bilton. Lucy, he thought, had done rather better in the romantic names department, as she occupied Minor Pars Altaris, the lesser part of the altar. Powerscourt looked around to see if he could find Major Pars Altaris. Perhaps he could transfer himself there. But it seemed, like so many of the statues outside, to have disappeared.

The choir had moved on to the Cantate Domino. 'Praise the Lord upon the harp; sing to the harp with a psalm of thanksgiving. With trumpets also and shawms: O shew yourselves joyful before the Lord the King.' Powerscourt looked closely at the decorations on the choir stalls. There was a little wooden orchestra of angels in here, singing along with the choir, angels with trumpets, angels with harps, angels with stringed instruments, even an angel with a drum. One rather superior wooden angel, carved those hundreds of years ago, seemed too important to have an instrument. It was perched just in front of the Dean's stall. Maybe it was the conductor.

Powerscourt could sense that Lady Lucy was becoming agitated as the choir sang an anthem by Purcell. She kept casting him anxious and worried glances, but he could not tell what was upsetting her. Then it was time for the closing prayers.

'Almighty and everlasting God,' the Welsh voice was at its most reverend, 'Send down upon our Bishops, and Deans, and Curates and all Congregations committed to their charge, the helpful Spirit of thy grace, and, that they may truly please thee, pour upon them the continual dew of thy blessing.'

Powerscourt found himself staring in disgust at the young man. How could he pray for the blessing of the Almighty God upon the clergy of this cathedral? At least one of its members, if not two, had been murdered, one of them virtually inside the precincts of the minster itself. What would God do, he wondered, if he found that one of his bishops or curates or deans was actually a murderer? Powerscourt didn't think the Almighty would be too pleased.

Lady Lucy held him back after the choir had departed. They waited patiently for the two old ladies, prayer books firmly clutched in their left hand, walking sticks in their right to descend the steps and tap their way out through the choir and down the nave. Powerscourt wondered if there was much future for the Christian religion in Compton with such a pitiful congregation. Then he remembered the Benedictines who had worshipped here for centuries after the place was built. Nobody came to their services at all, especially the ones in the middle of the night.

'Did you see it, Francis?' Lady Lucy was holding very firmly on to the sleeve of his coat just outside the main door.

'See what, Lucy? I don't think I saw anything unusual at all,' said Powerscourt.

'Did you see the choirboys, Francis, those poor choirboys?'

'Well, I think there were about a dozen of them altogether,' said her husband. 'Ages ranging from about eight, I should say, to thirteen. Differing heights, depending on their ages. One very tiny chorister indeed with blond hair, could just about see over the stall. All dressed for the service in red and white. All giving what is almost certainly a misleading impression of virtue, devotion and general good behaviour. Was there anything else I was supposed to notice, Lucy?'

'Sometimes, Francis, you can be really quite irritating. It's because your brain has wandered off somewhere that you can't see what is right under your nose.'

'What was I supposed to have seen, Lucy?' said Powerscourt, giving her arm a firm squeeze in recognition of his sins.

'They all looked absolutely terrified, every single one of them. That tiny one you mentioned looked scared out of his wits to me.'

Powerscourt tried to remember the looks on the faces of the choristers. He also remembered that the youngest of them could have only been a year or two older than Thomas. Maybe that was influencing Lucy.

'I think I should have said that they were looking solemn, Lucy. But surely the choirmaster must tell them they have to look serious in the cathedral. You couldn't have them climbing all over the choir and running races up and down the nave.'

'This was much more serious,' said Lady Lucy. 'I'm going to find out what's going on if it's the last thing I do. I can't bear to think of all those little boys being so unhappy.'

Anne Herbert thought Patrick Butler was looking particularly cheerful as he threw himself into her best armchair. Really, she thought, as the springs gave a slight shudder, he's not much better behaved than my two boys, just older.

'Patrick,' she said in an accusing tone of voice, 'have you been having lunch all this time with Lord Powerscourt in the Queen's Head?'

'Lord Francis Powerscourt and I are the best of friends. He calls me Patrick now,' said the young man.

'And have you been drinking all afternoon?' Anne pressed home the attack, in a voice that reminded Patrick Butler ever so slightly of his mother.

'We had a bottle of very fine red wine, Anne. I can't quite remember its name but I think it came from France. I can't see any harm in that.'

Anne Herbert poured him a cup of strong tea. 'You'd better drink some of this, Patrick. Maybe it'll wash some of the alcohol out of your system. What did he tell you anyway?'

Now that he thought about it, Patrick wasn't exactly sure how much Powerscourt had told him. He seemed to have done much more of the talking himself. But there was his scoop for the paper. 'He told me he's here to investigate the death of Arthur Rudd, the vicar choral.'

'But I thought you knew that already, Patrick. Was it just the one bottle you had, or was there a second one to help it down?'

Patrick Butler ignored that one. 'And,' he said triumphantly, 'Lord Powerscourt said I could use that in the paper.'

'I wonder why he did that, Patrick. But listen, I've got a piece of news for you about the murder.'

'What's that?'

'You know Mrs Booth, who comes to clean here for me twice a week? Well, she also used to clean for Arthur Rudd, in his little house in Vicars Close. She did just one hour a week for him. Well, the day before poor Mr Rudd was murdered was her day for

125

cleaning his house. She went back again the morning after he died to give the place another clean in case his parents or his relatives came to call. And she says, this Mrs Booth, that there were a number of diaries that used to be on Mr Rudd's little desk. He kept one of these every year, apparently. Now they've gone. They've disappeared.'

'Do you think the police could have taken them, Anne?'

'No, I don't, because Mrs Booth says the police didn't go to the house until the following day.'

'And has she told the police? Does Chief Inspector Yates know about this?'

Anne Herbert shook her head. 'The police don't know. She won't tell them either, that Mrs Booth. Her husband was locked up a couple of years ago and she blames the police for it. She won't talk to them at all.'

Vanishing Papers Key to Murder Mystery. Riddle of Disappearing Documents. New Clues in Hunt for Compton Killer. A variety of headlines shot through Patrick Butler's fertile brain.

'How did you hear about this, Anne? Did Mrs Booth tell you herself?'

'She told me this morning. I'm not sure I should have told you now.'

Patrick was hunting through his pockets for a pen. His reporter's notebook was in his coat in the hall. 'Just give me her address, Anne, that would be very kind. I've got to go. I've just about got time to call on her now before it's too late.'

With some reluctance Anne Herbert handed over the address. Mrs Booth lived in a small terrace near the railway station where the property and rental prices were depressed by the noise and smoke of the trains. Anne watched rather sadly as Patrick hurried off into the night in pursuit of another story for his paper. He didn't even finish his tea, she said to herself. And I had that nice new cake waiting for him too. Perhaps, she reflected, her friend had been right after all. Being married to a journalist could prove to be a rather unsettled existence.

11

Johnny Fitzgerald and the Powerscourts were having breakfast in Fairfield Park. Thomas and Olivia had gone back to London with their nurse. Olivia's favourite person in the whole world, her grandmother on Lady Lucy's side, was coming to help look after them until their mother returned.

Powerscourt was perusing the latest edition of the *Grafton Mercury*. Patrick Butler had told him about the missing journals the morning after his meeting with Mrs Booth. On that occasion Patrick had confined himself to the facts. The account in the newspaper, however, was slightly more fanciful. 'The *Grafton Mercury* has reason to believe,' Powerscourt read with a slight smile, 'that the contents of these volumes may well contain the key to the mysterious death of Mr Arthur Rudd. We call upon the authorities to display the utmost vigilance in the hunt for them. Not an hour, not a day must be lost. Even now the perpetrator of this atrocious crime may have burnt or destroyed them. They must be found before it is too late.' People reading the article, Powerscourt felt, would suppose the author to be some middle-aged reporter, grown cynical and disillusioned with age. It was hard to imagine the youthful and cheerful figure of Patrick Butler composing this report at his chaotic desk in the chaotic offices of his paper.

For the rest of the day, as for the previous days, the Powerscourts haunted the cathedral. Powerscourt had found, oddly enough, that the most illuminating guide to the building was not a member of the Chapter or the verger, but the policeman. As a boy, Chief Inspector Yates informed Powerscourt, he had wanted to be an architect when he grew up. The only problem was that he couldn't draw anything at all. Even his houses were scarcely recognizable.

So he had become a policeman instead. Powerscourt had tried hard to work out the connection between architecture and detective work and totally failed to find it.

'High altar, rebuilt late seventeenth century. East, my lord,' he had said to Powerscourt the day before, standing before the high altar in the sanctuary, 'east was the most sacred point of the compass for these medieval church builders. East pointed towards Jerusalem, towards Zion the Celestial City, linked metaphorically with the most sacred place in Christianity, the Temple in Jerusalem where God's presence was said to be strongest.'

Chief Inspector Yates was gazing up at the great stained glass window behind the altar. He was a tall man with a neat moustache and dark brown eyes. He was twisting his hat between his hands as he spoke.

'So, my lord, the high altar is at the east end of a church, the side altars are all placed on the east walls, the congregation faces east. The sun rising in the east is linked with the dawn on Easter Day when Christ rose from the dead. Even the dead bodies buried beneath the paving all around us, my lord, were placed with their feet to the east so that on the Last Day, when they rose from their vaults, they would stand up and face their Creator.'

Lady Lucy began her days with Matins. She knew by now the faithful, the regular attendees at the various services. The two old ladies with their walking sticks she had met at Evensong with Francis nodded to her politely as they passed. There was a tall, skeletally thin old man whose clothes no longer fitted him. Lady Lucy suspected he was dying, come to make his last peace with his Creator before he was called home. There was a tramp or a drunk, Lady Lucy couldn't quite decide which, come perhaps to pray for the forgiveness of sins. He looked, she thought, as if he could do with the Resurrection now rather than later. So few, she thought, so very few had come to Morning Prayer in this enormous building.

'All the earth doth worship thee, the Father everlasting.' The choir were singing the Te Deum, Lady Lucy's eyes fixed, as ever, on the faces of the choirboys. 'To thee all angels cry aloud: the Heavens and all the powers therein. To thee Cherubim and Seraphim continually do cry, Holy, Holy, Holy, Lord God of Sabaoth.'

The tiny choirboy had stopped singing. Lady Lucy wondered if he was going to break down and weep, here in the midst of the choir stalls.

'Almighty God, who hast safely brought us to the beginning of this day,' the Dean spoke the words of the collect without looking down at his prayer book at all, 'Defend us in the same way with thy mighty power and grant that this day we fall into no sin, neither run into any kind of danger.'

Lady Lucy sank to her knees and prayed for the choirboys. She prayed that no harm might befall them that day. She prayed that no harm had befallen them in the days gone by. She prayed that no harm would come to them in the days ahead. She prayed that the fear be taken from them. But, as she followed them out of the west transept, hoping to be able to speak to one or two of them, she suspected that, on this occasion at least, her prayers would not be answered.

Powerscourt and Chief Inspector Yates were walking slowly round the cloisters. The Chief Inspector looked up at the extraordinary carvings on the roof. 'Cloisters, my lord. Finished about 1410. Fan vaulting. Perpendicular. Last phase of English Gothic. There used to be a stream here next to these cloisters, my lord, but it was sent underground about forty years ago. The cathedral masons thought it was going to cause subsidence so they diverted it. They did leave a sluice gate that could be opened from somewhere in the cathedral so the building could be flooded in case of fire.'

'Could we come back to the cloisters in a moment, Chief Inspector? What do you make of these missing journals of Arthur Rudd's? Do you think they're important?'

'I'm not sure what to think about them,' said the Chief Inspector. 'We had to promise an increase in the number of visits to the husband in jail before that wretched woman would speak to us at all. Even now, I'm not sure she couldn't be mistaken. I certainly don't think they're as important as that young man Patrick Butler thinks they are.' The Chief Inspector fished around in his pocket for his copy of the *Grafton Mercury*. 'What did his paper say? "We call upon the authorities" – that means me in this case – "to display the utmost vigilance in the hunt for them. Not an hour, not a day must be lost." I can tell you this, my lord. We're looking everywhere for those bloody journals. I've even got a couple of my officers wading through all the rubbish in the Corporation dump. I don't suppose the young man on the *Mercury* fancies a day or two of duty squelching through all that mess.'

Powerscourt smiled. 'It all depends, surely,' he said, walking past the entrance to the chapter house, 'on why the journals were removed, if they were removed. Was it because this diary would have told us who the killer was? Not very likely, on the face of it, because most people have no idea they're going to be murdered, never mind who their murderer is going to be. Or was it because it contained something that would have led us to the murderer? Was he killed because of what was in the diaries? In which case how did the murderer know what was in the diaries? Did he pop in when Rudd was out and read the latest instalments? That doesn't seem very likely to me. Or did the murderer intend to kill him anyway and then remove the diaries afterwards to protect his own identity?'

The bells high up in the tower at the bottom of the spire tolled eleven o'clock. Powerscourt thought they sounded very loud. He thought briefly of all those monks long ago whose daily lives would have been regulated by the notes of Great Tom and Isaiah and Resurrection and Ezekiel a couple of hundred feet above.

'Had you ever thought of being a journalist, my lord?' Chief Inspector Yates was smiling now. 'If you can produce that many questions off the top of your head, think of the pages of the papers you could fill without ever leaving the office. For my money, my lord, the most likely explanation is your last one. The diaries might have given us all a clue as to who the murderer was.' The Chief Inspector stopped suddenly and stared at the snow melting on the grass in the centre of the Great Cloisters. 'This has only just occurred to me, my lord. Suppose the killer has just put the unfortunate Rudd on the spit. He's already dead, as we know. He pops three doors up into Vicars Close and does a quick check on Rudd's possessions and Rudd's diaries. There's something that would implicate the murderer. So they've got to go too. So the murderer trots back down into the kitchen and puts them on the fire. They'd be turned into dust and ashes long before anybody could find them.'

Powerscourt stared at the policeman. 'I wish I'd thought of that, Chief Inspector. It's so obvious when you think of it.'

They pulled back to the side of the cloister to let the choir pass on their way to Holy Communion at eleven fifteen.

'These cloisters here, my lord,' said the Chief Inspector, 'they're not as well preserved as the ones at Gloucester. Maybe that stream did them no good at all. I had to go there for a murder case two years ago and I made the time to go and have a look. The thing about this fan vaulting, my lord, is that all this tracery,' the Chief Inspector stopped and pointed up at the delicate and elaborate patterns in stone that ran in almost perfect order along the roof of the cloisters, 'they're all ornamental, they don't have any function at all. You could say that the masons were just showing off. And now, my lord, I must leave you. My Chief Constable won't be pleased if he finds out that we've been having architectural tours of the cathedral. I do have to pop back later on this afternoon, mind you. Perhaps I'll see you then.'

With a last look at the roof Chief Inspector Yates departed on his business. The patterns may have only been ornamental, Powerscourt thought, but they were incredibly graceful. They didn't look as though they were made of stone at all, but of some much lighter substance, as if a fifteenth century stonemason had managed to spray the roof with icing and it had set for five hundred years.

The congregation for Holy Communion was slightly larger than the one for Matins, Lady Lucy observed. The service was held in the Lady Chapel where the size or lack of size of the congregation was less apparent. The two old ladies were still there. Perhaps they never leave, she thought, hiding away overnight in some dusty corner of the huge building to pass the night with the rats and the departed saints. The drunk and the very thin old man had gone, but were replaced by a couple of elderly gentlemen in rather better health who spoke the responses in loud and self-important tones. There was an ascetic young man with a wide-brimmed hat on his knees who looked as if he was undergoing some profound religious experience, a mystic perhaps. Certainly he looked as if flagellation and hair shirts might not have been too far away. The choirboys were still there, looking, to Lady Lucy's eyes, even more frightened than they had done that morning.

'The Body of our Lord Jesus Christ, which was given for thee, preserve thy body and soul unto everlasting life. Take and eat this in remembrance that Christ died for thee, and feed on him in thy heart by faith with thanksgiving.' A look of rapture, a look of ecstasy crossed the face of the young mystic as he took the bread in his hands. Lady Lucy remembered Francis telling her about the bitter controversy that had racked the Church of England some years before. It concerned, she thought, something called the Doctrine of the Real Presence. Very High Church Anglicans known as ritualists, the ones closest in religious position to the Roman Catholics, believed that the bread and wine were transformed in the Communion Service into the real body and blood of Christ. The opposite party, principally Evangelicals, contended that such beliefs were incompatible with the doctrines of the Church of England. Anybody who believed in the idea of the Real Presence was effectively a heretic and should be expelled from the Anglican Church. One or two of these cases had actually ended up in court, one or two parsons had actually gone to jail, and, in the most farcical case, the Archbishop of Canterbury himself had eaten a consecrated wafer at the heart of the dispute. At the time of its consumption the wafer was over four months old.

The little congregation filed out of the Lady Chapel, the young man staying behind to kneel in front of the cross. Lady Lucy was closer here to the faces and expressions of the choirboys as they made their way towards the north transept and the cloisters. She could see no improvement.

Powerscourt spent most of the rest of the day reading the back copies of the *Grafton Mercury*. He had an appointment after evensong with Vaughan Wyndham, Organist and Master of the Choristers of Compton Minster, the employer and conductor of the late Arthur Rudd. Patrick Butler had assembled a great mountain of newspapers to the right of his desk. 'You don't mind, Lord Powerscourt, if they're not exactly in the right order, do you? I always mean to sort them out week by week but there never seems to be enough time. Now I've got to go and talk to a man at the printers.' With that Patrick Butler had grabbed his hat and rattled off down the stairs. He returned at various points during the day, searching hopelessly for some notes on his desk, crawling about on the floor to retrieve some material for the printers.

At first Powerscourt found the experience of reading these papers in the wrong order rather exhilarating. Reports of a bumper harvest in one paper might be followed by accounts of the longest period of rainfall in the county records in the next. Descriptions of cricket matches could be followed in the next paper in the pile with a sad account of the early departure of the local football team from the FA Cup. Eventually Powerscourt decided he had had enough.

132

He spread all the papers out on the floor and reassembled them in the correct order. It took, he checked, precisely thirty minutes. It could be his way of saying thank you to the editor. Then he read them all, a year and a half's worth of *Grafton Mercury* at a single sitting.

Powerscourt would have had to say, if asked, that there was not much in these newspapers that would have informed the citizenry about the wider world. Of events in the continent of Europe, of events in London, of events even in the neighbouring county there was nothing at all. The *Grafton Mercury* did not run to accredited correspondents in St Petersburg or Vienna, in Paris or even in Westminster or Whitehall. That was not its job. But its readers would have been very thoroughly informed about what was going on around them, a weekly budget of births, marriages and deaths, reports of the decisions of the county council, of the local court cases, of harvest festivals and outbreaks of bad weather, of the activities of every local society across the entire county of Grafton. Powerscourt thought the paper became livelier and more adventurous with the arrival of Butler as editor. Youth had replaced crabbed old age, he thought, and it showed on the page. As he read, his mind was registering what was not there in these papers as much as the printed stories themselves. There had been no murders. There were no reports of death in mysterious circumstances. There was only one unusual story about the cathedral in the seventy-eight back copies he read through. Some months before, strange pagan signs had been found, daubed on the floor beside the high altar. Powerscourt thought Return of the Druids might have been a little strong for the headline. He suspected Patrick Butler had written the headline and the story himself. It referred extensively to a prehistoric site just across the county border which was a centre for followers of ancient cults. But there were no reports of further incidents. Powerscourt felt sure that if Butler had been able to discover a scintilla of evidence for further pagan activity, however small, it would have featured heavily in the pages of the *Grafton Mercury*. There was one constant refrain that ran with increasing frequency through the pages. Powerscourt felt desperately sad each time he came across another report. The young men of the county had signed up for military service with the local regiment. There were glowing descriptions of their departure, the military bands playing, the young men marching off together to the war in South Africa. Now they were dying. Once a fortnight or so another death would be reported, another family heartbroken at their loss. There was talk of erecting a permanent memorial to the fallen in the cathedral when the war was over.

Powerscourt felt slightly disappointed as he headed back towards the minster across the windy expanse of the Green. He had hoped that there might be some clue hiding in the back pages that would bring him enlightenment. There was none. Evensong was nearly over when he returned, an anthem by Thomas Tallis soaring up to the roof. Lady Lucy was not to be seen. Powerscourt presumed she must have gone home. He was glad. He was growing increasingly worried about her obsession with the choirboys. He knew it all came from the highest of motives but he felt she was in danger of becoming ridiculous, something he had never encountered before in all his years of marriage.

He noticed that the builders had finally arrived. There was a battery of scaffolding in the crossing, the part of the cathedral where the nave met the transepts, underneath the tower that served as the launching pad for the spire. As he looked up Powerscourt saw that this must be the highest point inside the cathedral, a couple of hundred feet above the ground. The top of the scaffolding was next to a wooden trap door that led to the higher parts above. Waiting to be transferred the following day was an enormous pile of masonry slabs, destined to replace the broken sections further up. The workmen had spread thick dust sheets all over the surrounding floor. The Dean had complained to Powerscourt a couple of days before about the delays in the work, and about the enormous cost of having to operate at such high levels.

'The Lord is meant to provide,' he had said indignantly to Powerscourt, 'but our constant fear is that one day he may forget about us here. He may have better things to do. And then what will happen to his crumbling buildings?'

The choir had finished. The silver cross led the way towards the cloisters once more. The two old ladies were definitely leaving the cathedral, nodding politely to Powerscourt as they hobbled past, chatting quietly to each other about the service they had just attended. He watched them go, almost pleased to be the only person left inside. The lights were still on in the choir, casting a faint light back down the nave. The Cathedral of the Blessed Virgin Mary was completely silent as Powerscourt went back to stare up at the scaffolding.

Maybe it was the silence that saved him. He heard a very faint creak up above that might have been a rope running along a pulley. Powerscourt looked up. Then time stood still. The first thing that flashed across his mind was the memory of Beethoven's Emperor Piano Concerto which he had listened to with Lucy in London weeks before. There was one passage where the orchestra falls silent and the piano descends down the scale, falling, falling, falling, it had seemed to Powerscourt at the time, as though it was going to drop off the edge of the world. The descending notes didn't stay with him for long. For he realized that these great slabs of masonry stone were falling from their scaffolding and would land on top of him any second. He turned and dived full length through the entrance to the choir. He slid several feet along the polished floor and came to rest against the edge of the choir stalls. He hit his head hard against an ornate piece of wooden carving.

The noise was muffled by the dust sheets. The blocks of masonry smashed on to the stone floor of the crossing. Bits of broken stone ricocheted across the transept and down the nave. The dust of ages rose from beneath the cathedral stones and flowed outwards like a whirlwind. The Pillar of Smoke has come to Compton Minster, Powerscourt thought groggily, and we shall all be consumed. Shards of stone flew off and cracked the wooden seats at the top of the nave. Then the lights went out.

As he rose, very unsteadily, to his feet, Powerscourt could feel the blood flowing freely down his temple where he had hit the carving. His brain told him that he had stopped beside the stall of Chisenbury and Chute. Grantham Australis was next door. His leg must have been twisted in the fall. He limped off very slowly towards the high altar. The great gold crucifix beckoned him on towards the place of sanctuary. Then he heard the doors close. He was locked in, shortly after five thirty in the afternoon. There must be fourteen hours to go before they would open again to greet another day. Lord Francis Powerscourt sat down in front of the altar and tried to collect his thoughts.

12

As he sat there by the altar Powerscourt tried to remember his own actions just before the fall of stone. Had he touched anything by accident? Had he inadvertently pulled on some mechanism that could have caused the avalanche? No, he decided, he had not. There was only one conclusion. Somebody had just tried to kill him. That didn't bother him very much. People of one sort or another had been trying to kill him for years. He wondered suddenly if the killer was even now heaping the coal high on to the fire in the kitchen of the Vicars Hall. Tonight, ladies and gentlemen, we have another treat for you. After the earlier delicacy of the vicar choral, we now present another dish, Roasted Powerscourt. He shuddered and massaged his injured leg once more.

He staggered to his feet. He began to make his way slowly down the north ambulatory away from the altar. His hands felt the outline of the tomb of Abbot Parker, the last abbot but one before the Dissolution of the Monasteries. The Abbot felt very cold. His long thin face was wet. Powerscourt realized that he was leaving a trail of blood wherever he went. He looked back at the altar cloth, hanging stiffly in its place. No, that would never do. He took off his coat and jacket and ripped off one sleeve of his shirt. He folded it into a makeshift bandage and wrapped it round his head. With dust all over my clothes and a bloody shirt on my forehead, I must look like a tramp now, he said to himself, one of those lost souls who haunt the lonely services in the cathedral looking for salvation, or warmth. He abandoned the Abbot to his fate and moved across to the opposite wall. His fingers felt for the extraordinary memorial to the Walton family from the year 1614. There were two semicircular niches inside a marble frame. On the left was a little statue of the father, with a red cloak over a black robe, Powerscourt remembered from the hours of daylight, kneeling before a marble plaque, hands clasped in prayer. Facing him, also kneeling, also praying, was his wife, clad entirely in black, more pious perhaps than her husband. Beneath them, aligned according to age and height, were their eleven children, also kneeling in prayer, the boys beneath their father, the girls beneath their mother. The smallest was only a couple of inches high. Powerscourt wondered what terrible disaster had carried off the entire family. Maybe it had been the plague. Maybe Chief Inspector Yates would know.

Powerscourt paused beside the chantry chapel of Robert, Lord of Compton, passed away sometime in the fourteenth century, he remembered. The light from the great windows was very faint now. The stained glass didn't seem to let very much of it in. Powerscourt's hand felt the dust from the falling masonry already lying thickly on the stone. Half the monuments in the cathedral must be covered with it already. He wondered if the murderer was coming back to make sure he was dead. Or had the murderer watched the explosion from some high place up there on the scaffolding? Powerscourt didn't think he could have seen anything through the storm of dust that poured out of the broken floor. Had the murderer rushed off to close all the doors? Did he believe that Powerscourt was dead, one unfortunate victim of the accident to be discovered by the verger in the morning? Or was he intending to come back and finish Powerscourt off?

Powerscourt looked around for a means of defending himself. If he had the power, he reflected, he could raise a formidable host of warriors from inside the building itself. Those stone knights, facing east to meet their maker, could come clanking out of their tombs, stone swords in stone hands to terrify their enemies. There was a whole window partly filled with soldiery who had fought with Edward the Third in France in the Crécy campaigns in the fourteenth century. Powerscourt couldn't see the detail in the darkness, but he thought there was a good selection of cavalry, some infantry and some archers, sharpshooters he could deploy to cover all the doors. Across the choir from where he now stood was the Soldiers Chapel, with flags and banners from the past two centuries hanging proudly from the stonework. Fierce sergeant majors with enormous moustaches could come back from their earlier campaigns to lead the standards into the thick of battle. There was a stained glass window there too, Powerscourt remembered, filled with the bloodied infantry of Britannia's wars.

His shirt was not proving very effective as a bandage. Blood was dripping through it and trickling slowly down his cheek. Extremely gingerly, Powerscourt reached up and twisted it through ninety degrees so a drier part was now in place to stem his wound. His leg was throbbing fiercely. What, he wondered, had caused this attack by masonry? It couldn't be for what he knew about the deaths of John Eustace or Arthur Rudd, unless the murderers were appraised of Johnny's inquiries into the Eustace coffin. In truth he knew very little. It had to be for what he might find out, what he might discover in the future rather than what he knew in the present. Was the assault linked to his forthcoming interview with Organist Wyndham? Did somebody not want him to speak to the organist? Perhaps the organist knew too much. There must be some terrible secret at the heart of Compton Minster. To preserve this secret Arthur Rudd had been strangled, his body roasted on the flames, his journals stolen and almost certainly burnt. He must have known the secret. Had John Eustace known it too?

Powerscourt thought of Patrick Butler and what the *Grafton Mercury* might make of the attack. Murder by Masonry in the Minster? Investigator Inches From Death? He couldn't think clearly any more but he felt certain that he wanted no publicity for the events of this night. He thought of Lady Lucy, back in Fairfield Park by now, no doubt. She would think he had gone to talk to Johnny Fitzgerald and would be late home. He thought of the Chief Inspector, back home with his family, maybe looking through another of his architectural volumes. He tried to imagine the Bishop or the Dean or the Archdeacon or the Dean's enormous servant, two hundred feet above their transept, preparing to pull the rope that would pour all those stone slabs down on to their cathedral floor, killing somebody in the process. He thought of Thomas and Olivia, getting ready for bed, being spoilt by their grandmother, entirely ignorant of what had happened to their Papa. Maybe Compton is a more dangerous place than South Africa, he said to himself, for I went through a year and more of the Boer War without a scratch.

The bells made him jump. They were terribly loud in this empty building as they struck the hour of seven. Powerscourt felt sure that the dust moved again, swirling off the surfaces where it had settled before to find new resting places on chantry chapel or choir stall. Powerscourt knew he could not fall asleep in case his enemies found him in the dark. He looked at the choir, all dark outlines in the gloom. He needed to sit down, he decided. A sudden inspiration lightened his mood. I may be going to bleed to death in this bloody cathedral, he said to himself, but I shall go out with style. He hobbled slowly to the other side of the choir. He settled himself into the great chair. His fingers felt for the inscription on the back. This would be a good way to go. Episcopus, Beatus Vir. The Bishop, a holy man. Powerscourt, a holy man.

The real Bishop was hosting an important conference in the study of his Palace. The front of the building looked out over the Cathedral Green but the study was at the back. In daylight there was a peaceful view over the Bishop's garden, said to be one of the largest and finest of its kind in the country. On the desk, large enough to intimidate any passing prebendary, sat the wooden box found behind the coffin during the excavations in the crypt. Two gentlemen sat across from the Bishop, inspecting the documents contained inside. To Moreton's right was Octavius Parslow, senior keeper of documents at the British Museum, a man with a reputation for scholarship that stretched across the great museums and universities of Europe. To his left, Theodore Crawford, Professor of History at the University of Oxford and one of the leading scholars of the sixteenth century in Britain. They both wore fine gloves as they passed the document from hand to hand. From time to time Crawford, a thin man in his early forties with a goatee beard, would snort rather loudly and make a jotting in his dark red notebook. Parslow had placed a large magnifying glass in front of him and would raise it to peer earnestly at the writing. The Bishop had an enormous volume by his side, bound in fading brown leather, which contained the early records of the cathedral.

The Bishop coughed slightly and smiled at his guests. 'Gentlemen,' he said, 'you have now had over an hour and a half to peruse these documents. Would you be so kind as to give me your preliminary thoughts on them?'

The two scholars looked at each other, both reluctant to speak first.

'Could I ask you, if I may, Bishop, as to your own view on the matter?' Octavius Parslow was playing for time.

'Well,' said the Bishop, 'I am a mere country bishop, as you both know. My speciality is in the early textual analysis of the Gospels.

But I have consulted widely in the district. It is surprising how much expertise you can find in these rural parts if you know where to look for it.'

Four eyebrows shot up in unison across the desk. Surely the man wasn't going to suggest that Compton was a centre of learning to rival Berlin or Bologna. The Bishop noted the look of disdain on his visitors' faces and reminded himself of the obligations of Christian charity.

'It is my belief,' he went on earnestly, 'though I would never dare to lay claim to the wisdom you two scholars have brought to my Palace this evening, that the document is a diary, a record, kept by one of the monks when the present cathedral was still a monastery in 1530 or 1540, I am not at all sure of the dates. It would be a most magnificent find if it were true, for we celebrate one thousand years in the life of abbey and cathedral at Easter.'

Even Parslow and Crawford were impressed by the thousand years of history.

'Professor Crawford?' said the Bishop hesitantly. 'Perhaps you would like to give us your opinion.'

The Professor snorted slightly once again. He took off his spectacles and laid them on the desk. 'Interesting though your speculations are, my dear Bishop,' he just about managed a smile for Gervase Bentley Moreton, 'I feel it far too soon to pass any kind of authoritative judgement. There are a number of problems in my view. Even by the standard of Church Latin of the time, the language is very poor. I do not say that renders it inauthentic, but it raises the possibility, the strong possibility in my judgement, that it may be either a forgery, or a joke document written to impersonate what the author thought would be the grammar and vocabulary of a country bumpkin.'

Bishop Moreton had rather more respect for country bumpkins that either of his visitors. 'And what is your view, Mr Parslow?' He turned to face the man from the British Museum.

'I would have to say first of all, Bishop,' Octavius Parslow was tapping his fingers slowly on the desk, 'that I would wish to take issue with my colleague here about the Latin.' He bestowed a condescending smile on his fellow scholar. 'Crude, yes, ungrammatical, yes, but not, I would suggest, the work of a country bumpkin. There are records from one or two of the northern abbeys, Bolton, I believe, and perhaps Fountains, where the phraseology, while obviously not from the senior common rooms of Oxford, is not dissimilar. My reservations centre rather more on the sequence of legislation described in the documents. Surely the Act of Annates was passed before the Act of Succession? Yet here it would appear to be the other way round. There may be some perfectly innocent explanation as to why history seems to have been running in reverse order here in Compton, but for the moment I cannot see it.'

'I am not at all sure,' Professor Crawford returned to the fray, 'that the precise order of the various acts is significant. The fellow is not writing an academic thesis, merely giving his reactions to contemporary events. He could have made a mistake.'

This time it was Octavius Parslow who snorted. 'I don't think you will find that statement to be borne out by the historical records at all,' he said, turning slightly red.

'Gentlemen, gentlemen.' Bishop Moreton tried to restore some kind of order. 'Could I ask you a more specific question about the document. What date would you say it was?'

'Speaking for myself,' said Professor Crawford, 'I could not hazard my academic record or my professional reputation on that question at this juncture.'

'Mr Parslow?' said the Bishop.

'In my view, Bishop, it would be premature to attempt any precision at this stage.'

The Bishop felt himself growing drowsy. He had had a very busy day, with a diocesan meeting that had lasted for a full three hours. He lowered his head as if in concentration, but his eyes were closing. Various phrases penetrated his brain as the battle raged on across his desk. 'Need to see the whole question in its proper historical context,' 'further documentation to be consulted in the Bodleian,' 'a question not merely of the Dissolution of the Monasteries but of the wider evolution of Tudor religious policy in its entirety,' and this from the Oxford Professor Crawford, 'need to consult widely with colleagues, possibly even in Cambridge,' 'detailed textual analysis vital before any proper historical comparisons can be made at all.'

The bells of Isaiah and Ezekiel woke the Bishop at eight o'clock precisely. 'Gentlemen,' he said, 'this has been most illuminating. Perhaps we could continue our discussions over dinner.' As the Bishop led Professor Crawford and Octavius Parslow towards his dining room, he reflected on the idea of time in Compton running backwards. You could leave these two here, he said to himself as

141

he beamed happily at his guests, discussing this document and they'd keep going all the way back to the Dissolution of the Monasteries themselves in 1539. They might be able to keep the academic argument going right back to the foundation of the abbey in 901.

Lord Francis Powerscourt enjoyed being a Bishop to begin with. He wasn't quite sure precisely what a Bishop of Compton would do when he sat here. Maybe his job was simply to preside over the services, to give his seal of approval to all those Te Deums and Cantate Dominos that would have echoed round the choir down the centuries. Then the pain got worse. He was on the second sleeve of his shirt now and was seriously worried that he would be on his trousers or his waistcoat next. He limped painfully round the cathedral, checking all the doors. He passed the treasury, filled with ancient crosses and chalices and Communion cups. One of the past glories of the minster was in there, a small box said to contain relics of Thomas à Becket. This piece of treasure had brought great wealth to the cathedral in years gone by as pilgrims came from all over England to pay tribute. The money they left had been enough to repair the great crossing when the tower fell down in the fourteenth century. Above him, as he passed the mighty pillars, the jokes of the medieval stone workers were still there, a cobbler mending shoes, someone removing a thorn from his foot, a fox stealing a goose, a spoonbill eating a frog. The circuit of the doors took him over forty minutes. Normally it would have taken less than ten. His leg was still painful. He wasn't quite sure how much blood he had lost, spots of it marking his progress round the building.

By eleven o'clock Powerscourt was back in the sanctuary, sitting on the steps in front of the high altar. He wondered if he could last through the night without falling asleep. He was, he knew, on the edge of delirium. The pipes on the great organ seemed to dance in front of him. He heard over and over again the muffled thud of the falling masonry. He could see himself diving again and again through the entrance to the choir. The faint noises he had heard from outside earlier on, horses' hooves on the road, people talking to each other as they walked across Cathedral Green, had died out as Compton retired for the night. Sometimes he thought he detected scurrying noises at the back of the choir as if the cathedral mice had come out to play and sing some anthems of their own.

At twenty past eleven he thought he heard a creak coming from the west front. It was a prolonged creak, followed by a second one. Powerscourt remembered that there were two great locks on the door. The door opened very slowly. The murderer is coming back, Powerscourt said to himself. He's coming back to finish me off. When he finds no corpse underneath those masonry blocks in the transept he'll search the entire cathedral. He saw, or thought he saw – he wasn't very sure what was real and what was delirium any more – a lantern moving slowly up the nave about a hundred and fifty yards away from his position in the sanctuary. Powerscourt was dazzled by the unexpected light after his hours in the darkness. He couldn't see who was behind it. He looked around desperately at the high altar. He might have declined to remove the cloth to quench his wound but he felt the two heavy silver candlesticks might help to keep him alive. He didn't think God would object to that. He realized suddenly that while he could see the lantern, the person behind it couldn't see him. The light wasn't strong enough to reach all that distance. The footsteps were very loud. Powerscourt was planning an ambush. If he could reach the back of the chantry chapel of Sir Algernon Carew on the far side of the choir, he might be able to knock the murderer out with one great blow from his candlestick. He tiptoed off across the presbytery.

Then he heard the voice. At first he thought the delirium was back for it was the voice he knew best in the world.

'Francis?' it said in a doubtful tone. 'Francis?'

Powerscourt tried to run towards the voice but found he could not manage it.

'Lucy! Lucy, my love, I'm here, I'm coming.'

Husband and wife met on the edge of the transept where the falling stone had almost killed Powerscourt six hours before. Powerscourt held her very tight. 'Oh Lucy, I'm so sorry. I'm dripping blood on to your new coat.'

'Never mind my coat, Francis, you're injured. We'd better get you home.'

Powerscourt saw that the figure with the lantern was the enormous manservant of the Dean who had fetched him in the middle of the night Arthur Rudd was murdered. His shadow behind the lantern was enormous. Powerscourt pointed to the chaos in the transept.

'All these masonry blocks were up there,' he said to the two of them, pointing up to the roof. 'They very nearly fell on top of me. Had to dive into the choir to get out of the way. That's where I cut my head.'

With Lucy on one side and the giant on the other Powerscourt hobbled out of the cathedral and into the waiting coach. 'How did you know I was here, Lucy?' said Powerscourt, feeling giddy from the fresh air outside.

'Johnny came back alone an hour ago. He rode off back into town to see if he could find you. He's going to check back at the house at midnight to report progress. I came along in the coach to see if you were in the cathedral. I thought you might have been locked in. I had to wake up the Dean's household to get the keys.'

Lady Lucy did not tell her husband that she had never seen Johnny Fitzgerald ride so fast, nor that he was using language she had never heard before. The two of them watched as the Dean's enormous servant walked slowly back to his home on the other side of the Cathedral Green. Above them, on the west front, the remaining statues remained impassive at their posts, still depicting the story of their faith into the night sky.

Powerscourt was leaning back into his seat as the carriage clattered off towards Fairfield Park. One of Lady Lucy's finest handkerchiefs had been wrapped around his forehead.

'I didn't like to say it in front of the Dean's man,' said Powerscourt, holding firmly on to his wife's hand, 'but I don't think the falling masonry was an accident.'

'What do you mean, Francis?' asked Lady Lucy, wondering if the shock and the injuries and the long period of incarceration were affecting her husband's wits.

'Somebody was trying to kill me, Lucy. That's what I mean. If they had succeeded they could have taken my corpse away and done what they wanted with me. Maybe the force of the blow would have pressed me straight into the stone floor so I would have joined all those other bodies lying about all over the building.'

Lady Lucy thought of the terrible fate of Arthur Rudd and shuddered. She couldn't bear the thought of her Francis being roasted on a spit. She held his hand ever tighter. She knew it was useless asking him to give up the case and return to London. Giving up cases was something Francis and Johnny Fitzgerald never did, however difficult and dangerous they might be.

'But why, Francis? Why should anybody want to kill you here? You don't know who the murderer is, do you?'

'I have no idea at all,' said Powerscourt bitterly, 'about who the murderer is. But he sent me a message tonight. Either he was going to succeed, in which case we would not be driving back to the house a few minutes before midnight. Or he's trying to warn me off, a couple of tons of masonry to get me out of Compton before he tries again.'

'So what are you going to do, Francis?' said Lady Lucy, glancing across at her husband. Even in the dark she thought he looked drained by his ordeal, six hours locked up in Compton Minster with the dead of centuries and their strange memorials, with a bleeding forehead and a strained leg.

'Let me tell you, Lucy, precisely what I propose to do. I'm going to find this bloody killer. And I'd better find him soon, before he kills me.'

13

The Bishop of Compton would have described himself, if asked by St Peter at the gates of heaven to list his virtues, as a patient man. Patience and scholarship, after all, went together. For most of his adult life he had shuffled through the libraries of Britain in pursuit of his interest in the early versions of the Gospels. Books chained to their shelves, books that could not be removed from the floor where they were kept, books that nobody else had opened for a hundred years or more had been his daily bread for over a quarter of a century. In his youth the Bishop had dreamed of one spectacular discovery, a biblical Eureka, a modern version of Archimedes in his bath, that would make his name and secure his reputation. As time passed and no miracles were vouchsafed, he realized that steady labour and the accumulation of judgement were more valuable weapons in a scholar's armoury than the blinding light he hoped for in his earlier days. But patience, certainly he had acquired that. Or he thought he had, until the events of yesterday evening.

The Bishop was pacing up and down around the croquet lawn in front of his Palace where vicious battles with ball and mallet in the summer gave the lie to the concept of brotherly love among the clergy. It was ten to eleven on the morning after his encounter with the two scholars, Octavius Parslow, senior keeper of documents at the British Museum, and Theodore Crawford, Professor of History at the University of Oxford. Before their dinner they had refused to give any view on the authenticity of the documents found in the cathedral crypt which Bishop Moreton believed were a kind of diary, kept by a junior monk during the last days of the abbey at Compton before the Dissolution of the Monasteries in the sixteenth century. Two bottles of his better claret had failed to loosen their tongues into pronouncing a verdict of any kind. A bottle of the Bishop's vintage port, which his wine merchant assured him was the equal of anything in the kingdom, had also failed. The Bishop's patience finally snapped when Parslow inquired shortly after midnight if the Bishop had any more port in his cellar. 'This stuff seems quite palatable to me for the depths of the country,' he had said, pointing to his empty glass. Then the Bishop did something he had never done before in all his fifty-four years. He excused himself from his own dinner table and left his guests to their own devices. As he said his prayers by the side of his great four-poster he prayed for forgiveness, but even then, inappropriate words came to the Bishop from the book he knew so well. 'Forgive them, Lord, for they know not what they do.'

So this morning he had determined to take matters into his own hands. He had a visitor due to call on him in his study at eleven o'clock. The two scholars, he reflected sourly, asking for remission of his sins even as the thought crossed his mind, the two scholars could go to hell.

Lord Francis Powerscourt had returned to the cathedral, sitting quietly at the back of the nave. His forehead had been expertly bandaged by Dr Blackstaff in Fairfield Park the night before. He had a stout walking stick of Johnny Fitzgerald's to help him with his bad ankle. Johnny had taken great delight in explaining the secrets of this particular staff.

'See here, Francis,' he had said happily, as he fiddled with the top. 'This handle here unscrews. Inside is a secret phial, this glass container thing.' He drew out an object that looked like a very thin tumbler with a cork stopper at the top. 'In times of pain and difficulty, Francis, a man may find consolation in a drop of medicinal whisky or brandy, whichever you prefer. I never understood why they didn't make this glass container longer. It can only go about a quarter of the way down the bloody walking stick. They could have made it much longer. Then you could get nearly a full bottle in there.'

The two old ladies had passed Powerscourt earlier, nodding politely to him on their way to the Communion service in the Lady Chapel. He wondered if the consumption of so much sacred bread and wine might provide the secret of eternal life. The workmen had cleared away most of the debris from the night before. A new collection of masonry was being prepared for ascent into the higher regions.

Powerscourt wondered for the fifth time if the murderer had come back in the early hours of the morning to search for his corpse, if he had prowled all the way round the nave and the transepts and the choir looking for his victim. Or had he waited until the cathedral opened early in the morning before checking on his prey? The very first service of the day at seven thirty must have been a strange event, Powerscourt thought, the Dean or the Precentor or one of the canons reading the Order for Morning Prayer with the dust lying thickly over the choir stalls and broken slabs of masonry stone acting as hazards for the unwary across the great transept. He felt sure the service would have carried on as though nothing at all had happened. Worse things must have been endured in the past, Oliver Cromwell's soldiers in the Civil War looting all the gold and the silver they could find, tearing down the statues, Thomas Cromwell's Commissioners come to take a record of every valuable that could be stolen from the abbey before it was dissolved.

Powerscourt had arranged to meet Patrick Butler here after his meeting with the Bishop.

That young man was feeling uncharacteristically uncertain as the footman led him along the corridors that led to the Bishop's study, the walls lined with portraits of previous officers of the cathedral, surveying the present in their purple robes from the distant past. What did you do when you met a bishop? Did you bow? Did you kneel? Did you have to kiss his hand? He wasn't quite sure.

In the end the Bishop solved the problem for him, rising from his chair behind the great desk and shaking Patrick Butler warmly by the hand.

'Mr Butler,' said the Bishop, 'how kind of you to call on me at such short notice. I am most grateful.' He ushered them both into the two armchairs on either side of the fire. Patrick Butler had no idea why he was here. Perhaps it was to do with the accident in the cathedral the night before. But he didn't think it likely that the Bishop would have asked for a meeting to talk about that. The day-to-day running of the minster was much more the province of the Dean.

'Am I not right in saying, Mr Butler, that you are on friendly terms with Mrs Herbert, Mrs Anne Herbert, who lives on the edge of our Cathedral Close here?'

Patrick Butler blushed slightly. Surely he hadn't been summoned here to talk about Anne? Was the Bishop of Compton going to question him about his intentions?

'That is absolutely correct, my lord,' he replied.

'I knew her first husband very well, you know,' said the Bishop, smiling across at the young man like a benevolent uncle. 'I believe I am godparent to the first child. I'm afraid I keep forgetting his birthday.'

'That's easily done, my lord,' said Patrick Butler. Anne had never told him the Bishop was godfather to one of the children. Perhaps she had forgotten as well.

'Rest assured, Mr Butler,' the Bishop was beaming now, 'that if certain things should come to pass we should be only too happy to place the cathedral at your disposal.'

Patrick Butler hadn't thought about proposing marriage to Anne Herbert for at least three days. Was he being pushed towards matrimony by this prelate of the Church, nudged towards the altar by the weight of Bishop, Dean and Chapter? He blushed again.

'Forgive me, my dear Mr Butler, I did not ask you to come here to pry into your affairs or to interfere in any way. Forgive me if I have said more than I should. We are all so attached to Anne, you see, and eager for her happiness. But enough. Let me tell you the real reason for my invitation.'

The Bishop rose from his armchair and fetched the red folder containing the documents found in the crypt.

'I thought this might be of interest to your readers. In here, Mr Butler, is a document that was discovered by the workmen carrying out repairs in the crypt.'

'Is it old, my lord? Is it valuable?' The normal procession of headlines began to flash through the editor's mind. Secrets of the Compton Crypt. Priceless Manuscript Found by Minster Masons.

The Bishop smiled. 'It is certainly old, Mr Butler. I do not yet know how valuable it may prove to be. I must emphasize the preliminary nature of my conclusions at present. Nothing is yet definite or definitive. But I believe it to be a journal or a kind of diary kept by one of the monks in the years leading up to the Dissolution of the Monasteries.'

'Would that be 1538, my lord?' asked Patrick Butler who had been fascinated by the Reformation in history classes at school. He had had a special weakness for the burning of the martyrs and the priests' holes.

'Absolutely right, young man. Very good. If it is what I think it is, it should give us a unique insight into the last days of the abbey that stood here then.'

'Is it written in English, my lord?'

'Latin, Mr Butler, Latin, rather ungrammatical Latin in some places, I fear. Our monk might not have been the brightest boy in the class, if you see what I mean.'

'Would it be possible for me to have a look at the actual manuscript, my lord? I'm sure our readers would want to have a sense of the appearance of the thing.'

The Bishop opened his red file and held the first page up for Patrick Butler's inspection. 'You can certainly look at it, Mr Butler, but I must ask you not to touch it. You would have to be wearing very fine gloves for that, I'm afraid.' Untouchable by Human Hand flitted across Patrick Butler's brain.

'Could I make a suggestion, my lord? With your permission, we could serialize it in the *Grafton Mercury*.'

'Serialize it, Mr Butler? I'm not quite sure what you mean.'

'We could publish it in instalments, my lord, over a number of weeks. I'm sure more and more people would buy the paper to find out what the old monk was saying.'

The Bishop still looked doubtful. 'Isn't there a problem with that, Mr Butler?'

'Problem, my lord? I don't think so. It would be tremendous, a great honour for the paper.'

'I don't wish to sound disrespectful towards your readers, Mr Butler, but how many of them do you think would understand it?'

Patrick Butler was at a loss. 'Just at the moment, my lord, I must confess it is I who doesn't understand your reservations. Of course, if you feel that a serialization would be inappropriate, then I shall withdraw the suggestion. But with great regrets.'

The Bishop sighed. 'I know that educational standards are rising all the time, even in remote parts of the country like Compton, but I think most, if not all, your readers, would find it difficult to understand.'

Then Patrick Butler knew what the problem was. 'Forgive me, my lord. How silly of me not to have seen the misunderstanding. We would have to translate the document from the original Latin. Perhaps you could make a translation yourself, my lord, or suggest another scholar you feel would be fit for the task. But I am sure it would be much more widely read if we could advertise that the translation was the work of our very own Bishop. That would be a great coup for the paper.'

He would insert a great strapline into the text, Translated by the Bishop of Compton, the Very Reverend Doctor Gervase Bentley Moreton. It wasn't every day you could number a bishop among your correspondents. He wondered how often it happened in *The Times*.

'An excellent plan, Mr Butler,' the Bishop brought him back to Compton, 'I should be delighted to make the translation for you nearer the time. And I think you could also say, bearing in mind the reservations I have already expressed, that I intend to refer to the document in my sermon on Easter Sunday when we celebrate one thousand years of Christian worship in this community. I feel that would be perfectly proper.'

Patrick Butler was feeling elated as he made his way back to the cathedral for his second meeting of the morning. Two excellent stories discovered before twelve o'clock in the morning. A great accident overnight in the cathedral, falling masonry lying all over the place, a miracle nobody was hurt. One of the canons had given him the details earlier in the day. He wondered if he could hint that the ghost was walking again through the minster, a pale cleric clad in black robes said to come from the time of the Civil Wars when he lost his head to hostile soldiery. He would have to go to the County Library and look up the story of the ghost. There was, he remembered, a rather dramatic description of the spectral figure floating high above the choir around the time of the flight of King James the Second. And now this, the minster monk's last words, found in the crypt three hundred and fifty years after his death. And translated by the Bishop himself. Patrick Butler felt his cup was overflowing.

'Lord Powerscourt, my goodness me, sir, you don't look at all well. Have you been in an accident?'

Patrick Butler found his friend seated at the back of the nave, his face pale, the bandage clearly visible beneath the curly hair. He was leaning on his alcoholic walking stick and looking at the stained glass.

'Good morning to you, Patrick, and thank you for coming. I am going to tell you what happened to me, but I don't want it published in your newspaper at present.'

Powerscourt rose slowly from his seat and began a limping progress up the nave towards the main body of the cathedral, the sound of his stick tapping on the stone floor echoing up towards the roof.

'I don't feel happy telling you about it in here,' he said, 'I think we could go to the chapter house. They must have had lots of conspiratorial meetings in there over the centuries.'

Patrick Butler noticed that Powerscourt was carrying a large black notebook, rather larger than the ones his reporters used. He didn't think he had seen Powerscourt with such a thing before.

'Here we are,' said Powerscourt, lowering himself into a great stone seat opposite the entrance to the chapter house. In front of them the slender central pillar rose like an umbrella of stone, surrounded by carvings of foliage and unknown faces from long ago. In the centre of the tympanum above the doorway, the seated figure of Christ in Majesty, surrounded by the symbols of the Four Gospel writers, Matthew, Mark, Luke and John. The story of the Book of Genesis unfolded on the walls around them, Cain slaying Abel, the drunkenness of Noah, the city and tower of Babel, Abraham and the sacrifice of Isaac. Powerscourt wondered about taking a sip from his walking stick to ease the pain. He desisted, fearing that he might be turned into a pillar of salt. There were several such pillars ten feet to his left.

'I presume,' he said, 'that a man in your position must know most of the details of the accident in the cathedral last night?'

Patrick Butler nodded. 'Except for the time it happened,' he said, checking that nobody was coming to disturb them.

'I think I may be able to help you there,' said Powerscourt with a smile. 'It happened in the gap between the end of Evensong and the closing of the cathedral. It must have been about twenty minutes to six.'

'Good God, Lord Powerscourt, how do you know that? Nobody else has any idea at all about when it happened.' Then he looked at the bandage on Powerscourt's forehead, the walking stick by his side. 'You don't mean to say . . .'

'You're very quick this morning, Patrick. I do mean to say. I was here when it happened. I was nearly killed by that falling masonry. I hurled myself into the choir and banged my head on one of the wooden carvings. I must have twisted my ankle in the fall. Somebody was trying to kill me.'

'But this is terrible,' said Patrick Butler. 'How did you get out? Did somebody lock all the doors?'

'Yes,' said Powerscourt, pausing to look at a stone Adam and a stone Eve fleeing from the Garden of Eden, 'somebody did lock the doors. I don't yet know if it was the murderer in person or the member of staff who normally shuts the place up for the night. Lucy, that's my wife, came to find me shortly after eleven o'clock. But this isn't important now.'

'Somebody trying to kill you, Lord Powerscourt? I'd say that was very important.' He stopped to let a figure in clerical robes make his way down the steps into the cathedral, his boots loud against the stone. 'If I hadn't printed that story about your being here to investigate the death of Arthur Rudd, this might never have happened. I could never have forgiven myself if the murderer had succeeded.'

'Just remember, Patrick, that I asked you to print that story. I went out of my way to tell you to print it, if you remember.'

'Is there anything you have learnt from this horrible episode, my lord? Anything that can take your investigations further forward?'

Powerscourt paused. He could hear the rain falling on the roof. He looked round at all the empty seats where members of the Chapter had sat centuries before. He wondered if they could help him.

'Yes and No is the answer to your question, I'm afraid. I had quite a lot of time to think in here last night, wandering up and down with all those corpses and the chantry chapels. I am sure that there is a terrible secret here in this cathedral or in this community. I am sure the murderer is afraid I may discover it. The secret, or the revelation of the secret, may lie in the future rather than the past. That may be why he tried to kill me. And I need your help, Patrick.'

Powerscourt opened his black notebook at the two central pages. Butler saw that it was a plan of the cathedral and the Close. The minster itself was in the centre and the streets ran round it in a rough square, with an inlet opposite the east end of the cathedral for Vicars Close and Vicars Hall. Every house on there had a number, from the Deanery at Number One to the South Canonry at Number Twelve and Exeter House at Number Twenty-One.

'After the murder of Arthur Rudd up here,' Powerscourt pointed to the Vicars Hall on his map, 'I was virtually certain that the murderer must live very close to the cathedral, must be intimate with its workings, must know every detail of what goes on in the minster and the Close. The events of last night merely confirmed that. The murderer must have known how to get to the upper reaches of the great transept without being seen. Either he had himself a set of keys, or he knew precisely what time the place would be closed. If he didn't have the keys, then he must have allowed himself enough time to get down from the high place where he tried to tip the masonry over me.'

'Just as well the murderer didn't get locked in too, my lord,' said Patrick Butler.

'That would certainly have been interesting,' Powerscourt smiled. Single combat in the nave. Powerscourt's Last Stand on the edge of the high altar. Wrestling match to the death among the choir stalls. Anthem of celebration for the victor. Requiem Mass for the Dead.

'Assuming that most of the people involved with the cathedral live round here,' Powerscourt drew a great circle, an outer ring round all his numbered houses, 'then the murderer must live inside this territory here.' He drew a finger round the inner circumference of his map. 'I need to know the name of everyone inside it, servants, cooks, butlers, coachmen, clergy, cleaning staff, I probably need to know the names of every last cat and dog as well. Can be pretty sinister things, cats. There's a very evil looking one halfway up a pillar in the nave. Can you help me with that, Patrick?'

'Not sure about the cats, my lord,' said Butler, pausing again while another pair of clerical boots trudged up the steps and out of the door leading to Vicars Close. 'I can help with some of the people, but I know somebody who would be even more useful. He pointed to Number Nineteen on Powerscourt's map. 'That's Close Cottage, my lord. I have a very particular friend who lives there. She has lived in Compton all her life. We could try calling on her now, if you wish, my lord. I'm sure she would love to meet you.'

As they walked across Cathedral Green Powerscourt learned more about the young woman they were going to see: that Patrick Butler had known her for an incredibly long time, eight and a half months; that she was extremely pretty with a smile that could light up the county; that he often called on her for tea between four and five in the afternoon, no, often was not the right word, it was nearly every day and when business took him out of the town he tried to leave very early in order to make his rendezvous with Anne Herbert and her teapot.

'The Bishop hinted this morning that he would put the cathedral at our disposal,' Butler said. 'He didn't actually mention the word marriage, but that's what he meant.'

'And are you going to propose to the young lady, Patrick?' asked Powerscourt with a smile.

'That's my problem, Lord Powerscourt. I know it seems odd for somebody who makes their living using words, but I don't know really know how to do it.'

'Tricky things, proposals,' said Powerscourt, pausing to look back at the statues on the west front. 'I knew a man once who collected bets to the value of two hundred pounds that he could get engaged on the Underground Railway in London.'

'Which line?' asked Butler, with a journalist's interest in detail.

'The District Line, I believe. The story goes that he began his proposal between Gloucester Road and South Kensington. Perfectly respectable neighbourhood up above if you see what I mean. He could have made his offer somewhere much less salubrious, maybe between Wapping and Shadwell or some place like that in the East End.'

'And what happened?' asked Patrick Butler.

'I don't think it went very well, actually. You see, they weren't the only people in the carriage for a start. All the other passengers were listening in to this strange conversation. The young lady rose to her feet as the train pulled in to the next station, Earls Court, I believe. She uttered just one word to her suitor. "No," she said, and got off the train. He never saw her again.'

'And he never saw his two hundred pounds again either, presumably,' said Patrick Butler. 'Rather an expensive ride on the District Line. Think how much better he might have been if he'd hired a posh carriage above ground. She might have said yes then.'

'Well, she might have said yes. She might still have said no. But you can see some of the picture, Patrick. Privacy. Romantic setting certainly. I can't see even the most ardent devotee of the Underground Railway thinking it a place of romance, even between Gloucester Road and South Kensington. Some men favour candlelight and champagne, that sort of thing.'

The subject of these possible proposals opened her door and showed the two men into her little drawing room.

'I am delighted to meet you, Lord Powerscourt,' said Anne Herbert. 'I've heard so much about you from Patrick.'

'I made so bold as to tell Lord Powerscourt that you could help him in his work, Anne,' said Patrick Butler. He explained the attack the previous evening in the cathedral and Powerscourt's wish to learn the names of all who lived in or around the Cathedral Close.

'How very wicked of somebody to try to kill you, Lord Powerscourt. And in our cathedral too. I'm so glad you have survived. And I'll help in any way I can.'

Powerscourt opened his large black book at the centre pages and placed it on the table. 'I need to know the names of everybody who lives inside this ring here,' he said, outlining the area of interest with his finger. 'And anybody else who has business in the cathedral if they live outside this magic circle.'

Anne Herbert looked up at him, her green eyes troubled. Powerscourt thought she was pretty, very pretty indeed. It was easy now to see the appeal of tea every day at four o'clock.

'Do you mean to say, Lord Powerscourt, that the murderer lives inside this circle of yours?'

'I have to confess that I think it likely, Mrs Herbert, but I'm not sure.'

'Could I make a suggestion?' Anne Herbert felt quite excited at the prospect of helping to solve a murder mystery. Patrick would be so proud of her.

'If you leave the book with me for a day or so, I can fill in all the details for you. I'll write out the people who live in every house, numbered in the same way as you have them here. The ones I don't know about I can ask around about.'

'I'm afraid,' said Powerscourt gravely, 'that I should advise you to be very careful who you talk to. If word gets back to the murderer that you are helping me collect the names of every single person who lives around the Close, your life – let us not mince words here – could be in danger.'

'Rest assured, Lord Powerscourt, I shall be most discreet. I could say that I am compiling a list for one of the cathedral charities I am involved with. Nobody could object to that.'

'Very well,' said Powerscourt. 'But please be careful. I am going to see how up-to-date the electoral register is in the County Hall. But I fear it may be years out of date. They often are.'

'You're right there,' said Patrick Butler, 'we at the *Mercury* have simply given up on it as an accurate and up-to-date record.

Somebody in County Hall should take the matter in hand. But then, nothing ever moves very fast over there in County Hall.'

'Could I ask you one general question, Mrs Herbert?' said Powerscourt. 'I presume that most of the servants and other auxiliaries are local people, people from Compton or the surrounding countryside, I mean?'

'I don't think that's quite right, Lord Powerscourt, although it's what you would expect. The clergy, of course, come from all over the place. But there are quite a lot of foreigners in the servant population. The Dean has a French cook who's married to that enormous servant of his. The Precentor has a Spanish couple, one a cook, the other the butler, I think. The Archdeacon has an Italian friend who comes to stay for a week or so every month. He's always beautifully turned out, but rather superior in his manner.'

Anne Herbert paused and looked out of her windows, as if reminding herself of who lived in which house. 'There's another foreign couple somewhere, I remember now, it's the Sub-dean, he's also got a French cook with a wife who acts as housekeeper. And there are Irish everywhere, not just in service, but singing with the Vicars Choral. There's two or three of them from Ireland.'

The only common thread Powerscourt could wrap round this strange miscellany of foreign persons was that they all seemed to come from Catholic countries. He couldn't see the writ or the decisions of the Bishop of Compton cutting much ice in Turin or Tipperary or Toledo. But he thought little of it.

'I tell you what, Lord Powerscourt,' said Anne Herbert. 'You ought to go and talk to Old Peter. I can't even remember his surname. Do you know what it is, Patrick?'

'I'm afraid I don't. I've only ever heard him referred to as Old Peter.'

'No relation of the apostle?' said Powerscourt.

'No,' Anne Herbert laughed. 'But Old Peter was Head Verger in the cathedral for almost thirty years. Before that he worked as the Bishop's coachman, I think. He's lived in Compton all his life. He must be nearly ninety now.'

'He's ninety-one, actually,' said Patrick Butler. 'We featured him last year in an article on Compton's ninety-year-olds. There are only three of them left. The other two are sisters and live down by the railway station.'

'Anyway, Lord Powerscourt, I'm sure Old Peter would be able to help you. He's known everybody round here for years. He lives in a little cottage at the far end of the garden in the Bishop's Palace. I think the Bishop's servants keep an eye on him. I could come with you and make the introductions if you like.'

Powerscourt was doing rapid arithmetical calculations as he put his coat back on and collected his walking stick. 'Old Peter must be old enough to be the Bishop's grandfather,' he said cheerfully. 'He would have been five at the time of Waterloo, well into his forties by the Crimean War. Let's hear what this Methuselah of Compton has to say for himself.'

14

The most remarkable thing about Old Peter was his hair. He didn't seem to have lost any of it through his decades of service to the Cathedral. It was snow white and flowed down the sides of his face, giving him the air of a Druid functionary rather than a man who had spent his life in the service of the Church of England. His eyes were light brown and he fiddled constantly with an aged pipe that looked as if it might have been older than he was. He pointed Powerscourt to a battered sofa in front of his fire and returned to a faded leather armchair by the side. Anne Herbert had effected the introductions and returned to her cottage. Like many elderly people Old Peter gave his visitor a preliminary bulletin on his health.

'I can still see,' he said, pointing the pipe dangerously close to his eyes, 'and I can still smell. Hearing not what it used to be, my lord, so you may have to speak up a bit. The legs still work though the left one's going a bit rickety at the knee. Doctor says I may be getting a touch of gout.'

'I wanted to ask you about the people who live round the Cathedral Close, Peter,' said Powerscourt raising his voice slightly. 'Mrs Herbert told me you would know if there was anything unusual about them.'

'Unusual, my lord?' said Old Peter with a cackling laugh. 'If you think going to church every day at the same time morning and afternoon and wearing the same funny clothes and saying the same prayers each time for forty or fifty years is usual, then you're a better man than me.'

'You're not a believer, then, Peter?' asked Powerscourt.

'I'm not saying I am and I'm not saying I'm not,' said the old man diplomatically, 'but there have been some strange goings-on at this place, long before all this terrible murder.' He paused and began to refill his pipe with some strong black tobacco.

'When I started here, my lord, the whole place was more like a family business than a house of God. You'll have heard of the Fentimans, I suppose. One of them the bishop, another the Dean, every time there was a vacant canonry or prebendary, another bloody member of the Fentiman family popped up to take the position. Liveried servants behind every seat in the dining room of the Bishop's Palace every night, whether there were visitors or not. Fentimans taking every valuable living that fell vacant and putting in vicars to hold the service and paying them a pittance. Nobody could work out how to get rid of them, my lord. Had to wait for the grim reaper to do his work in the end.'

'I was wondering about more recent members of the Close, Peter,' said Powerscourt, reluctant to embark on a historical survey of Compton Minster, decade by decade, 'I was wondering about some of the foreigners. There seem to be quite a lot of them.'

Old Peter looked at him suspiciously. 'Plenty of foreigners here, my lord. Never did hold much with foreigners myself. Don't see why they can't stay where they were put, if you see what I mean. Still, I suppose Jesus Christ himself would be a foreigner round here so maybe we shouldn't complain. If you ask me,' Old Peter paused to fiddle with a match to light his pipe, 'the strangest one is that Italian who comes to stay with the Archdeacon.' There was a further pause as a cloud of smoke threatened briefly to make Old Peter temporarily invisible. 'Every month he comes, my lord, regular as clockwork, second week usually, and he stays for a week or ten days each time. He's got his own room on the top floor of the Archdeacon's house. Keeps himself to himself. And do you know the strangest thing about him? Every Tuesday I take my dinner with them over at the house and Bill, the Archdeacon's coachman, told me this only the other day.'

Old Peter paused and blew a great mouthful of smoke into his fireplace. 'Nobody's ever seen him at a service in the cathedral, this Italian. Not once in the eight or nine years he's been coming here. Wouldn't you say that was strange?'

Powerscourt was keen to move on. 'What about the French people, one with the Dean, I think, and another with the Subdean on the other side of the Close?'

Old Peter rummaged around in his pockets for his matches.

The pipe, in spite of its earlier clouds of smoke, appeared to have gone out. 'Whoever heard of a man being a cook, my lord. It's not natural. Women were meant to do the cooking ever since we all lived in caves if you ask me. Antoine, the Subdean's cook, is very thick with Mrs Douglas over at the Deanery. She's French too, you see. Local shops not good enough for them, my lord. Every couple of months they go off to London and come back with hampers and hampers of smelly oils and funny looking herbs and potions they put all over their food. They've even got some special French mustard they put on the Dean's rabbit. They say he's very partial to this Frenchified rabbit, the Dean. Maybe they even give him those frogs' legs with that horrible garlic, my lord.'

'And the Spaniards over at the Precentor's house, Peter? What about them?'

Old Peter scratched his leg. Maybe it was the bad one, Powerscourt thought.

'Them Spaniards are a lovely couple, my lord. He's strong as an ox, that Francisco. They say he was a great wrestler in his young days. And Isabella is as sweet a person as you could hope to meet. I heard the other day that she's expecting their first child but they haven't said anything about it.'

'And do all these foreigners belong to the Anglican faith?'

'They do not, my lord.' Old Peter spat into his fire. 'There's a little Catholic chapel down by the station. That's where most of them go. I don't think Francisco goes very often.' Old Peter brushed a couple of locks of hair away from his face. 'I expect you'll be wanting to know if I think any of these people round the Close could be the murderer, my lord.'

'Do you?' said Powerscourt, rather taken aback until he remembered that the *Grafton Mercury* had trumpeted his arrival to find the killer all over the county. The latest issue of the paper was lying on the floor beside him.

'It's a funny thing, Lord Powerscourt. Every day in that building over there,' he nodded behind his shoulder to the cathedral, 'every day in there they celebrate a murder, if you like, the killing of their God by the Romans, and a pretty terrible killing it was too, stuck up there on that cross for hours and hours drinking foreign vinegar. If you live with that week in week out it mightn't be too difficult to contemplate a killing or two of your own.'

161

'Anybody in particular?' asked Powerscourt, marvelling at the twisted theology of this ninety-year-old.

'All of them,' said Old Peter, puffing contentedly at his pipe.

Shortly after three o'clock Powerscourt presented himself at the choirmaster's front door. Vaughan Wyndham was a tall harassed-looking man with black hair turning to silver at the sides.

'Please forgive me for being unable to meet with you yesterday afternoon,' said Powerscourt, accepting a seat by the window looking out over Cathedral Green. 'I hope that now is not too inconvenient. I shall be brief. All I want to know is what you can tell me of Arthur Rudd, the late vicar choral.'

'First class voice,' Wyndham replied. 'I should say he would have been a credit to any choir in the country.' Wyndham spoke fast, with the air of one who wanted to finish the interview as speedily as possible.

'Please forgive me, it wasn't his voice I was thinking of, more of any personal problems he might have had.'

'I suppose,' said Vaughan Wyndham rather brutally, 'that what you really want to know is if I can think of any reason why somebody might want to kill him.'

Powerscourt nodded. 'Rudd wasn't married,' Wyndham went on, 'he wasn't, as far as I know, emotionally involved with anybody in Cathedral Close. When people live in very close proximity like the Compton choir, they very quickly learn everybody else's business, as you can imagine. He didn't have any expensive tastes. He didn't drink very much or you could have told it in his voice. But there was one thing about the late Arthur Rudd that always worried his colleagues.'

Wyndham paused suddenly, worried perhaps that he might have said too much.

'I do hope you will feel able to tell me what it was,' Powerscourt said, quietly but firmly. 'I'm sure you know that I am investigating the death on the Bishop's instructions. And I don't have to remind you that anything you say will be treated in the strictest confidence.'

The choirmaster was peering intently out of his window towards the great buttresses on the eastern side of the cathedral. 'Debt,' he said finally. 'Arthur Rudd was permanently, chronically, in debt.'

'Debts to whom?' asked Powerscourt. 'Debts to other members

of the choir, other members of the Chapter and the wider cathedral community?'

'Not any more,' said Vaughan Wyndham bitterly. Powerscourt wondered suddenly if he too had a large debt outstanding with the late Arthur Rudd. 'Nobody here around the Close would lend him any more. They'd all been burnt once too often. Sorry, Lord Powerscourt, I hadn't realized quite how offensive that was until I'd said it.'

'Don't trouble yourself,' said Powerscourt, his mind racing. Supposing Arthur Rudd had refused so often to repay a debt to one particular member of the choir, would that have been reason enough to kill him? To burn his body on a spit in the Vicars Hall? 'If Rudd couldn't borrow money here in this community, where did he go? Somebody else in Compton? Somewhere further afield? And did anybody know why he borrowed all this money? Surely there must have been a reason.'

'If he did have a reason,' said Wyndham, beginning to collect the music he needed for Evensong, 'he never told us. And I don't think he could have been borrowing money here in Compton. He must have gone further afield, Exeter perhaps, maybe even Bristol. And now, perhaps we could finish our conversation on the way to the cathedral, if you will forgive me.'

Powerscourt watched Vaughan Wyndham as he walked up the nave towards the choir, plucking at his red cassock as he went. Debt, he thought. Could you be killed for not paying your debts? The one certain fact about Arthur Rudd was that he was no longer in a position to pay off any debts in this world. But suppose he owed some unscrupulous lender a very large sum indeed. Would that lender have him killed *pour encourager les autres*, to act as a dreadful warning to others under obligation to the same lender? Pay up, or you'll end up like Arthur Rudd, dead and roasted in Vicars Close.

'Comfort ye, comfort ye, my people, saith your God.' Lady Lucy was walking up and down the drawing room of Fairfield Park the following afternoon, practising the *Messiah*. 'Speak ye comfortably to Jerusalem, and cry unto her that her warfare is accomplished . . .' She motioned her husband to silence as he tiptoed quietly into the room. 'The voice of him that crieth in the wilderness, Prepare ye the way of the Lord, make straight in the desert a highway for our God.'

Lady Lucy had joined the Compton Choir which gave occasional recitals in the city. The backbone, of course, was the Cathedral Choir itself, complete with choirboys. Lady Lucy believed she might be able to get close to them as they worked their way through Handel's masterpiece. The opening performance was less than three weeks away, in the Church of St Nicholas in Compton on the Wednesday and Thursday before Easter.

'Every valley shall be exalted,' Lady Lucy sang on, her soprano voice rising through the octaves. 'We haven't done the next bit yet, Francis, so you don't have to put up with any more. I'd better do some more work on the score. Oh, I forgot to mention that William McKenzie is here. He'll be down in a moment.'

Powerscourt had written to McKenzie the morning after the attack in the cathedral, requesting his immediate presence in Compton. McKenzie had served with Powerscourt and Johnny Fitzgerald in India and was famed for his ability to track man or beast without being detected. Powerscourt had collected his large black book from Anne Herbert's house as she was preparing tea for Patrick Butler. Powerscourt had declined an offer to join them, thinking that Patrick Butler could find worse places and worse times to propose marriage to his beloved. He saw that Anne had done her work very thoroughly. There were pages and pages of lists of the inhabitants of the Cathedral Close. She had helpfully added the date at which each person had first arrived when she knew it. Powerscourt noted that most of the members of the clergy had been there for less than ten years. He suspected that was unusual. He no longer intended to ask anybody connected with the cathedral anything about the place if he could help it.

A slight cough announced the entry of William McKenzie. As usual he seemed to have entered the room without going through any of the doors.

'William,' said Powerscourt, pumping the Scotsman's hand up and down, 'how very good to see you. You are most welcome. And, I fear, most necessary.' He told his colleague about the strange deaths in Compton, Chancellor Eustace passing away in mysterious circumstances, Arthur Rudd murdered and roasted on his spit in the kitchen of Vicars Hall, the attempt on Powerscourt's own life a few days before with the falling masonry.

'Do you have any suspects, my lord?' asked McKenzie, who knew from experience that Powerscourt would probably be running two or three theories through his brain at any given moment.

164

'That's the problem, William,' Powerscourt laughed. 'Sometimes I suspect all of them. Then I suspect none of them. It's so hard to imagine the deans and canons of an English cathedral engaged in murder. Now then, this is what I want you to do.'

McKenzie whipped a small notebook out of his pocket and began making notes.

'Today,' said Powerscourt, 'is Wednesday. Tomorrow therefore is Thursday. And on Thursdays the Archdeacon of Compton, man by the name of Beaumont, Nicholas Beaumont, goes on a mysterious journey very early in the morning from the railway station in the town. He always comes back the same day. You can recognize the Archdeacon quite easily, William. He is well over six foot tall and about as thin as a well-fed skeleton. He normally carries a large black bag on these journeys. Nobody knows where he goes on these Thursday expeditions. I think it's time we found out.'

'Do the locals have any theories about his destination, my lord? Locals usually do, in my experience.'

'I think the most popular theories have to do with women, William. The Archdeacon, like almost his brothers in Christ up at the minster, is not married. The respectable view is that he keeps a wife somewhere. The less respectable view is that he goes to visit the prostitutes of Exeter.'

In his youth McKenzie had belonged to a rather extreme Presbyterian sect in his native Scotland. Powerscourt saw an embarrassed look cross his colleague's face as he wrote that down in his book.

'Francis! Francis! Where the hell are you? I've got news!' Johnny Fitzgerald was clutching a bottle of Fairfield Park's finest armagnac and an enormous tumbler.

'William,' said Johnny, 'I needn't ask if you'll be joining me in a glass of this nectar but I'm well pleased to see you.' With that, he sat down beside the teetotal McKenzie and poured himself a very large tumbler of Auch's finest.

'What news, Johnny?' Powerscourt smiled at his friend. It was almost like being back in the North-West Frontier with the two of them here.

'Wednesday is half-day in Compton,' he began, 'so the two gentlemen who work for Wallace the undertaker repair to the Stonemason's Arms rather earlier than usual. And it so happened that the landlord has this very day taken delivery of a new beer from just outside the county border. Not only new, but strong, almost lethal, in fact.'

'Did you by any chance know that this fresh draught of ale was coming, Johnny?' asked Powerscourt.

'Funny you should ask that, Francis. I did, as a matter of fact. You see, I had recommended this ferocious brew to the landlord a week before. I said I would recompense him personally if it didn't sell well.'

'Is it selling well, Johnny?' asked Powerscourt.

'Just hold your horses there, Francis. The reason I advanced the cause of Fox's Extra Strong was this. Willie Dodds and George Chandler, old man Wallace the undertaker's two assistants, always drink five or six pints of beer in a session. By that stage they're almost ready to be indiscreet but they remember to clam up. After five or six pints they plod off to their homes or their burrows or wherever they live. I reckoned I could have poured the normal stuff in the Stonemason's Arms down them until the last trump sounded and they still wouldn't say anything. Hence the magic ingredient, the Fox's Extra Strong.'

'And would I be right in assuming, Johnny, that the vulpine concoction did the trick?' asked Powerscourt.

'Francis, it was wonderful, just wonderful to watch the stuff in action. After three pints they were more drunk than they usually were after five or six of the other brew. I struck at the beginning of pint five because I wasn't sure they'd be able to speak at all if they managed to get to the end of number six.'

Fitzgerald refilled his tumbler with another generous helping of armagnac. 'This is the story, Francis. I'll spare you their means of telling it as that grew increasingly incoherent. The two of them never had any dealings with the body of John Eustace. Normally they do all the lifting, all the carrying around, that sort of thing. They thought old man Wallace must have had somebody to help him, probably the doctor. They say Wallace is so old now he could hardly lift a copy of *The Times*. The only time they had any dealings with the body was after it was sealed inside its coffin. That is almost unheard of, but there's worse to come. At some point when the coffin was being put on the bier, I think, my informants were pretty groggy by this stage, almost at the end of pint five, it slipped. When they picked it up again they heard something rattling about inside.'

There was a pause, eventually broken by Powerscourt asking if the two men had any idea what it was.

'I think they knew perfectly well,' said Johnny, 'but this was the one thing they weren't prepared to tell me, even after a barrel of Fox's Extra Strong.'

'What do you think it was, Johnny?' said Powerscourt.

'Well, he was a sort of holy man,' said Johnny. 'He might have had one of those great big bibles buried with him. Something to read in there until the second coming.'

Powerscourt looked doubtful. 'I don't think it was a bible, Johnny,' he said with a slight shudder even though the room was warm from the fire.

'What do you think it was, Francis?' said Johnny.

'God forgive me if I'm wrong,' said Powerscourt sadly. 'I think it may have been his head.'

The police called for Powerscourt just after six the next morning. Chief Inspector Yates, the young constable informed him, wished to see Powerscourt in the Compton police station at once. Johnny Fitzgerald was muttering to himself as he mounted his horse about the lack of civilization in country parts, and how the police force should be prohibited by law from calling people out before they had eaten their breakfast. Powerscourt was trying to remember the names of all the inhabitants of the Cathedral Close from his black book as he rode along the silent lanes. He managed to reach fifty-three, suspecting there were a whole lot of people whose names began with M he had left out. He thought they were at the top of the fourth page on the left.

It was a clear night with an hour or more to go before the dawn. There was a cold wind blowing from the west.

'Francis,' said Johnny, 'what do you think is waiting for us at the police station? Apart from the Chief Inspector, that is.'

'Very good of you to turn out at this hour, Johnny,' said Powerscourt. 'I thought you'd be asleep for hours yet.'

Johnny Fitzgerald did not say, although he felt certain his friend knew, that Lady Lucy had made him promise to stick to Powerscourt like a limpet after the attempt on his life.

'Well,' said Powerscourt, 'look on the bright side. They may have apprehended the murderer. The police have been keeping a very close watch all over the Cathedral Close since Arthur Rudd was found.'

'You don't believe that, Francis, do you? If they had, the police boy up ahead would have told us.'

Chief Inspector Yates was waiting for them in a room at the back of the police station. There was a large table in the centre with a blanket covering a cylindrical object in the middle. Chief Inspector Yates despatched his young constable to bring some fresh tea.

'Not sure I would like the lad to see this, gentlemen,' he said. 'I used to play cricket with his father.' He pulled back the blanket to reveal a human leg, much bloodied at the top, wearing what must have once been dark grey trousers and a single black boot. Powerscourt inspected the break carefully, wondering what sort of instrument must have been used to cut it off from the body.

'We found this less than an hour ago,' he said, covering the leg up once more. 'A railway worker on his way to the station alerted his next-door neighbour who is a sergeant here in this police station. Dr Williams is on his way.'

'This is terrible, Chief Inspector,' said Powerscourt. 'I presume there are as yet no sightings of the rest of the body?'

'I have put out word for all my officers to report here as soon as possible,' said the Chief Inspector. 'At the moment there's only me and the young man on duty. The Sergeant is on watch at the front desk in case the rest of the corpse should be found.'

'I think, Chief Inspector, that it's possible the rest of the body may not be in Compton. It may be in one of the neighbouring villages,' said Powerscourt, not quite certain why he had made this particular statement.

'I think I'll go and have a look around,' said Johnny Fitzgerald, feeling that Powerscourt was perfectly safe in police custody. 'Do you have another of these blankets?'

'Blankets, Lord Fitzgerald? It's not that cold, surely. I'm sure we could find a police cape for you if you need one.' The Chief Inspector sounded rather disapproving.

'Sorry,' said Johnny, smiling at the policeman, 'it's not for me. It's just that if I found anything I'd like to be able to wrap it up. We don't want any old ladies terrified out of their minds if they see most of a dead body being carried along in full view of the citizens back to the police station.'

Dr Williams passed Johnny Fitzgerald on his way in. He lifted the blanket and inspected the top of the leg very carefully. 'Do you know, Chief Inspector, that I came to Compton from the East End of London because I wanted a quiet life. You have more dreadful murders in these parts than they do in Whitechapel. I will arrange to have this leg moved to the morgue later this morning. In the meantime I suggest you keep the room as cold as possible.'

'I don't suppose there's any chance, Dr Williams,' said Powerscourt doubtfully, 'that this isn't the work of human hand? There aren't any wild animals in the neighbourhood that could have caused this kind of damage?'

'The wolves left long ago,' said the doctor, 'and Compton is not in Africa. We don't have any lions or tigers reported missing, Chief Inspector, do we?'

'I wish we had,' said the Chief Inspector. 'Could I ask you, Lord Powerscourt, why you think the body may be lying elsewhere, in one of the neighbouring villages I think you said.'

'Well,' said Powerscourt slowly, 'think of the effort involved in hacking this leg off. Think of the amount of blood all over the place. For all we know other parts of the body may have been cut off as well. You'd need somewhere very secure to carry out all this butchery. It might be easier to take the dead man out of Compton altogether and perform your terrible work in a field miles from anywhere.'

Dr Williams was replacing a couple of medical items in his bag and preparing to depart. 'I can see the sense in that. But how did this leg get back here then?'

'I can only guess that the murderer brought it back with him. Maybe it's meant to be a sort of message,' said Powerscourt.

There was a loud rap at the door. 'Six men now reported for duty, Chief Inspector sir,' said the Sergeant who had been guarding the front desk.

'Right, Sergeant. I shall take those men on a search of the town. Man the fort here, Sergeant.'

'Chief Inspector,' said Powerscourt, 'Johnny Fitzgerald and I could search the cathedral and the Close if that would make your life easier.'

'Thank you very much, Lord Powerscourt,' said Chief Inspector Yates as he set off on his mission. Powerscourt lifted up the blanket and took another glance at the severed leg. He wondered if he could learn anything from the trousers. All he discovered was a set of keys in the pocket. If only he knew which door the keys opened, they might be able to identify the corpse. He covered the sad remains once more and set off to find Johnny Fitzgerald, the keys now jangling in the side pocket of his jacket.

Powerscourt found his friend on patrol just outside the Deanery, the blanket flung over his shoulder. They walked in silence right round the Close, peering into the front gardens, inspecting the railings. They criss-crossed the Cathedral Green, the west front with its host of statues looming in front of them. Nobody seemed to be awake in Compton yet, though lights were beginning to appear in one or two of the windows. The wind was stronger now, angry gusts shaking the branches of the trees.

'Do you think the rest of the body is here, Francis?' asked Johnny.

'I do not,' said Powerscourt, refusing to give any reasons for his answer.

They watched the two old ladies walking slowly along the path to the west door, the only worshippers for Holy Communion at seven thirty. Johnny Fitzgerald continued his circuit of the Close. Powerscourt sat at the back of the choir for the service, his mind racing. He felt sure that the dead man must have had connections with the cathedral, like John Eustace and Arthur Rudd. Maybe he was another member of the vicars choral. He remembered the two members of the vicars choral who had vanished over the previous eighteen months and who had never been found. It seemed as if the dark secret of Compton Minster might be contained inside the body of those with the most beautiful voices, in choirs and places where they sing. But that theory didn't work either. John Eustace had been concerned with the archives and the library, not the singing.

As the service finished he wandered round the cathedral, making sure the rest of the body was not there. The stone knights slept on. The dignitaries in their chantry chapels still waited for the second coming. The armies and the military men in their stained glass windows were still frozen in time as they had been for centuries. The little orchestra of wooden angels in the choir played on with their ancient instruments. But the dead of Compton had not been increased in number overnight. The rest of the body was not there.

As he left, he met Patrick Butler in a state of high excitement. But it was Powerscourt, searching for some piece of cheerful news on this terrible day, who asked his question first.

'Good morning, Patrick. Have you done it yet?'

'Done what, my lord?' said a bemused Patrick Butler.

'You know perfectly well what I mean, young man. Have you done it yet?'

'I'm not very good at riddles, Lord Powerscourt, and certainly not at this time of the morning.'

'My apologies, Patrick,' said Powerscourt with a smile, 'you would be surprised how often Lucy asks me for news on this important subject. It seems to be a matter of endless fascination for the females of the species. Have you proposed to Anne Herbert yet?'

Now it was the newspaper editor's turn to smile. 'I'm afraid I have not, my lord. I don't seem to have got around to it, if you see what I mean.'

'But have you made any plans? Sometimes you need to make a plan of campaign in these matters.'

'I did say I would take her to Glastonbury for the day when I can get away. That's a very romantic sort of place. I thought I might be able to manage it there, if you see what I mean.'

Powerscourt had been to Glastonbury years before when Lady Lucy was pregnant with Thomas. It was only an hour and a half from Compton by train. It wasn't a place he would have chosen himself with its melancholy ruins and legends of the body of Christ and Joseph of Arimathea, but he felt it might do the trick for some.

'But tell me, Lord Powerscourt,' the interests of journalism seemed to be stronger than those of romance this morning for the man from the *Grafton Mercury*, 'do you know what is going on here? There are policemen searching all over the city and they won't tell me what they're looking for. They're all as solemn as owls. You're wandering round the cathedral looking pretty sombre too. Has there been another murder?'

Sooner or later, Powerscourt felt sure, word would reach the newspaper that a fragment of a body had been found. 'I'm afraid there has, Patrick. But we don't know who it was. We don't know if it is connected with the other death in the Cathedral or not. All the police have so far is a human leg.'

'Leg, not legs, Lord Powerscourt?'

'Leg singular, I'm afraid. The police are searching all over the county for the rest of the corpse.'

'Male, I presume?' said Patrick Butler. Powerscourt thought you could almost see him composing the copy for his paper as he spoke.

'Male,' said Powerscourt, wondering how much detail the authorities would want to provide, if they ever found any details. 'I fear you may have to be restrained again in the reporting of this death, as you were with Arthur Rudd, Patrick. It's impossible to say at this stage.'

Patrick Butler was already on his way back to his office when he turned back for a final word with Powerscourt.

'I saw a very curious thing yesterday afternoon, my lord. It might interest you. The choir were processing over to St Nicholas, for another rehearsal of the *Messiah*, I think. The replacement for Arthur Rudd has arrived. He's a man called Ferrers, my lord, Augustine Ferrers. I was at school with one of his brothers in Bristol.'

'What's the curious thing, Patrick? No earthly reason why a chorister from Bristol shouldn't come to Compton, is there?'

'The Ferrers family,' said Patrick Butler, watching a detachment of policemen approaching the Green, their eyes scanning the ground like uniformed retrievers, 'are Roman Catholics, always have been.'

Part Three

Lent

March 1901

15

There were no reports concerning the rest of the body that morning. Shortly before midday the Dean reported to Chief Inspector Yates that a member of the choir, one Edward Gillespie, was missing. Powerscourt wandered between the Close, the cathedral and the police station. He wondered if you could write an architectural history of Britain based on the houses around the Close, their construction spanning five or six hundred years, the changing fashions in domestic design still standing around the cathedral. Just after lunch a report came in from Bilton, one of the neighbouring villages, that another leg had been discovered in the churchyard. The limb was being brought to the morgue in Compton with all speed.

Powerscourt went down to the offices of the *Grafton Mercury* and found Patrick Butler surrounded by his normal chaos. The editor informed Powerscourt that he was reserving a space for the details of the next Minster Murder. If they had the details before ten o'clock the following morning, he could include the story in the next edition. Otherwise it would be too late. He would, of course, have an alternative story ready to fill the space, probably a report on the rehearsals of the *Messiah*. Powerscourt found himself wondering if Patrick Butler would place his own engagement, assuming he ever got round to it, in the appropriate section of his paper. He took away with him Butler's best recollection of the Ferrers address in Bristol, 42 Clifton Rise, he had said, not far from that huge suspension bridge over the river.

At a quarter to three he called on Chief Inspector Yates at the police station. 'We've found the head, I think,' said the Chief Inspector, 'on the side of the road just outside Shipton. One of my men is bringing it in now. That only leaves the trunk and the arms, my lord.'

'When is Dr Williams going to examine it, Chief Inspector?' asked Powerscourt.

'At six o'clock in the morgue, my lord. The Dean is coming as well to see if he can identify the corpse.'

Powerscourt wandered off again. Faint outlines of a plan were beginning to form in his mind. He remembered an earlier case involving a morgue in the Italian city of Perugia, the corridor leading to it lined with pictures of the Virgin, where he had to identify the body of Lord Edward Gresham, the man who had confessed to Powerscourt that he had killed Prince Eddy, the eldest son of the Prince of Wales. There might have been a great deal of blood on that occasion, Powerscourt reflected bitterly, but at least the body was left in one piece.

He stood under the west front of the cathedral, staring up at the statues once more. He wondered if Cain's killing of Abel was somewhere in the limestone above, Abraham raising his knife for the sacrifice of Isaac. He felt angry with himself at his inability to catch the murderer. How many more mothers and fathers, wives and children were about to have their lives ruined for ever by the madman stalking the streets of Compton? By now Powerscourt felt sure that the murderer must be mad, not in the sense that he should have been incarcerated in an asylum, though the world would be a better place if he were, but mad with a consuming passion, a hatred that came from a source so deep that Powerscourt could not yet comprehend it. This was not a madman who saw visions or heard strange voices in his head or thought he was Napoleon or Ghenghis Khan or believed he could walk on water or jump safely from a high building. This madman, thought Powerscourt, is consumed with hate, with an obsession so strong that it drives him to terrible acts. A madness that permits of no remorse, no shred of human or Christian compassion even in a city devoted for a thousand years to the worship and the glory of Almighty God. Powerscourt felt sure now that the normal motives for murder, greed, jealousy, vaulting ambition even, did not apply to his particular madman. He was of a different order of madness.

Powerscourt abandoned the west front and wandered off, his brain far away, to the railway station where he absent-mindedly collected some train timetables. He was to tell Lady Lucy later that he was scarcely aware of doing this and only realized what he had done when he found the papers in his pockets later on that evening.

Powerscourt and Chief Inspector Yates were shown into an anonymous office deep inside Compton's little hospital shortly before six o'clock that evening. The Dean was staring moodily out of the window, pausing occasionally to look at his watch.

'Monthly meeting of the Diocesan Finance Sub-Committee at a quarter to seven,' he told the newcomers, still staring at the little garden outside. 'I hope this disagreeable business isn't going to make me late. They're always difficult, these financial meetings.'

He turned back to face the Chief Inspector. 'Have you managed to recover all the body now?' He made it sound as though he believed Yates was personally responsible for the event.

'We have, Dean,' said the Chief Inspector. 'The other two sections were discovered in Slape late this afternoon. They are with Dr Williams now.'

Bilton, Shipton, Slape. Powerscourt wondered where he had seen these names before. In one of the past editions of the *Grafton Mercury* he had read in Patrick Butler's office? On one of the walls or on the floor of the cathedral perhaps, past dignitaries from these neighbouring villages interred behind or beneath? No, he said to himself, and a feeling of great sadness overcame him as he remembered that these were some of the names on the choir stalls, names of the livings and the parishes belonging to the cathedral that had so enchanted him with their poetry earlier in his time in Compton. Maybe the corpse was the missing chorister whose body had been dismembered and sent to the very places that gave their names to the choir stalls where he had sat and sung the anthems of the Lord.

'Forgive me if I am a trifle late.' Dr Williams was wearing a white coat and looking rather tired. 'Perhaps you gentlemen would like to come this way.'

He led them about fifty yards along a dark corridor and opened a very heavy thick door at the end. The walls were painted an antiseptic green. A couple of feeble bulbs in the ceiling cast a fitful light over the room. In the centre of the little morgue was a long table, about eight feet long and five feet wide with a package that might have been a body on it, covered with white sheets. There was a very strong smell, carbolic and blood, disinfectant and death, Powerscourt thought.

'This should only take a moment, gentlemen,' said the doctor, positioning himself at the top of the table.

'I must ask you, Dean,' said Chief Inspector Yates, 'if you recognize this person.'

The doctor pulled the sheets at the top of the package away. 'We have assembled all the sections of the body now,' he said. 'I should tell you as a matter of record that the private parts have been cut off and the stomach and intestines appear to have been hacked out.' Dr Williams was pale but composed as he spoke. 'We have tried to clean up the head as much as we can. It is little consolation to anybody but I believe it was the knife to the throat that killed him. He was dead before the mutilation.'

The Dean stared in horror at the severed head revealed beneath the sheets, marks of his wounds purple and livid around the throat. 'I do recognize this person,' he said calmly. 'That is Edward Gillespie, one of our vicars choral.'

The Dean bowed his head in prayer. Dr Williams pulled the sheet back over the corpse. Powerscourt found himself thinking about the words of Old Peter who had watched the services come and go in the cathedral for fifty years or more. Every day, he had said, the Dean and the canons referred to an act of bloody savagery, wounds in the side, nails through his hands and feet, Christ bleeding to death on his cross to save mankind. Now they were inspecting a real butchered body in a hospital morgue at six o'clock in the evening.

'Dean, Chief Inspector,' Powerscourt and the two men were back in the little waiting room, 'I would ask you to consider how this information should be presented to the public. It is entirely in your hands. I spoke to Patrick Butler this afternoon and I believe he is aware that there may have been another murder. Should he be allowed to print all the details? Would it be of more assistance to you in your investigations, Chief Inspector, if the full facts were made public or not? And, Dean, you must speak for the cathedral.'

The two men paused. 'Let me say,' the Chief Inspector began, 'that we have, as it were, made a lot of noise today not only in Compton but all around these other villages, not just, I would remind you, in the ones where we found parts of the unfortunate Mr Gillespie, but in the ones where we didn't. I think it would be difficult to contain the truth. A lot would depend on how the information was presented, of course. But the more the public are on our side, dare I say it, the more frightened they are, the more they will be willing and eager to help us in our inquiries.'

Powerscourt wondered if the dead man would be referred to for ever after as the unfortunate Mr Gillespie.

'Lord Powerscourt,' the Dean was looking at his watch, winding himself up for his later meeting perhaps, 'what would your advice be?'

'I'm sure,' said Powerscourt, 'that the Chief Inspector is correct when he refers to the way the information is presented. Patrick Butler is a responsible fellow, after all. He won't want to offend his readers, especially the women, with the gory details. To say that the body had been cut up is much less offensive than what actually happened.'

'Very well,' said the Dean, preparing to leave, 'I shall send for the young man at once. If I have to interrupt my meeting, so be it. If I may so express it, finance may have to wait for death. There's just one other matter, gentlemen.' The Dean had suddenly lost a fraction of his normal composure, running his hands through his hair, looking anxiously at his watch. 'It's about Edward Gillespie,' he said nervously. The Chief Inspector was fiddling about in his pockets, looking for a notebook. 'It's bound to come out sooner rather than later. I'd rather you hear it from me rather than as a piece of chapter gossip.'

Powerscourt wondered what was coming. Was Gillespie also in debt, like his fellow chorister, the late Arthur Rudd? Was he about to be kicked out of the choir?

'I think, no, I am certain . . .' The Dean paused, as if he wasn't quite sure how to deliver his message. He was, Powerscourt noticed, turning rather red. 'Gillespie was carrying on with the wife of one of the shopkeepers in the Square,' he blurted out at last, 'a very pretty young woman called Sophia. He told me the other day that the husband had found out about it. He was a very worried man.'

'Had the husband threatened Gillespie with violence?' asked the Chief Inspector, looking up from his notebook.

'I'm not sure. I think he probably did. Now, if you'll excuse me I must go and chair my finance meeting. I'm late already.'

'Just two very quick questions, Dean, before you attend to your duties,' said Powerscourt quickly. 'The Chief Inspector and I will accompany you to the front door. What is the name of the shopkeeper, and what was the nature of his trade?' All three were now striding up the corridor towards the main entrance, their boots echoing on the stone floor.

'The man's name was Fraser, James Fraser,' said the Dean. He marched on. Chief Inspector Yates thought he knew the answer now, but he asked the second question once again.

'And his occupation?'

Again that pause from the Dean of Compton. Then he whispered it very softly. 'He was a butcher. The best butcher in all of Compton.'

'Oh, my God,' Powerscourt said very quietly. His brain was full of images of carcasses hanging on great hooks on the wall, of butchers' blocks and butchers' knives, long ones, thin ones, short ones, all of them honed to a pitch of sharpness that could dissect cows or sheep or pigs or lambs or humans. The best butcher in all of Compton.

'My wife has been a customer of Fraser's for over five years now,' said the Chief Inspector. 'His meat is excellent. But let me deal with this, my lord. Gillespie's affair with Mrs Fraser may have nothing to do with his death. I shall make inquiries now and let you know.'

Powerscourt stared at the disappearing figure of Chief Inspector Yates. Had John Eustace met a perfectly innocent death? Were the butler and the doctor telling him the truth after all? Had Arthur Rudd been killed for his debt? And Edward Gillespie, had he been butchered by a cuckolded husband? The best butcher in all of Compton?

Powerscourt was on his way to reclaim his horse from the police station and return to Fairfield Park when he bumped into Patrick Butler, just leaving Anne Herbert's cottage on the edge of Cathedral Close. Patrick already knew most of the story of Compton's latest murder. He grimaced with distaste when Powerscourt filled him in on the final details.

'I couldn't possibly print all that, Lord Powerscourt. Old ladies would be fainting in their beds. I'll have to keep it very simple.'

'You're about to receive a summons from the Dean, Patrick. I think he's going to ask you to be responsible.'

'I'll be responsible all right,' said the young man. Then he cheered up considerably. Powerscourt wondered for a moment if he had proposed over the Assam or the Darjeeling. He hadn't. 'I'll tell you one thing, Lord Powerscourt. I thought of the most fantastic headline while I was taking tea with Anne. I couldn't possibly use it, of course. But I think it's almost perfect.'

'What is this Platonic headline, Patrick?'

The young man laughed and whispered very softly into Powerscourt's ear.

'Hung, Drawn and Quartered.'

A musical medley, a rather confused musical medley, greeted Powerscourt on his return. He could hear one piano note, played very loudly. Then there were voices, singing out of tune. He wondered if Lady Lucy had managed to steal a couple of choirboys for the evening and then he thought better of it. Choirboys couldn't possibly be that out of tune. The piano note sounded once more.

'Hal,' sang a voice, in tune, which he recognized as Lucy's.

'Hal,' sang a second voice, out of tune.

'Orr,' sang a third voice, nearly in tune.

Then he remembered that his children were due to arrive that afternoon for a short stay. He listened on outside the drawing-room door. The piano and therefore the singing party were at the far end of the room.

'You're doing very well,' he heard Lady Lucy say. 'Let's just try to put the whole thing together.' She sounded out four notes on the piano. Then she played them again.

'One, two, three,' said Lady Lucy.

'Hallelujah,' sang the three voices, although Powerscourt thought Olivia was singing Orrerujah rather than Handel's preferred text.

'Hallelujah' they sang again, Thomas still out of tune. Powerscourt opened the door and ran to embrace Thomas and Olivia. He could still remember all those long evenings in South Africa when he would have paid thousands of pounds for an armful of his children.

'We've been singing, Papa,' Olivia told him proudly. 'It's called the Orrerujah Chorus.'

'It's from Handel's *Messiah*, actually,' said Thomas Powerscourt in his most grown-up voice.

'That'll do for today,' said Lady Lucy, smiling at her very own choir. 'We'll do some more practising tomorrow.'

'Can we come and watch you singing in the church?' asked Thomas. 'When you sing in front of everybody?'

'We'll have to see about that,' said Lady Lucy tactfully. 'You might put me off.'

181

'Why was that man called Handel?' asked Olivia. 'I thought that had something to do with opening doors.'

'It does,' said Powerscourt, 'have something to do with opening doors. But Handel the composer, the man who wrote the music for the *Messiah*, came from Germany originally. George Frederick Handel was his name.'

'Time for bed now,' said Lady Lucy briskly. 'Off you go. Papa will come and read you a story later.'

It was just before ten o'clock when a weary William McKenzie returned from his travels and took a seat in the drawing room, armed with a cup of tea and a plate of biscuits. Powerscourt remembered that McKenzie's reports were always couched in rather unfathomable prose in case they fell into enemy hands.

'I first encountered the subject at the railway station, my lord,' McKenzie began. Powerscourt mentally substituted the word Archdeacon for subject and listened on.

'He took a first class ticket to Colthorpe on the seven thirty-five train and spent the journey perusing various papers in the large bag he carried with him. I must confess I was curious about the bag, my lord. It was of much larger dimensions than gentlemen usually employ for purposes of business. He might have been going away on a visit.'

McKenzie paused and looked down at a tiny notebook. 'The journey from Compton to Colthorpe takes an hour and twenty minutes, my lord. At Colthorpe the subject alighted from the train and waited fifteen minutes for a local service going to Dunthorpe, Peignton Magna and Addlebury. The subject took a cup of Indian tea in the restaurant while he waited, and two slices of toast with marmalade.'

Powerscourt wondered where McKenzie secreted himself during all these activities. Did he peer in the windows? Did he conceal himself in the corner of the room? Could he make himself invisible?

'The subject did not make the full journey to Addlebury, my lord. He left the train at Peignton Magna at nine fifty-five,' McKenzie checked the precise time in his notebook, 'and was collected by a carriage. They must have known what time to expect him for those local trains are infrequent, my lord, and, I was told, rather unreliable. I nearly lost him there, my lord, for he was out of the station in a flash. Fortunately a cab drew up just after he had left, driven by a most reckless young man who said he knew where the clerical gentleman was going as he had taken him there several times in the past. At the tar end of the village we caught up with them, my lord.'

William McKenzie paused and took another drink of his tea. Powerscourt was trying to guess where the final destination might have been. So far the gossips of Compton could have been right. The subject might have a wife hidden away in the depths of the countryside.

'A mile and a half outside Peignton Magna, my lord, there is a long avenue of lime trees leading off to the left. My cabbie informed me that this was always the destination of the clerical gentleman. I paid him off and proceeded as rapidly as appeared prudent up the drive. The house is most handsome, my lord, Elizabethan in construction, I would hazard, set out in the form of a square with a courtyard in the centre and a moat running round all four walls. The moat appeared to be well maintained, my lord, unlike some you might see these days. I was just in time to see the subject disappear through the main entrance. The time was ten fifteen. I secreted myself in the trees and continued to observe, my lord.'

McKenzie was perfectly capable of waiting for his subjects for hours or even days at a time, Powerscourt remembered. One vigil in India, checking on the movements of the agents of a particularly vicious Nawab, had lasted three days and nights.

'There was limited activity I could observe from my position, my lord. One or two servants going to and fro, some produce being delivered from the home farm, a vet come to attend to a sick horse. All activity seemed to stop just before twelve o'clock, my lord, and there were strange noises from inside the house I could not quite catch.'

'Were there any bells at twelve, William? Ringing out from the neighbouring church perhaps?' asked Powerscourt.

'I heard no bells, my lord,' said McKenzie, beginning work on another biscuit and turning a page in his book. Powerscourt thought the fire needed more logs but he did not want to break the spell of McKenzie's narrative.

'Movement seemed to begin again shortly before one o'clock, my lord. There were cooking smells being blown my way and very pleasant they were too. At two thirty-five the carriage drew up again at the front door. At two forty-five the subject appeared again and was driven away.'

'Was he wearing the same clothes, William? Had he changed into something from his bag?'

'He was in the same clothes, my lord. The subject seemed in better humour from the brief glimpse I could get of him. The carriage took him back to the station. I ran after them as fast as I could, my lord. I was able to watch the subject board the train to Colthorpe at ten past three. There is a connection there back to Compton. The subject had purchased return tickets. He should have been back here by four fifteen. I remained in the village, my lord, and made some inquiries.'

William McKenzie paused in his report. He looked at several pages of his notes and proceeded.

'I must confess, my lord, that what follows is to some extent speculation. I have three main sources for my information. The young cabbie directed me to the village postmaster for information. The cabbie claimed that he was a notorious gossip who knew everything that went on in Peignton Magna and quite a lot that probably didn't. He was very informative. The vicar was tending his garden when I passed. The vicar, a most reliable witness I should say, had no knowledge of these regular visits by the subject. I found that most curious. He did not seem to be aware that the clerical gentleman from Compton was in the habit of making regular visits to his own parish. Late in the afternoon I presented myself at the house. I said I was working with a colleague on an architectural volume chronicling the moated houses of England. The butler gave me a brief tour of the house, my lord. It was most instructive.'

Powerscourt wondered why William McKenzie was taking so long to deliver his conclusions. Perhaps he didn't believe them.

'The house is called Melbury Clinton, my lord. It has been in the Melbury family for about twelve generations. They are an old Catholic family, my lord. They have priests' holes all over the place, enough to fox Sir Francis Walsingham's agents for days at a time, my lord. That's what the butler told me.'

Powerscourt had been more than impressed with McKenzie's knowledge of the key players of Elizabethan history.

'They're still Catholic, my lord. There is a little chapel where the Jesuits used to hide on the first floor. It's about as far from the front door as you could get. Mass is celebrated in there twice a week, the butler told me. Once on Sundays when a priest comes from Exeter. And once on Thursdays at twelve o'clock. Those noises I heard in the woods, my lord, must have been the service.'

'Are you telling me, William, that the Archdeacon goes all the way from Compton every Thursday to attend Mass in the little chapel at Melbury Clinton?'

'No, I am not telling you that, my lord. The subject does not go all that way to attend Mass. He goes to take the service. The subject has been officiating at Mass at Melbury Clinton for the past eight years.'

16

'God bless my soul,' said Lord Francis Powerscourt. 'Are you sure?'

'I can only go by what the butler said, my lord,' William McKenzie replied. 'And I didn't want to press him too hard about the Thursday services. It might have seemed suspicious when I was meant to be working on a book about the moated houses of England.'

'What exactly did he say about the Thursday services, William?'

McKenzie turned back a few pages in his notebook. 'I wrote all this down in the train on the way back. He said a Jesuit came to celebrate Mass every Thursday.'

Jesuits, thought Powerscourt. The shock troops of the Counter Reformation, the Imperial Guard of the College for Propaganda in the battle for the hearts and souls of the unconverted. Christ Almighty. What on earth was going on in this sleepy cathedral town?

'It makes sense of the bag, my lord. He must carry his Jesuit vestments to and from Melbury Clinton every week.'

'It certainly does,' said Powerscourt. 'William, you have done magnificently. I shall have another assignation for you in the morning.'

That night Powerscourt had a dream. He was in a church, not the Cathedral of Compton he knew so well, but a large church that might have been in Oxford or Cambridge. The pews were full of young men, every available seat occupied, latecomers standing at the back. The organ was playing softly. At first there were no priests to be seen. Then Powerscourt saw a figure floating above the congregation like a ghost from the other side. He knew that the spectre was the wraith of John Henry Newman, the most famous defector from the Church of England to the Church of Rome in all the nineteenth century. The ghost of Newman was beckoning the young men to follow him out of the side door into the world outside. Gradually the pews began to empty. Then it became a rush. Finally it turned into a stampede as all the young men followed Newman's lead and abandoned their pews, and presumably their allegiance to the Church of England. At Newman's side was another spectre, arms outstretched to summon the true believers. The other spectre was the Archdeacon of Compton Cathedral.

Early the next morning Powerscourt was seated at the desk in John Eustace's study, train timetable to one side of him, writing paper to the other. He wrote to the Dean, requesting the name and home addresses, if possible, of the two dead members of the community of vicars choral. Powerscourt was trying to avoid all human contact with members of the cathedral for fear it might endanger their lives if they were not the murderer, and endanger his own if they were. He still had occasional flashbacks to the falling masonry, his night vigil with the dead in their stone and marble. He wondered about the Bishop, apparently so unworldly, but with a record, Patrick Butler had informed him, of distinguished service in the Grenadier Guards. He wondered about the Dean, so impassive as he watched the horror being unveiled in the morgue. He wondered about the Archdeacon and his weekly pilgrimages to Melbury Clinton. He wrote to his old tutor in Cambridge, requesting the name and an introduction to the foremost scholar in Britain on the Reformation and the Dissolution of the Monasteries. He wrote to the Ferrers family of 42 Clifton Rise, Bristol, asking if he could call on them at four o'clock in the afternoon in two days' time. He explained that he was looking into the strange deaths in Compton and wanted to talk to them. He did not specify the reason for his visit. He wrote to his old friend Lord Rosebery, former Prime Minister in the liberal interest, saying that he proposed to call on him in five or six days to discuss his latest case. He particularly asked Rosebery if he could secure him, Powerscourt, a meeting with the Home Secretary. He wrote to Dr Williams asking for his co-operation in a very delicate matter.

'So which Archdeacon is the real one, Francis? The Protestant one or the Catholic one?' said Johnny Fitzgerald.

His correspondence complete, Powerscourt had joined the others over breakfast. Thomas and Olivia had gone to climb the trees in the garden.

'God only knows,' said Powerscourt. 'Maybe even God doesn't know.'

'Can you be a Protestant Archdeacon and a Jesuit Father at the same time?' said Lady Lucy. 'Doesn't each side think the other one to be heretics, if you see what I mean?'

'I don't know the answer to that one either,' said Powerscourt. 'But I'm going to find out.' He made a mental note to write a further letter to Cambridge requesting an interview with a theologian. 'The other question, of course,' he went on through a mouthful of bacon and eggs, 'is whether it is just the Archdeacon who is a Jesuit or a Roman Catholic. Maybe there are other members of the Cathedral Close who are secret adherents of the old religion.'

'Maybe they all are,' said Johnny Fitzgerald. Everybody laughed.

'Seriously though,' said Powerscourt, 'this investigation has become exceedingly difficult. I dare not ask questions of the Bishop and his people. I feel it would be too dangerous, either for me or for any of us here, or for them if they were known to have been asked those kind of questions.'

William McKenzie had been working his way through a small mountain of toast, thinly coated with butter but without marmalade, at the far end of the table.

'I've been thinking about the time, my lord. If the butler at Melbury Clinton is right, the subject has been celebrating Mass there for eight years. He travels in his Protestant clothes, if you like, and changes when he gets there. He's like a spy in some ways, isn't he, Johnny? But who is he spying on? It doesn't seem likely that the Protestant authorities in Compton want secret information about what goes on in Melbury Clinton. Nor does it seem likely that the Catholic family in Melbury Clinton want secret information about what happens in the cathedral at Compton. It's all very difficult.'

McKenzie consoled himself with a further intake of toast.

'It comes back to my original question,' said Johnny Fitzgerald cheerfully. 'Which one is the real one?' He picked up a fork and speared a sausage which he held up for general inspection. 'This,' he said, 'is the Protestant Archdeacon sausage.' With his left hand he impaled another sausage with his spare fork. 'And this is the Jesuit sausage. It seems to me that the Protestant sausage,' he waved the fork around in a menacing fashion, 'is taking a lot of risks going off to Melbury Clinton once a week for eight years to turn into the Jesuit sausage. No doubt he picked the place because it's so far away but somebody from there could easily have come to Compton and recognized him.'

'Unless,' Powerscourt interrupted the charcuterie display, 'the people from Melbury know all about his role in Compton and would not be surprised. We can assume from the distance and the precautions that the right-hand sausage, the Protestant Archdeacon, does not want anybody to know about his role as the Jesuit in Melbury.'

'Consider another factor,' said Johnny, bringing his two sausages side by side, 'what a strain it must be to alternate between these two lives.' He swapped the two sausages round at bewildering speed. 'We've all done bits of spying in our time, pretending to be somebody else for the greater good of Queen and country. It's an exhausting business. At any moment the whole thing can go wrong.' He dropped the two sausages back on to his plate and began to consume the Protestant Archdeacon. 'So why the eight years? Is he going to continue the pretence until his dying day? Is he waiting for a signal to emerge into his true colours?'

Powerscourt was running his right hand through his hair, a gesture Lady Lucy knew only too well. It meant that he could not see the answer. Johnny Fitzgerald had now carved the Jesuit sausage into small pieces. McKenzie was still eating his toast. Lady Lucy was sipping her tea.

'We're in the dark,' said Powerscourt, smiling at her as he said it. 'All I would hazard is that the Jesuit Archdeacon is more likely to be the real one. If you were going to betray one faith in the cause of another I'd be much more frightened of the Jesuits than of the Bishop of Compton. Today I'm going to have another rummage in John Eustace's papers. I may even go and call on Dr Blackstaff again. Tomorrow I am going on a journey. I think I'll be away for a couple of days. William,' he turned to McKenzie who had finally finished his consumption of toast, 'I think you should turn your attention to this Italian gentleman who stays with the Archdeacon. I'm not sure if he's there at the moment.'

'He's there all right,' said Johnny Fitzgerald. 'I saw him creeping about the town yesterday.'

'Excellent,' said Powerscourt. 'Follow him when he goes, William. Follow him wherever he goes. Find out where he comes from. I don't care if you have to go back to London with him.'

'Maybe he comes from Melbury Clinton,' said Johnny cheerfully. 'Maybe he's another bloody Jesuit. Pops over to Compton to keep the Archdeacon on the straight and narrow.'

'Johnny,' Powerscourt went on, 'I want you to try the impossible. We need to know if any other members of the Close are secret Roman Catholics. God knows how you do it. The last thing you can do is ask any of them.'

'I'll try,' said Johnny, picking up the last of his Jesuit sausage and popping it into his mouth, 'I'll certainly try.'

Later that morning Lady Lucy found her husband pacing up and down the drawing room.

'Francis,' she said quietly, 'I wish you weren't going away.' Powerscourt turned at the far end of the room, just past the piano, and stared back at her, his eyes still a long way from Fairfield Park.

'What was that, Lucy? Sorry, my love, I was miles away.'

Lady Lucy put her arm round her husband's waist and marched with him back down the room towards the doors into the garden.

'Let me come with you, Francis, this part of the way anyway. I said I wished you weren't going away.'

Powerscourt stopped and stared out into the garden. 'That child is very far up the tree down by the church,' he said anxiously.

'Is it Olivia?' said Lady Lucy. 'Don't worry about her. She's like a monkey in those trees. I'd be much more worried if you said Thomas was at the top of one of the big oaks.'

'I wish I wasn't going away either, Lucy. I don't think I'll be gone very long.'

'At least I've got the choir to keep me busy, Francis. Did I tell you, I've made friends with two of the little choristers, Philip and William? I think I'm going to ask them to tea to meet the children.'

'You be very careful with that choir, Lucy. I think everything's very dangerous in Compton at the moment.'

'Can I ask you a question, Francis?' said Lady Lucy, resuming their joint march up and down the drawing room.

'Of course,' said Powerscourt, giving her waist a firm squeeze. 'What is it?'

'Are you frightened?' said Lady Lucy, in a very serious voice.

'Do you know,' said Powerscourt, 'I don't think you've ever asked me that before.'

'Well, I'm asking it now.'

Powerscourt stopped by the side of the piano and sat down on the stool. His fingers picked out random notes with no pretence of a tune. They sounded rather melancholy in this grand room with the sun now streaming in through the windows.

'I think the answer is Yes and No, if I'm allowed to say that.' Lady Lucy put her hands on his shoulders. 'Yes, I am frightened in the sense that I find this killer so difficult to understand, so unpredictable, so terribly violent. And I can't find any sign of a motive at all. I feel as though we are all walking on eggshells. If we say or do the wrong thing, or our inquiries upset the madman, then he may kill again. So that makes me frightened, very frightened sometimes.' He paused and strummed some more random notes from the piano. Outside a battalion of rooks were flying across the ornamental pond, their harsh cries acting as a counterpoint to the black keys on Powerscourt's piano.

'I think, Lucy,' he turned to smile up at her, 'that it has to do with the combination of reason and imagination. Sometimes I think I'm lucky enough to solve these cases through reason, deducing how things must have happened. Sometimes it's imagination, trying to see how the emotional connections between the various parties must have worked. But imagination cuts both ways. It can help. But in this case it's often a hindrance because your imagination dwells on the terrible things this mad person has done and what he might do next.'

Powerscourt paused again. 'In another sense,' he went on, 'I'm not frightened. I think perhaps you can be frightened and courageous at the same time. I've seen some acts of terrifying bravery in battle, Lucy. The bravest people are the ones who admit they are terrified but carry on all the same. I'm not as brave as they are. But I think you must keep up your courage, whatever the circumstances. If I didn't, I think I'd feel I was betraying myself, betraying you, betraying the children, betraying all those families involved or yet to be involved in these terrible events.'

Powerscourt rose from the piano stool and embraced his wife. 'You know, Lucy, people are meant to have these kinds of conversations very late at night when the wine and the port may have been flowing freely. Certainly not at half-past eleven in the morning.'

The eight thirty train from Compton to Bristol seemed extraordinarily slow to Powerscourt, impatient to further his investigation. It stopped regularly at what seemed to be hamlets rather than villages. At one point, peering crossly out of his first class carriage window, he thought a horseman on the adjacent road was making faster progress than one of the great symbols of the modern age. A military-looking man joined him, turning immediately to the Births Marriages and Deaths columns of *The Times* and remaining enraptured there for over an hour. Powerscourt wondered if he was learning every entry by heart. He wondered too about the marriage prospects for Patrick Butler and Anne Herbert and whether the proposed trip to Glastonbury would enable Patrick to pull it off. Somehow he doubted it. He suspected he would have to propose to her by letter. Perhaps he could take out a quarter page in his own newspaper and propose marriage to her there alongside the advertisements for soap and bicycles. A suitable headline could be adapted from the nursery rhyme, Editor Wants a Wife. Anne, he felt, might find that rather embarrassing. At a small town on the county border a middle-aged lady joined them and began reading the latest Henry James. Powerscourt remembered Lucy telling him about an article she had read very recently which gave a clue to the central problem of Henry James' later novels – why were the sentences so long? This article claimed that he had stopped writing his books by hand and now dictated them to teams of typewriter operators. It was easy, Lucy had said, to imagine the Master wandering up and down his study, dictating exquisite phrase after exquisite phrase and totally forgetting to insert the full stops. Powerscourt read again the note he had received that morning from Chief Inspector Yates, telling him that it was most unlikely, but not absolutely impossible for James Fraser, the best butcher in Compton, to have killed Gillespie. They were still checking his alibi. Powerscourt's thoughts went back to the cathedral and its inhabitants.

After six and three-quarter hours the train finally arrived at Bristol Temple Meads. A cab brought Powerscourt quickly to 42 Clifton Rise, a respectable-looking house at the bottom of a hill. A maid showed Powerscourt into the little drawing room. Patrick Butler was certainly right about one thing, Powerscourt said to himself, looking at the Blessed Virgin Marys and the religious tapestries on the walls, the family Ferrers owed their religious allegiance to Rome rather than Canterbury.

'Lord Powerscourt, how very kind of you to call.' A handsome middle-aged woman came into the room and ushered him into a chair. 'Now would you like some tea?'

'Mrs Ferrers,' Powerscourt could not imagine this person to be anybody other than Mrs Ferrers, 'I am sure you have made the journey from here to Compton by train. There were times when I thought I could have walked it quicker. Tea would be delightful.'

'Now, Lord Powerscourt, you must be having a terrible time investigating these horrid murders back there in Compton! So upsetting to read about them in the newspapers!'

The adjectives, Powerscourt noticed at once, were delivered with remarkable force. Terrible and Horrid were underlined three or four times in Mrs Ferrers' diction. He wondered briefly how Mr Ferrers coped with it.

'They are certainly most distressing,' said Powerscourt diplomatically. 'And they must be deeply worrying for you with your son so close to the centre of events.' He just managed to resist the temptation to stress the word deeply.

'I'm sure all the mothers find it a great anxiety at this time, Lord Powerscourt. Anthony, that's my husband, and I have been most concerned.' Even simple words like great and most could be struck with the force of a great bell. She began pouring the tea.

'Forgive me, Mrs Ferrers,' said Powerscourt, his eye drawn to a picture of the Pope on the opposite wall, 'I have no wish to pry into your family's personal or religious affairs. But I must confess I am curious as to why Augustine comes to be singing in a Protestant choir.'

Mrs Ferrers laughed. 'Lots of people have asked us that. But it is perfectly simple really. Augustine, how should I put this, he is a dear dear boy, Lord Powerscourt, but he is not very bright. He was our seventh child.' Powerscourt noted the massive emphasis on the word seventh as if it had some cabbalistic significance. 'My husband says we had too many children and there weren't enough brains to go around. The one thing Augustine excelled at was singing. There aren't any choirs in Catholic cathedrals where he could be well paid, but Compton does pay moderately well, considering it's a rural place. Augustine has been on the reserve list for the vicars choral for some time and when that poor man Arthur Rudd died, they sent for him.'

Powerscourt took a cup of tea and a slice of chocolate cake. 'Were you worried about him going there,' he asked, 'with all the trouble?'

'Oh No,' replied Mrs Ferrers with a mighty stress on the No, 'Father Kilblane said he would be perfectly safe there. Father

Kilblane is our parish priest at St Francis of Assisi up at the top of the hill.'

Did he indeed? Powerscourt said to himself. How could a Catholic priest in Bristol be sure that one of his flock would be perfectly safe in Compton where the roll call of the dead and the disappeared was so long? Was he privy to the secrets of the cathedral?

'Did Father Kilblane say how he was so sure?' he asked.

'He didn't give any reasons, Lord Powerscourt. He gave us his word that Augustine would be as safe in Compton as if he were still under our own roof here in Clifton.'

'Just one last question, if I may, Mrs Ferrers, and then I shall be on my way. Did the Cathedral authorities in Compton raise any objections on the ground of Augustine's religious beliefs?'

'I don't think so, Lord Powerscourt. Father Kilblane fixed it all up with the Dean or the Archdeacon, I can't remember which.'

Powerscourt felt the ground shifting slightly under his feet. He thought he should make his excuses and leave as soon as he decently could. The last thing he wanted was any message going back from Bristol to Compton about his inquiries. He wondered if there was some perfectly innocent explanation. Perhaps Father Kilblane had been at school with the Dean or the Archdeacon or had had some dealings with them in the past. Perhaps he was the priest who served Mass on Sundays at Melbury Clinton. Christ, Powerscourt said to himself, I'd better stop speculating in here with Mrs Ferrers.

'Is he an experienced man, Father Kilblane?' Powerscourt tried to make it sound as innocent as he could.

'Oh No,' Mrs Ferrers replied. 'He's quite young, I should say in his late twenties or early thirties. I think he came to the priesthood slightly later than some. He was at the English College in Rome for three or four years. There was a rumour, but I've never heard it confirmed, that he was a convert from the Anglican Church.' Mrs Ferrers eyes lit up at the mention of conversion. 'He's been with us for about a year and a half.'

His eyes reeling from the Virgins on the walls, his ears still ringing with the force of Mrs Ferrers' adverbs and adjectives, Powerscourt took his leave of 42 Clifton Rise. God in heaven. A Catholic priest advising a member of his flock to take up a position singing the heretic hymns and anthems in a Protestant cathedral. A Catholic priest who felt able to assure the family that their son

194

would be safe in a city rent with murder and dismemberment. Did he know the dark secret of Compton Minster? Part of Powerscourt dearly wanted to make the short journey up the hill to question Father Kilblane in his sanctuary at the Church of St Francis of Assisi. But he felt it was too dangerous. Cambridge next, he said to himself, at least I shall feel on surer ground in Cambridge.

17

Anne Herbert had her private suspicions about why Patrick Butler should be taking her to Glastonbury for the day. Never before, in all the months she had known him, had he proposed an expedition out of Compton, not even to the seaside some twenty miles away. She had dressed in sensible rather than fashionable clothes, fearing that any trip to Glastonbury with Patrick might involve the ascent of Glastonbury Tor. He had chatted happily on the train, regaling Anne with details of the first excerpt of the monk's diary from the time of the Dissolution of the Monasteries which was to be published in the *Grafton Mercury* the following week.

'The Bishop seems to have done a splendid job with the translation, Anne. I rather feared it would all be very dry and boring. We don't know the fellow's name so he's just referred to as the monk of Compton. He seems to have spent a lot of time complaining about the food and the sloppy habits of his superiors.'

Now they were standing on the edge of the field that contained the ruins of Glastonbury Abbey. 'The farmer doesn't mind people wandering about,' Patrick assured Anne. 'I checked in that hotel where we had our coffee. Just have to be careful not to disturb the sheep.'

Glastonbury Abbey had once been one of the richest and grandest abbeys in Britain. It was famed throughout the kingdom for its relics and its collection of gold and silver ornaments. Now most of it had disappeared. Grass, moss and lichen had spent three hundred and sixty years creeping over the walls so they were now a dark green colour. The local birds had taken sanctuary here, rooks and starlings and sparrows building their nests in masonry that had once been nave and cloister. The sun was shining but a bitter wind swirled around what was left of the walls. The windows, once graced with the most elaborate stained glass the sixteenth-century craftsmen could produce, now gave vistas of distant hills or other sections of ruined wall. The doors through which the abbot and the monks had processed to their daily round of services now gave entrance to flocks of wandering sheep.

'How did it come to be such a ruin, Patrick?' said Anne Herbert, pointing across to the melancholy view.

'I expect somebody bought it for the stone after the abbey was dissolved. Then he'll have sold it off. I expect half the town is built with the stones that were here once. Come, Anne, if we go up there I think we'll be where the high altar must have been.'

Anne Herbert looked at him sadly. 'Patrick,' she said, 'do you think Compton Minster will look like this in a hundred years' time?'

'It might.' Patrick Butler laughed at the thought of the splendid spate of stories that would be produced by the Decline and Fall of Compton. 'We must have had two religious revolutions in this country at least, Anne. One when Christianity replaced the pagans and the Druids. Another when this abbey here was closed down. There's no reason why we shouldn't have another, this time an agnostic or atheist revolution. It's amazing how many of these people there are already. All churches to be abolished by order of the state. Building fabric to be used for the construction of dwellings for the deserving poor. That's what happened here, after all, except the dwellings were for the deserving rich.'

He took Anne by the hand and led her towards what he thought must be the remains of the high altar. That, she felt suddenly, would be an interesting place for a proposal of marriage. Perhaps that was what Patrick had planned all along.

An elderly porter who remembered Powerscourt from his days as an undergraduate pointed him in the direction of his old tutor's rooms.

'He's still in the same place, my lord, Mr Brooke, though he's very frail now. The Head Porter doesn't think he'll last the year out. Myself, I'm not so sure. Mr Brooke says the port will see him through.'

'Come in,' said the old man, rising slowly from his chair, leaning heavily on a stick. 'Good to see you, Powerscourt. Last time you were here was in '97. I looked it up in my diary. Some nasty business with Germans, I seem to remember.'

'How are you, sir?' said Powerscourt, slipping effortlessly into the mode of address of his student days.

'I'm less mobile than I was even then,' said the senior tutor, subsiding into his chair once more. 'College is in much better shape, mind you. That terrible man who was Master then, he's gone. Dropped dead in the Senate House Passage. I'd say the Good Lord called him home if I believed in the Good Lord. New Master believes in proper food. Thank God for that too. And proper wine. Place used to be like a second rate boarding school in the victualling department. Now it's more like a London Club.'

Powerscourt smiled. He noticed that the old copies of *The Times* were still piled high around the old man's chair. Soon they might be as high as his head.

'Now then, Powerscourt, mustn't keep you from your work.' Gavin Brooke reached across to a little table and brought out a letter. He searched all his pockets for his spectacles before discovering that they too were on the table.

'Reformation, you said in your first letter. That's what you want to know about. We've got just the man for you here in college. Young fellow by the name of Broome, Jarvis Broome. It's his special field of expertise. He's expecting you now. And then you asked about a theologian. After lunch I've arranged for you to see our Dean. He's very sound on all that sort of stuff.'

Powerscourt thanked the old man and was about to take his leave.

'I was thinking the other day, Powerscourt, about my books,' said the old man, gazing up at the shelves where a long row of works by Gavin Brooke, Senior Tutor and University Lecturer in Modern History, were prominently displayed. 'At the time I wrote the early ones on Europe in the first half of the nineteenth century, some of the participants were still alive. Did you know that the last surviving member of the British delegation to the Congress of Vienna didn't pass on until 1885? Now they're all dead, all those people I wrote about. Every single one of them.' The old man shook his head.

'Maybe you'll meet them all on the other side, Mr Brooke. You could give history lectures up in heaven. I'm sure your subjects would flock along. They can't have very much to do up there.'

'Be on your way, young man. I tell you what they'd do, all those people I wrote about if I met them in heaven or hell. They'd probably be like all the other bloody historians I've met down here.

They'd say I had the emphasis wrong. Even more likely they'd tear my books to shreds.'

Patrick Butler actually had three different proposals of marriage, carefully written out and currently incarcerated in his back pocket. First he had gone to the poetry section of the County Library and made copious notes. Then, late one evening when his reporters had all gone home, he composed them in his office surrounded by the normal detritus of his trade. The first was heavily dependent on the love sonnets of Shakespeare. The second was equally reliant on the work of John Donne, though even Patrick, who was not easily shocked, had been a little embarrassed at some of the language employed by the Dean of St Paul's. At least he hadn't ventured as far as Rochester. And the third was entirely his own work. Cynics might have said that it sounded too like one of his own leading articles in the *Grafton Mercury*, but it was late by this stage and Patrick was growing tired.

'Look, Anne,' he said, standing by a rectangular row of bricks, now only a couple of feet high and almost invisible in the long grass. 'This is where the high altar must have been. The choir must have been down there by that wall on the left.'

'Are you sure, Patrick?' said Anne, feeling that this was not after all a particularly romantic spot.

'I think so,' Patrick replied, leading her further down towards the remains of the nave. 'And I think they've put the Lady Chapel at the wrong end, if you see what I mean. It's right down at the far end. I think it should be up here somewhere. Maybe the masons looked at their plan the wrong way round.' The Lady Chapel, he thought, that might be better for his purpose. At least a lot of it was still standing.

Lord Francis Powerscourt was trying to work out how many times he must have walked this short route from the porter's lodge to the last staircase by the river in the three years he had lived there during his time in Cambridge. Five or six times a day, say forty times a week, three hundred and fifty a term, a thousand a year, three thousand times altogether. He was passing the hall and the kitchens now where the young Powerscourt, rather nervously, had intoned the Latin Grace before dinner. *Quid quid appositum est, aut apponetur, Christus benedicere dignetur in nomine Patris et Filii et Spiritus Sancti.* The words came back to him automatically. Powerscourt didn't think he would have described the food in his time as being like that served in the clubs of London, certainly not in any of the ones he belonged to. It was much worse than the second rate boarding school derided by his former tutor. Here was the staircase. He walked a few paces forward and peered down at the river, still meandering in its sluggish way along the Backs. To his left was King's where the famous Chapel was hidden from sight by the buildings of Clare. To his right the solid mass of Trinity and the glory of Wren's great Library inside.

Jarvis Broome was a handsome young man, cleanly shaven, with a large collection of ancient volumes stacked in neat piles around his desk. He showed Powerscourt to a chair with a view of the college lawns and a brief sliver of river.

'Gavin Brooke tells me you want to know about the Reformation, Lord Powerscourt. Is there anything in particular I can help you with? I'm writing a book on the subject, though God knows when I'll ever finish it.'

There, thought Powerscourt, is the world's difference between the scholar and the journalist. For Patrick Butler, surely more or less the same age as Jarvis Broome, not finishing an article, not finishing all the copy for his paper would be professional suicide. For Jarvis Broome, finishing too soon, finishing without having read all the available material, finishing without coming to a considered judgement, would leave him open to the savagery of his peers.

'I should explain, Mr Broome, that I am investigating a series of murders in a cathedral, Compton to be precise. They are about to celebrate one thousand years of worship in the cathedral, or the abbey, as it was, this Easter Sunday.'

Powerscourt did not give the young scholar any details of how the murders had been committed. 'What I would like to know,' he went on, wondering how long it would be before Jarvis Broome had a shelf full of his own books like Gavin Brooke, 'is how much opposition there was at the time. Not so much to the question of the King's divorce and the establishment of Henry as Supreme Head of the Church of England, as to the Dissolution of the Monasteries.'

'Now that is a most interesting question, Lord Powerscourt.' The young man got up from his chair and began pacing up and down the room, in exactly the same fashion, Powerscourt noted wryly, as he had done when writing his history essays over twenty years before.

'I'll try to be brief, Lord Powerscourt. I could go on all day about this. Let me say, as a preamble, that history is always written by the victors, as I am sure you know. I am certain that there was much more opposition to the various moves in the course of the Reformation than we know about. Some of the opposition will have fallen away, like water through a colander, as it were, and we shall never recover it, we shall never find out about it at all.'

A pair of college gardeners were trimming the edges of the lawns outside. Through the slightly open window Powerscourt could hear a couple of thrushes singing happily in the Fellows' Garden on the other side.

'Three points, I think, are worth considering,' said Broome. Powerscourt suddenly remembered the angry complaint of a fellow undergraduate of his, also studying history, but with a different tutor. 'Is it because bloody Gaul was divided into three parts?' he had said bitterly. 'Every time I take an essay to the wretched man there are always three points to be considered. Why not two, or four or five, maybe even seven? Why not just one, for God's sake? Why is it always three?'

'The Pilgrimage of Grace,' Jarvis Broome went on, '1536. This was a mass rising of the North of England against the King's policies, against his advisers, of course, rather than against the King himself. There were many reasons for the revolt, some to do with taxation, some to do with personal jealousies, the usual sort of mixture, but the principal reason was religious. The rebels objected to the changes that had taken place and the further changes they knew were coming, including the Dissolution of the Monasteries. They didn't want a Protestant Reformation. They wanted to keep a Catholic England. The banners and the symbols tell the story. They marched behind banners of the Five Wounds of Christ, which showed a bleeding heart, sometimes a Host, above a chalice, both surrounded at the corners of the illustration by the pierced hands and feet of Christ on the cross.'

'What happened to them?' said Powerscourt.

'They made the great mistake of trusting the King's word,' Broome replied. 'At one stage they could have marched to London and toppled the Tudors from their throne. But they were picked off bit by bit by duplicity and double dealing. The ring leaders were all executed.'

'How?' said Powerscourt suddenly.

'Most of them were beheaded. Their heads were left stuck in prominent places in the towns and cities where they came from. Anybody who tried to cut them down was liable to meet the same fate themselves.'

Patrick Butler had fallen silent as they peered at the ruins of the Lady Chapel in the ruins of Glastonbury Abbey. He had felt in his pocket for the three proposals he had written out. None of them felt quite right at this moment. He found that his brain had delivered to him a newspaper headline that seemed to sum up his predicament. Editor Lost For Words.

Anne Herbert thought the ruins of the Lady Chapel looked remarkably similar to the ruins of the nave and the high altar. Try as she might, she couldn't see much difference. She hoped her children were behaving themselves with their grandmother.

'They say King Arthur and his knights lived round here, Anne,' said Patrick, recovering his powers of speech. 'He came with a great army to rescue Queen Guinevere who had been imprisoned by his enemies in a castle on the tor.'

Anne Herbert tried to imagine Patrick as a Knight of the Round Table, Sir Galahad or Sir Lancelot or Sir Bedevere. She couldn't manage it. A monk perhaps, creating a Book of Hours or copying out the Gospels with occasional rude asides in the margins, yes, but mounted on horseback and riding into battle, no.

'Would you have liked to live in those times, Anne? Handsome young men on horseback pressing their suits?'

'I think I might have been the Lady of Shalott,' said Anne, 'floating down to Camelot behind that rotting barn over there.' Privately she felt that the knights would have said their piece by now, proposals of wedlock delivered from behind a visor in sub Tennysonian verse, the suitor clanking on bended knee before her.

'I don't think I'd have liked it much then,' said Patrick. 'Life can't have been much fun for a humble scribe. I tell you what,' he said, postponing things yet again, 'why don't we have lunch and then climb to the top of the tor.'

'What most historians have not realized up until now,' Jarvis Broome was back sitting at his desk, 'is the link between the violence, the savagery of the repression of the Pilgrimage of Grace in 1536 and the comparatively peaceful passage of the Dissolution of the Monasteries two or three years later. You can read many history books, Lord Powerscourt, which fail to make to make any link at all between those two facts. Previous historians talk blithely about how the acceptance of the Dissolution shows the monasteries were known to have been corrupt, or were not loved by the people. In fact the people were terrified by the reprisals handed out to the northern rebels. They were too frightened to risk their necks by opposing the end of the abbeys. I regard it as a complete failure of historical imagination and I hope to put the record straight.'

Powerscourt thought that mutual co-operation and brotherly love between the practitioners of the historian's craft was not going to get any better.

'Do we know how many people did oppose the Dissolution? And do we know what happened to them?'

'I fear,' said Jarvis Broome, 'that they were all executed. It is difficult to be precise about the numbers as the records have often been lost. Some of the Northern abbots were believed to have fled south to join their colleagues in other monasteries. They too were put to death.'

The sun had gone in while Anne Herbert and Patrick Butler ate their modest lunch in the George and Pilgrims Hotel. There was a wind rising as they set off out of the town towards the path that led to the summit of Glastonbury Tor, a round hill rising some three hundred and fifty feet above the surrounding plain.

'I came here when I was eleven or twelve with a history master from school, Anne,' said Patrick as they reached the path that led to the summit. 'Long ago, all this plain was water, it was the lake of Avalon. We had to learn bits of the *Idylls of the King* to declaim when we reached the top.'

'Can you remember any of it, Patrick?' said Anne, taking his arm as their route twisted steeply uphill.

Patrick frowned. The wind was very strong now, blowing fiercely through his hair. It was just beginning to rain.

'I am going a long way
With these thou seeest – if indeed I go -
For all my mind is clouded with a doubt
To the island valley of Avillion.

'It's Arthur speaking, Anne, on his final journey, somewhere round where we are now.'

Last Words of Dying King, Patrick Butler thought to himself, translating the Passing of Arthur into a contemporary headline for the *Grafton Mercury*.

'Can you remember any more, Patrick? It's lovely.'

He paused and put his hand to his forehead. 'I'm not sure. I think so. Maybe I should wait until we get to the top. If you still want to reach the top, that is, Anne. We'll both be soaked to the skin. We may even get blown away.'

'I don't think we should give up now,' said Anne, bending low against the wind and hurrying as fast as she could towards the little church on the summit.

The last hundred and fifty feet took them over half an hour. Sometimes the wind seemed to die down, then it would hit them full in the face as they moved on to another side of the slope. Once Anne slipped on the wet grass and had to be hauled back up again. The noise of the gale was very loud. They could see the branches of the trees bending and swaying below them. They kept their heads well down, eyes glued to the path. Overhead dark birds circled, keeping watch over their lofty kingdom. Sullen grey clouds were racing low across the sky. Patrick was cursing under his breath. Anne was exhilarated, rejoicing in their rain drenched adventure.

At last they reached the top and huddled under all that remained of the little chapel of Saint Michael. Patrick pointed dramatically at the valley beneath them and shouted into the wind:

'Avillion, where falls not hail, or rain, or any snow
Nor ever wind blows loudly: but it lies,
Deep-meadowed, happy, fair with orchard lawns
And bowery hollows crowned with summer sea,
Where I will heal me of my grievous wound.'

Now. It came to Patrick Butler in a flash. Now was the time to ask her. Forget all those proposals in his pocket. Forget about William Shakespeare and his sonnets. Forget about John Donne and his love poetry. Forget the pretty speeches he had rehearsed as he lay on the hard single bed in his lodgings. Forget all the business of waiting for the right moment. This was the right moment. Now or never. He turned towards her, his face drenched by the rain, his hair blown into an unruly sodden mass, flecks of mud on his trousers and his coat. But his eyes were bright.

'Anne, will you marry me?' he shouted into the gale, looking into those green eyes he knew so well.

'Is that another quotation from Tennyson, Patrick?' she shouted back.

'It is a quotation from Patrick Butler, my love, on this day in this place at this time and meant with all my heart.'

Anne Herbert squeezed his arm very tight.

'Of course I'll marry you, Patrick. Why did it take you so long to ask?'

Patrick Butler held Anne Herbert very tight and kissed her full on the lips. Relief was flooding over him like the rain that cascaded down both their faces. Then it came to him. He couldn't stop it. Maybe I'll always be like this, he said to himself. It was another headline.

Compton Couple Engaged on Glastonbury Tor.

18

'There are just a couple of other things to be said about the Dissolution of the Monasteries,' said Jarvis Broome, rising from his desk to pull down two dark red notebooks from his shelves. Powerscourt thought the young man must be a more lively teacher than Gavin Brooke had been in his own undergraduate days.

'For a start,' Broome went on, 'it would have been difficult to leave the monasteries as they were. Many of them directly or indirectly owed their allegiance to Rome. It would have been like offering the enemy a series of strongholds deep inside your own territory. But, more important, much more important was the money. Henry, in his later years, was always in need of cash. The income of the monasteries, from land and property, was much greater than his own. So under the pretence of extirpating these supposedly corrupt and Romish institutions, he could enrich himself and buy off a lot of the gentry who might not have liked his religious reforms any more than the monks did with the booty of the monasteries. I think it must have been the biggest transfer of wealth in England since the Norman Conquest.'

Powerscourt wondered if the man had detailed records on individual monasteries. He hoped he had.

'My last point,' Jarvis Broome went on, 'and then I shall be free to answer any of your questions after listening so patiently to all this ancient history, just goes to show how deeply entrenched opposition was to all these religious reforms. In the 1540s in the West Country – some of the people in Compton may well have been involved in it – there was another revolt called the Prayer Book Rebellion. It coincided with plans for the introduction of yet another new Book of Common Prayer, hence the name. Once again the insurgents marched behind the banners of the Five Wounds of

Christ. The rebels surrounded Exeter and the authorities had great difficulty in raising enough troops to suppress it. Like the Pilgrimage of Grace it failed. Over three thousand rebels were slaughtered. Even after that there were further minor uprisings all over the country in the years that followed. However, I plan to finish my first volume with the accession of Mary, so I have not looked into them very much as yet.'

With that Jarvis Broome leaned back in his chair and began to rearrange some of the old books on his desk.

'I am most grateful to you, Mr Broome. Just a couple of questions, if I might.'

'Of course.'

'I know this sounds rather morbid, but could you tell me in detail how most of these people were executed?'

'Well,' said Broome, 'if you were defeated in a battle you probably died in one of the usual ways that soldiers die in combat. Apart from that there were three main methods of execution.'

Here come those three points again, thought Powerscourt.

'The first was burning at the stake for heresy. That gave rise to the famous dying remark of Bishop Latimer to his fellow heretic Nicholas Ridley as they waited for the pyre to be lit around them in Oxford: "Be of good comfort, Master Ridley, and play the man. We shall this day light such a candle by God's grace in England as I trust shall never be put out." Sir Thomas More himself was not averse to the burning of heretics, you know. He sent quite a few sinners off to meet their maker in the fiery furnace.'

'I've always wondered,' said Powerscourt, 'if they thought they were being consumed in hell's flames, if all those paintings of the fires of hell weren't dancing in front of their eyes, as it were, as they were consumed, all hope of heaven burnt away.'

'I suspect, that for many of them their faith burnt ever brighter as their mortal lives ebbed away but we have no means of knowing.'

'And the second?' asked Powerscourt.

'The second was the most terrible of all. There's actually a very good description of it in the trial and sentencing of Sir Thomas More.' Broome pulled down a book from his shelves and turned to a passage near the end. '"Sir Thomas More, you are to be drawn on a hurdle through the City of London to Tyburn, there to be hanged till you be half dead, after that cut down yet alive, your bowels to be taken out of your body and burned before you, your privy parts cut off, your head cut off, your body to be divided in four parts, and your head and body to be set at such places as the King shall assign." It was a very popular mass spectator sport, I'm afraid, at Tyburn and similar places, rather like the Romans packing the Colosseum to watch the Christians being devoured by the lions. And the last method was a simplified version. You were beheaded and your head was later exhibited on a pole somewhere. That was what happened to Sir Thomas More as a favour from the King. He didn't have to go through with all the disembowelling business. He was killed with one stroke of the executioner's axe, his head was boiled, impaled on a pole and raised above London Bridge.'

'What a frightful business,' said Powerscourt. 'Thank God we seem to live in more enlightened times. Now, my last question is this. Do you have details of the executions at individual abbeys or churches or cathedrals? Compton is my main interest, as you will appreciate.'

If Jarvis Broome was wondering why Powerscourt should be so interested in possible deaths in Compton three and a half centuries before he did not show it.

'I might be able to help you there,' he said, reaching up towards a long series of black notebooks on the top shelf of his bookcase. 'We certainly know about three abbots who were put to death at Colchester, Reading and Glastonbury. I've been round all the major places over the past couple of years and taken notes on what was relevant in the records. Calne, Cambridge, Canterbury, Carlisle, Chester, Compton, here we are.'

Powerscourt leaned forward to look at the black notebook.

'It would seem, Lord Powerscourt, that there were a number of deaths in Compton round the time of the Dissolution of the Monasteries. One monk, killed the year before.'

'How did he die?' asked Powerscourt.

'He was burnt at the stake. Two more were given the full disembowelling treatment early in the year the monastery was dissolved. One last death shortly afterwards. The last Abbot was executed and his head put on display at the gateway leading into Cathedral Close. It seems that some more people may have lost their lives in the Prayer Book Revolt, but the records are unclear about the manner of their deaths.'

Powerscourt took himself off for a solitary walk after lunch. He had borrowed Jarvis Broome's desk and notepaper to send a brief letter to Dr Williams in Compton. He was, he wrote, now in possession of further information which confirmed, if confirmation was necessary, the substance of what he had said in his earlier letter. He asked the doctor to reply by return to his London address. Round and round the Fellows' Garden he walked, ignoring the neatly kept rectangle of grass, the flowers coming into bloom, the birds still singing happily in their trees. The manner of death, he told himself, gives little clue as to the reason for it. There was no sense in it. Cries of alarm drew him to the terrace overlooking the river. A party of visitors had taken a punt on the river and appeared to have no idea about the propulsion techniques required on the Cam. The boat was going round and round, disturbing the ducks who scurried crossly away towards the more peaceful waters of Trinity and St John's. Powerscourt wondered if he should offer instructions from his position on the bank. Then he saw that the pole had been abandoned and the party were going to proceed with the aid of two paddles in the stern of the boat. In the summer term, he said to himself, they would have been laughed to scorn.

The Dean's rooms were on the top floor of a tiny quadrangle off the front court. The chaos reminded Powerscourt briefly of the office of the editor of the *Grafton Mercury*.

'I only moved in here yesterday,' said the Dean. 'My apologies for the chaos.' Powerscourt saw that there was some form of order in the confusion. All the books were stacked neatly under the shelves by the side of the window. The pictures had been placed around the room underneath the places where they were going to hang. A large pile of papers, sermons perhaps, or unmarked undergraduate essays, were on top of the desk.

The Dean himself was a tall figure in his middle forties with jet black hair to match the colour of his cassock. He wore a silver crucifix around his neck.

'Thank you so much for taking the trouble to talk to me when you are in the middle of moving house,' Powerscourt began, 'and I fear you may find my questions somewhat unorthodox.'

'Fire ahead,' said the Dean cheerfully.

Powerscourt had already decided that there was no point trying to navigate his way towards the crucial query. He went straight to the point.

'Can you be an Anglican priest and a Roman Catholic priest at the same time?'

The Dean stared at Powerscourt. Powerscourt said nothing.

209

'God bless my soul,' said the Dean. 'Perplexed undergraduates reading theology – and most undergraduates reading theology these days are very perplexed indeed, Lord Powerscourt – ask me some pretty strange questions but I've never been asked that before. Just give me a moment to think about it, if you would.'

The Dean stared hard at the opposite wall. Powerscourt noticed that the Dean seemed to have a large collection of watercolours of derelict and desolate abbeys in the north of England. Fountains, he thought he could decipher at the bottom of one painting, Rievaulx on another. Desolate since the Dissolution of the bloody Monasteries, he said to himself. Were they never going to leave him in peace?

'I think this might be the answer,' said the Dean finally, his hands twisting at the chain of his crucifix for inspiration or consolation. 'In theory, the answer has to be No. You have to swear allegiance and fidelity to one particular faith when you take holy orders. But in practice the answer might be Yes. It might be possible, if the person concerned is prepared to lie to their superiors and believes that the sins committed in terms of one religion are outweighed by the advantages conferred by the other.'

Powerscourt had suspected that the answer might be something like this. No certainty anywhere.

'And do you think, Dean, that it would be possible to live this double life for years and years?'

The Dean's fingers were off again. Powerscourt wondered how often he had to replace the chain.

'I fear the answer is the same. In theory the answer would have to be No. In practice, if you were very careful and took great care to conceal your true allegiance, there is no reason why you should not keep up the fiction for a long period.'

'I realize,' said Powerscourt, 'that this is an impossible question. In these circumstances, of a man masquerading, if you like, as a Protestant priest and a Catholic priest at the same time, which is likely to be his true position?'

'Would he regard himself as a Catholic or a Protestant, do you mean?' said the Dean quickly.

'I do.'

Once again the Dean stared at his wall. Faint sounds of somebody practising the organ drifted in from the Chapel next door. Powerscourt thought it was Bach.

'This time,' the Dean said finally, 'you'll be relieved to hear that

I think the answer is more clear cut, even if it's not absolutely definitive.'

Certainly not, thought Powerscourt. In this world of scholarship and perplexed theology nothing was ever likely to be definitive.

'Let me give you an analogy, if I may,' the Dean went on, 'between republics and monarchies. I don't believe nations become republics because they want to be republics, if you see what I mean. They become republics because they don't want to be monarchies. Republics, by definition, are non-monarchies. Anglicans are Anglicans to some extent because they don't want or weren't allowed by their governments to be Catholics. Anglicans to some extent define themselves by being not Catholics. Previous centuries have seen a great deal of anti-Catholic hatred whipped up in this country. Even today the celebrations of Guy Fawkes and Bonfire Night are hardly a celebration of Christian unity. But Catholics don't define themselves by not being Anglicans, if you follow me. They have older, historically longer continuities. So I think it would be very difficult for this imaginary person to be really an Anglican purporting to be a Catholic. I think it is more likely to be the other way round, that he is truly a Catholic pretending to an Anglican.'

'Or, perhaps,' said Powerscourt, 'that he was an Anglican and converted to Catholicism but forgot to slough off his Anglican skin, as it were.'

'I doubt very much if he could have forgotten to get rid of the clothes, actually,' said the Dean. 'It would have been a deliberate act of policy, though why anybody would want to do such a thing I cannot imagine.'

'One last question, Dean.' Powerscourt was thinking about his return journey to London. 'Is there much traffic between the two religions, Anglicans defecting to Rome and vice versa?'

'There has always been a certain amount of traffic since the time of Newman and the Oxford Movement,' replied the Dean. 'Some people even buy season tickets for the journey. There was one wealthy man who travelled between the Anglican and the Catholic faiths and back again in the 1840s. Just before he died he reconverted to Catholicism.'

'Is Newman still important? I thought he'd been dead for years.'

'I don't know very much about Newman,' said the Dean, gazing at the great pile of papers on his desk. 'Student at Trinity Oxford, Fellow of Oriel, Vicar of the University Church, prime mover in the

211

Oxford Movement which tried to revive his Church, dithered about for a long time before he converted to Rome. Made a Cardinal as you know towards the end of his life. I do know a man, mind you, who knows all about conversions on the religious railway line. He's writing a book on Newman's legacy and his influence on subsequent converts. Man by the name of Philips, he's a Fellow of Trinity, Newman's old college at Oxford. Would you like me to write you an introduction?'

'I should be more than happy to call on him tomorrow afternoon, if that would seem acceptable,' said Powerscourt and headed for the stout oak that guarded the Dean's quarters. He was almost on his way down the stairs when the Dean called after him.

'Do you mind me asking, Lord Powerscourt, about the individual who might have been a Catholic and an Anglican priest at the same time? I presume he was purely hypothetical?'

'He is not hypothetical,' said Powerscourt. 'Would that he were. He is alive and well and going about his business in the West Country.'

'God bless my soul,' said the Dean in horror. His fingers flew once more to the chain that held his crucifix.

Old friends of Johnny Fitzgerald would have been most concerned about his behaviour on the day of Powerscourt's departure to Bristol and Cambridge. Many would simply have dismissed the reports as impossible. Others would have doubted for Johnny's sanity.

First thing in the morning he went to the seven thirty Communion service in the cathedral. He stared so hard at the Canon and the choir that the Canon later told the Precentor that another mad person had joined the ranks of the congregation. Then he went to the leading stationer's in the town and bought a series of maps of the locality and a small black leather notebook. He was back in the cathedral for Matins at eleven, after which he decamped to the County Library where he perused a number of county histories. Johnny, for some unaccountable reason, was not familiar with libraries of any description. At one point he walked all over the two floors of the building, looking carefully at all the doors in case a bar might be concealed inside. It stands to reason they must have some means of refreshment in this bloody place, he had said to himself, they can't sit cooped up here all day long without the need for a glass of something.

After lunch he returned to the library once more and engaged in a long conversation with the head librarian about the location and the times of service of the various Catholic churches within a twenty-mile radius of Compton. These details he entered solemnly into his black book. At four thirty he was back in the cathedral for Evensong, eyes firmly fixed once more on the faces of the clergy and the adult members of the choir. The choirboys, for some strange reason, appeared to have no interest for him.

Normality seemed to have been restored, however, on his return to Fairfield Park. He opened a bottle of Nuits St Georges before he had taken off his cloak and poured himself a generous glass. A few minutes later, cloak safely deposited into the arms of the butler, he helped himself to a second.

'Would you say, Lucy,' he found Lady Lucy in the drawing room singing something to do with a refiner's fire, 'that I am looking particularly virtuous this evening?'

'I'm not sure,' Lady Lucy replied, turning round from her piano stool to inspect him, 'that virtuous is the first word that springs to mind when people look at you, Johnny.'

'Come, come,' said Johnny Fitzgerald, 'you are looking at a man who has been to church three times today. And I've spent many hours working in the County Library. Is virtue not apparent? Surely the power of all those prayers must be visible in my face?' He poured himself a third glass.

'Three visits to the cathedral, Johnny? Libraries? Are you feeling all right? Do you need to lie down?'

Johnny Fitzgerald laughed. 'I've been trying to remember the faces of all those people up at the cathedral.'

'Forgive me for seeming obtuse, Johnny, and I'm sure it's good for your immortal soul opending all that time in the cathedral, but how is that going to help?'

'It's so that I'd recognize them if I saw them again,' said Johnny. 'Francis asked me to find out if any other members of the clergy up there are secret Catholics. Look, Lucy, I worked it out like this. Suppose, like me, you're fond of a drink. You need regular supplies of alcohol to keep you going. Well then,' Johnny Fitzgerald proved his point by helping himself to a fourth glass of burgundy, 'suppose it's the same thing with these crypto-Catholics. They're going to need a fix of the Mass or something every now and then, just like our friend the Archdeacon of Thursdays. I have here from my time in the library,' Johnny pulled his black book out of his pocket and proudly showed Lady Lucy the first four pages, 'a list of all the Catholic churches within a radius of twenty miles, and the times of all their services. So if any of our friends are going for a fix, they'll find me lurking in the back pew. And I'll know who the bastards are. There's only one problem with this plan.'

'What's that?' said Lady Lucy, smiling at her friend.

'Do you know what time they start their services, these Catholic persons? Wouldn't you think they'd wait for a reasonable hour? Give a man time to digest his breakfast? They do not. Most of them only have one service in the week. And that's Mass at half-past bloody seven in the morning.'

Powerscourt found two of William McKenzie's cryptic messages waiting for him. They concerned the movements of the Archdeacon's mysterious visitor, who had, apparently, decamped from Compton.

'My lord,' the first message began, 'the subject departed from Compton station two days ago on the 7.45 train bound for London, stopping at Newbury, Reading and Slough for local connections. Subject travelled alone in first class carriage except for final stage of journey when he was joined by elderly female in fur coat. Very little conversation between the parties. Unlikely to have been pre-arranged rendezvous.'

My God, thought Powerscourt, he's got a suspicious mind, that William McKenzie. Then he reflected to himself that so did he. Perhaps they were well suited.

'Subject spent most of journey reading documents in his case. Only caught sight of one of them when subject had gone to bathroom. Something to do with Consecration of Cathedrals. On arrival at Paddington subject did not take cab. Walked across London until he reached the priests' house attached to Jesuit church in Farm Street shortly after ten o'clock in the evening. Subject let himself in with own key. Did not venture out again that evening.'

How long had McKenzie waited, Powerscourt wondered. Eleven? Midnight? One? Did he stand in one place, behind a tree perhaps, or did he engage on regular patrols of the vicinity? What did he think about?

The second note was dated the following evening.

'My lord,' Powerscourt wondered what was coming this time,

'have further information to report on the subject. Subject's name is Barberi, Father Dominic Barberi. Believe him to be a member of the Jesuit order, but am not as yet absolutely certain. Subject only ventured out once today. Went to nearest branch of Thomas Cook and purchased return ticket to Rome in three days' time. Did not wish the clerk to make any hotel reservations in his name. Presume he must stay once more with religious order. Subject also said by housekeeper, married by chance to former corporal in our old regiment, to be member of secret Catholic society called Civitas Dei. Housekeeper unable to provide any details of said organization. Stressed it was secret.'

Civitas Dei? City of God, maybe community or polity of God. God's kingdom, that's it, said Powerscourt to himself. What on earth was that? Why was it secret? What did it have to hide? What was it doing in Compton? Maybe the man at Trinity would know something about it.

'Subject said to be very reserved and earnest individual. Not likely to be a bosom friend of Lord Fitzgerald. Subject works in his room during the day most of the time. Only known weakness said to be partiality for fish.'

Powerscourt decided that somebody should write a book about the different types of Oxford and Cambridge don. They spanned an enormous range after all, from the silent, the monosyllabic, the taciturn, the sarcastic, the arrogant, the superior, the rare ones who were almost normal, the talkative, the garrulous, the ones in love with their own voice, the ones in love with their own ideas, the ones in love with their own books, the windbags and the ones who couldn't shut up. Christopher Philips, Powerscourt was certain, sitting in his rooms overlooking the beautiful gardens of Trinity College Oxford, was in the gold medal class of the ones who couldn't shut up. Powerscourt had explained on his arrival that he was interested in the process of conversion from the Anglican to the Roman Catholic faith over the last twenty-five years. After ten minutes without a break, without even apparently a pause to draw breath, Philips still hadn't got as far as Newman's arrival in Oxford as an undergraduate. After twenty minutes Newman and his friends had launched the Oxford Movement and Powerscourt had decided that the only movement he was interested in at that point was movement out of Oxford as fast as possible. After forty-five minutes Newman had defected to Rome in 1845. There were, Powerscourt realized, another fifty-five years to go before they reached the present day. At the current rate of progress that was going to be some point well after sunset.

'Forgive me, Mr Philips, this is all most interesting, but I don't want to take up too much of your time,' he said. 'It is the conversions of the last twenty-five years that are of particular interest to me.'

'Of course, of course,' said Christopher Philips, and he was off again. The interruption did seem to have accelerated the flow of history, even if only slightly. The decades were now passing, Powerscourt calculated, at the rate of one every five minutes. Maybe he could escape in an hour and a half. He heard about Gladstone's sister Helen, a passionate convert to the Roman faith, who refused to have lavatory paper in her house. Instead her cloakrooms were liberally provided with the published works of Protestant divines. He heard about Newman's unhappy attempt to start a Catholic university in Dublin.

'In some ways, of course, the strange thing about Newman,' Philips said after seventy-five minutes with scarcely a pause, 'was not that some people followed him, but that so few did so. The Cardinal at the time believed that Newman would lead a positive stampede of some of the best and brightest of the youth of England into the fold. But it never happened.'

And then, miraculously, Christopher Philips paused. He looked up at his clock.

'My goodness me, Lord Powerscourt, forgive me. I have talked for far too long already. You want to know about the last twenty-five years, I believe.'

Powerscourt nodded. He wondered how long the man's lectures went on for. Did he start at ten in the morning and finish about half-past three? Was there anybody left in the hall by the end?

'The conversions are almost all one way, from Canterbury to Rome, as it were. They are isolated cases. They are steady but not very numerous. There are, of course, a variety of reasons for departure. You could put doubt at the top of the list, I suppose, doubt about the impact of modern science, doubts about miracles, doubts about belonging to a Church that is controlled by man in the form of the government of the day in the House of Commons rather than by a hierarchy of faith that has been in place for nearly two millennia. If you worked in the countryside you might wonder if you were in the wrong place. If you worked in the cities you might despair of ever achieving anything in the midst of such terrible social problems of dreadful housing that saps the body and the lack of work that saps the soul. Roman Catholicism offers faith to the doubtful. It offers certainty to the sceptics. It offers order to the confused. It offers hierarchy to the rootless. It offers historical tradition to those searching for authority. Once you can make the leap of faith to cross the drawbridge into it, as it were, your intellectual problems are resolved.'

'Have you heard, Mr Philips, of an organization called Civitas Dei?' Powerscourt fired his arrow into the dark.

Christopher Philips looked at him with great interest. 'I have, Lord Powerscourt. I have to say I am surprised to hear that you know about it. It is very secretive.'

'What sort of organization is it?' asked Powerscourt. 'And why is it so secret?'

'I don't know very much about it, I'm afraid. It's believed to be related to the Jesuits in some way. The headquarters are in Rome. Its aims are to advance the coming of God's kingdom, as the title would suggest. I believe it is secretive because they wish to use every means possible to obtain their objectives.'

'When you say every means possible, are you implying that they might be prepared to use illegal means?' asked Powerscourt, thinking suddenly of bodies roasted on a spit or cut into pieces and distributed about the countryside.

'I don't think they would do anything outside the law,' said Philips. 'I'm afraid that's the sum total of my knowledge.'

As Powerscourt began to say his thank yous and goodbyes Christopher Philips held him back. 'Just a moment, Lord Powerscourt, I think this might interest you.'

He reached into his desk and pulled out a fading place card from a dinner at High Table. 'This is the menu and seating plan for the dinner the Master and Fellows gave for John Henry Newman when they invited him back to Oxford in the late 1870s, over thirty years after he left. They say he derived more pleasure from his return to Oxford than he did when the Pope made him a Cardinal. Everyone who attended signed it on the back.'

He handed it over to Powerscourt as if it were a holy relic or the bread at the Communion service. Powerscourt glanced down the menu, thinking that Johnny Fitzgerald would certainly have approved of the wines. Then he turned pale. For in one place at the top table, three places away from the Master's left, was a Moreton. G.B. Moreton. Powerscourt remembered the Dean telling him about the two different Moretons who had been involved in the succession to the Bishopric of Compton. He checked the signatures on the back. There it was. Gervase Bentley Moreton. Then he had another shock. For seated at the bottom end of the table was one A.C. Talbot. Powerscourt checked the signature again. He knew it well. Like Moreton's he had seen it before. His head was spinning. Gervase Bentley Moreton was the Bishop, and Ambrose Cornwallis Talbot was the Dean of Compton Cathedral.

19

God in heaven, Powerscourt said to himself. Whose God? Whose heaven? Anglican or Roman Catholic? Not one but two of them. Not just the Dean but the Bishop as well. They must have been Anglican back then or else how could they have reached their present lofty positions in Compton Minster? But suppose they had been planning to convert to Rome even then, or maybe shortly afterwards, seduced perhaps by the beauty of Newman's prose and the luminous certainties of his faith. In that case they had been sleepers, moles burrowing deep into the Anglican hierarchy, for over twenty years. Hold on a minute, he said to himself, still staring as if hypnotized at the seating plan. It could all be a coincidence, an accident. The Dean and the Bishop could have been Anglicans all along. Maybe they still were. Then he remembered the Archdeacon and his furtive trips to Melbury Clinton on Thursdays. Perhaps there was not one but three of them. But what was the point? Why should they dissemble for so long about their true allegiance? Was there an end point, a time when the pretence could stop? An extravagant, an impossible thought shot through his mind. He put it to one side.

The bells of Oxford were ringing outside, Balliol following Trinity, Wadham following Hertford, the torch passed on down to New College and Queen's and Magdalen with its deer park by the river. Powerscourt suddenly realized that he had been staring at the menu and the signatures for a couple of minutes at least. He returned it with a smile to Christopher Philips.

'Sorry,' he said, 'my mind was far away.'

'You looked, Lord Powerscourt,' Philips replied, 'as if you were wrestling with some mighty problem. They say, you know, that Newman stayed in college for three or four days. Apparently he grew very friendly with some of the people he met at the dinner.'

'Really?' said Powerscourt. 'I don't suppose we know which people, do we?'

'One of them was certainly the man Moreton,' said Christopher Philips, totally unaware that he was setting off another depth charge in Powerscourt's brain. 'They say they had a lot in common with their interests in early biblical scholarship.'

'Of course,' said Powerscourt, 'I'm sure they must have had a lot to talk about.'

The rehearsal for Handel's *Messiah* was at its end. Vaughan Wyndham, the Compton choirmaster, and his choir were folding up their scores, the musicians returning their instruments into their cases. It was going well, the choirmaster thought. In a few days' time when they had finally mastered the more difficult sections of 'Unto us a Child is Born', he could have a full run-through of the entire oratorio.

Lady Lucy Powerscourt leaned forward and began a conversation with the two choirboys she had spoken to before. She was just about to invite them to tea when a loud voice interrupted her.

'Lady Powerscourt,' said Wyndham. 'Perhaps we could have a word after everybody has left.' The voice, Lady Lucy thought, was harsh, the tone rather menacing. Surely you could talk to one of these dear little boys, who always looked so frightened, without the intervention of higher authority?

'Forgive me, Lady Powerscourt,' said the choirmaster when they were the only two people left in St Nicholas' Church. 'I have seen you on previous occasions trying to converse with the junior members of my choir. It is strictly forbidden.'

It sounds as if he is German, Lady Lucy thought, memories of the word *verboten* coming into her mind from German lessons with her governess. 'And why is that, pray?' she said. 'I do not mean them any harm. I was only going to invite them to tea.'

'At this time, Lady Powerscourt, the choir have a great deal of work to do. Not only are they working on the *Messiah*. They are also learning a lot of new music for the thousandth anniversary of the cathedral. They must not be disturbed in any way.'

'I would not wish to interfere with their progress,' said Lady Lucy, wondering why the man had laid such emphasis on the new music for the thousandth anniversary. Maybe she should tell Francis about it.

'If you interfere any further, or try to talk to any of the boys again, I shall have no alternative, Lady Powerscourt.'

'No alternative to what?' said Lady Lucy, thinking the whole conversation was rather incredible.

'I shall have no alternative,' said choirmaster Wyndham severely, 'but to expel you from the choir.'

With that he stalked out of the church. Lady Lucy had never been expelled from anything in her entire life. She did not propose to start now.

The plaster primroses commemorating Rosebery's family name were in full bloom outside his front door in Berkeley Square. Leith the butler, famed throughout Rosebery's acquaintance for his encyclopedic knowledge of the train timetables of Britain and Europe, opened the door and showed Powerscourt into the library. Rosebery and Powerscourt had been friends since their schooldays and Rosebery had been an invaluable ally in many of Powerscourt's previous cases.

'Come in, Francis, take a seat. I shall be with you in a second.'

Rosebery was finishing a letter at the great desk by the window that looked out into the square. 'I'm trying to buy a library from a fellow down in Hampshire,' he said, adding an ornate signature to the bottom of his letter. 'He has an invaluable collection of documents and books relating to the Civil War. The only problem is that he thinks they are worth a lot more than I do.'

Powerscourt saw that portraits of the Rosebery children had replaced the racehorses on either side of the black marble fireplace. Maybe the horses were out of favour.

'Now then . . .' Rosebery seated himself opposite his friend. 'Thank you for your letter. I think I can help with one or two things. This disagreeable business of exhuming a body down in Compton. I take it you now have the relevant papers from the police? You do? Then I shall have it for you tomorrow.'

Powerscourt handed over a couple of letters that had been waiting for him in Markham Square.

'I mentioned it to Schomberg McDonnell the other day,' said Rosebery, sounding rather pleased with his ability to manipulate the system. Schomberg McDonnell was the Prime Minister's

Private Secretary. 'He said that after your invaluable service to the Crown in South Africa, an exhumation order was but a small thing to ask. He will obtain the necessary signatures.'

Powerscourt wondered if he could avoid the exhumation, the body brought from the grave in the middle of the night, the crowbars opening the coffin before its time, the medical people poring over the cadaver. He wondered if there was another way.

'I am most impressed, Rosebery,' said Powerscourt with a smile. 'I have two questions for you. Have you ever heard of an organization called Civitas Dei?'

Rosebery looked at his friend very carefully. 'You are moving in deep and dangerous waters, Francis. Yes, I have heard of it, when I was Foreign Secretary, I believe. There was a briefing paper on the organization from some of our people in Rome. They suspected that they acted as outriders, the auxiliaries, the unofficial wing, if you like, of the Jesuits and the College of Propaganda in the Vatican. Their function was to perform in the dark what the Church could not countenance in the daylight. If anything was discovered about their activities, it could, of course, be denied.'

'But what is their purpose, Rosebery, what are they for?' said Powerscourt, realizing that whenever anybody talked about Civitas Dei, they were grasping at shadows.

'Nobody knows for certain,' Rosebery replied, staring at the books on the opposite wall. 'I don't think they are going to nail a proclamation with ninety-five theses on to the door of Santa Maria Maggiore in Rome, if you see what I mean. Their objectives are to increase the power and influence of the Catholic Church by all means at their disposal. And people say they are none too scrupulous about the means, either. The former Ambassador to Rome, Sir Roderick Lewis, lives just round the corner from you, Francis. He would know more than I do. Or maybe not. But I could drop him an introductory note if you think that would help your inquiries? Could you call on him tomorrow morning?'

'That would be most kind, Rosebery. Let me now ask you my second question. I think I may need to get in touch with the Archbishop of Canterbury at very short notice. How do I do that?'

Rosebery looked closely at his friend.

'It's all right, Rosebery, I'm not losing my wits. Sometimes I think the conclusions in this case may be quite incredible, but I am not yet in a position to say what they might be. At first, you see, I thought there was just one riddle in Compton Minster. Now I think there may be two, perhaps three. And solving one may not mean that I have solved the others. They could each be in separate boxes. But to return to my question, what is the quickest route to the Archbishop of Canterbury?'

'His Private Secretary is a delightful young man called Lucas, Archibald Lucas. He was a scholar and fellow of Keble before taking up his new position.' Rosebery went to his desk and pulled out an enormous address book. 'He's to be found at Lambeth Palace most of the time, occasionally at Canterbury. Perhaps you'd like to take a note of the postal and the telegraphic addresses.'

The little town of Ledbury St John was right at the outer limit of Johnny Fitzgerald's collection of Roman Catholic churches. The church itself, dedicated to the Blessed Virgin Mary, stood at the very edge of the place as if the local council were slightly ashamed at having to give it house room. Johnny himself, feeling rather hungry after his long ride, was lurking at the edge of the graveyard. He could see two out of the three directions that potential worshippers might come from. A few locals passed, probably on their way to work in some of the outlying farms. Dawn was breaking over the town, a pale light seeping in over the rooftops. At twenty past seven two figures, dressed in black, he thought, made their way in through a side door. They seemed to have their own key, as there was a lot of rustling before the right implement was found. By twenty-five past the lights were lit inside the church, but no worshippers had yet appeared. At seven twenty-eight Johnny slipped in through the main door and took his seat at the very rear of the church. There was only one other member of the congregation, kneeling at the front, his face fixed on a painting of the Blessed Virgin Mary above the altar where the Blessed Sacrament was already in position.

The priest, not more than thirty years old, Johnny thought, kissed the altar. The worshipper at the front genuflected, Johnny following uncertainly behind.

'*In nomine Patris et Filii et Spiritus Sancti,*' said the priest, making the sign of the Cross. In the name of the father and the son and the Holy Spirit.

'*Gratia domini nostri Iesu Christi, et caritas Dei, et communicatio Sancti Spiritus sit cum omnibus vobis.*' The grace of our Lord Jesus Christ and the love of God and the fellowship of the Holy Spirit be with you all.

Johnny Fitzgerald was staring very closely at the man celebrating Mass. He tiptoed further up the aisle to a place with a better and a closer view of the altar. The service carried on.

'*Confiteor Deo omnipotente et vobis, fratres, quia peccavi nimis cogitatione, verbo, opere et ommissione.*' I confess to you, Almighty God, and to you, my brothers and sisters, that I have sinned through my own fault in thought, word and deed, in the things I have done and the things I have failed to do.'

The little congregation struck their breasts, lightly in the case of the priest, severely in the case of the lone worshipper, vigorously in the case of Johnny Fitzgerald. If only the man would turn round once or twice so he could get a proper look at him.

'*Mea culpa, mea culpa, mea maxima culpa.*' The fault is with me, the fault is with me, the fault is greatly with me.

Then Johnny knew. There was something in the profile of the man at the altar that made him certain. For he had seen him before. This priest celebrating Mass in the Church of the Blessed Virgin Mary in the parish of Ledbury St John was the same man who had been conducting the service of Evensong in the Cathedral of Compton five days before.

Sir Roderick Lewis, former Ambassador from the Court of St James to the Court of Umberto, King of Italy, was wearing a smock and had a paintbrush in his hand when Powerscourt was shown into his study. There were, Powerscourt discovered, a number of surprising facets to Sir Roderick's character. The first was that he loathed Italy. And, especially, he loathed Rome. Its inhabitants did not rate much higher in his estimation.

'Frightful place, Powerscourt. Perfectly acceptable if you're a tourist and only there for a couple of days. But to live there! All that terrible food! All that dreadful olive oil! And those vulgar wines they're so proud of that no proper Englishman would ever let into his cellar! I was never surprised the place killed Keats, you know. The bastards have even got Shelley's heart. Killed one of my predecessors, Lord Vivian, too. And the Romans! God only knows how they acquired an empire all that time ago, Powerscourt. Couldn't find their way out of a paper bag now, if you ask me. Intrigue, double dealing, treachery – diplomacy became a process of accommodation with a collection of particularly slippery eels.'

Powerscourt wondered if it was official Foreign Office policy to despatch the representatives of His Majesty to the places they loathed the most. Russia haters to St Petersburg, Ireland haters to Dublin, Americaphobes to Washington. Perhaps he could ask Rosebery.

'What's more,' Sir Roderick went on, staring balefully at the watercolour of Hampton Court taking uncertain form on his easel, 'Rosebery tells me you want to know about Civitas Dei. Civitas Dei means the Vatican. The Vatican means the Pope. The Pope means the Curia and the self-serving collection of the sycophantic, the devious and the ambitious who make up the Papal bureaucracy.'

With that he placed a blob of blue paint in the place where the sky should have been. It did not look right.

'Damn!' said Sir Roderick. 'Look what the bloody Vatican has made me do now. I'll have to wipe that off.'

'What do we know about Civitas Dei?' asked Powerscourt as the former Ambassador dabbed ineffectually at his watercolour with a piece of cloth. 'I mean know for certain.'

'We know nothing for certain about them, Powerscourt. If the affairs of the Vatican are shrouded in mist, the affairs of Civitas Dei are surrounded by impenetrable fog, much worse than we get in London.' He tried another splash of blue right above the roof of Hampton Court. Powerscourt was sure the roof was crooked but felt it might be better not to point this out. This time it worked. Sir Roderick's temper improved briefly.

'Very rich backers,' he went on, fiddling with his brushes as he spoke. 'Aim the improvement in fortunes if not the supremacy of the Catholic Church. Number of priests believed to be members. Very shadowy inner group based in Rome itself.'

'You make them sound a bit like Freemasons, Sir Roderick,' said Powerscourt.

'Don't think these characters have much time for aprons and funny handshakes, if you ask me,' Sir Roderick replied, 'much more like the thumbscrew alternating with the crucifix. What is amazing are the variety and the improbability of the rumours that circulate about them.'

The former Ambassador raised another brush full of blue. His hand hovered over where the river ought to be. Powerscourt hoped the Thames wasn't going to be the same shade as the sky.

'Rumour flows around Rome like the water supply, Powerscourt. There are pipes sunk into the ground to hasten its passage from place to place, aqueducts old and new to ferry it over the difficult terrain. Turn on the tap, ask a Roman to speak, and out it flows, sometimes hot, sometimes cold, more often, with their useless engineers, tepid if you want to take a bath. But the rumours flow, just like the water.'

Sir Roderick paused and raised his brush high above his canvas, as if poised to strike.

'In the last two years, Powerscourt, we have had to listen to the following fantastic accounts of the power of the Civitas Dei. They were responsible for the recent change of government in Brazil. Any sane person would have told you it was their disastrous economic policies that brought that about. They have recently, if we are to believe the rumours, been responsible for the appointment of a new Minister of Finance in Madrid. Previous fellow was caught with his hand in the till. Two out of three cardinals appointed this past year are said to be leading members of the organization. There was even a rumour that they had a great work afoot in England itself which would cause a sensation when it happened. Rumours, all rumours, not a word of truth in any of it.'

Powerscourt watched as the brush finally made up its mind and placed a perfectly formed strip of river at the bottom of the painting.

'I know they're all ridiculous,' he said, 'but sometimes even rumours can be useful in my profession, Sir Roderick. Was there any more detail about the English operation?'

Sir Roderick, emboldened by his previous success, tried to extend the passage of his river. The paint escaped into the lower sections of the building instead, rendering some of it extremely wet, if not uninhabitable.

'God damn and blast!' said the former Ambassador. 'I shall have to redo that whole section. All the fault of those bloody Romans, if you ask me. The only other thing they said about the English business, Powerscourt, was that it was controlled from Rome. Of course, you don't have to be Caesar Borgia or Niccolo Machiavelli to work that one out. Whole bloody business is controlled from Rome.'

As Powerscourt left the artist to his labours he found himself thinking about Hampton Court. Built by Cardinal Wolsey at the height of his power, he remembered. Appropriated by the King who could not bear a mere commoner to have a grander house than he did. So had Sir Thomas More, victim of the King, walked with him in counsel in the gardens and the corridors? And, as more of his recent history lessons came back to him, had Thomas Cromwell whispered his advice into his sovereign's ear inside that fantastic building? Was the Dissolution of the Monasteries conceived and planned inside Hampton Court Palace?

William McKenzie settled nervously into his first class carriage at Victoria station, feeling rather out of place. McKenzie was not used to travelling first class. Three compartments further down Father Dominic Barberi was also travelling first class. He had not required the services of a porter to bring his luggage on to the train. One black valise was all he had. McKenzie also felt rather nervous about the very large sum of money Powerscourt had stuffed into his pocket before he left.

'You never know who you might need to bribe when you get there, William. And I've hired a guide and interpreter to meet you at the further end. A former Ambassador gave me his name. The fellow is a retired journalist by the name of Bailey, Richard Bailey. He's married to an Italian and knows the place like the back of his hand.'

McKenzie hoped his old mother did not where he was going. For she belonged to an extreme Presbyterian sect which believed that the Catholic Church was the kingdom of the Devil and the Pope the permanent reincarnation of Satan. The minister in their local church was a man who prided himself on his physical resemblance to John Knox, the great Calvinist divine of sixteenth-century Edinburgh. Indeed, the minister had bought every single book ever published about Knox so he could imitate his mannerisms and recreate the patterns of his speech. How often had McKenzie sat there in his pew beside his mother, his mind miles away, while the man preached on and on about the Anti-Christ in the Vatican and the evils of the Church of Rome, its coffers bloated by the sale of indulgences and pardons, its members denied the basic rights of the study of the Bible and damned to all eternity by their idolatry and the worship of graven images. McKenzie had told Powerscourt in India once that he had learned patience by sitting through these terrible sermons, so filled with hate in the name of the love of God.

He remembered Powerscourt's last words to him in the drawing room at Markham Square. 'William, it is important that you find out as much as you can. But it is even more important that you do not get caught. I dread to think what might happen if these people suspect they are being followed, their affairs investigated. I cannot emphasize that enough.'

Outside, McKenzie saw that the great clock on the station platform had almost reached eleven o'clock. The last trunks and hatboxes were being loaded into the goods van, the porters throwing the late ones in before the train departed. McKenzie checked his ticket once more. London, Calais, Paris, Lyon, Mont Cenis, Turin, Pisa, Rome. The whistles blew, the green flags came down and the train moved slowly out of the station, a few relatives and friends waving at the carriages as they passed. William McKenzie was on his way to the Eternal City.

After his journey back to the West Country Powerscourt suspected he might be on the verge of solving one of the riddles of Compton. It was the one where he had started all those weeks before. If he had to, he could now arrange for the exhumation of the body of John Eustace, interred with such speed and secrecy in the grave-yard behind his house. But, if he was lucky, that might not be necessary. His first port of call the following day was with Chief Inspector Yates. He showed him the papers he had brought from London.

'Chief Inspector, thank you for the papers about the exhumation order on John Eustace. I have the Home Secretary's signature here. I think I am going to have one last attempt on Dr Blackstaff. But I need some ammunition. If the coffin is lifted and opened up, and we discover that Eustace did not die of natural causes, where does that leave the doctor?'

'Well,' said the Chief Inspector, 'we could charge him with murder straight away, if you like. He did stand to make a great deal of money out of the will after all.'

'I'm not sure that it would be easy to secure a conviction on those grounds. And a local jury would certainly be very reluctant to convict him. He's a very good doctor, I believe. Is there anything else you could charge him with?'

Chief Inspector Yates scratched his head. 'Obstruction of justice,' he said, 'concealing the manner of death, lying to the police forces? We could certainly rustle up something along those lines.'

Powerscourt found Lady Lucy sitting in the garden of Fairfield Park, watching the children throwing a ball to each other. He kissed her and smiled as she ran her fingers through his hair.

'I think we're making progress, Lucy,' he said. 'But the answers I am finding are so incredible I wonder if I am going out of my mind. I don't want to tell anybody yet, in case I'm completely wrong.'

'Surely you can tell me, Francis?' said Lady Lucy. A pair of sad blue eyes looked up at him. 'We've been married for years and years now, after all.'

Powerscourt kissed her again. 'I think this knowledge is very dangerous, my love. Believe me, I will tell you as soon as I can. Now, what has been happening down here?'

Lady Lucy told him about her strange encounter with the choirmaster, his comments about the amount of work the choir had to do for the *Messiah* and the commemoration service. She told him about Johnny Fitzgerald's discovery of one of the canons of the cathedral celebrating Mass at seven thirty in the morning in the little church at Ledbury St John. Two of them Catholic for certain, Powerscourt said to himself, Archdeacon and Canon, maybe two more. At that point Powerscourt rose from his garden chair and walked round the garden three times, collecting his children in his arms as he went so that three Powerscourts returned to join Lady Lucy on her chair.

'I must go now, or I shall be late,' he said, kissing all three of them in turn.

'Where are you going, Papa?' said Thomas and Olivia in unison, worried that he might disappear abroad again.

'I have to go and see Dr Blackstaff,' he said. 'I'm rather worried about my health.' As Lady Lucy watched him go out of the garden gate, she didn't think for one moment that it was his own health he was going to discuss, but the death that had brought them to Compton all those weeks before.

On his short journey to the Blackstaff residence Powerscourt thought about many things. He thought of the two dead bodies, one roasted all night on the spit in Vicars Hall, the other cut into pieces and distributed around the countryside. He thought about the extra music the choir were learning for the service commemorating one thousand years of the minster. He thought of the Archdeacon, travelling every Thursday to celebrate Mass at Melbury Clinton, his other religious identity concealed inside his bag. He thought of the dinner at Trinity College Oxford all those years before, the candles burning brightly along the tables, the dons resplendent in their gowns of scarlet and black, the long shadows of the servants on the walls as they moved up and down to serve the different courses, the red wine gleaming in front of Newman, his white hair shimmering like a beacon in the centre of High Table.

The daffodils in Dr Blackstaff's garden were swaying slightly in the early evening breeze as Powerscourt rang the bell at precisely six o'clock. He had sent word to the doctor from London that he proposed to call on him at this time. He was shown into the drawing room lined with medical prints where he had talked to the doctor about the death of John Eustace in January. He greeted the grisly portrait of an eighteenth-century tooth extraction like an old friend. He was, after all, he reflected, about to embark on a different kind of extraction. The truth might be more painful than an infected upper molar.

'Dr Blackstaff,' Powerscourt began, as he was ushered into a high-backed leather chair by the fireplace, 'please forgive me for troubling you once more about the death of John Eustace.'

Dr Blackstaff looked slightly irritated. 'I have already told you, Lord Powerscourt, all that I know about the death of my friend.'

'But have you?' said Powerscourt. 'That is the question, Dr Blackstaff. You see, I'm afraid I didn't believe the story you related about the manner of John Eustace's death the first time you told me, here in this room, all those weeks ago. I still don't believe it today. There are too many discrepancies in the account you gave me and what the butler said. You said, if I recall, that he was wearing a pale blue shirt. Andrew McKenna said it was grey. Maybe people could confuse one with the other. Perhaps. You said he was wearing black boots. McKenna said they were brown. But, you see, it wasn't just those variations that made me doubt you were telling me the whole truth. The demeanour of the two of you was most unsatisfactory. Not to put too fine a point on it, you sounded as though you were lying some of the time, the unfortunate butler, one of the worst liars I have ever come across, sounded as though he was lying almost all of the time.'

Powerscourt paused. The doctor was silent, staring at his fire. A couple of blackbirds were singing lustily in the fruit trees outside. Maybe even the birds, Powerscourt said to himself, had to learn new tunes for the celebrations of the thousandth anniversary of Compton Minster as a site of Christian worship.

'There was little I could do about the lack of truthful information, short of digging the body out of the grave. And then there were other murders which took my attention. But now the situation is different.'

Powerscourt took out the papers relating to the exhumation order and placed them carefully on the table between them.

'As you can see, I have the signature of the Home Secretary on the exhumation order already. I don't think your brother could oppose a request now.'

The doctor pulled on a pair of spectacles and read the documents very slowly. Then he read them again.

'Can I say at this point, Dr Blackstaff,' Powerscourt went on, 'that I would urge you now to consider your own position. If we go ahead with the exhumation, I believe there will be questions from the police about why they were not told the truth. There may be charges of obstructing the course of justice. It will all become most unpleasant in a personal and professional sense. But it need not come to that.'

Powerscourt stopped. At last the doctor spoke.

'What do you mean, it need not come to that?'

Powerscourt paused for a few moments before he replied. A gang of magpies had taken occupation of the top branches in one of the Blackstaff apple trees, noisily preparing for some malevolent mission.

Powerscourt was at his most emollient. 'I think one of the key factors in this terrible affair has been your intimate friendship with John Eustace and Andrew McKenna's loyalty to his employer. I respect you both for that. I suspect John Eustace must have been a very lovable man. Some people are just like that. And I think he was a very troubled man in the weeks and months leading up to his death. In some ways I think that what troubled him also led to his death. I shall come to that in a moment. I think he made you promise, or you felt such a promise was inherent in your friendship, not to tell a single soul what had been happening in the weeks before he died, or what had worried him previously. That is why you have been reticent with the true facts of the affair.'

Powerscourt paused and looked carefully at the doctor. The doctor held his peace.

'I said a moment ago that the exhumation need not go ahead. I am not going to ask you to break your solemn oath. I am not going to ask you to make your confession, if confession is the right word, which I rather doubt. All I ask is that you nod your head if the version of events I am about to give you is correct in the broad outlines. We need not quibble about the accuracy of the minor details. Do you agree, Dr Blackstaff?'

Dr Blackstaff looked once more into his fire. Powerscourt waited.

'I agree,' he said finally.

'Thank you,' said Powerscourt, 'thank you so much. Let me give you first of all my guess as to what happened on the night John Eustace died. You see, I don't think he died here in this house at all, as you said in your earlier account of events. I think he was dead when he came here. I think Andrew McKenna brought him here in the middle of the night. He died in Fairfield Park, not in your surgery after a long and difficult night. I say he died in Fairfield Park, I should have said he was murdered in Fairfield Park.'

Powerscourt stopped for a moment to see if there would be a nod from the medical department. Eventually there was a slow, but definite inclination of Dr Blackstaff's head. It was undoubtedly a nod. Inwardly Powerscourt rejoiced.

'The murder,' Powerscourt went on, remembering he was speaking to John Eustace's closest friend, 'was truly horrible. I think his head had been cut off. I think the intention of the murderer was to stick the head on a pole. Maybe he stuck it as a temporary measure on one of the posts on that great four-poster bed. The butler was terrified of scandal. You wished to be loyal to your friend and to his memory. You feared, above all, what damage might be done if the circumstances surrounding John Eustace's demise became public. So you rushed the body off to the mortuary as fast as you could. You also made sure that only the undertaker knew what must have happened to the corpse. Nobody else in his business saw anything other than a closed coffin.'

Dr Blackstaff looked as if he might speak. But he did not. Instead he nodded a weary nod.

'Thank you once again,' said Powerscourt. 'Let me tell you how your acceptance changes the position. We can leave the body where it is. The police will take no action. I am assuming the man who murdered John Eustace is the same man who murdered the man on the spit and the dismembered corpse. You cannot be hanged more than once, no matter how many people you may have slaughtered. The killer can hang for those two murders. It should not be necessary to bring a third charge. The body and the memory of John Eustace can be left in peace. I am sure that is what you would have wished, Dr Blackstaff.'

At last the doctor spoke. 'Do you know who the killer is, Lord Powerscourt?'

Now it was Powerscourt's turn to shake his head. 'I do not,' he said sadly.

'Do you think you will find him?'

'Yes, if he does not kill me first.' Powerscourt told the doctor about the attempt on his life in the cathedral, the falling masonry, his hours alone with the dead of Compton's past.

'One last request, if I may trouble you still further.' Powerscourt's eye was drawn to another of the doctor's grisly collection of medical prints on the wall opposite. It showed a long line of wounded men who snaked out of the picture into the fields beyond. Snow was falling. The head of the queue was in front of a barn which must have served as a temporary medical station, Dr Blackstaff's predecessors working furiously inside. It must have been a terrible battle, Powerscourt thought, Inkerman perhaps or Balaclava. Heaps of amputated limbs were stacked neatly against the side of the building. An orderly was bringing a bundle of the latest arms and legs to add to the charnel house. They were arranged separately, Powerscourt saw to his horror, arms in one pile, legs in another.

'We are still, I would suggest,' he went on, 'operating under the same rules as before. All you have to do is nod. I want to test out on you what I think must have been troubling John Eustace in the last weeks and months of his life. You see, I think we are in the middle, no, not the middle, I think we are very close to the end of a very daring conspiracy, a most ingenious conspiracy, a conspiracy that could have repercussions far beyond the boundaries of Compton Minster.'

Powerscourt spoke for about five minutes. He paused every now and then to collect his thoughts. He had never tried to put all the pieces together in conversation before, only in his mind, and then usually in the middle of the night. He left out a lot of the details. He did not mention the Archdeacon's pilgrimages to Melbury Clinton or the Canon's expeditions to Ledbury St John in case the doctor did not know of these. He spoke at length about the thousand year celebrations in the cathedral.

When he stopped he felt like an undergraduate who has just read a controversial, possibly heretical, essay to his tutor. He wondered what the verdict would be. Dr Blackstaff looked at Powerscourt in astonishment. Powerscourt wondered if he was going to be declared insane. He was not. Dr Blackstaff did not speak. He continued to stare at Powerscourt for what must have been almost a minute. Then he nodded. He nodded very vigorously indeed.

20

Ever since their engagement in the storm on the summit of Glastonbury Tor Patrick Butler had taken to dropping in on his fiancée at all hours of the day. Their earlier trysts over afternoon tea had been broadened into coffee in the mornings, chocolate in the early evenings and occasional suppers with the boys. But it was a perplexed Patrick Butler who joined his fiancée the morning after Powerscourt's conversations with Dr Blackstaff.

'I don't understand it, Anne,' he said. 'Weeks ago the Bishop more or less told me we could get married in the cathedral. I asked him for the date we discussed, a month or so after Easter Monday, as I am sure you remember.'

Anne Herbert nodded.

'Now he's saying,' Patrick Butler went on, 'that it will be impossible for us to be married that day in the minster.' Bishop Ruins Wedding, was running through his mind. Happy Couple Distraught. 'He says we could have the service in St Peter under the Arches instead.'

'But that's impossible, absolutely impossible, Patrick,' said Anne Herbert with unusual vehemence. Her late husband had been rector of St Peter's. 'He can't possibly think I'm going to marry again at the very altar where my dead first husband held his services. It would make a mockery of the service. Just think of what the congregation would say.'

'Maybe he's made a mistake,' said Patrick. 'But why the cathedral should be out of bounds beats me. All the commemoration services will be over by then.'

'This should cheer you up, Patrick,' said Anne. 'We've been asked out to dinner this evening. Lady Powerscourt dropped the invitation in on her way to rehearsals for the *Messiah*.'

'Is it going to be a very grand affair, Anne? Do I have to dress up?' Patrick Butler was the proud owner of two perfectly respectable suits. But they betrayed, here and there, the marks of his profession, ink spilt in unfortunate places, a permanent air of wear and tear. They always looked in need of cleaning. He had promised Anne he would buy a new one after they were married.

'I think it's only us and Johnny Fitzgerald,' said Anne.

'I say,' Patrick Butler was back to his normal excitable self, 'do you think he's solved the murder? Is he going to tell us who the villain is?' The headlines raced through his mind once more. Sleuth Solves Mystery Over Salmon Mousse. Compton Killer Unveiled Over Veal Viennoise.

The last course had been cleared away in the dining room at Fairfield Park. Powerscourt had given instructions to Andrew McKenna that they were not to be disturbed. Patrick Butler had chatted happily with Lady Lucy, telling her outrageous stories about the misbehaviour of journalists. Johnny Fitzgerald had discovered a common interest in birds with Anne Herbert and they had ended up discussing the different varieties of binoculars. Powerscourt himself said little during the meal. He had told Lady Lucy the upshot of his conversation with the doctor before she rushed off to choir practice. Lady Lucy had turned white. She was so shocked that she sang the wrong note in three different places during 'Unto Us a child is Born' and received a number of stern looks from the choirmaster.

Three different riddles, he said to himself, surveying his guests. One to do with the death of John Eustace. One to do with the cathedral. One to do with the murderer. He thought he could answer the second, but not the third. He looked down his table, Lady Lucy smiling at him from the opposite end. She knew what was coming. He tapped a fork on the side of his glass.

'Lucy, Anne, if I may be permitted to call you that,' he smiled broadly at Mrs Herbert, soon to be Mrs Butler, 'Patrick, Johnny. I would like to tell you what I think has been going on here. And to ask your advice about what we should do next. For the time being, Patrick, this must remain private, however difficult you may find it.'

Patrick Butler bowed his head in acknowledgement. Anne felt rather proud of him.

'I was called here originally, as you will recall, to investigate the death of John Eustace. I want to leave that to one side for the present. I want to concentrate on one thing only, on what has been and is going on in the cathedral. I'm afraid I should warn you before I start that my conclusions may seem incredible. I found them so myself in the beginning. Let me try to bring the evidence forward in chronological order.'

Patrick Butler had a notebook and pen in his pocket. He found it difficult to resist the temptation to start scribbling straight away. Johnny Fitzgerald was drawing imaginary pictures of birds on the tablecloth.

'Let us begin with the mystery of the Archdeacon and his visits to celebrate Mass in the private chapel in Melbury Clinton. He is either an Anglican pretending to be a Roman Catholic or a Roman Catholic masquerading as an Anglican. I think the truth lies with the latter proposition, that he is a Catholic pretending to be an Anglican. He is joined by the Canon of the cathedral found by Johnny also celebrating Mass in the outlying village of Ledbury St John. In my opinion, we can be virtually certain that two members of the Chapter are Catholic. There is a third, the young man Augustine Ferrers from Bristol, come to sing in the choir. His parish priest told his mother, even as the reports of the Compton Cathedral murders were filling the newspapers, that he would be perfectly safe coming to Compton if he was a Catholic. The implication of that, of course, was that he might not be so safe if he were a Protestant.'

Powerscourt paused and took a sip of water. Anne Herbert was looking alarmed, Johnny Fitzgerald seemed to be working on the outline of some enormous bird, maybe an eagle. Patrick Butler could not take his eyes off Powerscourt's face.

'And then there is the mysterious visitor to the Archdeacon who is a regular guest in the Archdeaconry. I now know that he too is a Catholic priest called Father Dominic Barberi, who often stays with the Jesuits in Farm Street in London. He is also a member of a mysterious and secretive body called Civitas Dei, dedicated to the greater glory and success of the Roman Catholic Church in this world rather than the next. I was told of a rumour that circulated in Rome by our previous Ambassador, Sir Roderick Lewis, a rumour that he discounted but which I suspect might be true.'

'What was the rumour, Lord Powerscourt?' Patrick Butler was unable to stop himself asking questions.

'I'm coming to that, Patrick.' Powerscourt smiled at the young man. 'The substance of the rumour was that Civitas Dei were mounting a great operation in England which would cause a sensation when it was revealed. And there's more to the Compton Catholic connection, as your newspaper might like to headline it, Patrick. There is another piece of evidence, flimsy in itself perhaps, but significant I believe in this context. Twenty years ago John Henry Newman, the most famous defector to Rome of the last century, was invited back to a special dinner or feast in his old Oxford college, Trinity. All those present signed the menu. One of the signatories is now the Dean of this cathedral. The other, who spent a lot of time talking to Newman, is the Bishop.'

Powerscourt took another sip of his water. He was saving his port till the end. Patrick Butler stared at Powerscourt open-mouthed. Anne Herbert had turned pale. Johnny Fitzgerald had suddenly abandoned his imaginary bird drawings on the Fairfield linen. He was working on an enormous crucifix. Lady Lucy kept her eyes fixed on her husband's face, trying to send whatever encouragement she could from one end of the table to another.

'So there we have some of the pieces of the puzzle,' Powerscourt went on. 'Ever since I have been here I have felt that there is a secret right at the heart of the minster. And the key to it, I would suggest, lies with the celebrations for the thousandth anniversary of the cathedral as a place of Christian worship. All along I have wondered about the secrecy. Why has the Archdeacon gone on his solitary communions to Melbury Clinton? Why does the other man ride out at the crack of dawn to Ledbury St John? Why don't they just come out in their true colours? I think they are waiting for something. I think they are waiting for the same thing as the members of Civitas Dei in Rome who are looking forward to a sensation that will shock England.'

Powerscourt stopped. His hand moved from the tumbler of water to the glass of port, a rich ruby red in front of him.

'What is it, Francis?' Johnny Fitzgerald whispered. 'For God's sake, what is it?'

Powerscourt looked directly at Lady Lucy as he spoke.

'On Easter Sunday, I believe,' he said, speaking very quietly, 'the Bishop and the Dean and the Chapter are going to rededicate the cathedral to the Catholic faith. The minster will be restored to its old religion before the Dissolution of the Monasteries. Compton will be made Catholic once again. It's not just a question of the

Archdeacon and the Canon and the young man from Bristol, you see. They're all Catholics now, every single last one of them. Even the mice and the rats have probably taken their vows by this stage.'

Patrick Butler had turned pale. Anne Herbert stared at Powerscourt open-mouthed. Lady Lucy was feeling rather proud of her Francis. Only Johnny Fitzgerald did not seem very surprised. But then he had been working with Powerscourt for years.

'Where does this fit in with the murders, Francis?' Johnny asked.

Powerscourt took a sip of his port. 'I would guess, and it's only a guess, that the victims were all signed up for the enterprise. Then they changed their minds. Maybe they threatened to go public about the whole scheme. Maybe they said they would go and have a cosy little chat with Patrick here. In any event, they were all killed. The secret had to be kept until Easter Sunday. I think it all ties in with John Eustace's wills. The first one, dated 1898, left almost all his money to the cathedral. The second one, from early last year, left it all to his sister Mrs Cockburn, but I've always suspected Mrs Cockburn herself was responsible for that will. And the third, from last December, left everything, more or less, to the Salvation Army. But the Dean was very persuasive that Eustace intended to leave his money to the cathedral, that he had talked to various people about how he wanted it spent. The point is that he intended to leave it to a Protestant cathedral, not one that was about to turn Catholic. Once he knew about that he changed his mind.'

'Do you know who the murderer is now, Lord Powerscourt?' said Patrick Butler, looking at his host as if he were a miracle worker.

'No, I do not,' said Powerscourt. 'I have no more idea about the identity of the murderer than I did the first day I set foot in Compton. And there's one enormous problem with this theory.'

Powerscourt stopped as if he expected that everyone present would know the answer. The one man who could support his theory, Dr Blackstaff, would never speak in public out of loyalty to his dead friend.

'What's that, Francis?' said Lady Lucy, coming to his rescue.

'It's very simple,' Powerscourt replied. 'It's incredibly simple when you think about it rationally. You see, I can make theories, join things together, a piece of damaged string here, a frayed rope there, maybe make two and two add up to eighteen. But I can't prove a bloody word of it.'

'Why do you have to be able to prove it, Lord Powerscourt?' Patrick Butler was already thinking about how he would tell the story in his newspaper, if he was ever able to tell it.

'Forgive me, Patrick, I'm not making myself clear. It seems to me that I have a responsibility to try to prevent this thing happening if I can. Compton going back to the Catholic faith will cause a sensation, not just here but all over the country. The newspapers will be full of it for days. There will be questions in Parliament. Nobody, least of all, I suspect, the Anglican Church, will have any idea what to do about it. I think the Bishop and his friends may be able to pull this thing off for a couple of days, but then some form of authority will have to intervene. Whether it's the Church or the State I don't know. Perhaps in these circumstances they are one and the same, I'm not sure. But what can I do? I can write to the Archbishop of Canterbury or the Bishop of Exeter, being the nearest see to Compton. I can write to the Prime Minister in Downing Street or the Lord Lieutenant of the county here. And what will they do? They may talk to the Bishop or the Dean. What nonsense, they will say. Powerscourt has gone mad. Pity really, he was quite a good investigator when he was younger. Ought to be locked up now, mind you. Poor Lady Powerscourt and the little Powerscourts, having a madman for a husband and a father. And then they will carry on with their plans.'

Lady Lucy smiled up at the maniac at the other end of the table. 'Surely, Francis, there is some evidence. There's the Archdeacon going to Melbury Clinton for a start. And the Canon celebrating Mass in Ledbury. And all these dreadful murders.'

'Of course there is some evidence, Lucy,' said Powerscourt, taking a further sip of his port, 'otherwise we wouldn't have got as far as this. But I'm sure the Archdeacon and the Canon could cook up some perfectly reasonable explanation. They've got all those Jesuits in Farm Street at their beck and call, not to mention the Civitas Dei people in Rome. Something would be concocted. But the scheme could still go on.'

'What about John Eustace, Francis, where do you think he fits into all of this?' Johnny Fitzgerald had finished doodling his crucifix on the tablecloth. He seemed now to be working on a cathedral spire.

Powerscourt sighed. 'I didn't want to go into the murders at this stage, but I think I'd better. There have been three of them.'

His little audience stared at him. Two, surely, not three. Perhaps he was losing his wits after all.

'Sorry,' said Powerscourt, 'I only learnt very recently – please don't ask me how – that John Eustace, last owner of this house where we sit, was also murdered. His head was cut off and placed on one of the posts in his great four-poster bed. Then there was Arthur Rudd, murdered and roasted on the spit in the Vicars Hall. Third but not least was Edward Gillespie, his body hacked to pieces and left lying all over the county. There is a connection, of course. I should have seen it sooner. I must have been blind.'

'What is the connection?' said Patrick Butler.

'The connection, believe it or not,' Powerscourt replied, 'is the Dissolution of the Monasteries. Let me make myself clear. For six hundred and forty years what is now the cathedral was a Roman Catholic abbey, devoted to the Blessed Virgin Mary. The break came with the Reformation and the Dissolution of the Monasteries in 1538. Compton was one of the last to be dismembered. Some time after that it became the Protestant cathedral we know today. A number of people in Compton opposed the transfer from one faith to another. They were put to death in a variety of ways. One was burnt at the stake, in the manner of Arthur Rudd. One was hung drawn and quartered in the manner of Edward Gillespie. The abbot himself, I believe, was beheaded and his head stuck on a pole at the entrance to the Cathedral Green. The fate of poor John Eustace. Whether his head was destined to go somewhere other than his own four-poster I do not know. So the murderer is after a certain symbolic symmetry, if you like. Three people who opposed the transfer from Catholic to Anglican all those years ago were killed in particular and very horrible ways. Three people who opposed the return from Anglican back to Catholic, presumably, have been killed in the last weeks in ways which echo those earlier deaths three hundred and seventy years ago. It's a warped form of Catholic revenge in a way.'

Patrick Butler was drumming his fingers on the table. He longed to reach inside his pocket for notebook and pen. Anne Herbert was feeling rather faint. Lady Lucy found herself humming one of the arias in the *Messiah* to herself under her breath. Johnny Fitzgerald had not touched his port for at least a quarter of an hour. Outside a lone owl hooted into the night.

'Surely, Francis,' Johnny said, 'this makes the case for the

Archbishop and the authorities all the stronger. All this history and stuff about the monasteries before.'

'That's the problem.' Powerscourt surveyed his little audience one by one. 'I don't think it does. You see, it seems quite possible to me that the people organizing the return to Catholicism are not the murderers. They may be just as upset and confused by it as we are. The murderer may be somebody completely different, though I doubt it. I suspect the two are so closely linked you couldn't get a hair between them, but I can't prove it.' Powerscourt suddenly realized, looking at Anne Herbert, that she might faint at any moment. Perhaps it had been a mistake inviting them here.

'And there, I suggest,' he said, smiling at Lady Lucy, 'we leave things for now. I was going to ask your advice but that can wait for another time. Just one last point. I think we should all pray very hard that none of those involved in the Catholic Compton conspiracy change their minds between now and Easter Sunday.'

'Surely, Francis,' said Johnny Fitzgerald, 'we should be praying the other way round, that they should repent of their ways and remain as Anglicans.'

'On the contrary,' said Powerscourt, 'if they change their minds, then the murderer will treat them in the same way he has treated their predecessors. Anglican or Catholic, even in Compton you're better off alive than dead.'

As Powerscourt rode into Compton the next morning to confer with Chief Inspector Yates he began thinking about the letters he knew he had to write to the Bishop of Exeter, the Lord Lieutenant and the Archbishop of Canterbury's Private Secretary. 'Please forgive me if the contents of this letter seem rather extraordinary,' he said to himself as his horse trotted down the country lanes. No, that wasn't quite right. 'Please rest assured that however bizarre the contents of this letter may appear, I am still in full possession of my faculties.' That wouldn't do either. Powerscourt was convinced that once he began telling people he wasn't mad, they would instantly jump to the opposite conclusion. Maybe he should confine himself to the facts. But a bald narrative of events might not be credible either. One letter he had written before his breakfast that day to one of his employers, Mrs Augusta Cockburn, sister of the late John Eustace, currently residing in a small villa outside Florence. He regretted very much, he told her, having to confirm her suspicions that her brother had been murdered. He did not give details of the manner of his death. He promised to write again shortly with the name of the murderer. He hoped that the Italian postal service was not too quick.

Chief Inspector Yates was reading a pile of reports in his little office at the back of the police station and making notes in a large black book. Inside, Powerscourt knew, the Chief Inspector was collating the movements and the alibis of every single resident of the Close. Powerscourt had already told him about the death of John Eustace. Now he told him about the plans for the mass defection to Rome on Easter Sunday. The Chief Inspector was astonished.

'God bless my soul, my lord, are you sure? This will tear Compton in half.'

Powerscourt went back over his reasons, the secret of the Archdeacon's visits to Melbury Clinton, the Canon's pilgrimages to Mass in Ledbury St John, the connections with the late Cardinal Newman. Above all, he told him about his conversations with Dr Blackstaff.

'Isn't it all illegal, this sort of thing?' said the Chief Inspector vaguely, only too aware that his previous training and experience did not equip him to quote section or subsection of Act of Parliament.

'I'm sure it's illegal,' said Powerscourt. 'But God knows which Act of Parliament it is. Before Catholic Emancipation I think it was illegal to celebrate Mass in an Anglican church, but I don't know if this still applies. But at the moment nobody has actually done anything illegal. You can't arrest people on suspicion of being about to do something in a week's time.'

'Do you think it helps with the murders?' asked the Chief Inspector.

'I'm not really sure that it does,' said Powerscourt. 'It may be that the Catholic conspirators are as upset about the killings as we are. What terrifies me is what the killer may do if we start asking around about the mass conversions. I think he may kill again. I'm sure he might kill again. He's not like any murderer I have ever come across before, Chief Inspector. I feel he's driven by a kind of madness that ordinary mortals simply wouldn't understand.

'You know as well as I do,' Powerscourt went on, 'about the most common motives for murder. Money. Greed. Hatred. Jealousy. Revenge. I'm not sure that any of those work in this case. Hatred perhaps. Revenge maybe.'

'Seems to me, my lord,' said the Chief Inspector, 'that there's domestic murder, and then there's state killing in war if that's the right word. Millions must have been killed in wars in the name of religion, isn't that right?'

Powerscourt thought of the Christians massacred in the Colosseum, of purges and pogroms throughout the Middle Ages, Cathars despatched in their mountain fortress of Montsegur in the Pyrenees or slaughtered wholesale in the amphitheatre at Verona, the ruinous wars of religion that swept over Europe in the sixteenth century, the list went on and on.

'I'm sure you're right, Chief Inspector,' said Powerscourt. 'It's only that the wars of religion seem to have returned to Compton a century or two after they finished everywhere else.'

'This has just come for you, Lady Powerscourt.' Andrew McKenna handed over a rather battered envelope with the address written in a childish hand. 'Lady Powerscourt, Fairfield Park.'

'Did you see how it got here, McKenna?' Lady Lucy asked, slitting open her missive.

'No, I did not, madam. It was found lying inside the front door. It must have been delivered by hand.'

'Dear Lady Powerscourt,' Lady Lucy read. The letters were large and sprawled across the page. 'Could you meet us in the south transept to the side of the choir just before five thirty this afternoon. William and Philip, choirboys.' McKenna took his leave. Lady Lucy was rejoicing. These were the two choirboys she had managed to speak to on a number of occasions after the rehearsals for the *Messiah*. Now they were asking for a meeting. Now perhaps she would discover the secrets of their fear and their unhappiness. Now perhaps she would be able to improve their situation. Never had she seen a collection of little boys so constantly crestfallen, so much in need of love and proper food and attention. She checked her watch. It was shortly after half-past four. Should she wait for Francis to return from his visit to the Chief Inspector? She knew how worried he had been about her interest in the choir, how often he had spelt out how dangerous it could be. She knew he might insist on accompanying her. Then she made up her mind. They were her special interest, these children. She had gone out of her way to try to get close to them. The presence of a man might put them off. Maybe the boys would say nothing at all. She scribbled a brief note to her husband, saying she had popped into Compton and hoped to return by half-past six at the latest. She did not specify precisely where she was going.

Lord Francis Powerscourt thought he could manage the first paragraph of his letter to the Prime Minister's Private Secretary on his ride back to Fairfield Park. He remembered Rosebery telling him that the Prime Minister himself was unwell, his mind now so exhausted by the pressure of work that he had had to give up his beloved Foreign Office, his mighty frame so weary that he frequently fell asleep in cabinet meetings. Schomberg McDonnell, Private Secretary, confidant, intimate, the man who knew where all the Prime Minister's political enemies were buried, he was the man to write to.

Powerscourt sat himself down at the desk in John Eustace's study and began his letter. Lady Lucy's note was still sitting, unseen and unread, on the table in the drawing room.

'I am currently engaged,' he began, 'on an investigation into some very bizarre deaths in the Cathedral City of Compton in the west of England.' Begin with the intelligence that is easy to understand, he reminded himself of his days in the Army, and move on slowly to the unpalatable conclusions. 'In the course of my inquiries,' he went on, 'I have discovered a plot so unusual and so potentially divisive in the country as a whole, that I felt duty bound to lay the details before you.' Make them curious, he said to himself, make them want to keep reading.

'But before I do, however disagreeable I find it to advertise my previous achievements, I felt I should remind you of my own earlier involvements in the fields of detection and some of my past services to Crown and Country.'

Lady Lucy was humming the 'Hallelujah Chorus' to herself as she walked up the nave of the cathedral. The late afternoon sun was casting great beams of light across the body of the cathedral, some of it multi-coloured as it was filtered through the stained glass. What a pity we couldn't sing the *Messiah* here, she said to herself as she peered into the choir stalls to the left of the south transept. The building appeared to be completely deserted. There was no sign of the two boys. Perhaps they were late, or were hiding somewhere to give her a surprise. Then she saw a light coming round an open door in the corner. Perhaps they're over there, she said to herself, and set off to investigate. As she reached the bottom of the steps she called for them by name.

'William,' she said softly, 'Philip, I'm here.'

There was no answer. She moved forward, away from the door and tried again.

'William, Philip, I'm here.'

Then two things happened virtually simultaneously. The light went out. There was a loud bang as the door slammed shut.

It was only a matter of moments before the minster was closed up for the night. And Lady Lucy Powerscourt was locked in the crypt in total impenetrable darkness.

Part Four

Easter

April 1901

21

Powerscourt gave details of his investigation into the mysterious death of Prince Eddy, eldest son of the then Prince of Wales, some nine years before. He referred to his role in the defeat of a plot to bring the City of London to its knees at the time of Queen Victoria's Diamond Jubilee in 1897. He mentioned his work in South Africa, undertaken at the request of the Prime Minister himself. Then he started a new paragraph about the three deaths in Compton. He left nothing out. He referred to the celebrations at Easter for the one thousandth anniversary of the cathedral as a place of Christian worship. He felt his letter was going well now. He could see his way to the end. Somewhere outside he heard Johnny Fitzgerald enthusing about the birds to Anne Herbert who had brought her children over for the afternoon.

Lady Lucy cursed herself for her folly. How could she have been so stupid? How could she have ignored every word Francis had said to her? The crypt was very low, Norman vaulting rising from great pillars in the floor. Lady Lucy felt her way very gently round her prison, realizing that a tall man would be continuously banging his head on the stonework. The walls were clammy to the touch. She remembered that the workmen in here had found the ancient volume supposed to have been written by a pre-Reformation monk and currently appearing in weekly instalments in the *Grafton Mercury*. Faint scurrying noises could be heard in distant corners of the underground chamber, which might have been mice. Or rats. There was a mouldy smell, as if things left down here centuries before were still rotting slowly inside the walls.

Then she remembered Francis's fears that the murderer might

strike again. Lady Lucy was not particularly frightened of the dark. She remembered games of hide and seek in gloomy Scottish castles as a child where she had been able to conceal herself in places virtually bereft of daylight. But then there had usually been a gleam from under a door, a distant shaft of light up some corridor lined with long-dead warriors in their rusty armour. Down here there was nothing. If she held her hand in front of her face she could see nothing at all. She wondered about the man roasted on the spit. She shuddered violently as she thought of the man hung drawn and quartered, his parts distributed around the county. She thought of Francis's vigil alone in the cathedral for hours until she found him. Huddled against a pillar, tears beginning to form in her eyes, terror in her heart, Lady Lucy Powerscourt began saying her prayers.

'Our father which art in heaven,' she began, her voice sounding strange in the deserted crypt, 'hallowed be thy name . . .'

It was nearly half-past seven when Powerscourt finished his letter. He read it through three times. Then he decided to leave it until the morning before he posted it and the two other versions he would send to the Archbishop and the Lord Lieutenant. He had decided to omit the Bishop of Exeter. Maybe he could improve it in the morning. As he set off through the drawing room to join Johnny and the children, he saw Lucy's letter on the table. He read it once and called for the butler in his loudest voice.

'McKenna! McKenna!'

The butler came running into the room. He had never heard Powerscourt shout before.

'Do you know why Lady Powerscourt went into Compton this afternoon?' said Powerscourt, staring hard at Andrew McKenna.

'All I know is that there was a letter, my lord. It came about half-past four, I think.'

'Did you see who brought it?' asked Powerscourt.

'No, my lord. Nobody saw the bearer. It was addressed to Lady Powerscourt at Fairfield Park. The handwriting might have been a child's.'

Or somebody pretending to be a child, Powerscourt thought bitterly.

'And did she go out straight away?'

'Yes, my lord. She rode off into Compton at about a quarter to five.'

'Right, McKenna,' said Powerscourt, 'can you ask the coachman to take Mrs Herbert and the two children back to the Cathedral Close. And ask him to wait outside her house.' He strode out into the garden. Johnny and Anne Herbert were looking sadly at the remains of a small bird that seemed to have fallen victim to one of the Fairfield cats. Johnny was proposing burial underneath the trees, the children nodding slowly in agreement. None of them had been to a funeral before.

'Mrs Herbert,' even now Powerscourt remembered his manners, 'the coachman will take you and the boys back into town as soon as you are ready. Johnny, we must go now. I think Lucy may be in danger.'

'Lighten our darkness, we beseech thee oh Lord, and by thy great mercy defend us from all perils and dangers of this night.' The closing prayer of Evensong, which Lady Lucy had heard so often less than a hundred yards from her dungeon, gave her some comfort. Fragments of prayers and bits of collects jumbled themselves up in her mind. She had prayed for the means of grace and the hope of glory. She had prayed for the hope of grace and the means of glory. She didn't think God would mind if the message was confused. This after all was one of his own on temporary sojourn in the valley of the shadow of death. Then she heard a noise. Only when she heard it did she realize that up till now, fifteen to twenty minutes after her incarceration, she thought, she had heard absolutely nothing. No human voice, no passing carriages, no songbird gracing the walls of the minster with its music, not even the trebles of the choirboys could be heard down here. The walls must have been ten feet thick, built to last at the end of the eleventh century, rendering the crypt the perfect place for the contemplation of one's soul in peace. Or the contemplation of your own death in peace, Lady Lucy said to herself, huddling ever closer to one of the central pillars. The noise was growing louder, a hissing noise, a gurgling noise, a noise that grew in volume as time went by. Lady Lucy was virtually certain what it was. Then she felt it running over her shoes. Water was flooding into the Compton crypt, not in a deluge, but in a steady flow that must surely fill the entire chamber if it continued. Lady Lucy began looking for the steps. Over there was higher ground. Twice she fell over and her dress and her blouse were soaked. What a frightful sight I'm going to be if anybody ever manages to find me, or if the monster decides to turn off the water, she said to herself. She thought of Thomas and Olivia grieving for a drowned mother. She wondered how Francis would cope on his own. Perhaps he would marry again. He didn't seem to have very much luck with his wives staying alive, she reflected bitterly. Two drowned, one in the Irish Sea, one in the crypt of Compton.

At last she found the steps and sat halfway up to wait for the flood that would engulf her to rise slowly up the Norman pillars. Sometimes she thought it was subsiding, draining away perhaps through some porous section of the walls. Then it rose again, slowly, steadily, stealthily, almost like some wild animal stalking its prey in a jungle and waiting to pounce. Lady Lucy found herself thinking of her grandfather in Scotland who had dreamed of her marrying the Viceroy of India. He had taught her to shoot in case she needed to defend herself against hostile natives or marauding wild animals. Bullets would not help me now, she said to herself. I must remain calm, she told herself. If I panic or turn hysterical I shall die even sooner. She tried to imagine what Francis would say. She thought she knew exactly what his message to her would be. Hold on Lucy, I'm coming.

Powerscourt and Johnny Fitzgerald were riding into Compton faster than they had ever galloped across the South African veldt the year before. Johnny had a dark bag on his back, filled with strange implements that would open doors and windows designed to keep intruders out. The sun was setting over to their right, the glorious greens of an English spring turning back to the anonymous grey of twilight. Once or twice Johnny glanced wistfully at some bird of prey hovering above the fields. Powerscourt was calculating how long it would take them to reach Compton. And how long the murderer had already had to kill his Lucy.

Lady Lucy had counted fifteen steps from the bottom of the crypt to the great door that had banged shut on her some time before. She was sitting on step number eight, peering at the tide of water that swirled about her feet. Not that she could see the water, but she heard its presence everywhere, rippling round the pillars, slurping along the walls at the back. She had drawn her feet up to the step beneath. As the water rose she was going to retreat higher until she ended up crouching on the top step with her back to the door. She had moved on from the prayers and the collects to St Patrick's Breastplate. One of her grandmothers used to recite it to her as a lullaby at bedtime. The words had never left her.

'Christ for my guardianship today: against poison, against burning, against drowning, against wounding, that there may come to me a multitude of rewards.
Christ with me
Christ before me
Christ behind me.'

Christ was not beneath her. The water was. It had risen again during her prayer. Lady Lucy retreated to step number nine. She found herself wondering why the murderer was so sensitive about the choir. Her mind went back to the conversation with the choirmaster when he had threatened to expel her for taking too much interest in the boys. They have a lot of new music to learn for the commemoration service, he had said, as well as the *Messiah*. What sort of new music? Catholic music? Music that would never gain countenance in an Anglican cathedral, perhaps? And the choirboys might have told her? Surely that was the answer. She would have to tell Francis when she saw him. Maybe the choirmaster was the murderer. Then Lady Lucy's courage broke down and the tears rolled down her face to add a touch of salt to the malevolent flood beneath her. She might never see Francis again. He would never know how much she loved him, how she had loved him ever since that meeting in the National Gallery nine years before when she had talked with such passion about Turner's *Fighting Téméraire*. The thought that Francis would never know how much she felt for him reduced Lady Lucy to bouts of uncontrollable weeping. The waters advanced again. Lady Lucy retreated. She was on step number ten now. Only five to go.

Powerscourt reined in his horse on the edge of the Cathedral Close. He felt very cold in spite of the vigour of his ride.

'Johnny,' he said, 'do you think you could pick up the cathedral keys from the Deanery over there? I'm going round to the choirboys' house. I'll see you at the west door in a few minutes.'

The choir were still practising as Powerscourt raced round to the Georgian house that was their home. He heard the singing from twenty yards away, the choirmaster not happy with his charges, making them sing the same phrase over and over again. Powerscour thought there was something unusual about this music, something not right, but he had no time to wait and listen further. He pulled vigorously on the bell. You would think the bell in this sort of house would be melodious, he said to himself as he waited for an answer, a Mozart or a Haydn among door bells. But this one was harsh and grating, a dissonant note with the heavenly voices on the upper floor.

An enormous man in his late thirties with a large black beard opened the door.

'I'm so sorry to disturb you,' said Powerscourt. 'My wife has gone missing. She is a member of the choir for the *Messiah*. I wonder if you've seen her at all earlier this evening?'

'We all know Lady Powerscourt,' said the man ominously, 'and I can promise you we haven't seen her at all this evening. Goodnight to you, sir.'

And with that the man closed the door very sharply in Powerscourt's face. There was some strange accent there in the man's speech, Powerscourt thought, but he hadn't time to wonder what it was. He led his horse back to the front of the cathedral. It was twenty-five past eight.

Lady Lucy was on step number twelve now. She had cried all she could. Now she felt very cold. The water was beginning to creep up around her ankles. Ever since she was a child Lady Lucy had believed in heaven. Now she felt she might see it rather sooner than she expected. She had given up all hope of rescue, all hope that the remorseless flood might stop rising. She wondered if they had cleaning and drying facilities for new arrivals up above. God's laundry, she said to herself, presided over by a couple of wrinkled female saints, dispensing good cheer and heavenly soapsuds in equal measure. She wondered suddenly if there were big queues at busy periods, remembering the long delays that sometimes occurred at her local laundry on the corner of Sloane Square. She would just have to wait and see.

She began rehearsing some of her sins for the questions higher up. She hoped she would get preferential treatment for being so wet. Most of the new arrivals must come in perfectly dry after all. She should have been kinder to her mother. Lady Lucy suspected the authorities must have heard that one before. Sometimes she had been too strict with the children. Another familiar refrain. The waters were rising again. Lady Lucy, on her very own ghastly stairway to heaven, climbed back another step. Number thirteen. Unlucky thirteen.

Johnny Fitzgerald was carrying an enormous bunch of keys. 'The Dean's man wasn't about,' he said cheerfully. 'I had to interrupt the Dean in the middle of a meeting for him to fetch me the keys. He looked pretty cross.' Johnny began inspecting the bunch for the key of the west door, Powerscourt trying not to become impatient beside him.

'I think it might be this one,' he said, inserting an enormous key into the lock. 'Damn,' he said. 'Backed a loser there. Hold on, Francis, sorry about the delay.' The second key didn't work either. Neither did the third, Powerscourt feeling desperate by his side. The fourth did. Johnny Fitzgerald handed Powerscourt a lantern and they set off together up the nave, dramatic shadows falling across the tombs and the chantry chapels of the dead. They kept together by long custom, remembering from years of experience that two might make quicker progress separately, but that one person on their own is easier to kill. The sound of their boots went echoing up into the roof. They spoke in whispers. Powerscourt felt relieved when they passed the high altar and found it empty. He had been wondering if the murderer's macabre imagination could have left Lucy on top of it, like the victim of a human sacrifice. He tried to remember if his historians had talked of any women being put to death during the agonies of the Reformation. There was only one he could recall, a woman widely believed to have been a witch who had been burnt at the stake. He shuddered as they passed into the Lady Chapel behind the altar. A host of medieval saints and sinners peered down at them from the stained glass. But of Lady Lucy there was no sign.

Lady Lucy was on the fourteenth step now. Just one more to go before the end. The tears were back in her eyes as she thought of her children growing up without her. She would never see Thomas and Olivia married, she would never hold their children in her arms. Perhaps Thomas would become a soldier like his father and ride off overseas in some resplendent uniform to fight his country's battles. She felt very cold, shivering now as the waters approached. Then she thought she could hear some faint noise outside the door. Down at the bottom of the crypt, in amongst the pillars and the thick stone arches, you could hear nothing at all. But higher up it was different. She decided to make one last try for life. 'Help!' she shouted. 'Francis! Francis!' She thought it would be fitting if she perished with her husband's name on her lips. But there was no reply, only the mocking swirl of the waters that were coming to envelop her. She carried on regardless. 'Help! Help! Francis! Francis!'

It wasn't Powerscourt who heard the noise but Johnny Fitzgerald. He stopped suddenly and held Powerscourt back with his hand. 'Listen, Francis, I thought I heard a noise, coming from down there somewhere to the side of the choir.' They strained forward. They were over a hundred yards away from the entrance to the crypt. The next time they both heard it. 'Lucy! Lucy' they shouted at the tops of their voices as they sprinted down the south ambulatory, bumping into the tomb of Duke William of Hereford as they went. They stopped in the south transept and listened once more. This time they heard it more clearly. 'Francis! Francis!' There was hope in the voice now. Lucy thought she heard the sound of footsteps drawing near to the crypt.

'The crypt, Francis, the crypt. Over there in the corner. God knows which one of these bloody keys it is. Christ, why do they have so many? There's enough here to maintain a decent-sized prison.'

Powerscourt was banging on the door, calling out to Lucy inside. Johnny found the key at last. They rushed down a narrow passageway of twelve large steps to the second door. Water was now swirling round their feet. Johnny took one look at the second door and pulled out a vicious-looking iron crowbar.

'To hell with this bunch of keys, Francis,' he said. 'God knows what the divine punishment is for damaging cathedral property but I'll take my chance.'

With that he struck two mighty blows at the lock. Then he produced another instrument from his bag and wrenched the lock out of place. The door fell forward and with it a very wet Lady Lucy. She was crying. Powerscourt took her in his arms and carried her back up to the body of the cathedral.

'It's all my fault, Francis, it really is. If only I had listened to your advice about the choirboys.'

'Don't worry, my love,' said Powerscourt, stroking her hair, and striding fast towards the west door. 'You're safe now. You can tell us what happened later. We're going to take you to Anne Herbert's house. I'm sure you can have a bath and borrow some dry clothes.' Johnny Fitzgerald was packing up his tools. Powerscourt suddenly remembered his conversation with Chief Inspector Yates in the cloisters where the policeman had told him about the diverted stream and the sluice gate.

Powerscourt shook his head. When was this murderer going to stop? he said to himself. John Eustace, Arthur Rudd, Edward Gillespie. He'd tried to kill Powerscourt once. Now he'd tried, perhaps, to kill Lady Lucy. Let Easter Sunday come quickly, he thought. Then there may be an end of it.

Two days later Lord Francis Powerscourt was walking up the cobbled street of the Vicars Close. Two rows of ancient houses, with pretty little gardens in the front, ran up the hill away from the cathedral. Not Compton Cathedral this time, but Wells, a couple of hours away by train. For two days Powerscourt had sat at Lucy's bedside. The long exposure in the crypt, the cold and the water, had left her weak and feverish. Privately Powerscourt blamed himself. They should have left her in Anne Herbert's house rather than bringing her on yet another journey back to Fairfield Park. Dr Blackstaff was a regular visitor and prescribed a couple of medicines and a lot of rest. When the fever was running high Lady Lucy would plead with Francis to find out about the music. She was certain that the Protestant choirboys were being forced to learn the tunes and the words of the Church of Rome. She was sure the boys were not allowed to tell their parents for fear of some terrible punishment. Only that morning, Palm Sunday, as the procession of palms made its way round the cathedral and then up to the high altar inside, she had pleaded with him again.

Powerscourt had not told her about the singing he had heard on the way to the rescue. But it had stayed in his mind. Dr Blackstaff, a veteran of many West Country choirs, had written on his behalf to the assistant choirmaster in Wells. The doctor understood only too well why Powerscourt might not wish to pursue his queries in Compton.

Michael Matthews opened the door himself. He was a cheerful young man, almost six feet tall, with curly blond hair and merry brown eyes.

'You must be Lord Powerscourt,' he said, 'Welcome to Wells. Do come in. We should have time to sort out your problem before Evensong.'

He showed Powerscourt into a little sitting room. His house was at the top of the Close, looking down towards the chapter house and the north transept of the cathedral. The first thing Powerscourt noticed was a large piano which occupied most of one wall of the tiny room. The second thing was a wall full of books, many of them lives of the composers. And the third thing was that the floor was covered with musical scores, Byrd and Thomas Tallis, Purcell and Handel, Mozart and Haydn, the great choral tradition of Western Europe scattered in random piles across the fraying carpet. In one corner of the room Powerscourt thought he saw some Gilbert and Sullivan, a touch of the profane hiding among the sacred.

'Please forgive me, Lord Powerscourt,' said Michael Matthews, waving towards his floor, 'I'm in the middle of a tidying-up session. If you'd been half an hour later, all of this lot would have gone.'

'Don't worry at all,' said Powerscourt with a smile, 'there's always a lot of confusion when you're in the middle of a clear-out.'

'How can I help you, Lord Powerscourt?' said Matthews, ushering him to a small chair by the side of the piano.

'I believe Dr Blackstaff told you I am investigating a series of murders in Compton,' said Powerscourt.

'He certainly did,' said the young man. 'I pray we may never be afflicted with anything similar here in Wells.'

'Things in Compton at present, how should I put this, Mr Matthews, are rather delicate. We have not found the murderer, though I hope we shall do so soon. However strange it may sound, I must ask you to keep our conversation absolutely confidential. You have not seen me. We have not spoken. We did not meet.' Powerscourt knew he was sounding melodramatic, perhaps a little mad, but just one scribbled note from Wells to Compton might spark another round of murder.

The young man began to laugh, then stopped when he saw how serious was the face of his visitor.

'Secrets,' he said cheerfully. 'Have no fear, Lord Powerscourt. I shan't tell a soul about today. Now then,' he moved away from his mantelpiece and sat down by the piano, 'what is this piece of music you want to have identified? Perhaps you could hum it or sing it if you can remember it.'

Powerscourt hummed about six or seven bars. Matthews tapped them out on his piano with his right hand. Then he added an accompaniment with his left.

'Something like that, Lord Powerscourt?'

Powerscourt shook his head. 'The last three or four notes sound right, but not the beginning.'

'Try to remember exactly where you were when you heard this piece. Now close your eyes. Now try again.'

Powerscourt delivered another opening, slightly different from the first. Again the young man picked out the notes with his right hand.

'Just one more time, if you would, Lord Powerscourt. I think I've got it.'

Powerscourt closed his eyes again, remembering the noise coming to him across the Close from the choristers' house as he searched for Lady Lucy. This time the young man was delighted.

'Splendid, Lord Powerscourt, splendid. Not exactly the piece of choral music you would expect to hear floating across an English cathedral close.' Michael Matthews played a very brief introduction. Then he sang along with a powerful tenor voice.

> 'Credo in unum Deum
> Patrem omnipotentem, factorem caeli et terrae.'

I believe in one God the Father Almighty, creator of Heaven and earth, Powerscourt muttered to himself.

'You might think it's a musical version of one of the Anglican creeds, words virtually identical,' said Matthews, abandoning his singing but keeping the tune going on his piano. 'But wait for the great blast at the end.

> 'Et unam, sanctam, catholicam et apostolicam Ecclesiam.
> Confiteor unum baptisma in remissionem peccatorum.
> Et exspecto resurrectionem mortuorum,
> et vitam venturi saeculi. Amen.'

Michael Matthews played a virtuoso conclusion, a great descant swelling through the higher notes.

We believe in one holy catholic and apostolic church, Powerscourt translated as he went, we acknowledge one baptism for the forgiveness of sins and we look for the resurrection of the dead and the life of the world to come.

'The music you heard, Lord Powerscourt, is the Profession of Faith of the Catholic Liturgy, to be used on Sundays and holy days. When the congregations get to the line about one holy and apostolic and catholic church, they belt it out as if they were singing their own National Anthem. No, better than that, it's their equivalent of the Battle Hymn of the Republic.'

Powerscourt looked closely at Michael Matthews. Matthews didn't think he was at all surprised. As Powerscourt made his way out of the little house and back down the Vicars Close to Wells station, the assistant choirmaster stood at his window and watched him go. What on earth was going on down there in Compton? Why were the choir singing the music of a different faith? Ours not to reason why, he said to himself and sat down once more at his piano. The window was slightly open. Powerscourt could just hear the strains of 'Jesu Joy of Man's Desiring', played with great sadness, pursuing him down the street.

There was a telegraph message from William McKenzie waiting for Powerscourt on his return to Fairfield Park. It seemed to have taken rather a long time to reach Compton, despatched from the Central Telegraph Office in Piazza San Silvestro on Wednesday morning and only arriving at its destination on Friday afternoon. Maybe, said Powerscourt to himself, the wires were down somewhere along the route.

'Subject reached destination safely,' the message began, couched in the normal cryptic of McKenzie's despatches. 'Subject has spent his days in conclave with high officials of the parent organization.' Christ, thought Powerscourt, McKenzie could have been describing the activities of a bank manager rather than a priest in conspiratorial meetings with the College of Propaganda. 'Evenings in restaurants with prominent citizens dressed in strange colours?' What in God's name was a prominent citizen dressed in strange colours? Powerscourt asked himself. A member of the Swiss Guard charged with the protection of the Pontiff? A member of the Italian

Upper House – did they wander round the streets of Caesar and the Borgias looking like members of the British House of Lords? Was McKenzie's prey, Father Dominic Barberi, dining with one of the cardinals, the scarlet robes of the descendants of St Peter tucking into some Roman speciality like *carpaccio tiepido di pescatrice*, brill with raw beef, or *mignonettes alla Regina Victoria*, veal with pâté and an eight-cheese sauce? Then Powerscourt reached the most important part of the message. 'Subject and two colleagues returning London, arriving Monday night. Meeting would be beneficial.'

Powerscourt looked up and saw that Johnny Fitzgerald had come in and was reading the *Grafton Mercury* on a chair by the garden. There was a final sentence, straight from McKenzie's heart. 'Local food inedible. Much worse than Afghan.' Powerscourt smiled. The unfortunate McKenzie suffered, indeed he had suffered all the time Powerscourt had known him, from a weak stomach. It was his only failing. Powerscourt remembered him surviving six weeks of an Indian summer on a special diet of hard boiled eggs for breakfast, hard boiled eggs for lunch and yet more hard boiled eggs for supper. Johnny Fitzgerald always maintained that McKenzie only attained dietary peace in his native Scotland where he survived on home-baked scones and a regimen of lightly boiled fish with no sauce.

'William's been having trouble with the food in Rome, Johnny,' said Powerscourt.

'I'm not surprised,' said Johnny. 'He's a lost hermit, that William McKenzie, he'd be perfectly happy with bread and water for the rest of his life.'

There was another letter waiting for Powerscourt. 'Here we go, Johnny,' he said, 'I think this is a reply from the Lord Lieutenant. I don't hold out much hope here.'

'Read it out, Francis, why don't you. I've reached the Births Marriages and Deaths section of our friend Patrick's paper. I think I might get through another few hours of life without any more of that.'

'"Dear Powerscourt,"' the recipient read, walking up and down the room, '"thank you for your letter. I am most grateful to you for bringing your views to my attention."'

'Frosty start, Francis,' said Johnny. 'Don't think you're about to receive an open invitation to Lord Lieutenant Castle or wherever the bugger lives.'

'Here we go, Johnny, second paragraph. "I have played cricket with the Bishop of Compton. I have hunted with the Dean. Both of them and their senior colleagues have been frequent guests at my table. I have had the honour of receiving Communion from their hands and instruction and enlightenment from their sermons. Five out of my six daughters were baptized in their font and three of them were married at their altar."'

'Five out of six daughters, Francis? Is this the case of the son that got away?'

Powerscourt continued. '"I do not intend to insult the probity or the intelligence of either of these elders of the Church by laying your preposterous charges before them. I regard them as beneath contempt."'

'That sounds pretty clear to me, Francis,' said Johnny Fitzgerald, staring cheerfully at his friend. 'Don't think his Lord Lieutenancy agrees with you. Would that be a fair interpretation of the letter so far?'   .

'There's more, Johnny,' said Powerscourt, holding the top left-hand corner of the letter in his right hand as if it smelt. 'Third paragraph coming.'

'I reckon this is where he says you're out of your mind, Francis. Terribly sad really.'

'"Permit me to say – "'

'People always say that when they're about to be really unpleasant.'

'Really, Johnny,' said Powerscourt, 'I'm not at all happy with all these interruptions. You may have to go to the back of the class. "Permit me to say how perturbed I was to discover that such a distinguished public servant, with such an exemplary record of achievement and success, had come to a point where he was unable to distinguish between the wilder fantasies of his own imagination and the realities of the true facts of the situation. Believe me, Powerscourt, I have seen this kind of thing before. During my long service in India I saw how the great heat in Oudh or the Punjab could rot men's minds and rob them of their sanity. It is most unfortunate. I have known a good many promising officers afflicted in this fashion."'

'Pompous old bugger,' said Johnny Fitzgerald. 'Do they select these people because they're stupid?'

'The Lord Lieutenant, as I'm sure you know, Johnny,' said Powerscourt sternly, 'is the local representative in Compton of the King Emperor himself. So there.'

'Does the Lieutenant – he sounds much better like that, Francis, don't you think, – have any more words of wisdom? I suspect he's going to recommend you to some dreadful spa in Germany.'

'Last paragraph, Johnny, here we go. "I feel I would be derelict in the execution of my duties if I did not offer you some advice."'

'Here comes the bloody spa, Francis,' said Johnny Fitzgerald triumphantly.

'"The seaside resorts,"' Powerscourt wagged his finger at his friend, '"to the south of Compton are highly regarded as places of recovery and recuperation for those afflicted in mind and body. The sea air can help disperse the malevolent humours that infect the brain. Others speak of the beneficent influence of twenty-mile walks. I can recommend most highly the services of a near neighbour, Dr Blackstaff, while you are away from the care of your own man in London."'

'At least you've missed out on the cold baths, Francis. It could have been worse. And you've escaped the spa with the Germans in lederhosen.'

Powerscourt held up his hand again. 'Here comes the parting shot, Johnny. You'll like this bit.' Powerscourt turned his letter over. '"Finally, Powerscourt, let me say how saddened I was by the contents of your letter and the revelations within it about your state of mind. I wish you a speedy recovery. Yours et cetera et cetera et cetera."'

'Tremendous, Francis, tremendous!' Johnny Fitzgerald was laughing heartily by the window into the garden. 'Do you think the other two will be as good as that? I haven't given up hope of the spa yet, you know, Francis. There's still a chance.'

Powerscourt folded the letter up and put it back in its envelope. 'This will always be one of my dearest possessions, Johnny,' he said. 'I may have to make special dispensation for it in my will. The British Museum? The library of my old college in Cambridge? We shall see. You ask about the other two. I don't think they will be as bad as this one. The Archbishop's man may be slightly more polite. I suspect he's the only chance of a recommendation of Bad Godesberg or Marienbad as a place of recovery and recuperation, to quote the Lord Lieutenant's very own words. Schomberg McDonnell will be the most respectful, I'm sure.'

'So do we just wait and let this mass defection take place, Francis? There must be something we can do.'

'There is, Johnny. Tomorrow I have to go to London to meet

William. Perhaps I could buy him a square meal. Or perhaps not. I'll be back on Tuesday night. In the meantime could you do a couple of things for me?'

'Just as long as I don't have to talk to that bloody Lieutenant Lord person, Francis. Otherwise I'm at your disposal.'

'Could you ask Patrick Butler to find out from his future father-in-law the stationmaster if there are any special trains coming down to Compton for the celebrations? And if so when they are due to arrive and so on.'

'No problem,' said Johnny Fitzgerald cheerfully. 'And the other thing?'

'The other thing,' said Powerscourt, staring out into the garden, 'is more difficult. I want you to get hold of some explosives.'

22

London seemed very noisy to Powerscourt. In Compton ten or fifteen people almost constituted a crowd. Carriages rushing through the streets were rare. The inhabitants never seemed to be in a great hurry. But here the streets were packed with people, hordes of them rushing in and out of the underground railway stations, the carriages stretching back along the King's Road towards Sloane Square, moving at a snail's pace, the passengers inside seething with fury at the long delays in reaching their destinations. Even the birds seemed to be in a hurry.

Powerscourt dined alone at home. He expected William McKenzie to be late. He knew he would track his Italian visitors to their final destination before his rendezvous in Chelsea. It was half-past eleven when a weary Scotsman presented himself in the drawing room on the first floor of 25 Markham Square.

'William,' said Powerscourt, 'how very good to see you. And thank you very much for your mission.'

'I wish I could say it had been more successful, my lord,' said McKenzie, perching on the edge of a chair and pulling a small black notebook out of his pocket. 'Let me give you the main points of my report.'

He checked through a couple of pages of notes, all written, Powerscourt observed, in McKenzie's microscopic but always readable script.

'Subject travelled to Rome. Journey uneventful. I made my rendezvous with the translator and guide. Very talkative gentleman, my lord. Following the subject difficult because the guide would not hang back and follow me at a distance. Always wished to be by my side. Two much more visible than one. Subject stayed in the building belonging to the Congregation of

Propaganda, close to the Piazza di Spagna, a body composed of cardinals and others which manages the affairs of the Roman Catholic Church in Great Britain and Ireland. Subject only came out once, my lord. Dined in fashionable restaurant with a bishop and another prince of the Church, so my guide told me.'

'William, you poor man,' said Powerscourt, 'are you telling me that you kept watch on this building for two days and the man only came out once?'

'That is correct, my lord. I did learn a lot about the building, mind you. The College, attached to Propaganda,' McKenzie peered closely at his notes at this point, 'I wrote this bit down out of the guidebook, my lord, because I thought it would interest you, "was founded in 1627 by Urban VIII for the purpose of educating as missionaries, entirely free of charge, young foreigners from infidel or heretical countries, who might afterwards return and spread the Roman Catholic faith among their countrymen."'

'And the bloody place is nearly three hundred years old,' said Powerscourt, wondering if Propaganda had tried to pull off a coup like the one in Compton in the past. Rarely could they have been so close to triumph as they were now.

'Subject now returned to London, my lord, accompanied by bishop person and the other fellow, a rather fat gentleman, my lord, in the mould of Friar Tuck perhaps. All received great attention and tribute from the railway staff en route through Italy and France. Rather less on the passage between Dover and London. All three gone to Jesuits' house in Farm Street. Believe they intend to go to Compton tomorrow, my lord. I overheard conversation about purchase of tickets.'

'Are you telling me, William, that you spent all your time waiting around these Propaganda buildings? That you had no time to see any of the sights of Rome?'

'That is correct, my lord. I had hoped to visit the Colosseum where they killed the Christians all those years ago. I would have liked to be able to tell my aged mother about that. But it was not to be. Should I follow the gentlemen back to Compton, my lord?'

Powerscourt was imagining the Compton murderer at large in the Colosseum, despatching Protestants reluctant to convert with sword, spear or trident, rejoicing as his victims met their deaths, their blood pouring out into the sand.

'Sorry, William,' said Powerscourt. 'My mind had wandered off. I think you should go back to Compton with the religious gentlemen, just to make sure we don't lose sight of them.' He suddenly thought of them as Father, Son and Holy Ghost, though which was which he didn't know. He explained to McKenzie the plan to rededicate the cathedral to the Catholic faith on Easter Sunday, the secret attendances at Mass, the fact that the murder victims had almost certainly been part of the enterprise and then changed their minds. When Powerscourt finished McKenzie looked at him closely and said very softly, 'Forgive them, Lord, for they know not what they do.'

Powerscourt spent most of the journey back to Compton staring out of the window, his mind debating with itself. When was it legal to break the law? Under what circumstances would a man be justified in causing damage to property, and possibly to other human lives, in a higher cause? Was it his duty to infringe the laws of England so that other English laws might not be violated, or not violated in front of so many people? As the train curved round the tracks towards the south-west he found himself measuring angles, possible explosion points on the line where the damage could not be repaired for days. Heaven knew Johnny Fitzgerald and he had done enough of this in India. When Powerscourt reached the inevitable philosophical question of did the ends justify the means he gave up and thought of other things.

He thought of a place to take Lucy when all this was over. St Petersburg, he decided, a city built on the water, a city built facing Europe to change the culture of the Russian nobility, a city built as a titanic social experiment to see if architecture and geographical position could alter the mindset of a nation. The Winter Palace, he remembered, all those other vast palaces, some with so many rooms that their owners never visited them all during their entire lives, humble servants squatting in squalor in the attics while their masters dined on eight courses of French cuisine down below.

Johnny Fitzgerald was poring over a huge map of Compton and its railway lines laid out on the floor of the Fairfield Park drawing room when he reached home. Lady Lucy was sitting by the fire, still looking pale but happier than she had been when he left. Powerscourt hugged her cheerfully and looked down at Johnny's map.

'There's two letters for you on the mantelpiece, Francis,' Johnny said. 'They're both from London.'

'I see you've been busy with the railway lines, Johnny.'

'Well,' said Johnny, 'when you asked me to find out about the extra trains coming to Compton and so on and then you asked me to get some explosives, I could see the way your mind was working. If we could blow up the tracks and stop some of these extra people coming, maybe the damage wouldn't be so bad. Not all of the wine would have got out of the bottle, if you see what I mean. I've got some explosives, I've got the maps of the railway lines and I know that there are a lot of extra trains booked to come here. Most of them are going to arrive on Saturday afternoon. Every hotel, every lodging house for miles around is full, Francis. It may not be the right season, but in Compton this Easter, there's no room in the inn.'

'I don't think we can do it, Johnny,' said Powerscourt rather sadly. 'I don't mean that we couldn't blow up the railway, we've done plenty of that in our time. But I've been thinking a lot about this in the train on the way down.'

He went and stood by Lady Lucy's chair, his hand absent-mindedly stroking her hair as he spoke. 'Even if we did blow up the lines, we couldn't stop the news getting out. I'm sure the Catholic faction in the cathedral have laid their plans already for broadcasting the news. Maybe they're going to have special announcements of their triumph in every church and cathedral in the country. Maybe even in Rome itself the College of Propaganda will announce the downfall of a citadel of the heretic English. And, even if we gave warnings, some of them might not get through, or be misunderstood. I couldn't bear it if we were responsible for the deaths of innocent people whose only crime was setting out to attend Mass on Easter Sunday. I don't want to sound pompous, but I don't think we can set ourselves up as the solvers of crimes and mysteries and then rush out in the middle of the night and commit some crimes of our own.'

Powerscourt paused. He realized suddenly that if they had carried on, they would have had to place the explosives on Friday night. Good Friday, the darkest night in the Christian calendar, Christ carrying his cross to the place of the skull called Golgotha where they crucified him on a cross with the inscription Jesus of Nazareth, King of the Jews, the last drink of the sponge filled with vinegar, Jesus saying it is finished and giving up the ghost. And he and Johnny Fitzgerald riding round the Compton countryside in the dark, blowing up railway lines.

Powerscourt found that Lady Lucy's hand had left her lap and travelled up to unite with his own on her shoulder.

'Never mind, Francis,' said Johnny, 'we might be able to find a use for the explosives after all. I didn't think you would go ahead with it in the end.'

'Neither did I, Francis,' said Lady Lucy in rather a weak voice. 'I even offered to place a bet on it with Johnny but he wasn't having it.'

'Always nice to know that you can both work out what I'm going to do,' said Powerscourt with a smile. 'I'm not offering any prizes for guessing what I'm going to do now. I'm going to read these bloody letters.'

Johnny folded up his enormous map very neatly. Powerscourt observed that it said Property of the Stationmaster, Compton. Not to be removed. Anne Herbert's father must have been prevailed upon to lend one of his maps. Powerscourt wondered if he had been told why they wanted it.

'Archbishop of Canterbury here,' said Powerscourt, holding up his first letter, written on expensive-looking notepaper. '"Thank you for your letter . . . It has been my custom, ever since taking up my current position, to maintain the closest links and personal relationships with all the bishops and senior dignitaries of the Church of England."'

'It'd be pretty odd if the bugger ignored all his colleagues,' said Johnny Fitzgerald.

'"I have known Gervase Moreton for nearly twenty years,"' Powerscourt carried on, '"and I find it simply inconceivable that he should contemplate the actions you describe. Under normal circumstances I should simply have thrown your letter into the wastepaper basket. Letters from the mentally disturbed are one of the smaller crosses an archbishop has to bear. Owing to your distinguished record I have taken soundings in the diocese of Compton. I can assure you there is not one single piece of evidence to support your wild allegations.'

'Last paragraph coming,' said Powerscourt. '"I shall add you to the list of those for whom I pray on Tuesdays. Yours sincerely . . ."'

'Tuesdays, Francis? You're not in luck today I'm afraid. It's Thursday. You've got five days to wait. But think how much better you'll feel early next week.'

'Do you think he has a rota like we did in the Army, Johnny? Burglars on Mondays, lunatics on Tuesdays, thieves on

Wednesdays, blasphemers on Thursdays, fraudsters on Fridays, murderers on Saturdays, heretics and unbelievers on Sundays? I am rather looking forward to being prayed for, I must say. Along with all the other lunatics. Lucy, you must watch me very closely on Wednesday mornings to see if there are any signs of improvement.'

Lady Lucy smiled at him. 'You've got one letter left, Francis. Do you think there's any hope there?'

Powerscourt slit open his last envelope. 'Encouraging start,' he said. '"The Prime Minister has no doubt of the veracity of the proposition you outline in your letter . . ."' He skimmed through the next section. 'Few more sentences along the same lines. Damn! Damn! Damn!' Powerscourt glowered at the letter, 'I think we've had it. The Prime Minister has gone away for Easter and asked his colleagues to deal with the matter. "I'm afraid I have to report," says Private Secretary McDonnell, "that there is a lack of unity among the colleagues. The Home Secretary believes it to be a matter for the Church of England. As the Archbishop does not take it seriously, the Home Secretary proposes to ignore it. The government law officers believe it would be impossible to act before a crime has been committed. Even then they are uncertain which particular law or laws would be broken. The foremost authority on ecclesiastical legislation is on a walking tour of the Pyrenees at present and cannot be contacted. The Lord Chancellor believes it is a matter for the Judicial Committee of the Privy Council which cannot be summoned before the week after Easter. The Chancellor of the Exchequer, who has always taken a keen interest in religious questions and in everybody else's business, is of the opinion that it is for the two Archbishops and the senior bishops to resolve. In short, Lord Powerscourt, you have fallen between the cracks in the shaky edifice of Church and State. May I offer you my commiserations and express the hope that you can find some means of settling the business without further bloodshed. Schomberg McDonnell."'

Powerscourt folded his two letters very carefully and put them back in their envelopes. He smiled at Lady Lucy.

'It's like that line in the *Messiah*, Francis,' she said, 'you're the voice of one crying in the wilderness.'

'Don't think I'd like to be John the Baptist very much, Lucy,' said Powerscourt, 'my head served up on a platter in front of Salome like a roasted ham. Mind you, I should get some better prayers from the Archbishop. I might have to move from Tuesdays to a different day.'

'It's like the poet says, Francis,' said Johnny, moving towards the cupboard with the drinks, 'a prophet is not without honour save in his own country.'

Powerscourt looked at him doubtfully. 'I don't think that's a poet, Johnny. That's St Matthew's Gospel, chapter thirteen if I remember right. And the unfortunate Christ had to walk on the water in the next chapter to convince the unbelievers. I don't think I'm up to that either. But that's what we need, a miracle. A miracle in Compton. None of the authorities are going to lift a finger. Maybe we should blow up the railway lines after all. We're on our own. Nobody can stop them now.'

23

All through Friday and Saturday Powerscourt and Johnny Fitzgerald kept a discreet watch on the comings and goings round the Cathedral Close. Sometimes they watched from Anne Herbert's upper window, regular supplies of tea and home-made cake fortifying them in their vigil. Sometimes one of them would walk round the streets, the cathedral itself standing impassive as it waited for the Resurrection.

On both days the pattern was the same. A quartet of clergy would set off from the Archdeacon's house shortly after nine o'clock, heading at a sedate pace towards the Bishop's Palace, the Archdeacon himself accompanied by Father Barberi and the two gentlemen from Rome. Then there would be a gap. Between ten and ten thirty a steady trickle of members of the Chapter and the choir would present themselves at the Bishop's front door. About half an hour later they would emerge, looking rather happier than when they had gone in. Sometimes Patrick Butler would join Powerscourt and Fitzgerald, taking careful notes of the times of entry and departure of all the participants.

'What a story,' the young man said cheerfully to Powerscourt on the Friday afternoon. 'I think it's the biggest story I've ever come across. Maybe I can make my name with the Saga of Compton, its murders, its conversions, like William Howard Russell did in the Crimea for *The Times*. Then Anne and I could be rich and move to London!'

Powerscourt smiled at the young editor. 'Do you know what's going on with all this religious traffic?' he asked. 'I mean, I think I can guess but I'm not sure.'

'I've been reading up on all this stuff, Lord Powerscourt. You have to in my business if you've got the time. Very discreetly, of course. I haven't asked anybody in the Close about it. But I think that all the members of the Chapter who weren't already Catholics are being received into the faith. Maybe the Archdeacon's friends are doing them in relays. And they may also be ordaining them as Catholic priests and deacons at the same time. Mass conversion, mass ordination, if you ask me.'

And with that the young man returned to his offices, dreams of fame and glory floating through his brain. Powerscourt was thinking of betrayal, the betrayal by Judas that led to the crucifixion on this day nearly two thousand years before, the betrayal of their religion by all these Anglican priests in the name of a higher calling. He didn't think it was going to be a very good Friday for Compton.

On the Saturday evening Powerscourt and Lady Lucy and Johnny Fitzgerald assembled at Anne Herbert's house on the edge of the Close. There were notices all over the town advertising the great bonfire due to take place on the Green late that Saturday night. Anne Herbert reported that her father, normally a phlegmatic and reserved individual, had been astonished at the number of people arriving at his station. The number of extra trains was greater than he had ever seen. Every railway worker for miles around was on duty to ensure safe passage for the visitors.

At seven o'clock a team of workmen began building the bonfire that was to be the centrepiece of the night's attractions. Powerscourt and Patrick Butler watched, fascinated, as cart after cart and wagon after wagon drew up alongside the site.

'Christ, Patrick,' said Powerscourt, 'it's going to be enormous.'

'They say in the town,' Patrick Butler replied, 'that it's going be to be the biggest bonfire Compton has ever seen. The wood was ordered from all over the county weeks ago.'

'I wonder how many heretics you could burn on it when it's finished,' said Powerscourt. 'I doubt it even Bloody Mary herself could have provided enough bodies for it.'

'Careful how you speak of the Catholic Queen in these parts at this time, Lord Powerscourt. Tomorrow you might be struck down or popped on to the pyre yourself for such blasphemy.'

Powerscourt was thinking about Arthur Rudd, burnt on the spit in the kitchen of the Vicars Hall. He thought of the monk of Compton, burnt to the west of this Cathedral Close in 1538. He had passed a small memorial to his life and death set into a wall during his perambulations round the Close the day before.

From time to time Patrick Butler would dash off into the town or to inspect the building of the bonfire at first hand.

'He's like a puppy, really,' said Anne Herbert affectionately, 'he just can't sit still. He has to be running about all the time. Do you think he'll calm down later on, Lady Powerscourt?'

Lady Lucy laughed. 'I'm not sure he will, you know. He wouldn't be Patrick if he wasn't like that, would he?'

Patrick Butler reported that another pair of carts were approaching the bonfire, bringing not wood but candles. He also reported that the streets of the city were virtually impassable. Shortly after nine o'clock the workmen began erecting a monstrous scaffold, whose peak was almost as high as the top of the bonfire itself. 'That's for the Archdeacon to address the crowd,' said Patrick. 'God knows if we're going to get a sermon. I do hope not.'

Powerscourt thought the platform was going to be high enough for Lucifer himself, come to Compton to preside over the flames of hell. At nine thirty the crowd closest to the bonfire fell silent. The silence spread slowly out across the Green until even the tavern opposite the west front, scene of much rowdy merriment throughout the evening, fell silent. It was now completely dark, the spectators by the fire faint shadows from Powerscourt's vantage point. Four men with blazing torches stood at the corners of the pyre. As if acting on a common signal they touched their flares to the faggots. Then they moved slowly and deliberately round the bonfire until the bottom section was a circle of light in the darkness. Sparks began to fly upwards and outwards, forcing the crowds back. Still the Archdeacon did not mount his scaffold. Powerscourt wondered what would have happened if it had rained. Maybe on this day the Lord their God delivered them the weather they needed.

It was hard to tell at first where the singing came from. Powerscourt stared forwards into the night. He could certainly hear singing, maybe a choir. He could also hear the sound of marching feet. Then he saw it, a great column of men and women coming down Vicars Close and passing not into the cathedral but along the Green and out towards one side of the bonfire. The choir, Powerscourt realized, was hidden in the body of the column, just as Napoleon's drummer boys were hidden among the Emperor's armies advancing to secure the destruction of their enemies.

'Faith of our fathers, living still,' they sang,

'In spite of dungeon, fire and sword:
O how our hearts beat high with joy
Whenever we hear that glorious Word!'

As the column, at least a hundred and fifty strong, Powerscourt thought, reached the light of the flames he saw that at the front were two men bearing an enormous banner. It showed a bleeding heart above a chalice in the centre. At the four corners were the pierced hands and feet of the crucified Christ.

'What on earth is that, Francis?' asked Lady Lucy, standing very close to her husband and feeling just a little frightened.

'It's the banner of the Five Wounds of Christ, my love. In the Pilgrimage of Grace, the northern revolt against a Protestant England in 1536, it was the chief emblem of the rebels.'

Still the Archdeacon did not climb to his position above the fire. Powerscourt wondered where he was. Perhaps he was in the cathedral, at prayer before his great ordeal. For this was a huge crowd, sections of it maybe rather drunk. It could be difficult to contain, much more difficult than preaching a sermon to the converted.

Then they heard another burst of singing, coming from the other side of the Green. Another column, at least as long as the one from Vicars Close, was approaching the bonfire from the opposite side to the first one. In the vanguard two men were carrying an enormous banner of the Virgin enthroned in glory. They were singing the second verse of the same hymn. People were now moving quickly through the crowd, circulating handbills with the words printed on them so that those unfamiliar with it could sing along.

'Faith of our fathers we will strive
To win all nations unto Thee:
And through the truth that comes from God
We all shall then be truly free.'

Sections of the crowd were now able to join hesitantly in the refrain.

'Faith of our fathers, holy faith!
We will be true to thee till death.'

275

The second column advanced across the Green and stood shoulder to shoulder with their colleagues who had marched down Vicars Close. Still the Archdeacon held his peace. The next column was coming from behind the cathedral. Powerscourt realized that they were advancing from all four points of the compass. The final column would come from behind them and pass right in front of Anne Herbert's front door. The third column was advancing behind no fewer than five banners. All of them showed the Five Wounds of Christ. They too joined the semicircle around the bonfire. Stewards were moving through the crowd again, handing out candles to the faithful. They started on the side nearest the Vicars Close and a ripple of lights winked up towards the night sky. Fathers with small children on their shoulders peered nervously upwards in case the candle dropped on their heads. And here Powerscourt saw just how carefully the evening had been organized. For the children's candles were tiny, a fraction of the size of those handed out to the adults. They wouldn't have looked out of place on a birthday cake.

Then they heard the last column. Powerscourt and his party were all out in the front garden by now, staring as if hypnotized at the bonfire. They too had candles in their hands. The hymn was growing louder. Peering into the dark behind the Green Powerscourt saw another banner of the Five Wounds of Christ at the head of the procession. This one had the letters IHS, an abbreviated form of the Greek word for Jesus at the top.

> 'Faith of our fathers, we will love,
> Both friend and foe in all our strife . . .'

The pilgrims were passing Anne Herbert's front door, advancing through a waving sea of candles towards the bonfire. Powerscourt doubted if much love had been shown to friend and foe in all the strife in Compton. Three dead bodies was not the greatest tribute to brotherly love.

> 'And preach thee too, as love knows how,
> By kindly words and virtuous life.'

The column had been intended to continue up the road and then turn left further up where the path led to the west front of the minster. But something, maybe the lights, maybe the noise, made them swing left and head straight across the Green. The crowd parted before them like the waters of the Red Sea, candles making sudden darts to the left and right. As this final column arrived at the bonfire the other three already there joined in the last verse.

> 'Faith of our fathers, Mary's prayers
> Shall win our country back to thee
> And through the truth that comes from God   · ·
> England shall then indeed be free.'

The chorus was deafening. Most of the crowd were holding their candles high above their heads. The fire was burning fiercely. Some of the banners of the Five Wounds of Christ had been stuck in the ground in front of the bonfire, swaying slightly in the light breeze.

> 'Faith of our fathers, holy faith!
> We will be true to thee till death.'

Then the trumpet sounded. At first nobody could see where the noise was coming from. Then a forest of candles pointed up to the parapet above the west front. Almost lost among the statues of saints and bishops, of Christ enthroned in glory, a young man played one short fanfare. 'Christ, Francis,' muttered Johnny Fitzgerald, 'are we going to have the four horsemen of the apocalypse riding across the sky in a minute?'

'You never know, Johnny, maybe it's the name and number of the beast, the whole book of Revelations coming next.'

The minster door opened. Four people bearing enormous candles escorted the Archdeacon to the scaffold. He mounted very slowly. Powerscourt saw that he was wearing the regalia of a Jesuit priest. Presumably these were the clothes that had travelled to Melbury Clinton with him on his furtive and clandestine missions to celebrate Mass. At last he reached the top. Powerscourt noticed that one of his companions, carrying a large bag, had accompanied him and placed the receptacle on a tall table beside him. Really, Powerscourt thought, as the acolyte retreated towards ground level, these people leave nothing to chance. The Archdeacon would not have to grope about at his feet for whatever religious rabbit he wished to pull out of the bag. It was ready by his right hand. They leave nothing to chance. Maybe somebody should ask them to organize Edward the Seventh's Coronation. The Archdeacon looked very slowly at the great throng beneath him. The crowd was inching closer and closer to the bonfire. He raised his hand very slowly and made the sign of the cross. Then he spoke.

'*In nomine patris et filii et spiritus sancti, Amen.*'

He paused again. There was an enormous outbreak of cheering. Powerscourt wondered how many of this crowd came from Compton and how many had come in the special trains.

The Archdeacon raised his hand for silence. 'Brothers and Sisters in Christ,' he went on, 'we are gathered here in this time and place to mark a very special anniversary.' Powerscourt realized why the Archdeacon had been chosen for this particular assignment. He had an extremely powerful voice which carried easily right to the back of the Cathedral Green.

'Tomorrow,' he continued, turning slowly so that each section of the crowd could see him in turn, 'is the one thousandth anniversary of this cathedral as a place of Christian worship.'

There were huge cheers from the crowd. Many of them punched their candles in the air.

'For nearly six hundred and fifty years the abbey belonged in the bosom of Mother Church, a dutiful servant of Rome.'

Again a mighty roar from the crowd. Many of them were crossing themselves. One or two were kneeling on the ground, eyes closed in prayer.

'And then, due to the political necessities of the King of England, this church was ripped from its rightful home.'

The men in the first cohort to reach the bonfire had pulled the banner of the Five Wounds of Christ out of the ground and were waving it aloft.

'Tomorrow,' the Archdeacon went on, his finger stabbing into the night, 'we are going to right that wrong. Tomorrow we are going to restore this church to its rightful home in the bosom of the Holy and Apostolic Church! Tomorrow we are going to rededicate this building as a place of Catholic worship! Tomorrow we are going to make the Cathedral of Compton Catholic once again! Tomorrow we shall celebrate Mass here for the first time in three hundred and sixty years!'

At each tomorrow he had pointed dramatically at the minster, the building still dark among the ocean of candles waving at varying heights on Cathedral Green.

'I have here,' the Archdeacon pulled a heavy-looking package from his bag, 'a gift for the cathedral from the Holy Father himself!'

Very slowly the Archdeacon took off the cloth that surrounded the bounty from the Pope.

'This is an altar stone, a slab that contains the relics of a saint and martyr who gave his life that his country might come back to the true religion!'

The crowd fell silent. Powerscourt wondered if it was a relic of Sir Thomas More.

'Compton will be graced,' the Archdeacon went on, 'with a relic of one of the most illustrious servants of the Church in England. Edmund Campion!'

He waved the slab in the air. There were gasps from the crowd. Powerscourt wondered how many of them knew who Edmund Campion was. He rather suspected that most of them did.

'At this time of renewal, of rebirth, of Resurrection, it is fitting that we should make a symbolic rupture with the past that deprived England of its true faith and Compton of its true religion! I have here some of the heretical Acts of Parliament that drove an unwilling Compton into the arms of heresy!'

The Archdeacon fished about in his bag once more and produced an ancient scroll, the paper on the front yellow with age.

'The Act of Annates of 1532 which stole from the Pope the revenue due to him from the bishops of England!'

The Archdeacon held it aloft, turning slowly so that all sections of the crowd could see it properly. Then he hurled it on to the fire. There was a quiet splutter at first, then a brief blaze of light as the Act was turned to ashes. For a second or two the crowd were completely silent. Then there was an enormous cheer.

The Archdeacon was back in his bag again. 'The Act in Restraint of Appeals of 1533 which ratified the sovereignty and independence of the Church of England!' Another vital piece of Reformation legislation was cast into the flames of hell. There was another burst of applause as the act caught fire.

'The Second Act of Annates of 1534 which proclaimed the heresy that the King and not the Pope selected the bishops of the Church!'

Again the Archdeacon hurled the scroll into the bonfire. The crowd had found a word they could chant now. Shouts of Heresy! Heresy! rang around Cathedral Green.

Now he was bringing laws out two at a time. The Archdeacon held two acts aloft, inciting the crowd with the cry of 'Further heresy! The Act of Succession of 1534 which pronounced Henry the Eighth's marriage to Catherine of Aragon null and void! Further heresy! The Act of Supremacy of 1534 which proclaimed that Henry was the only supreme head of the Church of England!'

The Archdeacon held the second act high above his head. 'This was the Act that led to the death of saint and martyr Sir Thomas More!'

Then he threw the two Acts on to the pyre to join the earlier cornerstones of Henry's Reformation. A great chant of Heresy! Heresy! Heresy! rang out among the crowd. Powerscourt wondered if they might get out of control. Lady Lucy was holding on to him very tightly. But the Archdeacon wasn't finished yet. He pulled another ancient scroll out of his bag.

'Yet further heresy!' he called out to the crowd. 'The Act for the Dissolution of the Smaller Monasteries of 1536! The Act that destroyed hundreds of faithful Christian houses, devoted to the service of their communities and to the worship of God! To the flames with it!'

Again he cast it into the fire. This time the Act stuck at the very top of the pyre. For a moment or two nothing happened. The crowd held their breath. Was this a sign from God? Was this one not going to burn? Then there was a loud whoosh as the flames took hold. Once more the shout of Heresy! Heresy!, sounding rather like a battle cry now, rose above Cathedral Green.

The Archdeacon had one Act left. He held it aloft and turned slowly on his scaffold so that the entire throng could have a chance to see it.

'And this!' he shouted, waving it in the air. 'This is the Act that saw the dissolution of our own abbey here in Compton! The Act for the Dissolution of the Greater Monasteries of 1538! This was the Act that tore the people of Compton from their mother church!' Still he held it high above his head. The crowd stared, mesmerized. 'Let it share, in part . . .' The Archdeacon was at full volume now. Powerscourt wondered briefly if his voice was carrying as far as Fairfield Park. Or heaven itself. 'Let it share, in part,' the Archdeacon repeated himself for greater emphasis, 'the fate of the blessed saints and martyrs who gave their lives to God in opposing it.' He brought it down to chest level and ripped the Act in two. 'Those martyrs were hung drawn and quartered, their bodies cut into four pieces.' He ripped the Act into four. 'This dismembered Act, cut into four pieces, I now commit to the fire!' The Archdeacon knelt down and placed each part separately into a flaming section of the bonfire. He rose to his feet once more. An enormous cheer erupted from the crowd, their candles held aloft, their eyes fixed on four little scraps of paper that had once been yellow and were now turning into wafer thin sections of black, then crumbling into ash.

'Francis,' said Johnny Fitzgerald, nudging him gently in the ribs, 'do you think those Acts were the real thing? Or did he just pick up a few bits of aged paper in an old bookshop?'

'They might have come from Rome for all I know, Johnny,' said Powerscourt. 'I'm sure Propaganda could rustle you up a forgery or two if you asked them nicely.'

The crowd were still cheering. Powerscourt wondered how the Archdeacon was going to bring them down from their ecstasy. He noticed that it was very close to midnight. He saw too that people were on the move. A new procession was forming with all the banners of the Five Wounds of Christ at the front. Then the four choirs that had sung in the marches to the bonfire swung into line behind them. They moved off into a new position in front of the cathedral doors.

Still the crowd cheered. Loud shouts of Heresy! Heresy! rang out towards the darkened minster. The candles were still flickering brightly all across Cathedral Green. The Archdeacon was holding both arms aloft, turning very slowly through three hundred and sixty degrees. He looked, Powerscourt thought, like one of those Old Testament prophets appealing for calm among the unruly Israelites as they hankered after the golden calf or graven images rather than the God of their fathers. Gradually silence returned. All eyes were on the tall figure on top of his scaffold. Only when total silence had been restored did he speak. And then he astounded every single person at the scene.

'Please extinguish all candles,' he said. There were gasps of astonishment. People had become attached to their candles, seeing them by now as friends and companions on this very special night. Powerscourt saw that the Archdeacon's shock troops, the choirs and the bodies who had marched together to the fire obeyed without question. Maybe that's Catholic discipline, he suggested to himself. Then he corrected himself. Jesuit discipline. With mutterings of regret and a great deal of blowing all the candles went out. There was not a single light to be seen across Cathedral Green. It was five minutes to midnight.

The Archdeacon began to address the faithful once again. 'On this day, of all days, at this time so close to midnight and Easter Sunday,' he said, 'we value the dark. The cathedral is dark. Christ's tomb, the sepulchre where he lies is dark. The darkness is the darkness of sin, of error, waiting for redemption from the light of Christ's Resurrection. The Gospel of St Mark: "And very early in the morning the first day of the week, they came unto the sepulchre at the rising of the sun. And they said among themselves, Who shall roll away the stone from the door of the sepulchre?"' Heads were bowed everywhere. The Archdeacon continued: '"And when they looked, they saw that the stone was rolled away for it was great. And entering into the sepulchre they saw a young man sitting on the right side and he saith unto them: Ye seek Jesus of Nazareth, which was crucified: he is not here: he is risen."'

The Archdeacon crossed himself. So did most of the crowd.

'On the last stroke of midnight,' the Archdeacon's voice was beginning to show signs of its labours during the night. It cracked ever so slightly on the word midnight, 'it will be Easter Sunday. I invite you all to take your candles into the church and leave them there. Stewards will show you the way. The paschal candles are by the door for you to relight your own. The light in the church will be the light of Christ's glory. The light in the church will be the symbol of the church's victory over its enemies.' Powerscourt wondered who he meant. Luther? Calvin? Thomas Cromwell, the architect of the Dissolution of the Monasteries? Henry the Eighth? 'People of Compton,' the Archdeacon held his arms aloft for the last time, 'I commend to you the words of the prophet Isaiah: the people that walked in darkness have seen a great light; they that dwell in the land of the shadow of death, upon them hath the light shined.'

The Archdeacon paused. *'Dominus vobiscum.'*

There was nearly a minute of almost total silence. Some of the choirs were trying to clear their throats. Some of the crowd were retrieving their candles from the ground. Then the trumpet sounded once again, the young man on top of the west front enjoying his second moment of glory. As the last note died away, the Cathedral clock began to toll the hour of midnight. Great Tom, cast in Bristol in 1258, who had spoken every day for centuries, gave forth once more. This was his six hundred and forty-third Easter Sunday. One, two, three. People began to shuffle forward from the back. The Archdeacon was still aloft on his scaffold, waving graciously to the people who passed beneath. Four, five, six. Powerscourt was holding Lady Lucy very tight, hoping she wasn't too cold. Patrick Butler had disappeared on another of his forays into the crowd. Seven, eight, nine. Powerscourt wondered if the Lord Lieutenant had abandoned his port to come into Compton for the bonfire. He tried to remember who the Archbishop of Canterbury prayed for on Sundays. Murderers? Heretics? Ten, eleven, twelve.

The great doors of the cathedral swung open. The inside was completely dark but at the door two stewards were holding out the paschal candles, large enough and broad enough to rekindle all those which had burned so brightly on Cathedral Green. The choirs processed slowly through the doors, preceded by men carrying the banners of The Five Wounds of Christ, and made their way up the nave towards the stalls. They were singing from the Resurrection section of the *Messiah*: 'Lift up your heads, O ye gates, and be ye lift up, ye everlasting doors and the King of Glory shall come in.'

Sconces to hold the candles had been placed all over the cathedral, in the aisles and the ambulatories, on the great pillars of the nave, in the north and south transepts, in the presbytery and the choir. Great empty stacks were waiting in the Lady Chapel and the side chapels to receive the surplus. Two orderly queues had formed outside the doors, shuffling forward to cast their light into the darkness.

'Who is the King of Glory? Who is the King of Glory?'

Patrick Butler reappeared as suddenly as he had vanished. He took Anne Herbert by the hand and led her off towards the cathedral, both of them clutching their candles. Powerscourt thought suddenly that they might prefer to be alone but he did make one request before they left.

'Could you see if you can find Chief Inspector Yates for me, Patrick? He must be about somewhere. I'd very much like to speak to him.'

The candles were beginning to have an impact now. The first arrivals were all instructed to leave theirs at the bottom of the nave. The lower section of the minster became incandescent with candles that flickered, candles that burned straight up, candles that burnt quickly, candles that looked as though they would burn for ever. It was a glacier of light, inching its way up the cathedral as the pilgrims left their tribute.

'Who is the King of Glory? The Lord, strong and mighty, the Lord mighty in battle.'

'You must be feeling very annoyed, Francis,' said Lady Lucy. 'You told everybody this was going to happen and it has.'

'Well, there's one consolation, Lucy,' said Powerscourt. 'You always believed in me. I can't tell you what a help that has been. Come, we'd better bring our candles. I think I'd feel incomplete if we didn't.'

The Archdeacon had finally come down from his scaffold. He inspected the remains of the bonfire carefully, as if trying to make sure all the Acts had been properly consumed. Inside the glacier of light had reached the top of the nave. The pillars and the soaring tracery were bathed in a golden light, glowing and glimmering as they had seldom glowed before in all their long history.

'Lift up your heads, O ye gates, and be ye lift up, ye everlasting doors, and the King of Glory shall come in.'

Patrick Butler found Powerscourt and Johnny and Lady Lucy very near the front of the queue. The editor of the *Grafton Mercury* was more than usually excited. 'Lord Powerscourt,' he said, panting slightly, 'I've been making inquiries as to where all these people came from. They've come from all over southern England, London, Bristol, Reading, Southampton. And they've all known about it for months. The thing's been organized like a military operation. The local Compton people think they've been invaded. They've all gone home. They're just going to wait until things quieten down.'

'Have you had time, Patrick,' said Lady Lucy in her sweetest voice, 'to think of a headline for tonight's proceedings?' Lady Lucy had grown rather attached to Patrick's headlines.

'Well,' said the young man, drawing Anne Herbert even closer to him, 'I've known what the headline should be for some time, but I'm not sure all my readers will understand it.'

'Share it with us, Patrick,' Lady Lucy smiled, 'we'll do our best to grasp it.'

Patrick looked sheepish all of a sudden. 'You're teasing me,' he said. 'I shan't tell you about my headline at all. You'll never get to hear about the Bonfire of the Vanities.'

'Who is the King of Glory? Who is the King of Glory? The Lord of Hosts, he is the King of Glory.'

Powerscourt was dazzled as he and his companions finally entered the cathedral, their candles rekindled by the paschal candle at the door. The glacier had reached the bottom of the choir. Looking back down the nave he thought he had seldom seen anything so beautiful. He transposed Wordsworth's daffodils into the candles of Compton in his mind.

Continuous as the stars that shine
And twinkle on the Milky Way
They stretched in never ending line
Across the margin of a bay:
Ten thousand saw I at a glance
Tossing their heads in sprightly dance.

Powerscourt placed his candle on a sconce at the top of the choir, Lady Lucy's behind it, Johnny's nestling very close to a wooden angel with a harp. The wounds of Christ on the banners were gleaming in the light. The choir were belting out Handel's most famous Chorus.

'Hallelujah! Hallelujah! For the Lord God omnipotent reigneth.'

The queues were still there as they left, shorter now, but still patient, snaking their way towards the west front. An extremely excited Patrick Butler was waiting for them.

'Lord Powerscourt, you must all come at once! I found Chief Inspector Yates with the Chief Constable. They've been looking for you, my lord. They should be in Anne's house by now. I didn't think you'd want to talk to them anywhere near the cathedral.'

Powerscourt remembered meeting the Chief Constable very early in this investigation. He had seemed a most capable individual then, sitting in the Dean's front room, discussing the murder of Arthur Rudd. Now he was distraught.

'Powerscourt, Lady Powerscourt, Lord Fitzgerald, please forgive me for the lateness of this visit. I would welcome some advice. Chief Inspector Yates informed me of your suspicions some time ago, Powerscourt. I wasn't sure whether to believe your theories or not, and it is difficult to take action when nothing has been done. But now I am convinced these people are going to rededicate the cathedral to the Catholic faith tomorrow. The Archdeacon said so. Even then I don't think I have the power to act until something has actually happened.'

'Do you think you can arrest them?' said Powerscourt.

'That's just one of my worries, Powerscourt. I'd have to arrest the Bishop, the Dean and the entire Chapter. I'm not sure we have enough cells to hold them all here in Compton. We'd have to throw out the current incumbents, two burglars, one suspected murderer and a couple of horse thieves. I don't think that would go down too well with the citizens.'

'Why don't you put them under house arrest?' said Powerscourt.

'Confine them all to their own quarters. Lock up the bloody cathedral for the time being.'

The Chief Constable smiled. 'I've thought of that. But I don't have the manpower to keep them all confined to their quarters. That's my other worry, you see. You all saw what that crowd was like on the Green this evening. They could cause a great deal of trouble. They might even decide to storm the jail if they thought their people were inside.'

'Are you saying, Chief Constable,' asked Powerscourt, 'that as things stand, you will be unable to take any action in defence of the laws of this country tomorrow?'

'I'm afraid that is the case,' the Chief Constable replied, looking even more miserable as he said it.

Silence fell in Anne Herbert's little drawing room. Outside they could still hear faint noises of singing. It was Johnny Fitzgerald who spoke first.

'Francis,' he said, 'you will recall that I did some reconnaissance into the military in the locality?'

Powerscourt nodded. That would have to do with Johnny's acquisition of explosives, not a subject he wished to go into in present company.

'Well,' Johnny went on, 'what the Chief Constable needs are reinforcements. Soldiers can be used like policemen, can't they? There's a crowd of infantry about twenty miles from here. I don't think they'd be able to get here in time. But there's cavalry five miles further away. I'm sure they could be persuaded to come to the rescue. They always like arriving at the last possible minute.'

'My dear Lord Fitzgerald,' said the Chief Constable, 'your suggestion is admirable. But I fail to see how they could reach here in time.'

'That's easy,' said Johnny, 'we just get go and get them, Francis and I.'

'But it's nearly two o'clock in the morning. Even if you set out at first light they couldn't get here in time.'

'Chief Constable,' said Powerscourt, sensing that Johnny was about to get irritated, 'what Johnny means is that we leave now. Once we can get changed and on to our horses.'

'God bless my soul,' said the Chief Constable.

'We will meet with you or your representatives outside the cathedral during Mass tomorrow morning,' said Powerscourt. 'With or without the cavalry.'

While he waited for Lucy to collect her things before the return to Fairfield Park and the horses, Powerscourt went to have a final look at the cathedral. The last pilgrims were making their way inside. Even at a distance it glowed magnificently, the light from hundreds and hundreds of candles streaming out of the doors. The choir were nearly finished.

'And he shall reign for ever and ever. Hallelujah! Hallelujah! King of Kings and Lord of Lords. Hallelujah!'

Powerscourt bumped into the Archdeacon on his way back.

'Shall we be seeing you at Mass tomorrow, Lord Powerscourt?' asked the Archdeacon.

'You might, Archdeacon,' said Powerscourt cheerfully, 'you very well might.'

24

By four o'clock in the morning Powerscourt and Johnny Fitzgerald were nearly halfway to the cavalry camp at Bampton. It was a clear night with a silver crescent of a moon. The road took them past a number of villages sleeping peacefully under the stars.

Powerscourt was thinking about the murderer. Chief Inspector Yates had told him as they left Anne Herbert's house that the final checks had been carried out on the movements and the alibi of the butcher Fraser. The police were convinced the man was totally innocent of the murder of Edward Gillespie. And all their inquiries among the murky undergrowth of moneylenders in Bristol and Exeter who might have had dealings with Arthur Rudd had been fruitless. The murderer must reside inside the great circle Powerscourt had drawn around the Cathedral Close in his notebook weeks before. But which of them was it? The Bishop with his service record in the Guards? The Dean with his passion for efficiency that would have been disturbed by defectors who changed their minds? The Archdeacon with that passion for the faith he had demonstrated so eloquently up there on his scaffold the night before? The choirmaster who had threatened to expel Lady Lucy from his choir? The mysterious member of Civitas Dei, Father Barberi, regular visitor to Compton, London and the College of Propaganda in Rome? Five of them, Powerscourt thought, three murders, two attempted murders, himself and Lady Lucy, to their name. Maybe they hadn't finished yet. Maybe it would take one more murder before the killer was unmasked.

'What do you know about these cavalrymen, Johnny?' said Powerscourt, panting slightly as the horses moved uphill. 'Did you borrow the explosives from them?'

'I got the explosives from the infantry over at Parkfield. I'd met one of the officers before. The cavalry are part of the Compton Horse. The commanding officer is a man called Wheeler, Colonel Wheeler.'

Two miles further on, Powerscourt signalled Johnny off the road. They moved into a clump of trees by the side. Powerscourt peered back the way they had come. 'Listen, Johnny,' he whispered, 'can you hear anything? I've thought for some time that someone was following us.' They waited for a full five minutes, straining to catch the sound of another horseman on the road at this time of night. All they heard was the wind sighing through the trees and various small animals scuttling around in the field behind them.

'Would you like me to go back, Francis, and see what I can find?' Johnny Fitzgerald was always eager for action. Powerscourt shook his head. They could have been spotted conversing with the Chief Constable in Anne Herbert's house. They could have been followed back to Fairfield Park and then on to the road. For months, for years, this murderer had been plotting and killing to secure this day when the cathedral would be rededicated to the Catholic faith. If it took a midnight ride and another couple of dead bodies to keep that secure Powerscourt had no doubt that the murderer would carry on with his deadly campaign. Still they heard nothing.

'Let's just give it a couple of minutes more,' Powerscourt muttered, advancing to the very edge of the trees to stare back at the road. A disturbed owl hooted angrily in protest. Johnny was looking at his watch, doing mental calculations about how long it would be before they reached Bampton and roused the cavalry. Another owl sounded off in the distance, back the way they had come. That seemed to make up Powerscourt's mind. He gestured them back on to the road once more.

Less than a mile from Bampton disaster struck. Johnny Fitzgerald's horse, which had carried him steadily all through their journey, suddenly stopped. Its legs gave way and it sank slowly to the ground. Johnny looked at it closely. 'Damn! I don't know what's the matter with the poor animal, Francis,' he said, 'I think she's had it for the time being. You'd better go on alone. I'll wait till she's better. And I was just thinking about a proper breakfast with those cavalrymen. They always like to start the day with a decent spread.'

Powerscourt too peered closely at the horse. He would have been the first to admit that his knowledge of the workings of horses was limited. 'You can't stop here, Johnny. It's out of the question. Leave her here and hop up behind me. We'll ask the cavalry if they can send somebody out to bring her in for repairs.'

Shortly after half-past seven, under a pale blue sky flecked with pink at the eastern corner, a weary Powerscourt and Fitzgerald presented themselves to the sentry on duty at the barracks.

'Colonel Wheeler is in the officers' mess, sir,' he said to Powerscourt, 'Please come with me.'

Military architecture had never been one of England's glories, Powerscourt reflected, as they were led across a dreary parade ground. Around it were nondescript military constructions, the cheapest the War Office could get away with, and handsome stabling for the horses off to one side. It seemed that the horses had better accommodation than the humans.

'Colonel Powerscourt, Major Fitzgerald to see you, sir!' The sentry raised his hand in a textbook salute. The Colonel was alone in the officers' mess, seated at a top table that would hold about a dozen officers, enjoying a generous breakfast. He looked to be in his late forties with an enormous moustache and greying hair.

'You look, gentlemen,' he growled, 'as if you haven't been to bed. Better have some breakfast before you tell me your business. Lance Corporal! Bring another two chairs! And a couple of As at the double!' Colonel Wheeler showed them into their seats. He scratched his head.

'Powerscourt, Powerscourt. You the fellow who was in India? And then in South Africa?'

Powerscourt nodded. 'We both served in those locations, Colonel.'

'Goddamit, man, you've both seen more active service in your lifetimes than this regiment has in a hundred years! See these pictures on the walls?' He waved a fork carrying half a mushroom around his officers' mess. 'See all these officers commanding the Compton Horse? Look carefully and you'll find the significant fact.' The Colonel paused and gave his full attention to a couple of kidneys. 'Do you see it? Let me tell you. Look at the bloody uniforms. Those four colonels over there,' he pointed dramatically at the left-hand wall, 'fought with Marlborough. Blenheim, Oudenarde, those sort of places. The other six,' Colonel Wheeler waved his fork once more, this time bedecked with tomato, at a collection of veterans on the opposite wall, 'they all went to Portugal in the Peninsular Wars, lucky devils. Fought their way right across Spain with Wellington into France. Talavera, Badajoz,

Salamanca, Vittoria, Toulouse. Sent home after Toulouse. Too far away to be called back for Waterloo. Too far away to be called up for the damned Russians in the Crimea or the bloody Boer in South Africa. We're the forgotten regiment, Powerscourt. Miracle the bloody War Office remembers to pay us.'

At that point two enormous breakfasts were placed in front of Powerscourt and Fitzgerald. Eggs, bacon, sausages, tomatoes, kidneys, mushrooms, fried bread.

'A is the full experience,' the Colonel explained happily, 'B doesn't have the fried bread, C doesn't have the kidneys and so on.'

'So G would just be eggs and bacon on their own,' said Johnny, tucking into bacon and mushrooms.

'May I talk as I go, Colonel?' asked Powerscourt. 'There is very little time. You will see why as I explain.' He took Wheeler through the events in Compton, the murders, the plans to defect to Rome, the bonfire the previous evening, the intention to rededicate the minster to Rome that morning and to celebrate Mass in what had been a Protestant cathedral at midday.

'Goddamit, man,' the Colonel had turned red, 'this is monstrous! This is a Protestant country! Catholics have their own places for conducting the Mass or whatever they do. What's wrong with those, for God's sake?'

The Colonel found temporary consolation in a combination of egg and tomato. Powerscourt looked quietly at his watch. It was five minutes to eight.

'The Chief Constable is short of men, Colonel. He sent us here to seek reinforcements.'

The Colonel stared at Powerscourt. He laughed bitterly. 'Whole century goes by, Powerscourt. Compton Horse rots quietly down here, not invited to any parties at all, no chance to destroy His Majesty's enemies. When the call comes we're to turn into bloody policemen and arrest a couple of canons and a rural dean. Never mind, Powerscourt. This regiment won't let you down. How many men d'you need?'

'Thirty,' said Powerscourt firmly, 'forty if you could manage it.'

The Colonel uttered an enormous roar that might have been Lance Corporal. He devoted his full attention to finishing his breakfast. Tomatoes, eggs, sausage, kidneys disappeared at breathtaking speed. Powerscourt wondered if he would suffer from indigestion on the ride back to Compton.

'Lance Corporal!' he bawled as the man appeared in the doorway at the end of the room. 'Get those bloody officers out of bed and in here at the double! Order the buggers' breakfast for them! Can't hang about while they dither about whether to have the kidneys or not. Find the Regimental Sergeant Major! Tell him I want thirty-five men ready to ride out at eight thirty sharp! Move!'

Compton Cathedral was packed to the rafters. All of those who had come from right across southern England to the bonfire were now filling the pews in the nave, standing in the two transepts and the ambulatories. The candles that had illuminated the night had been replaced with fresh ones to illuminate the day. The pillars in the nave glowed gold for the consecration of the cathedral and the ordination of a bishop. One of the men who had come from Rome was presiding over the service, clad in his bishop's robes, the ring clearly visible on his finger. The congregation were on their knees.

'*Sancte Michael, Sancte Gabriel, Sancte Raphael,*' two cantors sang, working their way down the Litany of the Saints.

'*Ora pro nobis, Ora pro nobis*, Pray for us,' the faithful repeated.

Gervase Bentley Moreton, one-time Anglican Bishop of Compton, about to become the Catholic Bishop of Compton, had strips of cloth, anointed with oil, wrapped around his forehead. He was lying prostrate on the ground while the roll call of saints continued.

'*Omnes sancti Pontifices et Confessores, Sancte Antoni, Sancte Benedicte, Sancte Dominice, Sancte Francisce,* All you holy bishops and Confessors, Saint Anthony, St Benedict, St Dominic, St Francis' and the reply rising up from the kneeling multitude, '*Ora pro nobis*, Pray for us.'

The Compton Yeomanry had not kept to their timetable. Two of the young officers Colonel Wheeler wanted in the expedition could not be roused from their beds. Only a terrible dressing-down from the adjutant brought them on to the parade ground, ten minutes late.

'I shouldn't worry too much about the delay,' Powerscourt said diplomatically to their commanding officer as they finally rode out, the troopers side by side along the road. 'Mass is at twelve. It shouldn't be over till one at the earliest. We've got plenty of time.'

The Colonel snorted. 'Disgraceful behaviour, disgraceful. Damned good mind to confine them to quarters for a month. No more balls and parties then, what?'

Johnny Fitzgerald was riding right behind the Colonel on a borrowed horse. He remembered the time, early on in their career, when he and Powerscourt had nearly missed a parade altogether owing to overstaying their welcome at the Viceregal Ball in Simla.

'Tell you what, Powerscourt,' said the Colonel, the ride restoring his spirits, 'do I get to bag the Bishop? That would be the nearest thing in this campaign to capturing the enemy colours, I should think. What chance of that?'

'Nothing is impossible,' said Powerscourt, wondering what exactly was going on in the cathedral at this moment. He had no idea what form the consecration of a cathedral would take.

Patrick Butler was watching the spectacle, mesmerized. He was writing almost continually in the small notebook hidden inside his missal. Anne Herbert beside him was thinking that her first husband would be turning in his grave. Hands were now being laid on Moreton's head by the Bishop sent from Rome. There was a prayer of consecration. Then the congregation stared at Moreton as he kissed a copy of the Gospels and fresh clothes were brought for him.

'What's going on now?' Patrick whispered to his next-door neighbour, a white-haired old lady from Southampton.

'He's only wearing an alb and stole at present,' she muttered, pleased to be able to explain the intricacies of the service to an unbeliever. 'They're going to clothe him in dalmatics that a deacon wears and a chasuble, a priest's vestment over the top of that.'

Patrick Butler wondered if dalmatics came from Dalmatia, wherever that was, but felt it better not to ask. The choir were singing an anthem now, the long litany of the saints sent back to their eternal rest. A pectoral cross was now hung round Moreton's neck, white gloves were put on his hands and the Bishop's ring was placed on the index finger of his right hand. The crozier or Bishop's staff was handed over. It was a few minutes after eleven o'clock.

The Colonel's cavalcade was now about eight miles from Compton. One or two villagers had come out of their houses to stare as they passed, the red uniforms and the gleaming horses a spectacular sight on Easter Sunday morning.

'Powerscourt,' said the Colonel, 'please forgive me. Never at my brightest first thing in the morning. Attention has to be devoted to breakfast. Did you say that all these bloody parsons had defected to Rome? Every last deacon and prebendary?'

'I'm afraid so, Colonel,' said Powerscourt cheerfully. 'Even the cathedral cat can now recite the Mass in Latin.'

'God bless my soul.' The Colonel was shaking his head as he trotted along the country lanes. 'One of them going mad I could understand. Two at a pinch. But all of them!' The Colonel stopped suddenly and looked back at his little column. 'It's as if,' he said, slapping his horse firmly on the thigh, 'all of my officers' mess were to defect and join up with the wretched infantry, the damned foot sloggers! It's not just treachery, it's damned bad form!' And with that he rode on to arrest the renegades.

Patrick Butler felt they must be nearing the end. The Bishop was seated now and the zuccheta or purple skull cap was placed on his head, followed by the mitre. Lady Lucy, sitting on the other side of Anne Herbert, felt the whole thing was a bit like a coronation though she doubted if Britain's new sovereign would be crowned with quite so much incense. And though the cathedral was packed with the faithful she doubted if the streets of Compton would be filled with loyal subjects of the new administration in the cathedral. Almost all these people at the service were visitors. The citizens of Compton had stayed at home again, waiting for time and officialdom to give them back their cathedral. Now Bishop Moreton had made the sign of peace to his fellow Bishop and the attendant clergy and was moving down the main aisle, blessing the congregation as though he were the Pope himself. When he had been led back to the sanctuary by the Bishop from Rome he was formally seated on his cathedra. Gervase Bentley Moreton, until twenty hours before the Protestant Bishop of Compton, was now the Roman Catholic Bishop of Compton. As the choir began to sing Mozart's Coronation Mass the Chief Constable slipped quietly out of the west door. He paced up and down the paths that criss-crossed the Cathedral Green staring at the roads that might bring reinforcements. Was Powerscourt coming? Had the cavalry refused the mission?

Without them the Chief Constable simply did not know what he was going to do.

The Compton Horse were now a few miles from the city that bore their name. Every now and then the Colonel would look back to check that his little troop were in their proper formation.

'Don't suppose you know how long the campaign will last, Powerscourt?' he said as the spire of the minster came into view. 'Short engagement, or long siege? Bloody boring things sieges, so they tell me.'

'I doubt if it will last more than a couple of days,' said Powerscourt. 'But without your assistance the whole affair would have been a complete fiasco.'

'Never thought we'd end up guarding a flock of treacherous parsons,' the Colonel continued. 'Don't suppose we'll be adding it to the regimental colours.'

'I'm sure that your role will be recognized,' said Powerscourt, wondering if they would be in time. Johnny Fitzgerald had ridden ahead to find out how long before the service would end.

'I'd better detach a couple of fellows to sort out the commissariat,' said the Colonel. 'I feel as though I could manage a bite of luncheon quite soon.'

The Bishop was addressing his congregation. Anne Herbert was feeling deeply irritated that all these men, who had cared for her so well after the death of her husband, were now desecrating his memory. Lady Lucy was wondering where Francis was and if he would arrive in time. Patrick Butler was trying to hear what was happening outside. Once he heard the horses' hooves rattling on the stones outside, he said to himself, he would slip out the side door. He checked once more the spot where the Chief Constable and Chief Inspector Yates had been sitting. They were not there.

The Bishop was holding up the box containing the words of the monk of Compton, recently serialized in the *Mercury*. 'This casket,' he told his congregation, holding it well aloft above the ornate pulpit, 'contains the link between Compton's past and Compton's future. It was discovered in our crypt earlier this year. It contains what I believe to be the last writings of a monk who dwelt here in the days before the Dissolution of the Monasteries in the 1530s.

Those of you who live in or around Compton may have read my translations of the earlier sections of the document in our local newspaper. For the visitors to our cathedral on this special day, our one thousandth birthday, I would merely say that it is like a diary, the fears, the reflections, the last words of this monk, whose name we do not know, as his end approached and he went to the scaffold for his faith.'

The Bishop paused briefly. Patrick Butler listened hard for noises outside. There were none.

'These are the last words of the monk of Compton before he was led away and put to death. "Tomorrow they are coming for me. It will be my last day on earth before I go to meet my father in heaven. They have brought me clean clothes. I would not have chosen to be hung drawn and quartered for my beliefs. But I cannot betray my conscience and my God by subscribing to a faith I do not believe in. I shall fix my eyes on Christ on the cross. May my blood flow in memory of his. May my wounds echo the sufferings of our Saviour in his last hours. May my agony contribute to the final victory of Christ over his enemies. And for my tormentors, secure in the faith of our fathers, I pray that the Lord will forgive them, for they know not what they do."'

The Bishop put away his notes. The congregation were very still. Patrick Butler heard no noises coming in from outside. The Bishop raised his arms high above his head.

'May the martyred monk of Compton act as a bridge between our glorious heritage of six hundred years in the true faith and the fresh dawn of a new Catholic beginning we are witnessing here today. For today is Christ risen. Today the stone has been rolled from the sepulchre of his dark entombment. Today is this cathedral risen from its own long entombment in the false religion so brutally imposed on God's people all those years ago. True religion cannot depend on the lusts of princes or the arrogance and greed of their ministers. True religion cannot depend on the fancies of a Parliament or the passing whims of an electorate that may be moved more by the lures of Mammon than by the faith of our fathers. True religion could never depend on the body of men now sitting in the House of Commons, a body peopled by ever-growing numbers of professed atheists and a host of unbelievers. Thou art Peter, our Lord said, and upon this rock will I build my Church. That rock, that Church have survived intact across the years since those words were uttered in Jerusalem. The authority of Christ's true Church stretches out across the centuries in an unbroken line to us here in Compton today. It is an authority above and beyond the reach of politicians and the fashionable doctrines of this unhappy world. That authority, slowly accumulated over the long ages of the Church's life, is stamped on the patterns of our worship and on the conduct of our lives.'

Patrick Butler was still scribbling furiously in his notebook. Lady Lucy wondered if the Bishop was longing for martyrdom like the monk of Compton. Anne Herbert was wondering if the new cathedral authorities would apply to Propaganda for the monk to be canonized.

'Let us give thanks on this day for the Resurrection of Our Lord and Saviour. Let us give thanks for the life and example of the monk of Compton, so brutally murdered for his refusal to betray the true faith. Let us give thanks for the Resurrection of our own cathedral, one thousand years old this year. Let us offer up our own sins and our own weaknesses and our own failings to God in his mercy.

'Let me close by invoking the name of one of the greatest English Catholics of the last century. John Henry Newman was born and baptized an Anglican. He was ordained as an Anglican priest. He became a leader of the Oxford Movement, a doomed attempt to reform the Anglican faith. Shortly before he was received into the Catholic Church he wrote a remarkable essay. At the time he was making a choice, a choice between the soft life of an Oxford academic, the companionship of its fellows, the quiet beauty of its quadrangles, the cloistered havens of its great libraries, the candle-light and the fine wine flowing beneath the portraits of scholars past at High Table, and the very different world of the Catholic faithful, a world he had never met and scarcely knew. Newman's words reach out to us all from the tiny parish of Littlemore outside Oxford where the future Cardinal wrote them seventy years ago. They call on us to make our choice of faith while we still have the chance. If we do not, the consequences may last for ever. Time is short, wrote Newman. Eternity is long.'

The Bishop bowed his head. A great silence had fallen over the cathedral. Nobody stirred. Nobody changed their position in the pews. Nobody checked the angle of their hat or crossed or uncrossed their legs. Many of them had their eyes closed in silent prayer. Maybe the spirit of John Henry Newman had descended on Compton's cathedral to deliver a final benediction to the faithful.

Then the Bishop turned very slowly and began his descent from the pulpit. The choir rose to their feet and resumed the singing of the Mass. Very faintly outside there came the noise of horses' hooves. The cavalry had arrived. Patrick Butler began to rise from his feet to find out what was happening outside. Anne Herbert placed a hand firmly on his arm.

'You can't leave now, Patrick,' she whispered. 'You'll never see anything like this again in your life. It would be like leaving Hamlet before the last act.'

Reluctantly he sat down again. The Mass carried on. He was wondering if Time is Short Eternity is Long could be fitted as a headline across one page or if he should run it, in the largest typeface his printers possessed, across a double page spread.

Shortly before the end of the service Chief Inspector Yates and five of his officers placed themselves very quietly in a line across the top of the nave. The Chief Inspector watched the Communion ceremony very carefully.

'*Et qui, expletis passionis dominicae diebus,*' sang the choir, 'You have mourned for Christ's sufferings, now you celebrate the joy of his Resurrection, May you come with joy to the feast that lasts for ever.'

The service was over. As the clergy moved slowly down the choir Patrick Butler saw that the police were directing them out of the cathedral not by the west door at the bottom of the nave but by the entrance that led past the chapter house towards Vicars Close. He could contain himself no longer. He ran at top speed out of the west door and sprinted off towards the south transept.

As the procession reached the top of the steps leading them out of the minster they were met by a body of eight dismounted cavalry men. Colonel Wheeler and the Chief Inspector ushered them into the chapter house. Powerscourt, standing a few paces behind, thought that the chapter house couldn't have been this full of clergy since before the Reformation. When they were all seated, the Chief Constable, the Colonel at his side, addressed them.

'My lord Bishop, Dean, Archdeacon, members of the Chapter, distinguished visitors,' the Chief Constable nodded to the Bishop from Rome who was scowling furiously in a corner, 'I have to tell you that you are all under house arrest. You have broken the laws of this country, more specifically, the Act for the Uniformity of Common Prayer and Service in the Church, and Administration of the Sacraments, passed in the reign of Queen Elizabeth the First.'

Powerscourt had remembered on the final lap into Compton with the cavalry that there was an Act of Parliament reproduced at the very beginning of the Book of Common Prayer. He had drawn it to the Chief Constable's attention shortly before the end of the Mass in the cathedral.

'Under this Act,' the Chief Constable went on, sounding, Powerscourt thought, as if he had learned the legislation by heart many years before, 'it is illegal to hold any service in any church or cathedral other than those contained in the Book of Common Prayer. The Catholic Mass, as you know as well as I do, is not included in that Book. Your fate will be decided by the justices, in accordance with the statutes of the Act of Uniformity, acting in concert with the civil and ecclesiastical authorities. Until such time you are all under house arrest. You may not leave your residences without permission. You may not leave Compton under any circumstances. The cathedral is closed until further notice.'

As the clergy were led away, escorted by police and cavalry, Patrick Butler found Powerscourt staring at the departing figure of the Dean.

'Well done, my lord, at least you and Johnny Fitzgerald brought the reinforcements here in time.'

'Well done, do you say, Patrick? Well done? I failed to prevent all this happening this morning. And there's another failure to be laid at my door.'

'What's that, my lord?' said Patrick.

'The Bishop and the parsons may all be locked up, Patrick,' said Powerscourt. 'I still have to find the murderer.'

25

Lord Francis Powerscourt was pacing up and down in front of Anne Herbert's cottage. Inside the Herbert household the Chief Constable was talking to a young canon from Exeter called Gill who had been an unobtrusive witness to the morning's events. Chief Inspector Yates and his men, accompanied by a section of Colonel Wheeler's horse, were ensuring the safe dispersal of all the visitors to their trains. Patrick Butler had departed to his office to write up his notes while they were still fresh in his mind. Johnny Fitzgerald and Lady Lucy were indoors, discussing the Bishop's sermon.

Powerscourt thought of the murder that had brought him to Compton in the first place, John Eustace, one of England's richest men, despatched in his own bed. He thought of Arthur Rudd, roasted after his death on the spit in the kitchen of Vicars Hall, the flesh falling off the cremated body. He thought of Edward Gillespie, hung drawn and quartered, sections of his frame dumped all across the surrounding countryside. He wondered again about the murderer. The Dean with those organizational skills? The Archdeacon, longest known convert to Catholicism, with his secret visits to celebrate Mass at Melbury Clinton? The Bishop himself, so secure and comfortable that morning in his new role? The Dean's monosyllabic servant, strong enough to tip that pile of masonry over Powerscourt in the minutes before the cathedral closed? The mysterious Italian from Civitas Dei, Father Barberi, companion of the Archdeacon? Five of them, he thought, like the Five Wounds of Christ. Then it struck him. There might just be a way to bring the matter to a conclusion. It would be risky, it would be dangerous, there could be yet another death in Compton. He rushed inside to fetch Canon Gill. As the Bishop had said, Time is short.

The two men walked along the path that led to the west front. The statues were still there in their niches, staring past the sinners below them towards John Henry Newman's long eternity. Powerscourt did most of the talking. Canon Gill was in his early thirties, clean shaven with a distant look in his soft brown eyes.

'I think it could be done,' the Canon said at last. 'It wouldn't be the real thing, of course, but then that wouldn't matter for your purposes. And I would need another Anglican priest. But I'm sure we could rustle up one of those from a neighbouring parish.'

'You do realize, Canon,' Powerscourt was very emphatic at this point, 'that it could be very dangerous. It could even prove fatal for somebody if we're not careful.'

The Canon smiled. 'Of course I realize that, Lord Powerscourt. But in my profession we are not meant to take any account of such things.'

'Forgive me if I ask this question, Canon. Do you have a wife and children? You do realize that you could leave them without a husband and father if things go wrong?'

'I believe, Lord Powerscourt, that you too have a wife and children. Shall we return and confer with the Chief Constable?'

Johnny Fitzgerald looked very closely at his friend as he came back into the room. 'I know that look, Francis,' he said cheerfully. 'I don't think you've been discussing the finer points of Reformation theology out there. I think you've been concocting some scheme or other.'

Powerscourt smiled. ' I have indeed. Lucy, Chief Constable, Johnny, Anne, Canon Gill from Exeter, let me put forward a plan that might get us out of some of our difficulties.'

He removed a one-legged teddy bear, property and victim of one of Anne Herbert's children, from the corner of a chair and sat down. 'In all the excitement of the past few days, I have not lost sight of one thing I am here to investigate a murder, not to participate in any religious wars. I want to see if you agree with my hypothesis about this murderer.'

He paused and accepted a cup of tea. 'We presume that he has killed to ensure that the service earlier today went ahead. His three victims were all slaughtered because in one way or another they threatened to expose the plans to make Compton a Catholic cathedral once again. I have been extremely concerned in the days of Holy Week that any possible threat to his plan would make him kill again.'

Lady Lucy was watching her husband's hands which were twisting round each other as he spoke. The Chief Constable was looking closely at Powerscourt's face. Johnny was watching Canon Gill from Exeter who was looking something up in the appendix to a very small and very battered Book of Common Prayer.

'Now,' Powerscourt went on, 'you might think that the murderer will be able to rest on his laurels, as it were. His mission has been successful. His work is done. But what do you think would happen if there was a sudden reversal in the position of the cathedral?'

'What do you mean, Powerscourt?' said the Chief Constable.

'My plan is very simple. We set a trap to catch the murderer. The cathedral should be reconsecrated to the Anglican faith at the earliest possible opportunity, tomorrow if it is not feasible today. The murderer will have to try to stop that, by fair means or foul, since it would mean all his efforts had been in vain.'

'But,' the Chief Constable interrupted again, 'the murderer is surely under house arrest. How is he going to stop it?'

Johnny Fitzgerald had seen Powerscourt carrying out a similar manoeuvre in a murder case in Simla. 'I presume, Francis,' he said, 'that you are going to suggest that word is put about to all those under house arrest that the cathedral is going to be rededicated at a particular time. Discreetly, of course. But the gossip must be swirling round all those houses like wildfire. Then you would flush him out.'

Powerscourt smiled. 'Absolutely right, Johnny. Your men, Chief Constable, would have to relax their guard at the appointed time. The murderer or murderers would have to be allowed to escape from their confinement to go to the cathedral. Johnny and I would be hiding inside. After ten or fifteen minutes from the start of the service your men and Colonel Wheeler's horse would surround every known exit from the building. We wait for the murderer to make his move. Then we pounce. Then this terrible affair might be at an end.'

The Chief Constable looked apprehensive. 'Could you do it?' he asked Canon Gill. 'Rededicate the cathedral, I mean?'

Canon Gill looked up from his prayer book. His voice was very soft. Outside they could hear the local children playing on the Green. 'The answer is No and Yes,' he said. 'No in the sense that I must confess I do not know the precise form of service to be used in these circumstances. But I am not sure that matters. I just need another Anglican priest to assist me. We can cobble together some form of service that might not be entirely correct but would be sufficient to convince the murderer. We could quote from the Act of Supremacy that you invoked earlier, Chief Constable. We could read the Thirty-Nine Articles. I'm sure I could make it pretty convincing.'

Lady Lucy intervened for the first time. 'Wouldn't the murderer know that it was the wrong form of service? If he's been pretending to be an Anglican all these years wouldn't he realize that this wasn't the proper way to do it? And therefore that the re-dedication would be invalid and the cathedral still be a Catholic one? So he wouldn't have to stop it.'

'What you say is entirely plausible, Lady Powerscourt,' Canon Gill bowed his head slightly in her direction as he spoke, 'but I don't think it's going to be like that. These gentlemen now under house arrest know all about how to rededicate the cathedral to Rome. But I don't think they will have thought for a second about the traffic the other way, if you see what I mean. You could spend your whole life in the Church of England, you could end up as Archbishop of Canterbury, without knowing what to do in these circumstances. Nobody's been here since the Reformation.'

Powerscourt turned to the Chief Constable. 'It is for you to decide, sir. You and Colonel Wheeler would have to make the plan work.'

'Is it dangerous, Powerscourt?'

'Yes, I think it could be. We have to assume that the murderer would want to stop the service. And that he might try to kill those taking part. I have discussed this aspect with Canon Gill. He is willing to proceed.'

The Chief Constable stared out of the window. A couple of the Compton Horse could be seen marching up and down on sentry duty outside the Dean's house.

'Dammit, Powerscourt,' he said at last, 'let's try it. These murders have been an intolerable strain on the citizens of Compton and on the morale of my force. What time would you like the curtain to go up?'

'Tomorrow morning,' Powerscourt replied. 'I feel that the service to rededicate the cathedral should commence at eleven o'clock sharp.'

Easter Monday dawned bright and sunny in the little city of Compton. The daffodils were waving brightly behind the minster.

Some of the trees around the Close were in bloom, blossom of white and pink adorning the green of the grass. At eleven o'clock precisely a small procession of four men in white surplices entered the cathedral by the west door, Canon Gill in the lead with Richard Hooper, a young curate from the neighbouring village of Frensham, at his side. The other two were several paces behind. The air in the building was musty, faint whiffs that might have been incense or perfume still lurking in the atmosphere. The hundreds of candles that had enlightened the proceedings the day before were all burnt out, wax lying about on the bodies of the dead interred beneath the floor. The chairs in the nave had not been put straight, resting in exactly the places the congregation had left them as they departed. There was no choir. Canon Gill led them to a large table, covered with a white cloth and a couple of silver candlesticks, placed across the great transept at the top of the nave. He began by reading the Lord's Prayer, followed by the Collect for the Day.

'Almighty God, who through thy only begotten son Jesus Christ hast overcome death and opened up unto us the gate of everlasting life...'

One of the white surplices was behind the table, facing the high altar beyond the empty choir stalls, eyes flickering from side to side. The other was on the opposite side, scouring the space towards the door, scanning the triforium and the clerestory, the upper levels above the nave. Both men kept their hands by their sides.

Canon Gill had moved on to the Thirty-Nine Articles, the defining statement of Anglican belief. He and Richard Hooper were reading them alternately. By twenty past eleven Hooper had reached the end of Article Number Twenty-One on the Authority of General Councils. Outside all the doors and passages leading into the cathedral were watched or guarded by Chief Inspector Yates's policemen and Colonel Wheeler's horse. The Chief Constable had decided that the murderer must be inside by now, if he was going to make his move. Patrick Butler, notebook in hand, was just behind the Chief Constable. Anne Herbert and Lady Lucy were staring at the cathedral from the front garden of the Herbert cottage. Along the roads that lined the Close cavalry in red uniforms were guarding the houses of the converts.

'"Article Number Twenty-Two,"' said Canon Gill, his soft voice disappearing upwards to fade away in the arches above, '"Of

Purgatory. The Romish doctrine concerning Purgatory, Pardons, Worshipping and Adoration, as well of Images as of Relics,"' the eyes of the white surplice facing the door were locked on a glint that seemed to be moving along the clerestory, '"and also invocation of saints, is a fond thing vainly invented – "'

'Down!' shouted Powerscourt. Johnny Fitzgerald in the other surplice hurled himself to the ground. Canon Gill dropped to the floor a fraction of a second before the shot rang out. The bullet hit one of the candlesticks and ricocheted off into a chantry chapel. Canon Gill's voice continued from underneath the table, '" . . . vainly invented, and grounded upon no warranty of Scripture, but rather repugnant to the Word of God."'

Johnny Fitzgerald fired back. There was a scream from high above. Powerscourt, tearing off his surplice, sprinted towards the little door that led up to the higher levels. Johnny fired again. The Canon continued reading from the ground the article on Ministering in the Congregation. Now it was Powerscourt's turn to provide covering fire for Johnny as he too shot across the nave. Powerscourt, panting slightly by the door, was wondering about the last time there had been Murder in the Cathedral. Thomas à Becket? Cromwell's soldiers on the rampage in the Civil War, despatching their foes who had sought sanctuary at the high altar?

Powerscourt pointed upwards. Johnny whispered very quietly, 'Better be careful when we get near the top of the stairs, Francis. The bloody man could pick us both off as our heads come out.' Powerscourt wondered who they would find on the next level. Was this the end for the Compton Cathedral murderer? And which one of them was it? He still didn't know. The stairs curved around a central pillar. The stone was very cold to the touch. There was only room for one person at a time. They paused from time to time to listen for sounds of the murderer on the move. Richard Hooper was speaking of the Sacraments. Powerscourt wondered when the clergy would stop.

They took the stairs at a run. When they reached the floor above, Powerscourt tiptoed up towards the light coming in through the windows. A foot or so from the summit he raised his hand above his head so it was level with the ground. He fired three shots at a different level and in a different direction each time. Another scream rang out. As Powerscourt and Fitzgerald charged into the clerestory they saw a man wrapped in an enormous black cape, leaning through an archway, preparing to fire once more at the

Protestant clergy below. He turned when he saw them and limped as fast as he could through the door into the lower tower. He left a trail of small puddles of blood behind him. It was the Dean. They heard his prayers, punctuated with mighty sobs, coming through the door.

'Hail Mary, full of grace, blessed art thou among women, blessed is the fruit of thy womb Jesus.'

A Protestant response rose out of the nave below from Article Twenty-Eight, Of the Lord's Supper. '"Transubstantiation or the change of the substance of Bread and Wine in the Supper of the Lord, cannot be proved by Holy Writ . . ."'

'Pray for us now . . .' from the wounded Catholic above.

'". . . but it is repugnant to the plain words of Scripture, overthroweth the nature of the Sacrament, and hath given rise to many superstitions,"' from the Protestant below.

'. . . and in the hour of our death, Amen.'

'Dean!' shouted Powerscourt. 'Are you badly hurt, man? Give yourself up and the doctors will attend to you!'

'I don't want to be taken alive!' The Dean was weeping with the pain as he spoke.

'Are you responsible for these murders?' Powerscourt spoke again. Johnny Fitzgerald was inching his way towards the door, preparing to rush in.

'I certainly was. They would have spoiled everything, those people. They wouldn't listen to reason.'

With that the Dean kicked open the door and fired two shots. One caught Powerscourt between the elbow and the shoulder of the left arm. The other hit Johnny in the leg.

They heard the sound of feet clattering up another set of stairs. Powerscourt fired defiantly after the retreating figure.

Johnny looked sadly at his leg. Protestant blood was now flowing freely on the upper levels of Compton Cathedral. 'Dammit, Francis, one more minute and I could have got the bastard.' He tore off a section of his surplice and wrapped it round the wound. 'Are you sure God is on our side, Francis? Is your arm all right?'

'Mine's only a scratch, Johnny. Not sure about God. Can you wait here for a while?'

Johnny Fitzgerald winced. 'Bloody hell, Francis, I'm not going to miss the last minutes of the match. I'll crawl if I have to.' With that he inched his way into the lower tower. Powerscourt was peering suspiciously at the stairs.

'That's the upper tower above,' he said. 'After that it's the spire.' The words of the Thirty-Nine Articles were still sounding from the middle of the great transept. Powerscourt thought he heard something about the marriage of bishops, priests and deacons. Surely they must be near the end by now. A gust of fresh air rushed into the lower tower. Powerscourt began to climb the wooden stair. Blood was still flowing from his arm. Very faintly now, they could hear the sobs above them. When Powerscourt charged into the upper tower it was empty. A door was open and the bright blue sky of Compton's Easter Monday was visible outside. He heard Johnny behind him, coming up the stairs backwards, swearing as he raised himself up step by step.

'Dean!' Powerscourt shouted into the open air. He wasn't sure if the man had jumped down or begun to climb the spire on the series of rungs and brackets that marked the way to the top. 'Why did you do it?'

Powerscourt poked his head out of the door. He doubted if the Dean would be in a fit state to fire down at him and hold on at the same time.

'I've waited and planned and organized for years for yesterday! Finest day of my life! ' Powerscourt saw that the weathered grey of the stone was flecked with the Dean's blood. The Dean was about twenty feet above him, making his way agonizingly slowly upwards. Powerscourt saw that blood was flowing fast from a great wound in his side.

'I've left you a letter, Powerscourt. I wasn't sure today was going to go well.' The Dean began speaking to the spire in front of him, then turned to look down at Powerscourt. Powerscourt saw that the Dean's face was white, turning grey. Down below a collection of tiny dots in uniform were staring upwards at the Dean's last moments.

'Come back! For God's sake, man, come back!' Powerscourt yelled at him. 'You can still come down the same way you went up! I could come and get you with a rope, if that would help!'

'For Christ's sake, Francis.' Johnny Fitzgerald had raised himself into a sitting position against the wall. 'I've heard of the Good Samaritan but this is ridiculous. Bloody man must weigh fifteen stone at least. He'd pull you both down to your deaths for sure. Don't think Lucy and the children would approve.'

Powerscourt looked at the rope he had found in a corner of the upper tower and put it down again.

'Dean!' he shouted once more. 'Turn back, man! For God's sake, turn back! You'll get yourself killed!' He looked up the face of the spire. The Dean was now over halfway to the top, moving ever more slowly. Powerscourt suddenly remembered that there was a statue of the Virgin at the top, next to the risen Christ. Another prayer began.

'*Anima Christi, sanctifica me*, Soul of Christ be my sanctification.'

Powerscourt heard the sound of footsteps rushing up the stairway to the clerestory beneath him.

'Body of Christ, be my salvation.'

Powerscourt leant out of the door as far as he dared and shouted up into the sky, 'Come back, man! Come back!'

'Blood of Christ, fill all my veins, water from Christ's side, wash out my stains.'

In the nave the voices of Canon Gill and Richard Hooper had fallen silent. The words of a Catholic prayer, the Anima Christi, Soul of Christ, punctuated with great groans, filled the air.

'Passion of Christ, my comfort be. O good Jesus listen to me.'

Powerscourt saw that the man had only another fifteen rungs to go before he reached the top. Somehow, in spite of the terrible deaths, he hoped that the Dean would reach the pinnacle. Then the investigator in him fired one more question up into the morning sky.

'Dean,' he shouted. 'Did you act entirely alone?' It was, he realized, an absurd question to put to somebody two hundred and fifty feet above the ground, blood pouring from his wounds, desperate to reach the statue of the Virgin before he died.

'Yes. Alone.' The voice was little more than a groan now. The prayer went on.

'In thy wounds I fain would hide. Ne'er to be parted from thy side.'

Chief Inspector Yates, panting heavily, was inspecting Johnny's wound. One of the other policemen tried to step out of the window on to the spire. Powerscourt pushed him back.

'Guard me when my life shall fail me. Bid me come to thee above.'

The Dean was but a few rungs from the top now, way above Powerscourt and the others in the upper tower. Then something seemed to happen to his lower leg. He looked as though he might fall. Just in time he reached aloft and pulled himself up, holding on to the feet of the Virgin. Then his other arm reached her waist.

'With all thy saints to sing thy love. World without end. Amen.'

It was hard to tell the precise sequence of events at this point. The statue, designed to withstand the storms and gales of centuries, was not designed to take the weight of a fifteen-stone man holding on to it for dear life. Very slowly the Virgin began to lean. Then she leant a little further. Then she fell, breaking into several pieces on the cathedral roof before tumbling to the ground. The Dean seemed to hang suspended at the top of the spire. Then he too fell, a last Hail Mary following his passage back to earth, bouncing off the side of the spire, rolling over the parapet of the upper tower, crashing on to the roof of the east transept, then a final sickening crunch of flesh and bones as he landed on the ground twenty paces from the Chief Constable. Ambrose Cornwallis Talbot, Dean of Compton Cathedral, was dead before he touched the ground. Pray for us now and in the hour of our death, Amen.

Two burly policemen were carrying Johnny Fitzgerald down to earth. Powerscourt sprinted along the clerestory and down the stairs. The cathedral dedicated to the Virgin was empty. Canon Gill and Richard Hooper had departed. A dark blue police cloak had been placed over the body of the Dean where he had fallen. Dr Williams, summoned to attend the morning's events by the Chief Constable, had made a cursory inspection.

'He's dead, of course,' he said to Powerscourt and the Chief Constable. 'Let's pray that he's the last.'

'He is,' said Powerscourt quietly, staring sadly at the dark blue cape that covered the battered body of the Dean. 'It's all over now.'

The Dean's letter was three pages long. Powerscourt found it on the study desk in the Deanery, addressed to himself, written in a flowing copperplate. Ambrose Cornwallis Talbot spoke of his growing disillusion with the Anglican Church, a disillusion that gradually turned into hatred. He said it was a Church that had turned its back on belief in favour of comfort, that had sacrificed the difficult truths of the Christian faith in favour of a quiet life in the countryside and the pomp and privilege of its bishops in the worldly surroundings of the House of Lords. Its buildings were in the wrong place, in the countryside rather than in the cities, where a national Church should be based with the vast numbers of the urban poor rather than in the upholstered comfort of parsonage and rectory. Soon, the Dean continued, the Anglican Church would be completely filled with the wrong sort of worshippers, devotees of the numinous cadences of Thomas Cranmer's Book of Common Prayer and the soaring beauty of the anthems of Purcell and Byrd. But a Church was not meant to be a place of pilgrimage for lovers of the English language or the anthems of centuries past. It should be rooted in the present, daily confronting the problems of God's people, preaching Christ's Gospel where it was most needed. It was in his own former parish in the slums of London's docks that his Anglican faith had finally ebbed away with the tides. So great was the personal crisis that his doctors ordered him to take a quieter position in Compton. Nine years ago the Dean had joined the Bishop in the Catholic faith. The Bishop, with a more acute sense of history than his, had first suggested the reconsecration of the minster to the true faith on the Easter Sunday of its thousandth anniversary. The Dean had organized it, the slow process of secret recruitment, the appointment of the Archdeacon to carry out the negotiations with Rome. Reluctantly they had sanctioned his mission to Melbury Clinton, realizing that it was a terrible risk, but believing him when he said he could not carry on out without the consolation of regular celebration of the Mass. All three had been members of Civitas Dei for the past seven years. The two missing vicars choral had found out about the Archdeacon at Melbury Clinton. The Dean had packed them off to a new life in Canada with six months' wages in their pockets.

Powerscourt had hoped for more information about Civitas Dei, but suspected that Talbot was being faithful to its principles of secrecy to the last.

Single human lives, the Dean went on, had little meaning to him in comparison with the glory of the enterprise and the reclamation for the Catholic Church of a cathedral that had been stolen from it at the Reformation. He had, throughout, acted entirely alone. He hoped and prayed that the events of Saturday and Sunday would mark the sounding of the tocsin, a trumpet call that would signal the beginnings of the return of the people of England to the Holy and Apostolic Church, that the lives of the isles would once more be carried out to the slow rhythm of the Church's calendar and the central mystery of the Mass.

John Eustace had changed his mind about making the journey to Rome. So had Arthur Rudd, who had referred extensively to his doubts in the diaries he had kept which had perished with him in the flames. Edward Gillespie had been overheard telling a colleague that he proposed to tell Powerscourt in person all about the conspiracy. He had, the Dean went on, deliberately echoed the deaths in Compton at the time of the Dissolution of the Monasteries as a tribute, a memorial to those faithful Catholics who had given their lives for the true religion in 1539 and 1540. He reminded Powerscourt that as a gesture to a more squeamish age he had killed all his victims before the burning and the disembowelment. He had no regrets, for he was the servant of a higher Truth, the pupil of a greater authority, the handmaiden of the only true faith.

'Let me conclude, Powerscourt,' the Dean's letter ended, 'with the words of Thomas Babington Macaulay which have been an inspiration to me for years: "The Catholic Church is still sending forth to the furthest ends of the world missionaries as zealous as those who landed in Kent with Augustine, and still confronting hostile kings with the same spirit with which she confronted Attila. She was great and respected before the Saxon had set foot in Britain, before the Frank had passed the Rhine, when Grecian eloquence still flourished at Antioch, when idols were still worshipped in the temple of Mecca. And she may still exist in undiminished vigour when some traveller from New Zealand shall, in the midst of a vast solitude, take his stand on a broken arch of London Bridge to sketch the ruins of St Paul's."'

Powerscourt read the letter twice. Then he folded it up and put it into his suit pocket. He felt numb before the Dean's diatribe, sad that his life had ended in such a terrible fashion. Then he thought of the families of John Eustace and Arthur Rudd and Edward Gillespie and grew suddenly very angry that one man could think he had the right to play God, to take away human lives, to leave behind broken families who would mourn for years. Not only mad, he said to himself, but bad. He wondered about the people the Dean had betrayed, the baptized he christened in one faith while believing in another, the young couples he had married in his deception, the funerals and burials of those who believed they were under the care of a Protestant priest and going to a Protestant destination.

Two days later Powerscourt and Lady Lucy were making their way once again across the Cathedral Green. The sun was still

311

shining but there was a bitter wind. They were going to say their farewells to the minster at Evensong. They would both be back, in a month's time, for the wedding of Patrick Butler and Anne Herbert. Patrick had threatened to expose him in the pages of the *Mercury* if they failed to turn up.

Johnny Fitzgerald was recovering fast in the upstairs room of Anne Herbert's cottage, entertaining her children with tales of four-eyed giants who lived in caves in the Punjab and six-legged horses who galloped at incredible speed across the veldt in South Africa. The Bishop of Exeter had arrived to take charge of the ecclesiastical proceedings. The Catholic Bishop from Rome and his party were sent back to the eternal city, escorted by the police as far as the Dover boat. The Bishop and the other members of the Chapter who had converted were to be dispersed around the Catholic churches of England and Wales. The Chief Constable was preparing a report for His Majesty's law officers on the strange events at Compton. Patrick Butler had scarcely been seen since the service of dedication, working around the clock on a special edition of his paper. Powerscourt had written again to Mrs Augusta Cockburn, naming her brother's murderer and telling her that he had been brought to a kind of justice. There would, he said, be no trial with its attendant publicity. He passed on the opinion of Mr Drake, the Compton solicitor, that it was unlikely that the legal wrangling about the will would be complete before Christmas. In Drake's view maybe even next Easter would be too soon.

'Lighten our darkness, we beseech thee O Lord,' Canon Gill and Richard Hooper were taking the service, spoken not sung in the absence of the choir, 'and by thy great mercy defend us from all perils and dangers of this night.' The two old ladies who had attended all the earlier services were back in position. Powerscourt looked at Lady Lucy, now fully recovered from her ordeal in the crypt. Tonight, over dinner at Fairfield Park, he was going to propose an expedition to St Petersburg, a place as remote from Compton as he could imagine. In the morning they were to return to London.

Richard Hooper was reading the Nunc Dimittis. 'Lord now lettest thou thy servant depart in peace according to thy word.' His clear tenor voice rang out across the wooden angels and the wooden instrumentalists that adorned the choir stalls. Powerscourt was drawn once more to the names on the back. Fordington and Writhington. Grantham Borealis. Alton Australis. Yetminster Secunda.

'May the Lord bless you and keep you.' Canon Gill's soft voice caressed the great cathedral as he spoke the closing prayer. 'May the Lord make the light of his countenance shine upon you and be gracious unto you and give you his peace.'

Hurstbourne and Burbage. Minor Pars Altaris. Netherbury in Terra. Shipton in Ecclesia.

'In the name of the Father and the Son and the Holy Ghost, Amen.'

Perhaps they're a message, Powerscourt thought, a message from the distant past into the unknowable future, inscribed here on the wood of centuries. Beminster Secunda. Lyme and Halstock. Wilsford and Woolford.

And their names liveth for evermore.

Winterbourne Earle. Gillingham Minor. Chardstock. Teynton Regis. Bishopstone.